Tamsin Harte

Tamsin Harte

Malcolm Macdonald

St Martin's Press ⚏ New York

For
Click & Clack
The Tappet Brothers
with whom I wasted
many a good hour

ISBN 0-312-20628-3

First U.S. Edition: February 2000

10 9 8 7 6 5 4 3 2 1

Contents

Part One

The Morrab

Shelter

1 She saw them from quite a way off, strolling along the Esplanade toward her — the Father, the Mother, the Young Master hanging back a bit, trying to look as if he didn't belong, and the Dutiful Daughter, clinging to her father's arm. There were dozens of families like them in Penzance that summer but something about this particular group held Tamsin's eye. Step by step, as they drew nearer, she began to evaluate them, as she was learning to do with everybody nowadays.

Paterfamilias, as he doubtless called himself, ought not to wear those mutton-chop whiskers; they were far too straggly and thin. And too pale to count. The cream blazer with the broad red stripes was a mistake, too; it made his face look all bleached and it showed up the ancient straw of his boater. Still, he could be quite rich. Men so careless of their person and dress often were.

Matriarch was a little harder to pin down (as her maid probably said to herself each day). Any woman of mature years who could choose to go abroad by day in an outfit like that was either devoid of all taste and sense or she was so rich she could afford to do it for a lark. The skirt was borrowed from a hospital matron; the blouse from a French matelot, collar and all; and the hat from Ascot, 1899 — eight years out-of-date (and ten out-of-fashion even back then). She could at least have chosen *white* gloves; what was going through her mind when she selected the lavender instead?

Young Master was interesting, though — and only partly because he had just set eyes on her and now, seemingly, could not take them off again. He stood two inches taller at once and began to walk with a swagger. The Man who Broke the Bank at Monte Carlo. He may have been of their flesh but he was of a different mould. For a start, he had a keen sense of dress and fashion, with his tapering trousers and spotless kid spats over white leather shoes, and his white blazer with silk edges and thin stripes, both of a blue to make you notice his eyes, and his blue cotton square tied with nonchalant care to thrust aside the dazzling ramparts of his shirt, which had fashionably short, rounded collars — the first she had seen in Penzance this summer. And then there was his neat, military moustache with its waxed points, pricked in perfect symmetry, and his merciless but very kissable lips, and ...

But that was enough, or he'd start leaping to all the wrong conclusions. Tamsin would never be interested in him, except as a means to an end. Everything and everyone was just that nowadays — a means to an end.

The Dutiful Daughter was the most interesting of all. The long, white, virginal dress, short enough to show schoolgirlish ankles in patent white kid boots, told of one who had not as yet come out. The red sash revealed a desire to complement, if not compliment, the Paterfam. The sailor collar might have done the same for the Matriarch if it had not been so obviously more appropriate for the younger female herself. And the straw boater, worn at the same insouciant angle as her elder brother's might indicate a touching desire not to leave him out of these flattering sartorial quotations, either. In short — a girl so incapable of making up her own mind that she borrowed willy nilly from the little world around her.

Perfect!

Tamsin blessed the instinct that had led her to the Esplanade this afternoon.

She gazed out to sea, wondering which of those lobstermen were hauling cognac today — and which of those French barques had dropped it — until the little family drew level. Then she 'noticed' Young Master's eyes upon her and gave an impatient little toss of her head. Pater and Mater, having already sailed by, saw nothing, but Dutiful D, turning to smile at her big bro, caught the gesture and giggled. Twenty paces farther on they both turned and looked back at her again. She saw them reflected in the glass of the shelter where she sat, for an obliging woman in widow's weeds had seated herself in the other bay, on the far side of that glass, turning it into a mirror.

"Some high-quarter folk, they!" said an old man at her other side, a man she had barely noticed until now.

A seaman, perhaps, to judge by his blazer and roll-neck pullover, both navy blue. Did he have 'Saucy Sal' stitched across the chest?

No.

Still, the salt-tanned skin and yachtsman's cap said Old Man of the Sea.

"Do I know you?" she asked, meaning to cut him for his impertinence.

"Benny Peters," he said and touched the peak of his cap with the tip of his thumb.

She hesitated. Benny Peters? It rang a bell. One of the housemaids had mentioned the name only yesterday. A tragedy at sea ... a drowning ... the loss of two sons? Tamsin had listened with only half an ear. But her present hesitation lost her the indignant moral ground from which she could have spurned his advance.

"Miss Harte," she said. She even managed a smile.

"So what does Miss Tamsin Harte think to *they* folk, then?" He jerked his head after the family group, who were now half way toward the end of the constitutional mile.

"You know my name?" she replied.

"I've heard tell of 'ee — you and your mother. Plymouth folk, they do say."

"Do they!"

"High-quarter folk fallen on harder times, they do say."

"*They* do say an awful lot, it would seem."

"Not true, then, is it?"

"It's none of your business!"

"That's a fack and no mistake." He chuckled.

She could not feel as cross with him as his impudence demanded; he was so mild and jovial.

"I only thought as one high-quarter young lady might have a better eye for what you might call the niceties of the situation than what I got. That's all. Sorry I spoke, I'm sure."

"Oh, I didn't mean to be rude ..."

He bounded back at once: "So what do'ee reckon, then? High quarter or not?" Again he jerked his head toward the family group. "Hardly can't see 'em now."

"Hard to tell," Tamsin said. She still felt awkward at discussing people of quality with *hoi polloi* — though she did it perforce with the chambermaids, Bridget and Catherine, almost every day of the week.

" 'Tis the new sport in Cornwall," he said. "Tellin' apples from horseapples."

"So what d'you reckon to them?" She, too, nodded after the strolling family. She injected a little experimental tinge of Cornish into her voice — educated Cornish, of course, or else she would have said, 'to they.'

"They'm worth more'n they do show," he replied. "That's a fack, that is."

"You think so?" She made herself appear mildly surprised, though, of course, she had reached the same conclusion herself. Surprised and admiring.

Her condescension flattered him into an explanation he might not otherwise have bothered to give. "See they five there?" He inclined his head toward another family — a boy, a young man, a girl in-between, and their parents — walking up from the Newlyn end; the mother was glancing right and left with ferret eyes. All were in brand-new summer outfits. "That's new money, that is," the Old Salt added. "First generation."

"Parvenus!" She laughed. "You come down here to play the same game as me, Mister Peters!"

"How's that, then, Miss Harte?"

"Guessing which niche to put each Tom, Dick, and Mary into. How far d'you go?"

He winked. "All the way, maid — if I'm left."

Six months earlier, Miss Tamsin Harte of Elburton Villa, Plymouth, might well have slapped his face for such gross insolence; but that Miss Tamsin Harte had been in the market for an eligible husband — who would want his wife to be as unsullied by the vulgarity of the world as possible. *This* Miss Tamsin Harte, however, could no longer afford to hold herself so aloof; vulgarity had to be renamed — re-evaluated, in fact, as part of life's rich rough-and-tumble. Her livelihood now depended on it.

So all this new Miss Tamsin Harte did was dig him in the ribs with one finger and say, "Now, now! None of that. Don't you try to guess their trades and occupations? Take this *parvenu* family, now — what d'you think *he* does for a living?"

"Attorney's clerk? Floor walker? Highways surveyor? That sort o' caper. How about th'others — the high-quarter lot?"

"My guess is the father doesn't work at all. He's 'consoled up to the eyeballs,' as my father used to say, God rest him."

"Ay-men," he said automatically. "And the young 'un — the one as couldn't take his eyes off of 'ee?"

"Really? I wasn't looking too closely."

" 'Course not. Still, you got some opinion, I speck?"

"He's still at school, I'm sure — not for the lessons but for the sake of the football. The 'Idle Rich,' eh — what a life!"

" 'Twas yourn once, so I heard tell."

"What I meant was it's no sort of life at all, Mister Peters."

He chuckled. "So if some ol' piskey now was to jump out o' thin air and offer 'ee such a life back again, you'd say no thank'ee, Mister, would 'ee?"

"If it meant bringing my father back to life, then ..."

"That's not what I meant — and you do know it very well."

She insisted: "I was going to say that *even* if it meant bringing my father back, I'd say 'no thank'ee, Mister' if it also meant I had to go back to living in idleness." She looked him up and down. "I think you'd have said the same at my age. You may live in idleness now but I can see you've *earned* it. You deserve it. That's different."

"Now we're cutting closer to the bone!" He sat up straighter and rubbed his hands. "What would 'ee do, then, maid — with all the piskey's gold you could carry?"

"Oh, what *wouldn't* I do!"

"Such as?"

She wondered whether to tell him her secret. Then she thought why not? After all, it was nothing to be ashamed of — they were quite alone in this bay of the shelter and there was no one else within earshot.

Her eyes strayed beyond him, fixing on a point near the western end of the Esplanade. "I'd build an hôtel," she told him. "Just there — where there's a vacant lot. The best hôtel in Cornwall. Better than the Tregenna Castle. Better than the Falmouth Hôtel. Better even than the Queen's." She nodded toward it, for it stood directly opposite the shelter, on the landward side of the Esplanade. Then, feeling she had bared too much, she laughed and added, "I don't need your piskey gold, though. I'll have it all one day, you'll see. I've already started saving up." She opened her purse and showed him two sixpences. "There!"

He laughed, too, but she realized he wasn't entirely fooled into dismissing it as just one of those passing-cloud dreams.

"Two tanners!" he said. "I had two tanners once. 'Bout your age, I was, too. And I belonged to dream of a vessel of my own — just like you and your hôtel."

"And did you get it?"

He raised his walking stick and aimed it like a telescope at a fishing boat, about two miles out. "The *Merlin*. My son do sail 'er now. My son Peter, that is, my little Benjamin."

She knew then that her earlier half-memory had been correct. He was, indeed, the Benny Peters who had lost two sons at sea.

Meanwhile he reached out and gave her wrist a hesitant squeeze, "It can be done, maid."

"If you're a man," she said, "yes. A man can go off whaling, or drilling for oil in Texas, or hunting diamonds on the African coast ... I know all the ways a *man* can fund his dreams."

"I went whaling, me," he said, not even pausing to offer token sympathy for her plight. "And there was a maid along of us — though none knew it. 'Course, she bound her chest and cut her hair ... and chawed baccy and swore worse'n any man aboard."

The possibility intrigued her, though not in any practical sense. "But if none of the crew knew of it ..." she began.

"Till we come ashore," he added.

"And then?"

He grinned and patted his breastbone.

"And then?" she insisted.

"Well," he replied, "let's just say that if I *hadn't* found her out, 'twould be some other son by some other woman out there now." He gestured vaguely toward his boat.

The Idle Rich, having reached the end of the Esplanade, by the pasture earmarked for Tamsin's dream-hôtel, had turned and were starting to stroll back again.

Benny, seeing that her eyes rarely strayed from them for long, said, "I daresay *they* got 'nuff money for your hôtel, just in loose change round the house."

"People like that?" She laughed thinly. "They wouldn't even give me the time of day."

"Ah!" He raised a finger and grinned knowingly. "That would depend, now."

"On what?"

"On your nimbleness of wit — that's what." He glanced all about them, including through the glass behind, where two boys were crossing the road. One was carrying a bucket and the other had two spades, to dig for lugworm bait. He turned to her quickly and said, "Would it be worth one o' they tanners to become 'persona greater,' as they say — with the Idle Rich? Yes or no — quick?"

"Yes!" She swallowed heavily, for sixpence was a small fortune to her — a week's tip from a guest at their boarding house. "Yes," she said again, just in case she changed her mind.

"Give it us, then." He held out his hand and then, raising his voice: "Boy! Come 'ere!"

The boys were going to ignore him until they caught sight of the silver coin. "I was first," said the first to arrive.

"Mebbe you won't be so keen when you do hear what you must do to earn 'n," the old man said. "See these four fine-feathered folk coming up? When they do reach the steps 'ere, they'll go down to the beach. The boy who earns this tanner" — he wafted it under their noses like toasted cheese — "is to throw sand at the young maid's dress. And this maid 'ere" — he jerked a thumb at Tamsin — "she'll be right behind of 'ee, and she'll clip thee round the lug'ole and tell 'ee to be off. And she'll say she knows your mother and she's gwin to tell on 'ee. And all you do do is run off, baalin' like a calf on a dry cow. *Now* who do want the tanner?"

The first volunteer lost interest; his companion stepped into the breach and tried to claim his reward now.

But the old dog made it disappear with a magician's flourish. "Forehand pay is the worst pay of all," he said. "You shall have 'n once you've done your half o' the bargain. Step lively now — here they come!"

Tamsin held her breath. Half of her wanted to carry out this exciting plan; the other half longed to take back the sixpence and run all the way home.

The moment the family started down the steps, she asked old Peters how he knew they'd do that.

"They belong to do it every day 'bout this-here time," he replied simply. "Go on now, maid. Carpet dee-em!"

For a moment she thought he was going to place a hand behind her b-t-m and propel her out of the shelter (and, for a moment, he even considered it, too). All he did, however, was take her elbow delicately between finger and thumb and gently ease her on her way.

The world swam around her as she crossed to the edge of the Esplanade. She had to keep swallowing, beacause her heart seemed to be trying to climb up out of her throat. She also had to keep remembering to breathe out.

The bribed boy came down behind her; his companion wisely stayed by the railings at the top, guarding the bucket and spades. The lad wasted no time but picked up a handful of dripping wet sand as soon as he reached the bottom of the steps, where the last tide had scooped out a small pool. He was no fool, either, for he threw that first handful directly at her, Tamsin. *Thwack!* it went, right between her shoulderblades. She had no need to *act* her outraged cry.

But even as she turned, a second handful went whizzing by and hit the Dutiful Daughter square on her left thigh — and with enough impact to stick to her dress, her dazzling white dress, and leave a dark-grey streak all the way to the ground.

"You little devil!" Tamsin cried as she ran toward him, again without calling on her thespian reserves.

He was good, though. He stood, apparently aghast at his own miscalculation, until she was close enough to fetch him one good wallop. Then he fled like the wind.

"I know you!" she called after him. "I know where you live! I'll make you laugh on the other side of your face!"

She turned to the Idle Rich. "Sir! Madam! I am so sorry!" To the daughter she repeated the words: "*So* sorry! Here — let me see what can be done."

She ran to the girl and, without a by-your-leave, began brushing away the clinging sand.

The girl, embarrassed, kept trying to say it was not necessary, that the sand was clean and would surely leave no mark once it dried ... and then she, in turn, started to brush the sand off Tamsin's back.

The sight was, apparently, comical enough to set the other three laughing — at which the two girls stopped their mutual grooming and joined in.

The Young Master's eyes were on the boy, still, who was running to the far end of the beach. He was the first to speak. "What is that little wretch's name, Miss ... er?"

Tamsin bit her lip. "Did I call him a d-e-v-i-l?" she asked, spelling out the cuss-word. "Do forgive me, *je vous en prie!* I was just so *angry*." To him she replied, "I don't actually know his name. I just said that to frighten him. But I have a fair notion where he lives, so he shan't escape chastisement, Mister ... er?"

The mother smiled and relaxed somewhat. This young lady obviously had enough *savoir faire* not to introduce herself to a gentleman before he had done her the same courtesy. "Allow me to present my children," she said. "This is my son, Victor Thorne, and his sister, Charlotte."

"Tamsin Harte." She bowed her head in Victor's direction and offered her hand to Charlotte, who shook it eagerly.

This emboldened Tamsin to offer her hand to Mrs Thorne, too, though she responded with somewhat less enthusiasm. Her husband made up for it, though. She had an inkling that this was the most exciting thing that had happened to them for weeks.

"Would you care to walk a little with us, Miss Harte?" Victor asked. "The sea breeze is so pleasant today and it will help dry off your beautiful dress."

He spoke in jest, surely, for this vaunted sea breeze smelled of low tide and dead sea creatures.

"You have a companion?" Mrs Thorne asked as she scanned the esplanade. "A lady's maid, perhaps?"

This, Tamsin realized, was the moment when it might all come crashing down around her. There was nothing for it but to take the point head-on. "Ah, Mrs Thorne, those days are over for me, I fear."

The woman frowned. "How so?"

"Once I dwelled in marble halls," she replied gaily, stretching the truth a little. "My father was one of the most respected shipping merchants in Plymouth. Indeed, in the West Country." She waved a lordly hand eastwards. "False modesty aside — he *was* the most respected one in Plymouth. He employed sixty clerks and we had a villa on fifty acres at Elburton." She smiled, as if that were the end of the tale.

"And?" Mr Thorne prompted.

She shrugged and said, "Smash."

Then, seeing they did not understand (which was, in itself, understandable), she added, "My mother and I now own a guest house in Morrab Road." She waved a hand vaguely in the right direction. "A most superior guest house, to be sure, but undeniably a guest house nonetheless." She smiled at the mother. "I suppose you'd rather I didn't walk with you now? Believe me, I'd quite understand."

It was the simple truth but Mrs Thorne naturally felt obliged to deny that such a snobbish thought had so much as crossed her mind. Her husband and children chimed in with more genuine enthusiasm. Charlotte even took her arm to prove it.

Victor, who looked as if he'd like to join in on the other side, was still keeping an eye on the boy, Tamsin noticed. His lips looked even more kissable close-to. The lad had now run to the far end of the beach and was climbing the steps to the promenade (which, for some reason, did not become the Esplanade for another three or four hundred yards).

"To tell the truth ..." Tamsin began, and then thought better of it.

"Yes?" Charlotte squeezed her arm encouragingly.

"Well, I was heartbroken when Papa died — naturally — especially when his death revealed that we were almost penniless. I thought there was surely nothing left to live for ... everything gone ..."

"But you have kept your faith?" Mrs Thorne tried putting the words into her mouth; that little hesitation had bothered her. "You believe that God is working in His own mysterious way."

"Of course," Tamsin agreed. "And that faith you mention has been richly rewarded, too. You may dismiss it as sour grapes but I assure you — I would not go back to our old way of life, now, not if ..." She hunted for some image strong enough to convince. "Not if the celebrated Cornish piskey were to pass his bottomless purse into my keeping — there!"

She could feel her words had stirred Charlotte somewhat. The tension communicated itself directly. But Mrs Thorne was staring at her in disbelief. "You mean to say you actually *prefer* filling your house with inferior strangers and waiting on them hand and foot?" she asked.

"Well, Mrs Thorne, I don't exactly wait on them. We have servants for that — as many as we ever employed living-in at Elburton, I suppose. No, I supervise the running of the house while my mother looks after the books and the kitchen. I had no idea that the world is such an interesting place and is full of such interesting people, inferior or no! I would not go back to those endless garden parties and yacht-club balls and croquet afternoons and" — she shuddered at the word — *"cricket!"*

"Steady the buffs!" Victor complained.

"Plays for Devon sometimes," Charlotte murmured, suppressing a giggle.

"Oh, I should love to *play* cricket," she protested. "It's the sitting on the boundary and watching it all happen a couple of hundred yards away."

"I think we should turn about now," Mrs Thorne said. "We are probably keeping Miss Harte from her, ah, exciting duties?"

"Not a bit, Mrs Thorne — though it is so kind of you to consider it. I work mornings and evenings. The afternoons are all my own. I am often down here on the beach or the Esplanade." She squeezed Charlotte's arm to make sure she understood why she was dropping this pearl of information.

Charlotte squeezed back.

They turned and began their return stroll to the steps. Victor was pleased at this, for now he could watch the boy without having to turn round.

Mrs Thorne monopolized the conversation most of the way, outlining the many planned excursions she and her brood would be making over the coming days, all, alas, to places that would not allow her, Tamsin, time enough to get back for her evening duties. So unfortunate! Tamsin suspected that the planning had all taken place within the past thirty seconds. She remembered how she herself had been able to cut unwanted people from her life by assuring them that they must all meet for a good chinwag one day soon.

When they reached the steps, Charlotte looked down at her dress and said, "It's quite dry."

Tamsin brushed away all that had not already fallen of its own accord and said, "There! It's as if it had never happened."

She smiled at Mrs Thorne as she spoke. The woman seemed to take it as a promise not to presume upon their accidental acquaintance and too-hasty introductions; she smiled back happily. "I do hope we run across each other again, Miss Harte," she said, carefully not extending her hand.

"After you have completed all your adventurous excursions," Tamsin agreed. "We can have a good old chinwag about it."

She let go of Charlotte's arm, reassuring her with one last squeeze, and glanced toward Victor, who, she decided, might be quite fun, actually, for a brief summer fling. And if he were rich in his own right … no, best not to think *too* far ahead.

Victor was still watching that wretched boy. Her eyes followed his and she saw that Mr Peters had come forward and was now leaning on the rails — much too close to the stairhead for the youngster's comfort. He kept plucking at the old man's sleeve and glancing back over his shoulder to see if they were coming to get him.

When the promised sixpence changed hands, they had drawn close enough for anyone on the lookout to see it. Victor, who had been on the lookout ever since the incident itself, chuckled and looked at Tamsin. Finding her eyes upon him, he gave her a reassuring wink.

Deception, she had just discovered — even a petty deception like this — is something of a two-edged sword.

2   When David Peters walked into the kitchen with a half-dozen fresh mackerel for their tea he called out to his father, "I saw *you* this afternoon."

"I seen 'ee, too," the old man replied as he came down the passage. "Out there. And I never needed no spyglass, neither." He sniffed at the fish, which were already gutted and scaled. "Call they wisht little things mackerel, do'ee?"

David ignored the jibe. "What's her name, then?" He asked as he picked off a few lingering scales around the gills of a couple of them.

" 'Oo?"

"You know who — the pretty maid in the white dress, that's who. Lucky I had the spyglass today and not the old woman!"

Benny started guiltily and put his finger to his lips.

"It's all right," David assured him. "I saw her next door with Mrs Oates." He laid the fish out head to tail to head to tail ... "These would make a good starry-gazey pie."

"You wouldn't be interested in the likes of that young maid," he told his son. "Anyway, she'd not give 'ee a second look."

"She spent enough breath on you."

"That's as maybe. *You* wouldn't hardly be interested," Benny said again. "And no more would she." He refused to be drawn any further.

He had his reasons, too.

Victor Thorne, dressed for dinner, tapped lightly on his sister's boudoir door.

"Victor?" she called out.

He let himself in, closing the door silently behind him.

"You can do up my pearls," she said. Then, to her maid, "All right, Dobbs. Just make sure everything's in order for tomorrow and then, if Mrs Harper doesn't need you tonight, you may take the rest of the day off."

The 'day' in question had already lasted thirteen hours.

"Miss Harte has frightened dear Mama out of her wits," Victor said when they were alone. "D'you think there's any danger she might actually arrange for us to go on all those dismal excursions?"

"Well — what do *you* think of her?" Charlotte asked, smiling at him archly.

"That was going to be my first question to you," he replied.

"But I got in ahead of you." She waited while he pretended that the clasp to her brooch demanded all his attention. "Go on!" she had to say at last.

"I'm thinking," he said.

"I don't believe you. I'm sure you already know precisely what you think about the young lady. I know *I* do."

"Not thinking about that," he replied.

"About what, then?"

"About whether to discuss her with you at all. All right — I'll risk it. She rigged the whole thing, you know. And that old sea salt was in cahoots with her."

Charlotte, torn between wondering what he was talking about and why he would have reservations about speaking his mind to her, asked, "What does that mean?"

"In cahoots? It means they were in league with … they were in it together."

"No! I know very well what the *words* mean, but …"

"I'm telling you they bribed that urchin to pretend to throw stuff at her and to hit you instead. I could read it in his eyes. And later I saw the old man give him a threepenny bit — or it could even have been a sixpence. I wonder if he's some sort of relation of hers? Anyway, that whole scene was rigged."

"But why?"

"Why d'you think?" He tweaked the fine points of his rampant waxed moustachioes and surveyed himself in her looking glass.

"Are you asking me?" Charlotte said.

"Not really." He was plainly satisfied with his image.

"Well, I'll tell you, anyway. Contrary to *your* conceited opinion in the matter, I think she did it all in order to become acquainted with *me!* So there!"

"I suppose we all need our daydreams," he replied loftily, "but I always find that fantasies which lack even the faintest grounding in reality are just so unsatisfactory. That's my humble opinion, anyway. I could tell with half a glance that it is, in fact, *me* with whom she wishes to become acquainted. In fact, *more* than merely acquainted, I hope."

"Such airs, Maggie!" Charlotte told her favourite doll. *"You* know it's me she's interested in. And *I* know it's me. So that's all that matters. Let us leave him blinded by his own vanity."

"Well, there's one sure way to settle the business," Victor said. He had, of course, intended provoking some such argument from the outset.

"What's that?"

"Shall we take a little stroll along the Esplanade tomorrow afternoon, sister dear?"

*   *   *

Tamsin intended saying nothing to her mother of that afternoon's encounter with the Thornes. The trickery involved in engineering the meeting would give the poor woman a seizure. But Harriet Harte had already been told something of it by their neighbour, Mr Vissick, who ran Chynoweth, the guest house next door. She was now eager to hear more.

"Tell me about Mister Peters, dear," were her first words after they sat down to dine that evening. "Do the Peterses know anyone we know? Or knew?"

The thought that Mrs Peters, the woman who cut off her hair and bound her breasts to go whaling — and who drank and cussed worse than any man aboard — might have any friends in common with her mother was just too comical. Tamsin had to struggle not to laugh.

But she also needed time to discover how much her mother already knew, for she would have to tailor her own story to that.

Now it so happened that dinner was the one daily occasion on which Harriet Harte would not countenance the slightest mention of business; all such affairs, no matter how urgent, had to wait until the moment when, if there had been gentlemen present, she and her daughter would have retired to the drawing room. 'One may be poor,' she often said, 'but one still has to maintain one's standards wherever possible.'

So Tamsin replied, "Most of what I could tell you would have to wait until after we retire to the drawing room, Mama."

This fitted a common turn in their nightly talks with each other. Tamsin felt that her mother's restriction on commercial conversation belonged to their former life of leisure and frivolity; here, now, in their present straitened circumstances, it merely got in the way of all sensible dialogue. She often said as much, too, so her mother's hackles were well primed to rise at this first hint of tonight's instalment.

"Don't be absurd," she snapped. Then, curbing her annoyance and forcing herself to seem jocular once more, "Next you'll be telling me you engaged in *commercial* conversation with him — a total stranger!"

Tamsin smiled apologetically, "And if I did? We'd still have to wait until we reached the sanctity of the drawing room. Or — God send the day! — are you beginning to see sense at last? Are you now saying you *want* to hear about it? Commercial or not?"

Her mother, realizing she'd been led into a trap, said nothing. Her lips worked as if she were chewing vigorously — although she had not yet taken up a single spoonful of the fish soup before her.

Her daughter tasted a morsel. "No one can cook seafood half so well as Mrs Pascoe," she said.

Her mother did not know it but this was, in fact, the first shot of her daughter's latest campaign to improve their income. "One does not discuss such things either at table, dear," she replied. "You know that. And it's 'half *as* well,' anyway."

"One did not discuss them in the days when one's livelihood did not depend upon it. I know *that.*"

"We shall maintain our standards for as long as we are able."

"However inappropriate they may be?"

Harriet fell silent again, though the excellence of Mrs Pascoe's fish soup had almost tricked her into agreeing.

Tamsin persisted. "And even if it actually *harms* us?"

Still silence.

"I declare that if the house went on fire, you'd not let me run out of doors before putting on my gloves!"

"Who says a whale's a bird?" her mother responded lightly. It was a family saying — meaning 'you are no longer talking any sense so let's change the subject.'

After a further silence, Harriet said, "I merely wondered how you happened to engage in conversation with Mister Peters in the first place."

"You mean did I break the ice or did he?"

" 'Break the ice'? Where do you pick up such lamentable expressions?"

"Which would be more dreadful in your eyes — me speaking to him first, or him speaking to me?"

"Tamsin, dear, I am trying my best to be pleasant and civil. Anyway, the correct English is *my* speaking first — not *me* speaking first."

"It's a wonder anyone can speak at all, sometimes," Tamsin said to no one in particular. "While you are merely trying to be civil, I, on the other hand, am trying my best to *make* something of our present situation."

"Oh? And do you suppose I am not?"

Tamsin adopted a conciliatory tone. "I'm sure that, by your own lights, Mama dear, you are. But your lights warn of rocks we have already left far behind us. We sail in new, uncharted waters now, and there is so much more we could be doing — *should* be doing."

"If your father were still alive ..." Harriet's lip trembled. But then she recalled that appeals to the dead father's memory had been proving less and less rewarding lately. Her lips compressed to a thin, bitter line. "... you wouldn't be talking to me like this," she concluded.

"If Papa were still alive," Tamsin said, "we should still have lost all our money. We should still have bought this place, or something very like it. And we should be doing our very best to recover our fortune."

"Then where's the difference? You still seem to be implying I'm *not* doing my best. I demean myself every single hour in this hateful business." She shuddered at being forced to utter the dreaded word. "Your father would call you a most ungrateful child, I'm sure."

"Well, Mama, there we must agree to differ."

"You wouldn't be speaking like this — I know that."

"I quite agree with you — but not for the same reason. I think Papa would already be doing all the things that we are neglecting — things I'd like to see us doing."

"Oh! You keep trying to worm the conversation round to topics that you *know* are unseemly at a civilized dinner table — it is most vexatious!"

"This house, this *business,* is our ..."

"Tamsin! Stop it this instant! I will not tolerate commercial discourse at my dinner table. I never have done and I never shall. So please respect my wishes, young lady. *I* know you're far too old to be sent to bed without supper — so try to behave as if *you* knew it, too."

Tamsin wondered whether or not to develop a convenient headache. She decided against it, recalling that that particular tactic had been proving less and less rewarding lately. Instead she remarked, "I thought the Morrab Gardens looked especially lovely this morning."

"Yes, dear." Her mother agreed eagerly, glad to see her daughter was being sensible at last. "It must have been the overnight rain. The green — so bright!"

"And so *many* greens. That is their glory, of course — the infinite variety."

"The thought crossed my mind the very first time I saw them."

"Every green in the box."

"Just so."

"Viridian, emerald, leaf green ..."

"Yes, dear — we can agree that there are many greens to be found there."

"Chrome green, olive green, sage green ... even khaki, I shouldn't wonder ..."

"Tamsin!" Harriet rang the bell for Bridget, the maid, to collect their soup bowls and serve the main dish, which was cold cuts of yesterday's beef joint with sautéd mashed potatoes and new season's maincrop peas.

Several minutes later, after Bridget had withdrawn again, Tamsin said, "And then there are all the greens you can get by mixing. Chrome green and emerald, for instance, would give you the green of that cactus by the first terrace."

"Tamsin!"

"Yes, Mama?"

"I shall hurl something at your head in a moment."

"You mean not talk any more about greens?"

"Not another word."

"Very well."

They ate in silence — and with relish, for Mrs Pascoe was pretty good at roast beef, too. Then Tamsin said, "Of course, what shows them off so well is the rich *brown* of the soil and the multicoloured *greys* you get in the granite. One forgets how important grey is in any colour scheme."

Harriet recalled how, when Tamsin had cried as a little girl in the nursery, Nanny Pickford had cured it by cupping her ear and singing out, 'Loud-er! I can't he-ar you. More!' and, of course, poor bewildered little Tamsin had soon dried up. So now, in that same spirit, she said, "I know so little about the truly artistic mixing of colours, darling. Do tell me — it sounds absolutely fascinating, I must say."

"One thinks of grey as just the simple blending of lamp black and flake white," the girl replied. She knew very well what her mother was about but she was determined to win this one — eventually. "Yet in the right hands it can become the subtlest colour of all. Take the colour sold as 'Payne's Grey' ..."

It was the start of an impromptu verbal essay that lasted until, had there been gentlemen present, the ladies would have retired to the drawing room. Long before it was over, Harriet was listening in genuine fascination — not so much at the content but at her daughter's ability to keep it going. George, her late husband, had compared their daughter to the eternal drip that can wear away the strongest granite — which, of course, made it all the more important to keep her under control now.

As she'd said to Mr Vissick next door, when he told her of the encounter on the Esplanade that afternoon, "She's still a girl in a woman's outer form. She's young. She's headstrong. She's missing her father much more than she'll ever admit to. And, through some misguided form of bravado, she's actually embracing our decline in fortune as if it were the finest thing that could possibly have happened. She used to love balls and picnics and amateur theatricals and parties of every sort — as any young girl ought, indeed, to do. But now she'll pretend it used to weary her beyond all measure. She'll tell you she'd far rather be supervising the maids and dealing with guests — some of whom, as I'm sure you know very well, dear Mister Vissick, are dreadfully common persons — and indulging all sorts of commercial fantasies."

Mr Vissick tut-tutted sympathetically. Normally he would have glanced in horror at his watch by now and rushed off pleading the call of duty. But he was a widower — and not happy at it — and Mrs Harte was a handsome woman, alone in the world ... and the two houses, run together, would make an admirable private hôtel. So he fixed her with a large and sympathetic gaze and tut-tutted avidly.

"Of course, it will pass," Harriet went on. "The novelty of our new way of life will wear off while the drudgery remains. Then she'll meet a handsome young fellow with an income and prospects, who will sweep her off her feet and remind her where a woman's duty and best interests lie. And somehow" — she sighed — "we must contrive to keep the lid on things until that happy day."

The moment she heard herself say 'keep the lid on things' she regretted the phrase. More and more these days — and for reasons she could not divine — common and even slangy expressions were creeping into her speech — to say nothing of Tamsin's. While she struggled to think of a respectable alternative, words like 'assuage ... mollify ... propitiate ...' flitted through her mind but refused to settle. Vissick saw his chance. His parting words were: "If there's anything I might do ..." Later, Harriet wondered how he might have finished that sentence if he had stayed.

'It will pass,' she would say to herself whenever Tamsin's forceful personality threatened to sweep everyone else up in her enthusiasms. 'This is not the real Tamsin. She will calm down soon — O Lord, pray let it be soon! — and she will forget all this nonsense.'

She found herself rehearsing silent incantations to more or less that effect throughout the rest of their meal.

"Now!" she said magnanimously as they settled to a final cup of tea in the drawing room. "What have you been bursting to tell me all this while?"

"Oh, it hardly matters now," Tamsin replied curtly. "It's gone off the boil."

"Oh good!" Harriet took out a box of bonbons. "Just for that you may have *two* tonight."

Tamsin took one and said that, hot or cold, she'd better state the facts, just in case Mr Vissick's no-doubt third-hand account had got it all wrong.

"I was sitting in the shelter there — I didn't even notice this old sea dog beside me. But after a while — you know how one does — we got chatting and he ..."

"What about? Who started it?"

"Does it matter? There were several hundred people all around us, if that's what worries you. Oh, I remember now! There was this family — father, mother, daughter about my age, son a couple of years older — and they were obviously a cut above your average day tripper."

"Indeed?" Harriet's attention doubled suddenly.

"Yes. Old clothes — holiday clothes — nothing fashionable — except Victor, of course — the son. He's a real masher ..."

"Victor?" Harriet almost screamed. The horror of that vulgarism, 'masher,' was entirely swallowed up inside the larger horror of the Christian name. "You knew them? They were our friends once? But I don't remember a young Victor ..."

"*Calme-toi, chère Mamman!* I didn't know them from Adam — then."

"So when *did* you ...?"

"If you'll only listen, I'll tell you! The old sea dog, whose name is Benny Peters, by the way — a retired fisherman of Newlyn, but a man with a thousand tales of adventures on the seven seas, I feel sure — anyway, he made some remark about them."

"A remark? A low fisherman making *remarks* about his betters? Tamsin! Did you permit it? What were you thinking of? I hope you put a flea in his ear? I mean ... oh, botheration!"

"D'you wish to hear about this family or not?"

"Oh ... very well — go on. But I warn you — I don't warm to one single element in this tale so far."

"Captain Peters" — she decided to promote him, to ease her mother's mind — "likes to play this harmless but amusing little game. He sits in that shelter on the Esplanade and he tries to sum people up by their dress, their demeanour, the way they walk, and so on."

"And how does he know whether or not he's right?"

"He doesn't need to. It's only a game — and if you think about it, we're all playing it, all the time. Anyway, he said he was sure that the members of this unfashionably dressed family were 'high-quarter folk,' as he put it. So I followed them down the steps to the beach, hoping to overhear them — to see if he was right, you understand."

"Tamsin!"

"It was only a game, Mama. However, some wretched little urchin took exception to a remark I made — I told him not to splash about in the pool near the foot of the steps. So he threw a sandball at me — which missed and hit Charlotte instead. She's the daughter. Charlotte Thorne."

"Thorne?" Harriet's ears pricked up at the name. "Mrs Cunningham, who came from Dawlish Warren, she was a Thorne —

originally from Somerset. Yeomen farmers but they made their
money out of quarrying that glorious honey-coloured limestone. I
wonder if that's them? Go on." She suddenly remembered they
had left Charlotte with a wet sandball on her dress. "Oh, good
heavens! What did you do?"

"I apologized, of course, introduced myself ..."

"And, of course, they could hear at once that you are one of
us and not one of *them!*"

"And we went for a little stroll along the beach — and that
was all."

"All? Did Mister Thorne not give you a card for me? Will they
call upon us?"

"I doubt it. I must say they seem to have planned a remarkably
busy holiday."

"But you cannot possibly pursue a friendship with people
who have not called upon your parents! Or parent, in our case.
It's quite unthinkable."

"I said nothing about a friendship. It was a casual encounter
on a holiday beach. It had an unfortunate beginning but a happy
ending — I mean, we parted on good terms."

"But ...'Victor' and 'Charlotte' ... You seem familiar with
their Christian names yet you call it a casual encounter? How
can that be?"

"Oh dear, Mamma — you know how young people carry on
these days."

"I don't, my dear. I don't know you. I don't understand you.
And what is more — I'm afraid I never shall."

"Anyway," Tamsin decided to strike while not appearing to,
"I was far more interested in Captain Peters."

"Oh?"

"As a source of the freshest possible fish — straight off the
quayside, in fact."

"Oh dear!" Harriet slumped. "Business!"

"Yes. *New* business."

"Worse and worse!"

"But perhaps it had better keep for some other day."

The seed was planted, anyway, she told herself. Give it time to
do what seeds usually do.

3 It drizzled most of the following morning, but come noon there were small patches of blue and by early afternoon there was enough to make a sailor's shirt. At half-past two, when Tamsin changed into a summer frock and white lawn gloves and set out on the short walk to the Esplanade, the cloud was thin and high, the breeze had stilled, and the evaporating rain raised the humidity to the point where nobody wanted to do anything at all strenuous.

Ladies with parasols drifted along the Esplanade like stately galleons of old, half becalmed; their attendant gentlemen were no more animated than the carved figureheads that would have graced such vessels then. Men and women who had 'seen the Great God Pan' — as the common euphemism had it — thought of lying naked and entwined in shady groves, lost in forests of spice trees, and making slow, soporific love together. Those who, like Tamsin, had not yet experienced that sublime vision wondered at the restless stirrings in their sinews and could not interpret the curious sensations of hunger that filled them, even after a good, sustaining luncheon.

The moment she moved into the shelter she understood why it was empty, despite the languid crowds all around. The glazed partitions shielded her from the slightest breeze while seeming also to magnify the rays of the sun, making them even more pitiless. She felt suffocated and moved out again without even sitting down. She raised her parasol again and crossed the Esplanade to stand at the railings, looking out to sea. What little breeze there was came fitfully from that direction.

For a while she watched the horses on the Ladies' Bathing Beach as they backed the bathing machines out into waist-deep water, where the attendant uncoupled the horse and led him ashore again — after ensuring, of course, that each lady was safely secured to the machine by a rope buckled about her waist. Tamsin envied the women as they bravely launched themselves into the cool, slick-calm water and lay there, bobbing gently up and down in perfect safety until their time was up. She envied the gentlemen more, swimming off the rocks at Battery Point. No one told *them* that diving and vigorous swimming was injurious to their health. They could horse around for hours, 'bombing' one another, swimming to Chimney Rock and back, or even farther, to the mouth of the Larrigan River, almost half way to Newlyn.

If she were the last person in the world now, she'd take off everything and skip down to the water and swim as boisterously as any man, all the way to Newlyn and back. Even to imagine it made her shiver with pleasure. There was something so tawdry about the men skulking away over there on Battery Rocks and the women floating like tethered, dismasted hulks over here. A wave of anger passed over her. She wanted to pick up something and shake it. It soon passed, dissipated in the cloying heat, but it left behind a residue of frustration.

Thoughts of Newlyn led her back to practical affairs, to Benny Peters and the fresh fish he landed daily — or on any day when there was wind enough to put to sea. On this windless afternoon his son was probably tending lobster pots, which could be done in a rowing boat from the shore. Not that any fisherman did much rowing hereabouts; they all seemed to prefer sculling with one oar over the stern. She wondered about his son, David. The old man was in his sixties, she guessed, so the son was probably in his forties. On the other hand, he'd been described to her as the youngest — the little Benjamin — when his brothers drowned, so he could be quite a bit younger.

Two friends in the fishing trade would be twice as good as one if her present plans came to anything.

And talk of the devil — or think of him, anyway — there was Captain Peters coming along the Esplanade now. Just when she was beginning to think that neither he nor the Thornes were venturing abroad today. He walked as if the heat had not yet reached him, striding out and swinging his cane. Tamsin compared him with other old men on the Esplanade, sour creatures hunched in bath chairs or walking on eggs and all looking as if they had never done a day's hard labour in their lives. It confirmed everything she had come to realize of late — that undeserved leisure was more of a disease than a blessing.

The day grew brighter at the mere sight of him. "I rather think your boat won't be out today, Captain Peters," she said as he drew near.

He accepted the title without complaint. He had trimmed and shaped his beard since yesterday; now it fringed his face like the rim of a white plate.

"Not so, maid," he replied, joining her at the rail. "See the lobster boat, the one nearest?" He pointed out a rowing boat with a single oarsman standing at the stern as he hauled up one of a line of pots.

"Your boy?" she guessed.

"The same." He drew out a spyglass and placed it to his eye.

"Is it lobsters or brandy today?" she asked.

He glanced at her sharply.

"I've heard tales," she told him.

"And tales is all they are, maid. The days of Harry Carter and brandy-smuggling in hogsheads by the dozens — they'm long gone. There's not a man left in the whole o' Newlyn could tell 'ee the first thing about smuggling now. How many bottles do'ee want, then?"

She laughed and said she'd have to consult with her mother about that. "So it couldn't possibly be brandy in those pots today?" she added.

He passed her the glass. "See for yourself."

The magnification was so great that she could not hold the image still. However, it was good enough to show the dancing silhouette of a youngish man hauling line but that was not good enough for her. She bent at the knees and rested the tube upon one of the knobs of the Esplanade railings. And then, with its restless hunting reduced to a mere tremor, she saw a slim, well-built young man, clean shaven and with dark if not jet black hair. The haze made colours hard to distinguish. All his movements were lithe and assured. She could imagine him being just as much at home in the roughest of seas. He did not look much over twenty-five.

There is a pleasure in watching anyone skilled at work — weaver, thatcher, juggler, trapeze artiste — their skills hold the attention long after they, as people, would have exhausted us. And that, Tamsin told herself, was why she continued to watch young David Peters at his toil. She kept it up so long that her unused eye protested and sent patches of blackness to overlay the view.

"Would I be able to come to Newlyn and buy fish from you direct?" she asked as she straightened up again. She collapsed the spyglass and passed it back.

"Miss Harte!" Before the Captain could answer, Victor's greeting, from no more than a dozen paces away, intervened.

She was about to turn and reply when the expression on the old man's face held her attention. It was a very particular expression and a perfect replica of one she had seen on someone else's face quite recently — just before they left Plymouth to come and settle here, she thought. Alas, the precise occasion eluded her, and she could delay no longer in greeting the Thornes; but it haunted her the rest of that afternoon.

"Miss Thorne! Mister Thorne!" She faced them with a smile though her heart was beating fast and she felt that strange, angry restlessness hovering near again. "What a pleasant surprise. I thought you would be lost amid the thousand-and-one antiquities of Land's End this afternoon. Are your parents cogging it all on their own?"

"I'll leave 'ee be," Peters said.

She turned back, intending to ask him to stay, but he was already moving off. "My question?" she called after him.

"You must ask your old woman, maid," he replied over his shoulder. "I must ask my young man. See 'ee 'gain."

"Strange man," she murmured. "I wonder why he came all this way, just to turn round and go back again?"

"That was the old sea dog you were with yesterday," Victor commented. "A friend of your family's?" Today he wore a cream blazer with a thin, dark-blue stripe and ice-blue binding, and he had a matching blue cane with a plain silver knob.

"I hope he soon will be — though I met him for the first time yesterday. Shall we walk a little?" She offered Charlotte her arm and they set off westwards, following the Captain by at least a hundred paces.

"You are swift in your alliances, Miss Harte," Victor said as he stepped to her side. He offered her his arm, too, but she tapped it with the butt of her parasol and said, "Not quite that swift, Mister Thorne."

He smiled, unabashed. "See!" Charlotte taunted. She was wearing another sailor-girl outfit, down to her ankles today.

"Not another word," he warned her. Then, to Tamsin, "What was the object of maritime interest?"

She was about to tell him the truth when something inside her refused. Instead, she told him a tale she had heard a few weeks ago. "D'you see the rocks that are just beginning to be exposed by the tide? There's an ancient mineshaft there, which goes down many fathoms. It's got an iron cover now and they say the sand is slowly infiltrating and filling it up. But in the days of Captain Peters's grandfather they extracted tin worth over seventy thousand guineas from it. There was a building over it, of course, to hold back the sea."

Charlotte tugged them to the railings and peered down at the sands and rocks. "It was only a century ago," she said, "and yet there's not a trace of it left. Vanity of vanities!"

Victor raked the heavens with his eyes and smiled apologetically at Tamsin. "Do tell us more about life among the *hoi polloi*, Miss Harte."

"Not if you simply wish to mock, Mister Thorne — and anyway, *hoi polloi* does not need 'the' before it. The Greek words already express the definite article." She stamped her foot. "And now you've made me sound like my mother! I warn you — I have never found it easy to forgive any man who causes me to sound like my mother. I shall not speak to you for five whole minutes."

He drew breath to protest but let it out unused when she added, "And if you attempt to address me, I shall make it ten. So tell me, dear Miss Thorne, how long shall you be staying here? And, indeed, *where* are you staying? I felt so sure yesterday that we were never to meet again that I neglected to ask."

Charlotte replied that they were staying at the Queen's Hôtel until the end of July. And would Miss Harte kindly consider calling her Charlotte? Tamsin thanked her for the compliment and asked her to reciprocate.

"And he's Victor," Charlotte added.

"No, he isn't, I'm afraid. He is *still* Mister Thorne. Tell me — I never had a brother, younger or older. It must be beastly?"

The girl caught her drift and fell in at once. "Pretty beastly," she agreed. "They think they are protecting one by frightening all their best-looking friends away."

"Perhaps they judge their friends' intentions by reference to their own — toward their friends' younger sisters and other females, I mean."

Charlotte giggled. "I think you must be right, my dear. He is a terrible masher."

"He? Oh! I assumed we were talking about brothers in general. Are we talking just about him?" She tilted her head in Victor's direction but paid him no heed. "Very well then. I hesitate to criticize people I barely know but I have to say I think it was imprudent of your parents to give him — to give any boy — the name Victor. The poor dear!"

The poor dear gazed skyward and whistled through his teeth.

Charlotte said, "I'm sure you're right, Tamsin, but I should adore to hear your reasons."

"Well, if they had named him ... oh, I don't know ... Admiral, say. Would they not have condemned him to a life before the mast, behind the mast, above the mast, toiling night and day until he had exchanged a snotty's spyglass for an admiral's gold epaulettes and fore-and-after? And just think what a laughing stock he'd be if he never rose above commodore! I feel sure that your brother — when we see fit to talk to him again — will break down and confess that all his life he's felt compelled to make conquests wherever he goes. His name compels it. How his friends would laugh if the Victor were more often the Vanquished! And oh, how he *longs* to climb off that treadmill of endless empty conquests and engage in warm, sincere friendships with all those young females whose hearts he feels driven to possess — driven by his slave-master of a name. Oh dear!" She stopped and bit her lip.

"What now, Tamsin dear?" Charlotte asked.

Victor sauntered on as if unaware they had halted.

"I hope he doesn't blub when he confesses it. I admire any man who's strong enough to admit he has a softer, weaker side to his nature — but not to the extent of blubbing. They always want to use my handkerchief. I draw the line at that."

Still Victor strolled on, head in air, hoping to compel them to call him back.

Tamsin put a finger to her lips, executed a full hundred-and-eighty degree wheel, and steered her friend back toward the shelter near where they had met — and also, as it happened, toward the Queen's, where they were staying.

They must, she reasoned, have taken several front-facing rooms — and, of course, several cheaper ones at the back for their servants. And therefore, even if Victor and Charlotte had been watching with only half an eye, one of them must have seen her out there with the Captain. Victor must have been the one, in fact, for Charlotte was so eager to meet her again that she would probably have rushed out hatless and gloveless. So why had Victor delayed?

It could be because of the enormous vanity of his wardrobe — she had to allow that. He would take longer to prepare himself, even for a simple stroll, than most women even. Or it could have been because he wanted to observe her at his leisure. Through binoculars, perhaps?

The idea both thrilled and angered her. What right had he ...? asked one half of her. On the other hand, she felt flattered. Simply by *being* — not doing anything special, just being — she had compelled him to notice her, to watch her, to think about her, to be intrigued enough to observe her.

So she was intriguing!

The sense of power it gave her was not exactly new; she had experienced it before at picnics and balls, ever since spotty boys had started eyeing her in that special, hangdog, hopeless way. But then she, too, had been trapped inside the gilded cage of social conventions. Now she was free. Or free-er. As far as her own behaviour was concerned, three-fourths of the pages in the etiquette books could be ripped out and discarded. And the sense of power was still there, as strong as ever — and as unfettered by rules as never before.

Tamsin did not reason it out in so many words, of course; but the feeling was all the stronger for that. Intuitions that remain unspoken cannot be tested (nor diminished) by mere logic.

In a curious way Charlotte now confirmed the general drift of those same intuitions. "We've shaken him off," she said, thinking that had been Tamsin's intention all along. "Now tell me about the freedom you spoke of yesterday — you know — the liberation you've felt since withdrawing from Society. I want to hear it all before he comes back."

"Really?" Tamsin's Society days were now so remote — in psychological if not in calendar weeks — that she did not immediately understand Charlotte's fears. "Why shouldn't he hear of it, too?"

"Oh, I'm sure he's *dying* to hear it all — and to ask a thousand questions beside — just like me. But he'd hate *me* to hear of it. Your words might unsettle me, you see." She glanced over her shoulder. "Damn! He's coming! Oops — sorry I said damn!"

"I say it ten times a day, don't worry. I say it even louder than that, too." A thought struck her. "You must have *some* sort of power over him. Why did he warn you — 'not another word' — back there?"

"Oh lordy! I couldn't tell you that! Not so soon, anyway."

"You don't need to tell *me*. Just remember what it was and threaten to use it if he starts getting uppity with you. Here he is!" She turned what she hoped was a dazzling smile upon him and, offering her arm, said, "Victor! Dear boy! You've decided to give up your sulks and join us at last. I'm *so* glad."

It unsettled him, as, of course, she had intended. Why should she be alone in this restlessness?

"What d'you mean — sulks!" he exclaimed in a wounded tone, though he was so eager to link arms with her that he could not complain too much.

"Now don't start all that again," she said, giving his hand a squeeze between her arm and ribs. "I was just about to explain those things I said to your mother yesterday afternoon. I fear she was rather shocked — though, of course, she's far too well bred and good natured to show it much. However, if I'd had time enough to explain myself more thoroughly, I'm sure I could have relieved her apprehensions entirely." She smiled at him again. "But perhaps you'd rather I didn't?"

Trapped between that smile and his own inner certainty that Charlotte could only be polluted by the no-doubt subversive sentiments this divine young woman would pour into their ears, he was paralyzed.

"I'm so grateful," Tamsin went on, "that when we were in Society my dear father encouraged me to study a wide variety of opinions — even those with which he violently disagreed."

"Did he by Jove! But why?" Victor asked in amazement.

"I remember asking him that same question once. He told me that he and Mama could not possibly hover at my elbow day and night until they passed me into the safe-keeping of a husband. The day would surely come when some engaging serpent would spring upon me some false idea — atheism, communism, socialism, suffragism, colonial freedom, love of Wagner ... the list was long ..."

"Can you talk like this at the drop of a hat?" Victor asked.

"You can go away again," Charlotte told him. "You don't *have* to stay, you know. Tamsin and I can perfectly well chaperon each other."

"Anyway," Tamsin insisted, "my father's point was that if I'd met the false ideology before, exposed in cold print rather than on the honeyed tongue of some beguiling wit, I would be armed against it. And indeed I am. Wild horses would not drag me to see *Lohengrin,* for instance."

Victor laughed hopelessly. "There must be some way of telling when you're being serious."

"You know very well the points I'm making, Victor," she replied evenly. "And what is more, you know it's right. Young ladies today cannot be shielded from the world as their mothers were. It is far too dangerous for them."

"You said 'points.' That's only one."

"You know the other one, too — it concerns you."

"I'd like to hear it!" He was rash enough to speak in that challenging tone which believes the other's words to be hollow.

"Then you shall," Tamsin said. "I know what went through your mind yesterday afternoon. You saw far more of what really happened than the other three members of your family ..."

"He thinks you conspired with the Captain and that urchin to make it all happen," Charlotte blurted out.

"And he was quite right."

The two of them halted in amazement. Indeed, Victor was so amazed that he quite forgot to crow over his sister at being proved so right so swiftly. "You admit it?" he asked.

"I'll do more — I'll even explain it. In fact, I could not honourably continue our new-found friendship without explaining it — d'you agree?"

"You are the strangest young woman," he said.

"I'm not at all what you had in mind, eh? The simple truth is that I saw two interesting-looking young people who looked as if they would have made wonderful companions in the days when I, too, moved in Society. I was explaining my circumstances to the Captain, whom, as I say, I had only just met — sometimes one can unburden one's soul more easily to total strangers, don't you think? Anyway, I was pointing out that you were now so far above me in rank that even to think of striking up an acquaintance was impossible. And so, while you continued walking on down here and back, he persuaded me I was wrong. Or at least to give it a try. And so, between us — and the handy arrival of those urchins — we devised our little stratagem. It deceived you, Charlotte, for which I apologize deeply. But your sharp-eyed brother saw through it all at once."

Victor basked in this apparent praise until she added, "Not that it has benefited him much!"

"Oh?" He was stung.

"Be honest, now, Victor," she urged. "You thought I was simply flirting with you. Your aspirations did not rise above a brief 'fling,' as they call it — a seaside fling — and I'd be one more notch on your own private tallystick of conquests."

When she was only half way through, he jerked his arm out of her grasp. By the time she had finished his nostrils were flaring, the strings of his neck looked about to snap, and he had trouble forcing his clenched teeth apart long enough to tell her he'd never heard so much rot in his life. He added, moreover, that she must be some kind of madwoman and that the rest of his holiday could not be more improved than by a decision, here and now, never to see her again. He was so angry that he strode off without commanding Charlotte to join him.

But Charlotte herself knew it was bound to come. "That's the end of that," she said bleakly, and very close to tears.

"D'you think so?" Tamsin replied evenly. "I think it's more like the real beginning." The truth was she did not greatly care which it might be, beginning or end. She was alive with pleasure now and that strange, unsatisfactory restlessness had been lifted from her.

4 There was a curious tailpiece to Tamsin's encounter with the young Thornes that afternoon. She suspected that Victor would go straight to his room and sulk until his self-esteem was restored. Doubtless he would gaze out of his window now and then and she wanted to be sure that every time he did so he he would see her out there, enjoying the day and never, *never* looking up to try to catch his eye. If nothing else it would show him that *she* had not been reduced to sulking at home.

But she needed something to underline the point. Or, better still, someone. To be seen as the the centre of a small, jolly group would be just the thing now; but even one conversational partner would do.

And that was when she remembered David Peters, who, she now saw, was still sculling round just beyond the Wherry Rocks. Surely he had lifted and rebaited all his lobsterpots long before now? Could it be that he was just drifting out there, trying to summon the courage to come ashore and introduce himself? Even if the Captain hadn't mentioned yesterday's encounter, his son must have been aware of their meeting today. And if his eyesight was any good at all, he must have noticed the pair of them watching him through the spyglass. She felt a slight rush when she realized he must have seen how long she had remained glued to the eyepiece.

If he was just sculling around, waiting for courage, it was a further example of that strange power young women like her seemed to have over men. But this time her response was different. She would not welcome such power over this David Peters, whom she had not even met. Over Victor, yes. She was already fairly sure she wanted something more than a simple friendship with him — precisely what, she couldn't say, but whatever it might turn out to be, she wanted it on her terms, not his. Hence her little battle of wills with him today; if he wasn't willing to accept that ... well, the sea was big and full of fish. And her choice out there was much wider than his.

But David Peters was not to be considered in that light at all. She already had a place earmarked for him in her scheme of things; he was part of quite a different battle of wills — the one against her mother. Young Mr Peters's part in it was to be commercial. Not *strictly* commercial, maybe. If they also became friends, it would do no harm. Indeed, it could help the commercial connection through difficult patches — and every commercial connection must certainly have such patches from time to time.

But that was all. She had no room for anything else. None of those games young ladies in Society might play — setting one suitor off against another ... making half a dozen young men dance through the hoops. There was no time in her life for such idle games. She would decide from the very outset, even before they became acquainted, which young man should occupy *this* rôle in her life and which should occupy *that* one. And which should have no rôle at all.

She had already decided that Victor would do very nicely in the romantic part — for the moment, anyway. If he should turn out to be unsuitable after all, well, the Thornes would be leaving Penzance soon enough, and no doubt someone else would come along. On the other hand, if he proved suitable, she'd find ways to encourage him to return, on his own. He was probably over twenty-one and he must surely have private funds. All in all, then, he was, for the moment, by far the most suitable young man for that particular part.

So, if David Peters was milling around out there, trying to summon the courage to come ashore and make the first romantic overture, she really owed it to him to disabuse him of the notion as soon as possible.

She descended to the beach and walked straight down to the water's edge, at the nearest possible point to him. He noticed, of course. In fact, he stood stock still and watched her all the way. He was too far off for her to want to shout but she lowered her parasol behind her and used it as a mask behind which (or, from his viewpoint, in front of which) she waved.

She had to repeat the gesture several times before he dared pick up both oars (so they did carry two, she realized, even if they preferred to use only one) and row the boat in the conventional way. Around the rocks he steered and into the shallow, low-tide inlet between them and the beach. As he drew near he rowed even more vigorously — showing off to her, she suspected, until she realized that the extra speed would carrying him farther into the shallows. In fact, so powerful were his strokes that the prow of his boat finally came to rest on dry sand — or undrowned sand, at least, for his feet, as he leaped ashore with the painter seemed to draw up the water and turn the dull sand into shimmering circles the size of dinner plates. He walked on circles of light.

"If there's one thing a fisherman hates," he said jovially, "it's getting his feet wet. There's nowhere on board for him to get them really dry again."

His educated speech, notwithstanding his marked Cornish accent, surprised her after his father's strong dialect. "Mister Peters?" she said. "I was talking with your father earlier."

She felt ashamed of herself. It seemed such a lame greeting, especially after his opening words.

"You have the advantage of me, Miss ...?" he replied.

"Oh, I'm sorry. Miss Harte. Do forgive me."

"Forgiven," he replied lightly. "D'you want a lobster for your tea, Miss Harte? The sea has been generous today."

"Oh, how kind." She wondered how she'd carry it back.

"I'll tie his claws," he said. "And I can probably find an old bag under the seat."

"That's *very* kind."

He tilted his head toward the bay. "Care for a little trip? Round the Wherry and back?"

"Oh ... well ..."

She realized that a little competition — or the long-distance *suggestion* of it — would give Victor lots to think about. However, a half-hour trip alone in a boat with another young man would hardly do, especially coming right on the heels of their parting. She wanted to give Victor a chance to reflect, to return, to beg forgiveness, and to be more reasonable in future — not to give him an excuse to walk away entirely, muttering something about sour grapes.

He grinned. "My father was right. He said you wouldn't give me the time of day."

As he spoke his eyes quartered the Esplanade, looking, she realized, for the Thornes. From out in the bay he would not have been able to guess the nature of their parting; for all he knew they might have gone back to the hôtel for another pair of gloves or something equally trivial.

And suddenly — seeing a younger version of his father in the son's features — she remembered where she had previously seen that rather curious expression in the old man's eyes, the moment Victor Thorne had appeared. It was last year in Plymouth, on the Hoe, about a month before her father's death. There had been some kind of naval pageant there, part of which had involved a Græco-Roman wrestling contest between the crews of two ships. She had managed to get quite close to one of the teams before her mother hauled her away, saying it was not seemly for a young lady to stand so close to the wrestlers.

But just before that she had been watching the petty officer who coached one of the teams; he would massage the muscles of the young man who was about to go into the ring, and he'd talk to him all the while about his opponent. During that time, he, the coach, never took his eyes off that opponent. And the look in those eyes was identical to the one she had seen in the old Captain's as he surveyed young Victor from head to toe, or from straw boater to summer shoe.

This memory came back to her in a flash, so that the young man's words were still in her ears: 'He said you wouldn't give me the time of day.' Her memory and his words coalesced into a sudden understanding of what was really going on here. Then, too, she knew the answer to her own earlier question as to why the Captain had bothered to walk all the way round the seafront from Newlyn to the Esplanade, just to look at his son for half a minute through the spyglass.

"I'll bet he nags you about not settling down, eh?" she guessed, suggesting by her tone that she, too, was more than familiar with the experience.

"Often enough." He smiled ruefully but now his air was relaxed. His earlier, slightly amused wariness was gone. He half-sat half-leaned against the gunwhale of his boat, just to one side of the bow stem. "Parents!" he added. "What are we to do with them, Miss Harte?"

"What indeed, Mister Peters!" Her mind was still racing over the implications of this discovery.

"We could discuss it out on the water," he suggested hopefully.

"Ah, Mister Peters!" She shook her head sadly. "Agreeable though that would certainly be, I think we should postpone it to some other day."

"Tomorrow?" he suggested.

"Some other day," she insisted. "Meanwhile, I should tell you that I have put a certain question to *your* parent. A commercial question about the supply of fish directly off the quay. It will be interesting to know if he sees fit to pass it on."

"Perhaps he has other fish to fry!" He kept a straight face. "However, I shan't mention this conversation if he does. What sort of fish, may I ask? And in what quantities?"

"That's the thing." She shrugged. "I don't know yet. But let me explain. My mother and I operate the Morrab Guest House — in Morrab Road, of course."

"Bed and breakfast?"

"Yes — and that's my point. We have a kitchen that can turn out two dozen lavish breakfasts each morning and then, from mid-morning on, it reverts to being an ordinary domestic kitchen catering for Mama and me — and up to eight servants. It's absurd. It's as if a factory owner decided to operate his factory for an hour and a half each day. The cook who copes with twenty hot breakfasts could just as readily cope with forty dinners — and be glad of the extra wages. And the maids who serve ..."

"Twenty breakfasts?" he interrupted. "But *forty* dinners?"

"She can as easily cook forty as twenty — so why not open up to the public as well? I tell you — if we could somehow serve meals round the clock, I'd say *that's* using our facilities to the full. Even just serving breakfasts and dinners, we could be so much more successful than we are. Anyway — that is my challenge, to bring my mother to this point of view. And I've hardly started yet."

"But you will prevail?"

"What do you think?"

"I'm sure you will."

"Yes. So am I — it's so logical, isn't it. And when I do, I shall need a sure and steady supply of fish of the very highest quality. I have in mind an evening restaurant that serves only seafood. There isn't a single such place in the whole of Penzance ..."

"Nor yet in Newlyn, either. Even in Falmouth there's only one, from what I do know."

"Thank you — that's useful to know. But what a shame, eh? What a *shameful* shame! You fishermen risk your lives out there to catch some of the most succulent fish in English waters. And what happens? A few baskets of them end up as the third or fourth choice in the table d'hôte of our local restaurants. It's an utter scandal!"

It was an argument she had mulled over for use at some vaguely future date on the quayside at Newlyn, for the past several weeks. Delivered face-to-face in these more intimate circumstances it sounded rather bombastic. Even so, it caught his imagination; she could see a new excitement in his eyes.

So she fired the second barrel, also prepared earlier: "Such a restaurant could pay well above auction prices for reliable supplies of premier quality fish."

"I was just thinking that, myself," he replied.

"So then, Mister Peters, we both have something to think about between now and whenever we next meet."

"Which will be after you've beaten your mother?"

She jibbed at that. "I don't look upon it as beating her," she replied. "Dear Mama has both our interests at heart, you know. She's most eager to do what's best by us. It's just that she doesn't realize that this restaurant idea of mine *is* what's best."

"Yet," he said.

"Exactly."

He fished her out the fattest of his lobster haul, tied its claws, and then was surprised to discover a remarkably dainty linen bag, beautifully embroidered and wrapped in paper, beneath the helm thwart.

It did not deceive her, though. "I think we had better meet sooner rather than later, Mister Peters," she said as she took it and thanked him. "Before somebody misses this beautiful bag."

This time she did not bother to mask her farewell waves behind her parasol.

5 Cicely Thorne was outraged to learn that her children had disobeyed her and consorted with the Harte girl — so outraged, indeed, that she led herself into a foolish blunder. As soon as they had arrived back at the hôtel the previous day, she had sent telegrams to friends in Plymouth inquiring into the characters of Tamsin and Mrs Harte. It was the least precaution that a cautious mother could take. The replies, which had come that afternoon, had not been reassuring. To avoid stirring up a scandal in the locality she had sent the inquiries — in French, of course — from Penzance, directing the replies to a *poste restante* in Newlyn.

ELLES SONT NQOC, was one opinion; NQOC being Society code for 'not quite our class'.

ELLES SONT CREVEES D'ORGEUIL read another, with Saxon disregard for French niceties. DEFENSE DE REPAIRER — which may be accurately rendered: THEY ARE BUSTED WITH PRIDE. DON'T RE-COUPLE.

So, on strolling back from Newlyn, it had pleased her greatly to observe the Harte girl talking with a common fisherman down by the water's edge. Well, she noted with quiet satisfaction, *today* at least, the creature has found her true niveau. But her pleasure was short lived. On entering the hôtel she almost ran into Dobbs, Charlotte's maid.

"How dare you use the front entrance?" she demanded of the impertinent girl.

Dobbs was not even faintly abashed. "It's because of the ale and the fish, madam," she replied.

A typical Dobbs response, this. It was meaningless on the surface and yet, if you probed and probed, you'd find justification in it at last — except that by then you'd have played the inquisitor so fiercely that you *almost* felt obliged to apologize. Cicely had been burned that way too often even though the maid had been with them for less than two months; indeed, she'd have dismissed her within the first week if she hadn't been so good at her work that every lady in Cicely's circle would have snapped her up at once. Good servants of every grade were becoming as rare as hens' teeth nowadays; the last assistant cook she'd tried to engage had had the temerity to spend most of the interview questioning *her* — and then had said she, meaning Cicely herself, 'wouldn't suit!'

"Well, I suppose you know what you're talking about, Dobbs," was all Cicely said now. "I'm blessed if I do, that's all I can say. The real question ..."

Dobbs cast a further small pearl: "Deliveries through the staff entrance, madam."

"The *real* question," Cicely insisted, "is why are you going out of the hôtel at all?"

"On a message, madam."

"I should hope so. That's not the issue, either."

By now they were blocking the entrance for other guests, one of them a craggy old gentleman with eyebrows like furze bushes. "May I go, then?" Dobbs asked.

"Not until I learn for whom this message is ... er, for — you know very well what I mean. Intended. For whom is it intended?"

Harrumph! The bushy eyebrows throbbed with impatience. Indeed, the man's whole body probably did the same but the eyebrows were all Cicely noticed. Intimidated by them she plucked the maid aside and tried to soothe the fellow with a smile. Unsoothed, he forged his way across the lobby with his jaw set like the prow of an icebreaker.

The maid produced a letter from her bag. "I'm to deliver it in person, madam," she said.

It was addressed to Miss Tamsin Harte, The Morrab Guest House, Morrab Road — in Victor's hand.

"Just around the corner," Dobbs added.

Cicely was trying to contain her anger. One did so hate all public displays of feelings of any kind — and the gentleman with the eyebrows still had half a malevolent eye upon her. "I know very well where *that* creature lives," she said grimly as she tore the envelope and its contents in two. "You may return this waste paper to my son this minute. At once."

Dobbs, who had remained quite calm throughout, turned to go back above.

Cicely immediately had second thoughts. "A moment, if you please," she said, following the maid to the foot of the stairs. "This way." She drew her into the ladies' lounge, where she took back the fragments of the letter and laid them out. They proved simple enough to piece together for the entire message comprised a mere couple of lines:

Dear Miss Harte,
You have impugned my honour as a gentleman. In the circumstances there can be no further intercourse between us.
    Yours (alas) sincerely,
    Victor Thorne.

Now Cicely cursed herself for her impetuous action in destroying a letter that could, at a stroke, have achieved her dearest present wish. However, it did raise the question: When was this impugning of Victor's honour supposed to have occurred? Not yesterday, certainly.

"Did they consort with Miss Harte while I was out this afternoon?" she asked the maid.

"Miss Harte?" Dobbs frowned. "That's a lady I do not know."

"Very diplomatic! Did they consort with anyone?"

"I believe they took a stroll along the promenade, madam. I was preoccupied with Miss Charlotte's gown for this evening."

So they must have met the Harte creature, Cicely mused. It was particularly annoying that she had been reading her telegrams and their solemn warnings at the very moment her two children had been cavorting upon the Esplanade with the NQOC girl herself. Still, all was not gloom, it now appeared. The little hoyden must have insulted Victor in some way, and it must have been serious enough to occasion this letter. It was vexing that they had disobeyed her, of course, but the outcome could not be grumbled at — except that she had, by her impulsive passion, nipped it in the bud. However, a scheme to undo that particular damage was beginning to form; after all, Miss Harte had no idea what Victor's handwriting looked like. "Wait," she commanded the maid.

She seated herself at the escritoire, took a fresh sheet of hôtel notepaper, and wrote out Victor's message once again. She sealed it in an envelope, as before, and dropped the fragments of the original in the waste-paper basket.

"You may take this instead," she said to Dobbs as she swept on out.

Dobbs, who knew that one *never* left drafts of letters in public waste-baskets, dutifully retrieved the original before setting off up Morrab Road.

They were a queer lot, the Thornes. Well, *all* masters and mistresses were a queer lot when you really got down to it. Jenny Saunders, whose mother had worked for the old queen at Osborne, said she was one of the very best. Any servant in her employ for more than ten years or thereabout became like one of the family. Of course, you still had to respect her majesty and mind your ps and qs, but even the lords and ladies of the court had to do that. But she'd tell you her thoughts and she'd expect you to share yours as well. And she knew all about your family and who was ill and needed asking after and such like. And she noticed if you were out of sorts and she'd give you little bottles from her own homeopathic cabinet. All the servants agreed that a real toff, a lord or a lady who was sure of their place in Society's ranks, was the best sort of master or mistress. Or 'employer,' as it was now more popular to call them — among servants themselves, anyway.

And they were all agreed that the worst employer of all was an ex-servant — someone who'd just moved up one rung of the ladder and wanted to make sure those on the old rung didn't forget it. They were the ones who paid in farthings, who never said 'Take the rest of the evening off,' and who'd 'never heard of such impertinence' when you asked for leave to attend a funeral.

Mrs Thorne came suspiciously close to the lower end of the spectrum that stretched between those two poles, Dobbs decided; she herself had only been with the family for six weeks and so had not had the chance to pry into her mistress's origins — yet. Whispers in the servants' hall tended to confirm her suspicions, but she was long enough in service to know that tittle-tattle was one thing and certain knowledge quite another.

She paused outside the Hartes', a large, imposing house that swept the eye around a bend in the road. It was built, or at least faced, in granite ashlars, with two semicircular bays that ran the full three floors — semi-basement, ground floor, and first floor — and ended in romantic, conical turrets such as you see on French chateaux. Small lights among the slates revealed that these turrets housed attic rooms, as well. She enjoyed a brief daydream of living in such a room, not as a servant but as one remote from the life of the world, content with the smallest portion. A woodman's cottage in a forest glade was another favourite of hers — and even less likely to find her in possession of it.

Tamsin opened the dining-room window. "Can I help you?" she asked.

Dobbs liked her at once, just from the sound of her voice, which was somehow warm and mellow. Inviting. "Miss Harte?" she asked, though she had no doubt of it.

"Yes."

The maid opened the gate and started up the short path to the front steps, speaking as she came: "I'm Miss Thorne's lady's maid, Miss Harte. I've been sent to deliver a message to you."

"Dear me!" Tamsin left the window and, moments later, reappeared at the door. "I hope it's one I shall want to hear."

"Read, Miss, not hear." She handed over the letter Mrs Thorne had given her.

"Who is it from? It's in a woman's hand, I see. Is an immediate reply expected?"

"It's from Mrs Thorne. She said nothing about a reply. Miss."

"Well, come in, anyway." Tamsin stepped aside. "I expect you could do with a cordial or something on such a warm afternoon." When the maid hesitated, she added, "No one is to know how long it took you to walk here ... much less how long it took the staff here to find *me*. We'll go into the lounge. There's no one about at the moment."

As they passed down the passage she rang a bell on the hatstand. A maid opened the servants' door and peered into the gloom of the hall. Tamsin said, "Two tall glasses and a jug of lemonade, Bridget, please."

She motioned her visitor toward a wicker chair and seated herself in one facing it.

"Well, that's short and sharp!" she said after scanning the two-line message. "Tell me, what's your name?"

"Dobbs, Miss."

"Just Dobbs?"

"Daisy Dobbs."

"And which d'you prefer?"

She smiled awkwardly. "Daisy, Miss."

"Good, Daisy Dobbs. In that case, I am Tamsin."

"Oh, Miss! I couldn't." But even as she said it she was thinking, *I jolly well could!*

"Suit yourself, Daisy, but I shouldn't mind in the least. You said this note was from *Mrs* Thorne?"

"I saw her write it — and seal it, Miss ... Tamsin." She contrived to make the name seem an alternative rather than an adjunct to the title.

Tamsin passed her the single sheet of notepaper, saying, "It's a lady's hand, as I said, but ..." She left the rest unspoken.

Daisy read it, frowned, and then, without thinking (except that later she suspected the not-thinking had been ever so slightly deliberate), pulled out the remains of the original. She extracted the torn contents, put the two halves together, and burst into laughter as she handed them over to Tamsin.

"I suppose," Tamsin said, "that, given time, I could imagine some circumstances in which a mother would intercept a note from her son to an unwelcome female, tear it up, and then copy it word for word in her own hand before sending it onward. But for the moment, I confess it quite baffles me."

Daisy explained what had happened, adding as a postscript: "I remember she quizzed me very particularly as to whether Mister Victor and Miss Charlotte had met with you upon the promenade this afternoon."

"And what did you tell her?"

"I said I had been busy with Miss Charlotte's evening gown — which was also the truth."

"Excellent."

Bridget brought their cordial and poured out two tumblers.

"Are you disappointed to read that?" Daisy nodded at the note in Tamsin's hand.

Tamsin relished her drink. "How serious d'you think he is?"

"He means everything at the moment he does it. Later he often regrets it, though."

"Well ... a man cannot expect to write a note like this" — she waved Victor's torn original — "with or without the support of his mother" — she waved the copy — "and expect to go *entirely* unpunished. Don't you agree, Daisy?"

Daisy giggled so much that a small quantity of lemonade went up into her nose, making her sniff and then cough. Tamsin rose and patted her on the back.

And somehow that small, even trivial act of intimacy sealed a bond of trust between them. Without the need for words or declarations, they were on the same side from that moment on.

"Tell me what you know of *Mister* Victor Thorne," Tamsin said. "Is he a plague to pretty young maids like you?"

"Nooo." Daisy drew the word out as if she suspected it might surprise her new friend. "Miss Charlotte says he's like the fox that'll never kill the rabbit that burrows beside its den. Did you ever notice that?"

"I can't say I have done."

"Well, it's true. There's a patch of woodland in the grounds of Peveril Hall — that's the Thornes' home, up Exeter way. It's a corner where they draw all the old treestumps after felling, and it's home to both rabbits and foxes, and the foxes never touch *those* rabbits. I don't know why."

"I can guess," Tamsin said. "It's so that when an angry farmer comes to confront the wily foxes with a couple of dozen dead chickens they can say, 'What, us? How could you suspect us when — as you see — we don't even kill the rabbits at our own front door!' At least, they could say it if they were in one of Æsop's fables. So!" She chuckled. "Young Mister Victor plays the virtuous innocent at home to hunt the more fiercely abroad, eh? I must say I had formed the same opinion of him as you. And Miss Charlotte is no dewy-eyed innocent, either — is she. I mean, she knows the ways of the world even if only as a spectator."

Daisy drank a deep draught of her lemonade this time. "Shall I carry a message back, then?"

Tamsin stared at the ample blank spaces around Cicely's copy, was tempted, but did not yield. "It would only get you into trouble, dear Daisy," she said. "I shall deliver it myself — and tip the porter there to be sure to get it to him without his mother's knowledge or interference."

"What'll you say?" Daisy rubbed her hands eagerly. "May I tell Miss Charlotte? She won't let on."

"Oh ... it'll be something vague, I'm sure. Something that sounds full of meaning but isn't. The main thing is to write it on the back of his mother's copy — that'll *really* put the cat in the dovecote!"

"Write it now," Daisy urged. "Miss Charlotte'll give me no rest if I can't tell her word for word."

"How did she respond to her brother's threat to cut me?"

"She knows nothing of it. Not yet, anyway. The fur will fly when she does!"

"Oh?" Tamsin leaned forward with abrupt interest.

"Oh, indeed. She couldn't stop talking about meeting you last evening when I was helping her dress. How you'd ..." She hesistated, suddenly awkward.

Tamsin smiled. "How we'd come down in the world? I don't mind — except that I don't think of it as 'coming down' at all. It's been a most wonderful release from ..."

"Yes! That was it. That's what she kept saying. How lucky you were. How you were no longer imprisoned by all the rules and conventions that *she* has to obey. You're a star to her."

"Goodness! Not a guiding star, I hope. I had to be pushed here, you know. I didn't jump of my own free will." She giggled again. "I say — I've just thought of what to write back."

She crossed the lounge to the bureau, taking her drink and Cicely's note with her. *The sea is unbreakable,* she wrote, *as any mariner will avow, yet it breaks eternally on every shore. Shall a woman's heart be otherwise? — T.*

Daisy read it three times — frowning, dubious, and finally laughing. "You keep thinking you know what it means," she said, "and then you realize you don't. It's like those drawings of faces that keep turning into other faces and every time you fix on one of them it turns into the other."

"And what two faces show here, d'you think?" Tamsin pointed at the page.

"One is heartbroken and the other is sneering."

"Good," Tamsin said. "Will you have some cordial?"

The nuances of this innocent-sounding query were not lost on Daisy. A well-brought-up person offering a second helping to a social equal would never use the word 'more' in such a question, for it would constitute the teeniset hint of criticism on the grounds of greed or gluttony. She held out her glass and said, "I thank you."

"I wish I knew just a wee bit more about the mother, though," Tamsin mused, leaning back in her chair and fixing her eyes upon the ceiling.

"You're not the only one," Daisy replied.

Still gazing upward, Tamsin continued, "We met so briefly and yet I felt a sense of ... what's the word? Unease? Uneasiness? The minute I mentioned our transition from being *in* Society to being decidedly outside it, I felt it. Like a sudden change in temperature. Of course, we've had similar experiences with other worthy matrons in the district, even in this backwater they like to keep the barriers up. But this coldness from Mrs Thorne was something more than that. It was almost as if ..." She fixed her eyes on Daisy at last but said no more.

"Almost as if what?" Daisy had to ask.

Tamsin laughed mildly. "Oh, I'm probably being much too fanciful. And I'm certainly being unfair in trying to engage you in a discussion of ..."

"Pay no heed to that!" Daisy protested.

"Really? Are you sure?"

"Quite sure! A servant's loyalty has to be earned nowadays. Cicely Thorne hasn't even made a down-payment on mine."

"Cicely Thorne, eh? Do we know her maiden name?"

"Cunningham, I believe. Mrs Slocombe, our cook, says the family were ironmasters in Wales somewhere, or so she heard."

"The reason I'm asking — I want to be as frank with you as you are with me, Daisy — is that I had this fleeting suspicion that Mrs Thorne recognized something in me — or in my particular situation — something that other Society matrons have failed to see. It's very hard to pin down."

Her vagueness forced Daisy to express her own intuitions about her employer. "I've sometimes had the feeling she wasn't *always* as top-drawer as she'd like everyone to think."

"I say! Do you suppose that's it?" Tamsin behaved as if Daisy had suddenly cleared up the mystery for her.

"She's *such* a stickler for correct form ..." Daisy began.

"You've absolutely hit the nail on the head!" Tamsin cut across. "My father used to collect ancient books on etiquette and how to write and speak good English and things like that — going right back to the middle ages. I remember an Elizabethan one that told men not to wipe grease off their fingers into their beards at table. And ladies shouldn't do the same in the fur of passing dogs or cats. He asked me why I thought such prohibitions had disappeared from modern books on good behaviour, and, of course, I said it was because you don't *need* to tell people such things nowadays because they wouldn't do it anyway. 'Just so!' he said. 'So what does that tell us about the behaviour of lords and ladies in Elizabethan days?' "

Daisy took it as a question intended for her and answered: "They were wiping greasy fingers in beards and dogs all the time!" She laughed.

"You see the point, though," Tamsin went on. "The *Don'ts* in all the etiquette books are an excellent guide to what people actually *Do!* So all those sad people who take them as gospel — the sticklers for 'Good Form' — merely betray their ignorance of actual behaviour in Society."

"That's Cicely Thorne to a tee," Daisy said. After a thoughtful pause she added, "How would one go about finding out things like that ... people's backgrounds and things?"

"A birth certificate is a good place to start," Tamsin said. "There's that revealing column headed 'Occupation of Father.' Mine says, 'Ship's chandler.' "

"Mine says 'Head Butler' which he was at the time."

"And now?"

"Now he's a civilian diver at the navy dockyards in Plymouth. I remember your father's firm there — Harte's the Chandlers."

"Really? How splendid! Do the Thornes give you much time off — while you're down here, I mean?"

She shrugged. "There wouldn't be much point ... I mean, there's not a lot to do in Penzance, is there!"

"You could come here. And if I'm free, we could go for a stroll, and if I'm busy, you could sit and read or sew or whatever, knowing *they* couldn't interrupt with some annoying request. Think about it anyway."

There were noises in the hall. Guests were returning, scattering sand, bits of seaweed, tiny dead crabs, and clutching what they felt sure were semiprecious stones, half-polished by the sea.

"No rest for the wicked," Tamsin murmured as she rose to deal with them. She winked at her new friend — not to say ally.

6 Newlyn's postmistress was Oenone Peters, widow to Captain Peters's cousin. She often dropped by for 'a bit tay and chat' — especially when she knew that David had been lifting lobsters, for she almost always got invited back for supper. She was relishing her second slice of saffron bread when the young fellow arrived, and, even though he'd given the cream of his catch to the Harte maid, the best of the remainder was enough to make the mouth water all over again.

"What? No more'n thirteen?" Benny said. "I seen 'ee lift fourteen for sure. You haven't sold none?"

"If you saw me lift fourteen," David replied, "you'll also have seen me give one to Miss Harte."

"You admit it then!"

"Why should I deny it? She has the makings of a good customer, that one."

"Harte?" Oenone put in. "Is that a Miss Harriet Harte?"

"Tamsin," David said. "Harriet is Mrs Harte, the mother."

"They have a guest house in Morrab Road?"

"I believe so. Why?"

"Never you mind. How could she be a good customer, then?" David explained. "What d'you know of her?" he asked.

She gazed at the writhing heap of lobsters.

"You'll stay to supper, I 'speck?" Benny's wife, Peggy, put in. She spoke rarely but missed nothing.

"I'll come back," Oenone replied, already rising to go. "I shall have something for 'ee then, too, I daresay."

She hastened up the hill to her shop, hoping to catch the Penzance office before it closed; her aunt's husband's niece was married to Andrew Harvey, the postmaster there. In Cornwall such a relatively short hop across the family tree made her and him only slightly more distant than brother and sister; in fact, business and kinship conspired to keep them in closer touch than most siblings. So it was no surprise to David or his parents to be regaled with the contents of certain telegrams — a piquant sauce to their lobster supper that evening. Three of the exchanges were between Mrs Thorne and friends in Plymouth; the other two were between Mrs Harte and friends in Exeter.

Strictly speaking, these disclosures broke half a dozen of the strictest post office rules on confidentiality; but when family and business combine — to say nothing of a whiff of romance — what price rules made in London by men who may have high principles, and even higher collars, but who know nothing of the world and its ways?

"Here's a how-d'ee-do!" David said as he committed the brief messages to memory.

"This-here Victor Thorne," Benny said. "Is the Harte maid and him all hurrisome-like?"

"If they were, d'you suppose she'd tell me?" David replied. Then, when he guessed his father was trying to think of another approach to the same question, he added, "Can you imagine Miss Harte going all hurrisome over *anything*? Other than her own ambitions, of course."

His mother smiled at him approvingly. "That's right, my lover," she said. "Don't 'ee go courantin' with no maid like she. They'm nothin' but trouble."

David had not, in fact, meant to imply he found Tamsin's ambitions disagreeable, but he let it pass.

"I had a splendid bit of news today, darling," Harriet said as she and Tamsin sat down to dine that evening. "Can you guess?"

"There's been a new edition of your favourite book — *The Manners and Morals of Good Society* by 'A Titled Lady' — and it says a truly modern family may discuss its own business at ..."

"If you're going to be tedious at every single mealtime, dear," her mother said wearily, "we shall simply have to eat in silence. Guess again."

"You sent telegrams to friends in south Devon — inquiring discreetly about the Thornes, I imagine? And you have received satisfactory replies?"

Her mother's face fell throughout this response, passing from puzzlement through disbelief to anger. "Have you been rifling my bureau?" she asked.

"I have been emptying your waste-paper basket — a task I never entrust to the maids, as you know. Two envelopes torn from telegrams — taken together with the gleam in your eyes when I spoke of the Thornes last night — lead me to ..."

"Yes, yes, dear. All very clever, I'm sure. Take care not to become *too* sharp, though, or you'll cut yourself. What d'you think they said?"

"More guessing — this *is* fun! Well, since you called it 'splendid news,' I must assume that the Thornes have consols enough to paper their ample acres, that young Victor has somehow earned the distrust of the parents or guardians of every suitable spinster in the entire West Country, and that they are therefore reduced to seeking his bride among spinsters who would be suitable were it not for a blush or two at the bank."

Harriet supped her soup in stony silence.

"Am I warm?" Tamsin asked.

The news was too good to keep back, despite the girl's provocations. "He is promised to no one. It is quite certain. In fact, he has just concluded an acquaintance with one particular female, an acquaintance that might have led, in the fullness of time, to an engagement."

"Oh dear! Is the air now heavy with the stench of a costly breach-of-promise suit?"

"I'm sure Eleanor would have warned me if that were so."

"Good. We have an empty field, then."

"Quite. But that's only the beginning. At the age of twenty-two, it seems, he will inherit a substantial portion of his uncle's — I had this from Madge Cunningham, by the way, whose maiden name was Thorne, as I said — and, indeed, she is a cousin to Walter Thorne, your young man's father — and she says ..."

"*My* young man?" Tamsin protested, though the news that Victor was to inherit a worthwhile fortune was interesting to her. "He is no such thing. In fact, he sent me a letter this very afternoon to inform me that there could be no further intercourse between us."

Harriet dropped her spoon into her bowl, which was fortunately empty. "He *what?* But what on earth have you done to provoke ..."

"I merely told him that if he had come to Penzance looking for a brief, seaside fling, then ..."

"*Seaside fling?* You used such a disgraceful vulgarism to him? Oh, Tamsin!"

"… then he would be wasting his own time in pursuing me. Was I wrong? Should I have encouraged him to look upon me as one of those discardable girls that men like him have no difficulty in finding? Even miles away from the shoreline?"

Her mother said nothing, being unable to say the honest no that would also condone her daughter's insulting brashness. "There are ways of saying these things, dear, without provoking letters like that." She rang the bell for Bridget to clear the soup and bring the entrée.

"Why are we so keen to discuss him?" Tamsin asked as they set about their second course. "With or without his inheritance, he is not the most interesting young man one could ever hope to meet. In fact …" She hesitated. She had been about to say that David Peters was ten times more interesting but she realized it was a thought she did not wish to pursue, not even with herself.

"In fact what?" Harriet asked.

"In fact, he's pretty dull."

"No man with prospects of an inheritance is *dull*, dear."

"Ah! So it is wealth that makes him interesting?"

"Of course it is."

"Wealth? As in money? As in filthy lucre? Are you quite sure this is a fitting subject for the dinner table, Mama dear?"

She ignored this new provocation. "You must reply at once. Ask his forgiveness. Say that whatever insult he may have inferred, you certainly did not intend it. Put it down to your innocence and youth — and stress innocence and youth. It will do no harm to remind him that you possess both those qualities in abundance …"

"You mean, allow him to understand I would make a docile and subordinate wife?"

"Not at all. I know you're trying to vex me again, so I shan't rise to it. You must allow him to understand you would not be a virago, a termagant …"

"A shrew, a frump, a tigress, a scold …"

"Tamsin!"

"Shall I write in blue ink? Or green?"

"What d'you mean?"

"Or I know — turquoise! Mix the two! The colour of my eyes — so daring!"

"What on earth are you talking about, girl?"

"Well, you seem to be laying down the law as to every dot and comma in this letter I am to write — why on earth should you balk at the choice of ink?"

"I'm only trying to suggest what's best for you, dear — for us both. And don't close your eyes and shake your head like that. You know it's true. Our best way out of our present difficulties is for one of us to marry, or marry again, and to marry jolly well. And so, since your prospects are a hundred times brighter than mine, you owe it to both of us to swallow your pride and write a letter that ..."

"And grovel, you mean. Honestly, Mama! I know you think you're doing everything for the best, but times have changed. We've moved on. The sort of letter you're proposing would have been the bee's knees in eighteen-eighty, I'm sure. Today it's the spider's ankles."

"Bee's knees! Spider's ankles!" Harriet fanned herself with her napkin.

"In any case, I've already replied."

"You have?" The colour drained from her cheeks and the fanning stopped.

"I scribbled a few words it on the back of his letter and sent it back to him."

It was Harriet's turn to close her eyes and shake her head. "Dare I ask?" she murmured.

Tamsin told her what she had written.

Dread yielded to bewilderment. "But what does it mean?" she asked.

"It means whatever he cares to read into it. If he wishes to think of it as a 'docile and subordinate' reply, he's free to do so. Why should any girl go out of her way to feed a man with flatteries when his own gift of self-delusion will do it all for her?"

Harriet's mood swung yet again, this time to consternation. "Where did you learn such cynicism, child? Not from me, I'm sure. Nor from your poor, dear father."

But there she was wrong. Tamsin had, indeed, learned her views of the world and its ways in many a conversation with her late father — though he would have called it practical common sense rather than cynicism. It wasn't that he had had some foreboding of the impending crash in their fortunes — and was therefore giving his daughter a few hasty insights into the ways of the world. From the time she was ten he had always tried to provide her with a tactful counterweight to her mother's views, about which the very harshest words he'd ever used were 'sheltered' and 'rose-tinted.'

But then again, perhaps he had *always* feared for some catastrophe — in the way that any prudent businessman must keep the possibility of bankruptcy forever in mind. In which case he would have realized that to leave his wife and daughter with their heads stuffed with the naïve and gullible innocence that had seemed so desirable among well-bred young ladies of the 1880s would be a peculiar sort of cruelty.

He would also have realized that his wife was beyond persuasion. Naïvete was almost her second religion. It had secured her the husband of her parents' (and her own) choice at eighteen and it had delivered all its promises right up until the crash — which was, of course, an Act of God but of a different God. Little wonder, then, that he had concentrated his efforts on his daughter, instead.

For all these reasons, however, Tamsin could not directly enlighten her mother; she could do nothing to reveal that the father had been quite different from the husband. Not only would her mother simply refuse to believe it but she would also close her ears to any future discussion where her 'sheltered, rose-tinted' views clashed with her daughter's more pragmatic ones. All she could do was seek to chip away at the edges with a thousand tiny 'provocations,' as her mother called them.

So, when Harriet said that Tamsin could not possibly have obtained her views from her father, the girl let it go. "What I *did* get from both of you, though," she replied, "is a good pair of eyes. And I can see that two females in our circumstances do *not* get the same treatment from the world in general as the two ladies we once were. Shopkeepers do not come fawning to our carriage. Nor do they offer us credit. Nor do people call with cards ..."

"Yes, dear," Harriet sighed wearily. "We know it all too well."

"Then let's behave as if we know it. Let's realize that we must now do things that those two ladies would have found distasteful.

And let's do them before even more distasteful things get done to us. Strike or be stricken, Mama — that's our choice now."

Bridget brought in the main course and set it before Tamsin to serve.

"Lobster thermidor!" Harriet exclaimed. "My dear!"

"What now?" Tamsin asked innocently. "It's one of your favourites, I thought."

"So it is — but the expense!"

"Really we ought to have a nice Bollinger with it," Tamsin said as she lifted the shell. "But I took the liberty of decanting some white *vin ordinaire* into the soda syphon and making it fizz — as we used to do for our servants' balls, remember?"

Harriet shuddered.

"And — once again — Mrs Pascoe has produced a culinary triumph. This is pure ambrosia. She is wasting her talent on kippers for breakfast."

Harriet ignored the by now familiar litany. "How much ... I mean, I hope you weren't too extravagant?"

"No, Mama, you mean 'what did it cost'? Well, it cost no more than a smile and the time of day."

An image of David Peters filled her mind's eye ... his strong arms, bronzed by sun and salt ... the muscles rippling as he pulled at the oars ... the lithe strength of all his movements ... his smile ...

No! Enough! She was not going to yield to silly, girlish daydreams of that nature.

"This fisherman-sea-captain who spoke to you so impertinently yesterday?" Harriet asked. "Did he ...?"

"His son David. His only surviving son, now."

"He has accosted you, too? Oh, Tamsin!"

"It was the other way round, if anything. I wanted to buy a lobster from him — they're not expensive directly out of the boat, you know. But he presented me with one instead."

"He'll want something in return, of course. People like that — they always do."

"Of course he does. And not just any old 'something'. I know exactly what he wants."

Harriet stared awkwardly at her plate; this conversation had taken an embarrassing turn.

"He wants me to persuade you that Mrs Pascoe's talents could be better employed than they are at present."

Harriet held her breath and counted slowly to ten. Unfortunately it gave time for the flavour of her latest mouthful of succulent lobster to bathe her senses. Tamsin's 'ambrosia' was an understatement, if anything. The steady drip of the girl's arguments must have eroded more ground from beneath her feet than she had realized; that and the ecstasy of her taste buds tipped her off balance enough to ask, "In what way?"

The tone was guarded, the eyes suspicious, but the question had been asked. The door was open. Even so, Tamsin had nous enough not to go rushing through it all at once. "Imagine!" she exclaimed. "Being able to dine on seafood of this quality any evening one wished! Think!"

Watching her daughter at that moment, Harriet felt an entirely novel emotion — at least, it was novel as far as her feelings toward her daughter were concerned. And it was not something she could easily name. To call it 'fear' was too crude; 'anxiety' was too feeble; 'alarm' too fleeting. Until this moment, Tamsin's persistence in arguing for her own point of view and badgering to get her own way had provoked little more than weariness in her mother; but now that she had been forced to concede, even in so slight a matter, she began to see it all in a different light.

She realized that Tamsin was going to win every such battle in which the two of them engaged. Her trivial concession on this particular occasion somehow confirmed it. Tamsin would see it as a reward for her persistence and it would make her doubly resolute in future. But even that was not the core of her mother's disquiet. Without admitting it to herself in so many words, Harriet realized that her concession was much more than a simple permission to break a firm rule of etiquette, just on this one occasion; it was, in effect, an admission that Tamsin might be right — that the rule itself was inappropriate — that the standards to which she had adhered since childhood might have to change. It was a moment as shattering as that other great watershed in her life — when Desmond O'Rourke, the family solicitor, had broken the news of their bankruptcy to her.

Perhaps, after all, 'fear' was not too strong a word.

7 Victor had been sitting out there in the shelter on the Esplanade, staring at the letter for a good quarter of an hour, when Charlotte came upon him. "What can ail thee, wretched wight?" she asked. "Shall we walk up an appetite before breakfast?"

He handed the sheet to her with a sigh. "I'm hemmed if I can make it out. See what you think."

"We are probably being watched," she warned, taking care to keep the paper below the solidly boarded part of the shelter.

"I know. The minute one of us passes out of sight they'll send a servant after us. I'm beginning to see what Miss Harte was talking about — freedom and all that. Turn it over. Read what's on the back."

Charlotte read Tamsin's response two or three times and said, "Extraordinary."

"Is that all you can say? I could have told you that. I send her a letter breaking off all intercourse and instead of returning it ..."

"*You* ...?" Charlotte began

But he continued: "Instead of returning it, she copies it out word for word and then scribbles that odd rigmarole on the back. What am I supposed to make of it?"

"*She* copied it out?" Charlotte's tone was filled with doubt. She turned the sheet over and read the letter again. "This is her hand? It looks very like Mama's, you know."

He snatched the letter back from her and examined it closely. "Oh, my God!"

"I'm right, aren't I?" she pressed him.

He nodded morosely. "But that only makes the whole business all the more mysterious. Why on earth should Mama ...?"

"Tell me from the beginning. You wrote her a letter ..."

"I've been sitting here trying to cudgel my brains as to why on earth Miss Harte should want to copy out my letter and then write her reply on the back. I could only think she wanted to preserve my original."

"Next to her heart, no doubt!" Charlotte sneered. "That would feed your vanity! Why, I daresay you might almost forgive her for that."

"What I wrote was identical ... I mean, those are my exact words. It means mother must have intercepted the letter ..."

"After you posted it? Actually, come to think of it, she did go to the post office in Newlyn ... no, that was before your little tiff with Miss Harte. Did you post it in the box in the lobby? That's not an official GPO box. She could get at it there."

"I didn't post it anywhere. I gave Dobbs sixpence to run round the corner with it."

"Then clearly Mama intercepted Dobbs."

"Yes, well, that's obvious now. But the wretched girl didn't say a word to me about it."

"Be fair. She's hardly had a chance. If we're not going for a walk, we could go in to breakfast now. I've already worked up my appetite."

He rose wearily and tucked the letter into his breast pocket.

"Who brought the reply back to you?" Charlotte asked as they crossed the road to the hôtel.

"The porter gave it me. He said Miss Harte called and left it with him. Yesterday evening."

"Called in person! She wanted to be sure you got it, then. Ah, there's Dobbs now."

Daisy, who had been hovering near the staff door, waiting for them to return, came forward in some agitation as they reentered the lobby. "Oh, Mister Victor!" she exclaimed. "Pardon me but I've been that eager to speak with you ..."

"Never mind all that now," Charlotte told her. "We've pieced together most of the story. My mother must have intercepted you and ..."

"Here, miss. On this very spot. And she took me to the ladies' lounge and got my message out of me ... well, I couldn't tell an untruth, could I." She turned again to Victor. "I did warn you it was tempting fate to ..."

"Yes, yes," he said. "What's done is done. But why did she send you onward with a *copy* of my letter? What happened to the original — the one I wrote?"

Daisy was now in a quandary. The last thing she wanted to do was admit she had retrieved the original from the waste paper basket — much less that she had shown it to Tamsin and had discovered the two letters to be identical.

"The way I saw it, sir," she replied, "is that the mistress tore up your letter, then sat down and wrote one of her own, and sent me on my way with it. She didn't tell me it was a copy of yours."

"And what happened to my original?"

Daisy shrugged. "I think she threw it in the waste-paper basket, sir."

"She tore it up *before* reading it," Charlotte guessed.

Daisy nodded.

"What difference does it make?" he asked glumly. "Tearing up is tearing up."

"Don't you see? She tore it up in a rage because she thought it was a *billet doux*. But when she calms down and actually reads it, she realizes what a mistake she's made. She wants us to have nothing to do with Miss Harte and now she's gone and torn up a letter from you that puts the identical sentiment in the strongest possible terms. So of course she copies it out again and sends it on, hoping Miss H won't notice it's in a woman's hand." She turned to Daisy. "Did she?"

"Beg pardon, miss?" Daisy was playing for time.

"Did Miss Harte notice the letter was in a lady's hand?"

"I believe she did say something to that effect, miss."

"And I asked you to hang around and try to study her face while she read it," Victor put in. "Did you manage that?"

"Yes sir. She read it and then she smiled."

"Smiled!" Victor was taken aback. "What, a putting-on-a-brave-face sort of smile?"

"No sir. More like *amused,* I'd call it."

"Devil take her!" He spun on his heel and would have left the building again if his sister's shocked cry had not halted him. "What now?" he asked truculently.

"I will not have you using language like that in front of my maid. Now come back here and apologize."

"Oh, miss ..." Daisy was embarrassed. "It's not necessary. Really and truly ..."

Charlotte ignored her. "Otherwise I shall have to ask Mama to deal with the matter."

He made a parade of his petty humiliation, rolling his shoulders and lifting his eyes to the ceiling to suggest that he'd humour her even though he thought she was over-reacting in a most childish way. "Sorry, Dobbs," he said in the least contrite tone he could manage. "Did she ... no, I don't suppose she did."

"Did what, sir?"

"Discuss ... you know ... the contents of this letter ... her response ... no, of course she didn't. Shouldn't have asked. Forgive me."

"Of course she didn't," Charlotte scolded.

"I already said that."

"And even if she'd tried it, Dobbs wouldn't have permitted it for an instant, would you, Dobbs."

"Not for an instant, miss," Daisy replied, glad her mistress had chosen 'an instant' rather than, say, 'half an hour.'

"She asked no questions about the letter? About us? Nothing?"

"Stop pestering the poor girl!" Charlotte cried.

"She gave me a glass of lemonade before I returned," Daisy volunteered. "There is just one thing, sir ... miss?"

"Yes?"

"Mrs Thorne didn't specifically order me not to tell you what happened, but she won't be too pleased to hear that I did."

"Mum's the word, Dobbs," Victor replied cheerfully. "I say — that's rather good, what? Mum's the word!"

"There's still the question of what Miss Harte's enigmatic reply actually means," Charlotte said as they went into the dining room.

Their parents were not about as yet. They helped themselves to porridge and chose a table as far as possible from the other diners, all of whom seemed to have chosen their tables on the same principle — such is the inordinate love of the bourgeois for their fellows.

"The sea is not breakable ..." Charlotte paraphrased from memory. "But it breaks every day on every shore. Shall my heart be any different? That was more or less the gist of it, wasn't it?" She chuckled.

"I see nothing funny in it," he grumbled.

"That's because she's won, Victor, dear."

"She most certainly has not!"

Charlotte darted her hand across the table and snatched the letter from his pocket. "Then we might as well tear this up and talk of other things. We'd save a lot of breath."

"Give it back," he said menacingly. "I'll throw it away, right enough — just try and stop me! But not before I've managed to work out what it means."

"Then she *has* won," she insisted. "Because the only way you'll ever learn what she meant is to ask her. You're going to have to seek her out and ask her." She grinned sweetly.

He stared into his porridge and said, "You could ask her for me instead."

"And disobey Mama?"

"Oh, of course, you've never done such a thing in your life before, have you!"

"I have. Of course I have. But only for my own benefit. Anyway, I don't need to ask her. I already understand completely what she meant."

"Am I permitted to …"

"But I already told you — she chose words so perfectly ambiguous that you'd be forced to break your own implied promise never to see her again and ask her."

He turned the letter over so that Tamsin's reply was face-up. Then he spun it side-on to him, as if some new meaning might then emerge from between the lines … the few, short lines. None did, of course.

"Is she trying to say I've broken her heart?" he asked.

"Or is she saying, 'I know you'd like to believe you've broken my heart and so, if it amuses you, think away to *your* heart's content. I am quite indifferent.'?"

"I'm asking the questions," he grumbled.

"*Her* questions — she's the one who put them into your mind. Don't you see?"

"I'm going for some more porridge. You?"

As they crossed the room to the buffet he said, "You might show a fellow a little sympathy?"

"I don't see why," she answered amiably. "This is a mess entirely of your own making."

The craggy gentleman with the bushy eyebrows entered the dining room and made straight for the buffet. Victor could not respond until they were on their way back to their table, where the waitress had, meanwhile, brought their toast and marmalade. They sent it back and asked her not to bring it until after they had finished the hot course from the buffet. They had asked for the same delay at every breakfast since the start of their visit.

"I don't see how it's a mess of my own making," Victor grumbled when they were relatively alone again. "Everything was perfectly straightforward until she weighed in with this ... this ... one can't even call it a reply."

"Riposte?" Charlotte suggested. "A flankonade. A hit! A palpable hit, egad!"

"I had no choice," he protested.

"Of course you did," she scoffed. "There was absolutely no need to climb up on your high horse like that. 'No further intercourse between us'! Faugh!" She mocked his tone. "You always regret it when you go all pompous like that."

"She made a quite scurrilous suggestion about me, to which I could hardly ..."

"All she said was that if you merely intended to trifle with her affections, you'd be wasting your time."

"And that's an insult. There you are!"

"You mean you *didn't* intend to trifle with her affections? Are we to believe that?"

"I don't care what you believe. It's the truth."

"What is the truth?"

"That I had no idea *what* I intended. For heaven's sake — we'd only just met. Why should I have any intentions at all?"

"Then, brother dear, why didn't you simply say so? You could have laughed it off and we'd have been spared all this confluffle. The very fact that your hackles rose at the merest suggestion that you might trifle with her affections suggested at once that there was something in it, after all."

"Suggested to whom?"

"To me, for one — and I'm sure to her, too. That's why I say you brought it on yourself."

"Well ... all I can say is I didn't mean it that way."

"Famous last words!'

He breathed deep and let it out in one long sigh. "I'm not really hungry," he said. "I wish we hadn't sent the toast and marmalade away now."

Charlotte smiled sympathetically. "Go and grovel to the waitress," she said. "It'll be good practice."

8 Walter Thorne threw up the sash window and breathed great draughts of what the town guide-book called healthy sea air, laden though it was with salt and marine decay. His intention was to gauge the weather for the coming day, to assist him in his choice between his club tie with a soft-collar shirt or a plain cotton square with an open-necked shirt. But the odour of decay started a different train of thought. "It's amazing, really," he said, "when you think of it, my dear. The sea is a vast liquid graveyard. Everything that lives in it also dies in it — to say nothing of all the activities they get up to while still alive ..."

"Walter, dear," said his wife, "I think that is quite vivid enough. There is no need to pursue the thought. Meanwhile, we have a much more pressing ..."

"Yes but my point is, you see — all these doctor johnnies keep going on about how healthy it is to bathe in the stuff and breathe the air that comes off it — it's a bit like advising people to haunt the cemeteries and sewage farms and to breathe the air that rises off the graves and ... you know, those things that go round and round."

"Walter!"

"Is it red sky in the morning, shepherd's warning?" he asked.

Cicely glanced up from her dressing table, where Daisy was sorting out the curl-papers from her hair. "But the sky isn't red at all," she said.

"Just so. Therefore no shepherds are warned. Therefore it's going to be a fine day. So I'll wear my cotton square, I think. Until lunchtime at least."

"Luncheon," she corrected him automatically. "We have a much more pressing problem — *nos enfants et mam'selle coeur.*"

"Ker?" he asked as he crossed to the door of his dressing room. "Teacup Ker and her parents? Are they in Penzance?"

The Kers were friends from Devon; their daughter was called 'Teacup' because she had been born minus one ear. Her dowry was fabulous.

"*Coeur*, dear — as in *Coeur de Lion!*" She tapped her breast. "Think!"

"Heart? Oh! Ah! See what you mean. Say no more."

Cicely's eyes raked the ceiling − or, rather, they raked the image of the ceiling in the mirror before her. Unfortunately it was at such an angle that Daisy stood between her and it and so, naturally, assumed she was being invited to share her mistress's despair at the master's obtuseness; she, too, raised her eyes heavenward in sympathy. Mrs Thorne had never thought to ask her if she spoke or at least understood French, and she, for her part, had never felt the slightest need to volunteer the information that she could.

The mistress realized there was no way to make it clear to the servant that she had *not* invited a comment on the master's behaviour; she did not conduct that sort of household. However, she simply had to swallow her annoyance. "Dobbs," she said. "You may go and tell Greenhill that the master is ready to shave and dress."

Greenhill was Walter Thorne's valet.

The moment Daisy left the room, Cicely turned on her husband. "You could at least try to be a little more *au fait,* my dear," she said, laying a venomous stress on the word *dear.* "This sorry situation *vis-à-vis* Miss Harte and our own two youngsters is fraught with danger."

He stood with his hand to the doorhandle of his dressing room. "I'm not aware of any difficulty. I thought you said all was well. Didn't you tell me Victor had written …"

"That was last night. I've had ten hours to sleep on it − not that I did much sleeping − and not that *you'd* be aware of that. But you know yourself how impetuous Victor is. He'll explode like that one day and, come the next dawn, he's apologizing to all and sundry."

"I still don't understand why he exploded in the first place. Something about impugning his honour? What on earth was that all about?"

"I don't know − and I'm certainly not going to inquire. It's a hornet's nest."

"It must have been quite harsh. I mean, he wouldn't have flown off the handle unless she'd said something that cut him to the quick."

"More to the point, dear, he wouldn't have been upset at all if he was indifferent to her opinions. He obviously cares what she thinks — which means, equally obviously, that he cares about her. So when he recovers from his fit of pique ... well, it's quite clear what he's going to do."

"Bow and scrape."

"Quite."

"In other words," Walter added, "he'll concede the first round to her."

"Yes, well there's no need to sound quite so brusque. One would almost think you were cheerful. We mustn't let her win anything. We must stop the contest *now* — so that there isn't even a first round."

He let go of the handle and sat in the chair beside the door. "We could cancel the rest of our holiday here," he suggested. "Go to Torquay? Or" — he sought to conceal a note of rising hope in his voice — "to France? What was the name of that absolutely splendid hôtel at Deauville?"

Cicely shook her head vehemently. "Certainly not! Cut and run? Let the gold-digging intrigues of a scheming little hussy like her ruin all our plans? No! We shall do as I said in the very hour of our first encounter — fill our days with excursions and engagements that make any sort of meeting impossible. If it hadn't been for having to send those telegrams ..."

"And our evenings? And nights?"

"Miss Harte has to attend to their paying guests in the evenings. And as for the nights, well, we must simply exhaust the youngsters enough by day to ensure that they desire nothing but a firm mattress and a soft pillow at night."

To Walter it sounded a pretty forlorn sort of plan — like trying to prevent schoolboy vices with sports and cold showers. Also he had little doubt which generation of Thornes would be the first to succumb to the exhaustions of each such day.

Cicely, aware of his unspoken misgivings and having no adequate answer to give, tut-tutted with vexation. "Where *is* that girl?" She picked up the hairbrush and made a few incompetent stabs at her own coiffure where the curl papers had been removed. "I hate these miles of corridors. We should have taken rooms for the servants on this floor."

*   *   *

Tamsin was in the kitchen, preparing the breakfast pats of butter in a new way. When she had delivered her reply to the porter at the Queen's last night, she'd asked the fellow to let her out by the back way, just in case one of the Thornes spied her out front. On their way through the kitchens she had spotted the housekeeper in the still-room, using a machine that squeezed butter out in a sort of sunflower shape and simultaneously cut it into slices anything from one-to three-eighths of an inch thick. They fell into a large bowl filled with ice-cold water — indeed, there were fragments of ice floating in it. Stored in a chill cabinet overnight, they remained firm and crisp until sent to the breakfast table next morning. Seeing Tamsin's interest, the housekeeper had shown her how to make attractively curly butter-balls with an ordinary teaspoon; it was simply a matter of keeping the butter cold enough to stay firm yet not so cold that it broke into fragments.

"The advantage," the woman added, "is not just that it looks nice but you need only send out half the amount of butter to each table that you would if you sent it in blocks. A block as small as two of these star-shapes would look far too mean."

The Morrab Guest House had no chill cabinet (*yet,* Tamsin would have added); but a large earthenware jar, glazed only on the inside and kept moist under a slowly dripping tap, could get finger-numbingly chill inside, especially if stood in a draught and out of the sun. So the curly butter-balls she had made after returning home last night were as crisp now as they had been then. She doled them out carefully, so many per person, into little glass sorbet bowls for Bridget and Catherine to serve along with the toast. She put three per person in the smaller bowls, four in the larger ones; if none of the threes asked for more, or complained, it would be three per person from then on.

Mrs Pascoe, the cook, watched her out of the corner of her eye throughout the breakfast service. "You done that afore, have you, miss?" she asked when there was a lull in orders.

"Never. That's why I waited until no one was around last night before I tried to make them. You should have seen my first efforts!" She gauged the size of the butter block that remained, "Still, I think we can cut a pound or two off our weekly butter order at the Home and Colonial."

The arrival of another family in the dining room cut short their conversation. Tamsin went out to greet them and to see how much butter was being left at tables where guests had breakfasted and gone. It was gratifyingly little, and none of the threes complained.

"Very nice!" One young guest caught her eye. Briefly his fair hair turned to a cauliflower head and an equally imaginary pig's trotter was clamped between his jaws, like a gun-dog retriever holding a partridge.

This was her system − or her father's system, in fact − for remembering the dozens of names she had to hold in her head, so that she never called a guest Mr Er-um. The more absurd the pictorial association, the better it stuck in the memory.

The cauliflower was a veg, which rhymed with Reg; so this was Reginald Trotter, staying here with his mother. The generally expressed opinion among the staff was that he was convalescing after some quite serious illness − consumption, perhaps; the generally *un*expressed opinion was that he was sweet on her. But Tamsin did not agree; in fact, she detected something rather cold − or at least indifferent − in the young man, though he was charming enough in every other way.

"The butter," he added. "Very elegant."

"Thank you, Mister Trotter." She paused just long enough to leave him feeling unsnubbed. "We learn as we go along and we try to improve a little each day. I hope your mother is well? Shall I send up to see?"

"No. I heard her thumping about before I came down."

She moved on to the new arrivals. In her mind's eye the man had a box made of thin cardboard on his head; on each of its sides was printed a single letter L; carton plus L equals ...

"Good morning, Mrs Carlton ... Doctor Carlton. I trust you slept well − your first night in new beds?"

They hadn't slept so well in years; it must be the sea air. The doctor had his practice in Gloucester. Always a great believer in sea air and salt-water bathing, he had seen remarkable cures. They usually went to south Wales for their holidays but this year they thought they'd try Cornwall, instead. Where was the best place to buy buckets and spades? And a canvas windbreak? And did the town council rent out deck-chairs by the day? What about a packed lunch? Could Miss Harte oblige? It was ten minutes before Tamsin escaped — miraculously without naming a price for the packed lunch, which she wouldn't have done without first discussing it with Mrs Pascoe. And her mother, too, possibly.

Five minutes later she was able to inform Mrs Carlton that she could do a packed lunch, consisting of an apple, a stick of celery, two full-round sandwiches (tongue and pickle, cheese and tomato), and a slice of rich fruit cake at sixpence each. She did not say it but she was prepared to knock twopence off the children's packs even though, at ten and twelve, they had appetites as large as their parents'.

Mrs Carlton said that Dr Carlton would have onion instead of tomato, which he believed was poisonous.

"And the same goes for you and the children, I suppose?" Tamsin asked.

"No, he doesn't mind us poisoning ourselves," she replied cheerily. "Would you consider charging less if we placed an order now for every lunchtime this week?"

Tamsin regretted that the price only just covered the actual cost of putting up the meals; however, as a gesture of goodwill, she would lend them a spirit stove on which they could brew a cup of tea whenever they liked. It might as well be gaining them goodwill, she thought, as gathering dust in the attic.

"What a very obliging young woman," Tamsin heard the ten-year-old daughter whisper as she returned to the kitchen.

"Lady, dear," her mother replied. "She's a lady. One can always tell."

Tamsin smiled to herself and wished her mother had been there to hear it. She drew a little notebook from her pocket and wrote, 'Find out prices of beach chalets on the eastern strand.'

If the Morrab Guest House could rent three or four of them throughout the season — at a good discount, of course — they could hire them out to their guests at a small profit and it would look good in their brochure and advertisements: *Exclusive beach chalets also available at nominal rates.*

"What are you grinning at?" her mother asked as she passed the office door.

"We may be poor," Tamsin replied, "but we do see life."

9   For two days Victor did nothing about Tamsin's ambiguous rejection of his over-hasty note — which is not to say that he mooned around the place doing nothing at all. Indeed, he and Charlotte, having a long experience of dealing with their mother's dictatorship, threw themselves body and soul into her plans to exhaust them by day and so leave them with no energy for evening mischiefs. For instance, on their tour of the Stone Age antiquities of the Land's End peninsula, if her guidebook spoke of some 'rock-embosomed tarn nestling in a nook upon a wild Atlantic headland, to which they simply must ascend,' they would race her and their father to its shore and there espy some noble, craggy eminence at an even greater altitude, from which the visitor simply must enjoy a commanding view of the mighty deep beyond.

"It's like in the Bible," Charlotte pointed out as they scaled the new height, leaving their exhausted parents trailing far behind. "If a man should compel you to go a mile, go with him twain … that sort of thing."

On Sunday morning, after several days of this biblical retribution, Cicely fell asleep at matins — during a rousing hymn, no less — and it became clear that some less demanding way of occupying her children would have to be devised.

"Deauville it is, then," Walter suggested brightly as they returned to the Queen's along the promenade.

"Deauville it most certainly is not," she replied. "We stand upon this ground and fight."

Tamsin was meanwhile kept in touch with events by Daisy, who had time on her hands while the exhausting excursions were in progress. Chores that would normally have taken three hours were dispatched in one, leaving two to spend at the Morrab Guest House. If Tamsin were busy, she rolled up her sleeves and pitched in; otherwise they went marketing together or simply strolled around the town, criticizing houses, gardens, colour schemes, shop windows, and what passed for fashion among the ladies and gentlemen they encountered on their way.

They approved of fair hair in a woman as long as it was not silver or ash; gold was tolerable if slightly hackneyed; but pale auburn, strawberry, or honey was best of all. Brown hair was fine, too, as long as it was light enough to show off its chestnut richness — dark brown being just too dull to consider. Daisy was a rather pale auburn, Tamsin a rich, light chestnut, but they did not believe that swayed their taste in the matter.

As for dress material, stripes should enjoy a come-back, they decided. Especially the rich silks of the 1890s with their broad, boldly coloured verticals, which were so flattering to the figure. But, please, not the big bustles that went with them then, and all the frothy frills and tucks and gathers they, in their turn, required. The modern bustle, which you could almost believe was natural, was so much more becoming. And convenient.

On the other hand, there was something to be said for the plain homespun of the arts-and-crafts fashions, with no bustle at all and a sensible hang to the dress. It allowed a woman complete freedom of movement and didn't touch the ground, or, as Tamsin put it, 'didn't do half the crossing-sweeper's work for him.'

Daisy was less certain. "It would be a great nuisance, though. Think of all the attention we'd get from errand boys and street-corner loafers if we showed our ankles. Even now, if you lift your hem to step over a puddle ..."

"Yes but if we all did it, they'd soon tire of it. Like with the Greek dancing craze, remember? All the men flocked to join at the beginning — and we know why — but now the only ones left are those who actually enjoy the dancing itself. If all ankles were on display, you'd soon have to show a knee before the errand boys would whoop. If you suddenly came into a fortune, Daisy — if they found you were the only heir to some diamond king, say — so you could do anything you liked and no one could stop you, how would you dress?"

Daisy answered without hesitation: "I'd buy a little cottage in the middle of a wood — I'd buy the woods, too, of course — and I'd wear simple rustic clothes, which I'd make from cloth I'd weave myself from yarn I had spun myself ... you know — that sort of thing."

"You, Daisy, are a simple-lifer!"

But now the dream was tapped, the flow of it was not to be stemmed with a single friendly-facetious comment.

"And I'd grow all my own food and I'd make up songs and poems and be friends with all the woodland creatures ..."

"And for company? You couldn't live entirely without ..."

"I'd have my cats and dogs, my pigs, my ducks and geese, my goats ..."

"And if you fell ill?"

"I'd find some berry or herb that'd cure it. There must be books that'd tell me such things."

"An herbal."

"If that's what they call it."

"And you wouldn't feel the lack of a husband? You wouldn't want a family of your own?"

Daisy shot her such a withering look that Tamsin almost felt she had committed a social trespass, though she knew it was a question most other women would not only understand but also feel obliged to answer. At the same time, the idyllic picture the maid had painted was seductive enough to make her wonder if her own ambitions had not been leading her down the wrong track entirely.

"More is less," Daisy said. "My mother was housekeeper to Lady Foster of Bledisloe Hall, up in Wiltshire. My father was head butler there, like I said."

"Yes, I meant to ask — how did he go from that to diver in the Royal Navy docks?"

"His elder brother, my uncle Joe, was head diver there. He trained him and got him the job. It's not *what* you know, it's *who* you know, he used to say. Anyway, Bledisloe Hall had one hundred and fifty-three rooms and each one was crammed to the cornice with pictures, china, silver, fans, butterfly cases, tapestries, stags' heads, suits of armour, old clocks, swords and shields ... and as for books! You could have lost the average town library among them."

"How does that make more equal to less?" Tamsin asked.

"Because when she died none of her children wanted any of it. And I didn't blame them. They'd watched her collection grow. They knew it was what killed her in the end."

"From nervous exhaustion, I suppose?"

"From *physical* exhaustion — just walking round, supervising the cleaning, keeping everything in working order, repairing damage … fighting woodworm, bookworm, dry rot, wet rot, foxing …"

"So what happened to it all?"

"Sotheby's cleared the lot. The auction went on and on and on for three weeks."

"Oh, *that* was the place, was it? Bledisloe Hall — yes, I remember reading about it now."

"When it was all over I came upon the Honourable Gwendolen, one of the daughters, standing by one of the ballroom windows … a great, empty, echoing room by then, of course — I was only fifteen at the time — and she pointed out the woodland down one side of the lake, which her great-grandad had planted, and where her grandad had built ruined temples and things …"

"Follies," Tamsin said.

"That's what they called them, yes — including a rustic cottage — very ornate like in fairy tales — and she said to me, the Honourable Gwendolen, she said, 'You know, Daisy, if Mama had only been content to live in that little cottage, she'd still be alive today.' Tears running down her face there were. I've never forgotten it."

"No … obviously."

"So!" Daisy laughed. "That's enough of me. What'd you do if you won a four-horse accumulator and could tell the world to go and boil its head?"

"I'd build an hôtel."

It stopped Daisy dead in her tracks — they were strolling around Morrab Gardens at the time. "You'd *what?*"

"You heard." They flicked some raindrops off the slats of a bench and sat down. "I dream about it every night before I go to sleep. I can close my eyes and walk through every room — from the wine cellar and boiler room down in the basement all the way up to the water tanks under the roof."

"But why?" Daisy's tone was part intrigued, part appalled.

"Before we went smash I used to dream of being the owner of a vast Atlantic liner — the family connection with the sea, I suppose. What always intrigued me was the business of the public face and the private face. It's the same with the stage, even with amateur dramatics. Did you ever take part in anything like that, Daisy?"

"We did a play at school — *Tom and the Water Babies.*"

"Then you know what I mean — the secret backstage life and the public show out in the limelight. It's the same with a big luxury liner like the *Celtic* or the *Kaiser Wilhelm II* — a round-the-clock theatre for the benefit of the first-class passengers in which all the *real* workings of the ship are hidden away. Two worlds — that's what it is — two worlds that are joined together yet never truly mix. Even in our humble little guest house we've got a hint of it — but you must see it even more in the Queen's?"

Daisy gave a hollow laugh. "I don't think the guests would approve of everything that goes on in that other world."

Tamsin's eyes glowed. "Do *tell!*"

"Well ..." Daisy rolled her eyes. "It's all little things. For instance, did you know you can serve cold cuts off yesterday's joint as if they were from today's fresh roast?"

"How?" She squirmed with pleasure.

"Say it's lamb — which is what the chef there did for dinner yesterday, Friday. All you need is good lamb stock — which he made last Tuesday when he roasted the joint. He cut thin slices off the leg, cold, of course, and put them on a hot plate with a teaspoon of the stock. Then into the bain marie and ..."

"What's that — a bain marie?"

"It's like a steam cabinet. You stack the plates inside, with rings, and you cover them so's they don't get wet with condensation. Then you just heat them with steam. It keeps them piping hot without drying out, see? And after ten minutes the cold meat has softened and taken up the stock and you'd swear it was fresh-cut off a roast joint."

Tamsin laughed and clapped her hands, which surprised her friend somewhat. "That's what I mean, Daisy — the difference between the public show and the secret reality behind it all."

"And there's another thing. The barman told me that if they've got a guest who's already had enough to drink and he keeps on ordering brandy and soda or gin and tonic — stuff like that — he just wets the rim of the glass with the brandy or the gin and then fills it up with the soda or tonic."

"And they never notice?"

"Not according to him. He says they're more interested in pouring out their woes to a sympathetic ear. So as long as you're the most sympathetic listener in the universe, they're not going to suspect you of anything like that, much less accuse you."

"Oh, Daisy!" Tamsin rubbed her hands with glee. "I'm so glad we had this conversation. It makes me think I'll try for a place at the Queen's when we close over the winter — which we probably will have to. Even if I do it for next to no wages, like an apprentice. It'd be worth learning all these little tricks and things."

Daisy giggled. "Funny — you've almost got me thinking your daydream's a lot more tempting than mine."

Tamsin joined her. "What's really funny is that I thought the same about yours!"

After a short silence Daisy said, "You seemed a bit surprised I don't want a husband and brats hanging around — they don't seem necessary to your plans, either."

"No," Tamsin admitted, "except insofar as the men in this world seem to have most of the money. Your dream is cheap compared with mine. You could probably buy fifty acres of woodland for a thou' — with a cottage thrown in — and you could set yourself up with livestock et cetera for a couple of hundred more. So your daydream isn't impossibly out of reach. Mine would need thirty thou' at least. Fifty to do it properly."

Daisy drew a deep breath and said, "Thirty is about what Mister Victor is going to earn — if you can call it earning — it's going to be his annual income after next year, anyway."

There was quite a pause before Tamsin asked, "D'you think I'm being disgustingly mercenary?"

"It's not for me to say," Daisy replied awkwardly. "Me not feeling the slightest want of a man, anyway, I mean."

"Dear me, Daisy! Do you even *like* the creatures, I wonder?"

"I do not," was the emphatic response. "They're hairy, bony, knobbly, smelly things … weak and domineering and …"

"Weak?" Tamsin queried.

"Of course. Look how they moan and snivel when they get so much as a little cold — something that wouldn't keep a woman in bed a minute longer than usual. And they're weak in the head, too — they can only ever do one thing at a time. I've watched gardeners walk empty-handed past a wheelbarrow that needs bringing back to the yard — ten times in an hour I've seen them do it — and it's always because they're on some other errand each time. How soldiers can march *and* sing as they go is a complete mystery."

This concluding remark allowed them both to laugh off her earlier vehemence. Tamsin wanted to ask her where and how she'd suffered at the hands, or behest, of men; nothing else, she thought, could explain such passion. However, she felt that, for all the warmth of their new friendship, they had not yet developed sufficient intimacy to permit it.

Daisy continued: "I suppose, if you've got to have a man ... well, Mister Victor's not among the worst of them."

"He's very good looking — well, *quite* good looking."

Daisy shrugged and made a noncommittal noise.

"You don't agree?"

The maid sighed. "I've carried his shaving water away when Greenhill's been snivelling with the so-called flu. I don't see how any woman can have much opinion of a man once she's gazed into his shaving water." She shuddered.

Tamsin, who had often 'gazed deep' into her father's shaving bowl, loving the smell of his special soap and of the astringent cologne he had used for closing his pores again — to say nothing of the swirly patterns she could make with the razor among the little black hairs on the surface — did not challenge the opinion. Instead she said, "It doesn't necessarily have to come to marriage. I'd never marry for money and ambition if there wasn't also some degree of loving in it as well."

Daisy, who could think only of being wife or mistress, was glad she had not spoken when Tamsin continued: "There's partnership, too — business partnership, I mean. A man with lots of money and not much ambition could make an ideal partner for someone who has no money but lots of vision. And who's willing to work day and night to make it profitable. It could be even better than a love match, in fact."

"A lot better," Daisy said at once. "He'd only own the hôtel."

Tamsin saw a way to tease her — and possibly learn a little more about her into the bargain. "Suppose Mister Victor was to fall in love with you, Daisy ..."

"Ha!"

The sudden loud cry put up a flock of town pigeons on the terrace behind them.

"No, seriously — suppose he got to hear of your ambition to live the simple life, and offered you the chance as long as he could share it with you, would you take him up?"

But Daisy was cannier than she'd thought; the maid just grinned and asked if those herbal books had a chapter on deadly nightshade and death caps, and such like. "And what about yourself?" she dared to ask, now that Tamsin had opened the door to the next stage of intimacy between them. "Are you more inclined to marriage or to partnership at the moment?"

"Marriage, I think. Maybe that's just shades of my upbringing coming out, though."

"With Victor?"

"Well … there isn't anyone else, is there!" She thought fleetingly of David Peters and said more firmly, "No, there isn't anyone else."

10 That Sunday morning Tamsin woke at half-past four and was unable to get back to sleep. She turned this way and that, finding each new position comfortable for no more than five minutes … and throughout her stirring, yesterday's conversation with Daisy in Morrab Gardens, replayed itself over and over in her mind. The more she thought about it, the less certain she became of her own ambitions — or, at least, of her tactics for achieving them. With her background and upbringing it was understandable that she should think that the world of commerce was almost exclusively the preserve of men. The few women in that world became by that very fact remarkable, no matter how undistinguished they might be in every other way. So from there it had been a short and entirely logical step to assume that her dream's fulfillment would depend upon a man — financially at least, even if he took no active part in the day-to-day business.

Actually, as she now realized, she had not *thought* about it at all. Her thinking (if one could even dignify it with that name) had all been downstream of those basic assumptions. In effect, she had said to herself, 'Of course there must be a man and of course he must be rich enough and it would be almost impossible for him *not* to be my husband into the bargain — so let's take all that for granted and get down to planning the details.' And *bargain* was just about the most appropriate word for such a 'love,' when you put it in those stark terms.

In short, she had not even begun to think; she had merely toyed with pipedreams and assumptions. The trouble was, she suspected, that she was not very good at thinking. If only her father were still ...

Yes, well, that was a pretty profitless line to start down, too.

She remembered asking him once what philosophers did and he told her they sit in chairs and think.

"What about?" she asked.

"Life and non-life ... existence ... reality ... good and evil, some of them ... logic ..."

She had tried it — sitting in a chair and just thinking — about good and evil, as it happened. Her train of thought called at some pretty bizarre stations before she gave up: good, evil, last Sunday's sermon, Rev. Ransome, bad breath, the dentist, the taste of cloves, apple tart ...

That was *thinking* for you.

Really she needed someone to think with. To think aloud with. Because if there was someone else, she wouldn't dare go chasing all those butterflies. That was where Papa had been so good, because you could talk about anything with him and he not only listened, he seemed to know where your own thoughts were going next; so he was always ready with a new idea or a new question. And it didn't matter whether you took him up or rejected whatever he was suggesting, he went along with you — ahead of you, even — and was ready to cast the next little pearl. 'Playing devil's advocate,' he called it.

She missed him more now than she had in the immediate aftermath of his death. There had been so much to do then. And the almost simultaneous blow of his bankruptcy had, in a curious way, helped them, bringing as it did the need to think quickly and act decisively to salvage what they could and get out with enough to start the guest house here in Penzance. So they had experienced grief in short, intense intervals between dealing with the most mundane and petty decisions about liquidating the business and settling with creditors.

That was when Mr Samson of Low, Beadle & Samson, their Plymouth solicitors, had complimented her and told her she could probably run a business better than most men he knew. She'd laughed it off, saying that her seemingly passionate involvement was just a way of coping with the grief — which was true enough. But his words had struck a chord within her and then, when she and Mama were planning the guest house, she began to realize that she was always the one who 'played Devil's advocate.' In fact, she played the part so well that Mama had more or less yielded the day-to-day management of the business to her, even before they first opened their doors. And at the end of this month, July, when she reached her majority and could open a bank account *with recourse,* she'd start pressing for some financial control, too.

But somehow she had leaped directly from that to the idea of owning a big hôtel. As she had confessed to Daisy, it had been a land-based version of her earlier pipedream about owning a luxury liner. What she hadn't admitted, though, was that Mr Samson's compliments had somehow made it seem achievable. And because *that* was the target out there in front of her, she had automatically assumed a Mr Moneybags to help make it real — preferably a husband, so he couldn't simply pull out and walk away.

Now, however, thinking about it for the first time — sweeping all those half-thoughts and assumptions aside — she began to glimpse a different route, one in which a rich husband played no part. Indeed, it was one in which no husband at all was needed, rich or poor. All she had to do was make the Morrab so successful that she and Mama could progress from there to one of the small private hôtels along the seafront, and then from there to … well, one step at a time; but you could easily see how an enterprising team of mother-and-daughter, hard working and with a good head for business, could end up with the controlling interest in a big luxury hôtel.

At least, you could if you were Tamsin Harte, *almost* twenty-one, and full of the confidence of youth.

All of which brought her back to her deepening grief for Papa, the only person in all the world with whom she could possibly have spoken such thoughts aloud. Mama was no good

— not for that purpose, anyway. You only needed to say a 'what if' to her and she immediately assumed you were going to rush out and spend a fortune on it that very day; and then, even if you did manage to get it into her head that 'if' meant IF and you might be talking about next year, or ten years from now, she'd relax and say something like 'let's cross that bridge when we come to it, darling.' With her, there was nothing between the immediate panic decision and the long-term complacency that things would sort themselves out, somehow.

By half-past six Tamsin realized there was no point in even trying to rest; and she had long since abandoned all hope of sleep. Besides, the mattress was growing harder by the minute. So she might as well earn a little merit mark by attending Holy Communion at St. Mary's, up near Battery Point. But after the service was over, she felt even more of a sinner than before, for she could not recall a single moment of it. Every minute had been filled with a churning and rechurning of the thoughts that had kept her awake since the small hours.

Outside she saw the young man with the cauliflower hair and the pig's foot in his mouth — Reginald Trotter. Her first instinct was to pretend she had not noticed him and to hasten home with her head in the *Book of Common Prayer*. But he had spotted her the moment she left the church porch so there was nothing for it but to call out, "Good morning, Mister Trotter," and wait for him to shamble across the road to join her.

"Not a very good morning, actually, Miss Harte," he replied as he drew near.

"It'll lift," she assured him as she set off at a brisk pace homeward. "This kind of early morning sea mist — 'wrack,' they call it down here — usually lifts before noon to reveal cloudless skies above. In fact, you can already see a tinge of blue if you look directly up."

"Ah, yes — oops!" He stumbled over a large pebble, probably brought up off the beach and then abandoned by some youngster.

"I'm not going too fast?" she asked. "I ought to be back supervising the breakfasts."

"Not at all," he panted. "I don't believe in all that stuff — Christianity and so on."

"It's a free country."

"I used to. I used to walk out of the house every morning of my life and feel the weight of God pressing down on me. It doesn't bother you?"

She laughed, more from mild embarrassment than from amusement. "No, I don't have that picture of Him — some sort of engineer-in-the-sky."

"Really?" He walked a cycle of three paces and two trots to keep up. Appropriate, really. "No picture at all? Long beard ... flowing robes ... nothing like that?"

"This is an extraordinary conversation for us to be having, Mister Trotter."

"D'you think so? Sunday morning — bells ringing all over town — swings chained and locked in the park — highly appropriate, I'd say."

"Between people who are already intimate, yes."

It was his turn to laugh, in between panting for breath. "I'll let you go," he said. "You obviously don't want to talk with me."

She stopped and turned back to face him. "You are most vexing," she said.

"I know." He grinned. "It's almost my profession."

"Come. I'll walk a little slower — as long as you don't talk about God and such like."

He drew level with her and offered his arm — which she pushed firmly away with her prayer book. Unabashed, he said, "You've not been in the guest-house business long, I'd imagine."

"Would you!"

"I would. I'm also a professional guest-house guest — me and my mater."

"Goodness! What a lot of professions!"

"They're all related."

It suddenly occurred to Tamsin that someone whose recent life had probably involved staying in a succession of guest houses would have useful tips and insights to pass on. "And how does our humble little establishment measure in your scales, may I ask?" Her tone was more cordial now.

"Oh, pretty good, don't you know. Near the top."

" Only near? What little extras would be required to place it *at* the top?"

"An evening meal — at a supplementary rate, of course."

"Mister Trotter!" She slipped her hand through the crook of his arm. "Do tell me more!"

He patted her hand and said, "That's better. You may not have been in the business long, but I see you learn fast."

She hesitated, considering how best to reply.

He continued. "Explain? Very well. I've been convalescing for the best part of two years now. In fact, I've long since recovered from the original consumption — which was never severe in any case. Now, the mater and I continue because we find it congenial. In the winter we travel from pension to pension around the Mediterranean and in summer we return to England. Migrants to our native haunts, you might say."

"You must enjoy it," Tamsin offered.

"Of course. Or we wouldn't be doing it. The mater likes novelty for its own sake — sightseeing, churches, museums, galleries, theatres, the opera ... et cetera. And I? I enjoy meeting new people."

"And pestering them." Her tone was humorous now.

He took the challenge seriously. "It sometimes comes to that, but usually not. The thing about a limited stay in any one place — particularly when all involved know it is limited — is that people are much more forthcoming than they would be if I were a new permanent arrival in the neighbourhood. Let me ask — you're regular churchgoers, you and your mater?"

"Yes."

"And you've been living here five or six months?"

"Thereabout."

"And how many new friends have you made in that time?"

"Well now, running a guest house — especially when you're new to it, indeed, to any sort of business at all — leaves little time for ..."

"None, in short. All these houses we're passing" — he waved a hand along the parade — "there isn't one of them of which you could say you know a little family secret that's hiding in there behind those curtains?"

"As I said ..."

"And yet," he continued, "I'll bet you already know a secret or two about some of the guests you've had — things that amazed you at the time?"

"That's true!" Tamsin exclaimed. Each separate incident hadn't seemed very dramatic in itself but now that Mr Trotter drew her attention to them all — en masse, so to speak — it did begin to seem quite remarkable.

"For instance?" he asked. "I don't mean names and addresses but what sort of things did people tell you that you may be quite sure they would never tell a neighbour back home?"

"There was a girl who sobbed her heart out to me one evening when we were alone in the lounge, all about some unrequited love. I was pretty embarrassed. That was the first. I remember thinking that was quite amazing — opening her heart and soul to a stranger like that."

"And?"

"There was an ex-officer who told me all about why he resigned his commission — protesting against some terrible injustice he'd been forced to connive at. He was very upset. He obviously had to get it off his chest to someone."

"And who better than someone who didn't really know him from Adam and whom he's probably never meet again!"

"I suppose that's it." Mischievously she added an invented instance: "And there was another young man, too, who thought along very similar lines. He supposed that, since I 'didn't know him from Adam' and would probably never cross paths with him again, we could gaily indulge in a brief romance and no harm done."

It didn't fool him. "And, may I ask, what on earth did you tell the poor chap?"

They had reached the bottom of Morrab Road, so the conversation was inevitably drawing toward its conclusion.

"That's my secret, Mister Trotter," she replied.

"Well now, shall I tell you what you *should* say? Should have said, I mean."

"If you feel you have to."

"You should have said you'd think about it."

"And if he kept on pressing for an answer?"

"Just keep on saying you're thinking about it."

"Why?"

"Because you're in business, and he's part of it, and in business you should never shut a door until you absolutely have to."

Now more than ever she realized that this strangely cool — even cold — young man might have a great deal to tell her in the way of running the business.

"To be serious, Mister Trotter ..."

"Oh? Weren't we that already? I thought we were."

"All right. To be practical. You've stayed at a great many guest houses, in England and abroad. You must know a thousand little things ... little ways in which we could do better. Could you possibly ... I mean, would you be willing ..."

"How much would you knock off our bill?" he asked.

"I ... oh, well ..."

"Or would you do it for kisses? One good tip, one delicious kiss — fair exchange?"

For a moment she actually considered the proposal seriously! Then, with a hidden kind of internal shaking of herself, she looked him in the eyes. They were as cold as before. It wasn't that she couldn't imagine herself kissing him — she could, though with little feeling — quite the opposite: She couldn't imagine him kissing her.

"How much pleasure would that give *you?*" she asked.

She hadn't meant to lay so much stress on the word but what was done was done. His response was rather strange, even for such a strange young man. He lowered his gaze and she'd have sworn there was the hint of a blush about his ears and cheeks as he murmured, "No, you're right. Bought kisses are never worth the price, are they."

Bought kisses?

There was no time to ask what he meant, for they were at the front door by now and the air that sprang out to greet them was laden with the reek of burned toast.

11 Was Trotter on the lookout for her or she for him — or, Tamsin wondered, was her father still lingering in that twilight world between this and the next, nudging events, shaping them into a sort of learn-as-you go education for her? Whatever about that, Trotter was there on the seafront as she set out on her Sunday-afternoon stroll to Newlyn — a favourite summertime

walk for those who lived in the western end of the towm. Newlyn's harbour was exclusively for fishing, and the sight of all those little boats tied up for the sabbath was most picturesque. Penzance, by contrast, was a commercial port as well, with all the *un*picturesque and scandalous sights that go along with such places; respectable persons avoided it — and the western end of the town was inhabited almost exclusively by respectable persons.

She strolled as slowly as possible past the Queen's, pausing twice to make unnecessary adjustments to her parasol (for her prediction about the lifting of the wrack had come true), hoping that Daisy would spot her and find some occasion to come out and join her when the coast was clear. She would surely have the afternoon off — and the evening, too, if the Thornes had any conscience at all.

A hundred paces farther on she saw Trotter by the Esplanade railings. He was easy enough to make out because everyone around him was gazing out to sea; he alone was leaning back against the top rail, watching the promenaders instead. Also, he was dressed with unusual elegance this afternoon, with a large hothouse carnation in his buttonhole.

He was probably wise, too, she thought, for, apart from half a dozen sightings of smoke or sail upon the horizon at any one time, the sea was dead calm and empty. People cried 'Ooh look!' when cormorants dived or resurfaced.

He had not yet noticed her, so she kept pace with those around her, not to stand out, and observed him. She soon realized he must be a very lonely young man; he clearly craved the company of other young men of his age. Groups of young women would saunter past, looking him over, as is the custom on those Sunday promenades, and he would barely give them a second glance; but any similar group of young men would hold his attention and keep it until another such group went by.

Just as Tamsin was about to attract his attention a young gentleman, also elegantly attired — and also, curiously enough, sporting a carnation — stopped to speak to him. From the way they looked each other up and down, she gathered they were strangers, and yet they were soon talking freely enough. She wondered if the flower were the emblem of some secret male society, like the Freemasons and their handshakes. Much of their conversation seemed to be secret, anyway, for they often leaned close together, almost as if whispering; also they looked about them every now and then, the way people do when they suspect others might be eavesdropping.

During one of those surveys Trotter's eyes happened to fall upon her. He broke into a broad grin, nudged his friend, pointed her out and said something, and then turned back to her with a welcoming smile.

"Mister Trotter!" she exclaimed as she went to join them. "I didn't wish to intrude."

"Not at all," he replied. "May I present a friend of mine, Mister ..." He turned to the fellow.

"Coverley." The man removed his glove and shook her hand. "Standish Coverley."

"Miss Tamsin Harte," Trotter said.

She knew all about Mr Coverley. He owned the Queen's Hôtel! Her heart began to beat double, for he was also quite a good-looking young man. Well, young-*ish*. Thirty, maybe.

While they engaged in the usual pleasantries, Tamsin studied their *habillement* more closely. Coverley was in white from head to foot except for his amethyst-blue gloves and the matching trim on his panama hat and blazer; even his silver-knobbed cane was lacquered white. His eyes were amethyst blue, too. And as for Trotter, it really was an extraordinary departure from the respectable but quite ordinary dress he wore about the house. He had shoes and spats of grey suède, and a grey cane with an ebony knob. His trousers, too, were of dove grey with the thinnest possible white stripe, and they tapered to hug his ankles; they must have elasticated gussets on the ankle seams, she thought, otherwise he'd never be able to thrust his feet through those openings. He wore a lavender-and-white striped blazer, edged in pale mauve silk — the same silk as trimmed his straw boater. The deep pink of that massive carnation was a bit of a clash, in her opinion, but, on the other hand, that was what made it stand out, too.

As the pleasantries flagged she told them she was thinking of strolling to Newlyn and back.

"Well now," Coverley said, "I was about to propose a drive out to Land's End. My motor is garaged at the Queen's. I'm sure

I speak for both of us when I say that Miss Harte's company would be an additional pleasure."

Trotter seemed slightly surprised at this but he agreed readily enough. What else could he do, Tamsin wondered, since his friend was so positive on the point? "A motor car!" she exclaimed. "I haven't so much as sat in one since last November."

Her father's beloved Wolseley had been one of the first items to go under the hammer.

"Shan't be a tick," Coverley said. "You may wait here. And don't worry — I have goggles and dusters and things for all and some to spare."

When he had gone, Tamsin said, "I'm quite willing to walk on alone to Newlyn, Mister Trotter — if you'd rather I didn't accompany you and your friend?"

"I'm sorry. Was it so obvious? I was just so happy to have met him that ..."

"For the first time, I think?" she risked saying. "Is the carnation some kind of secret emblem."

He stared at her in a curious mixture of doubt and incredulity, not quite knowing what to say.

Now she felt embarrassed; he was, after all a guest. "Forgive me! None of my business — except that you're far too polite and good natured to tell me so. Now it's my turn to apologize."

"Not at all," he said. "As a matter of fact, the carnations *are* a sort of emblem, or signal. How clever of you to spot it! I can't name the sociey, of course, but our purpose in driving out to Land's End was to discuss certain matters ..."

"Then I shall decline this invitation. And thank you for ..."

"No no! I assure you it will not be necessary. You really are welcome. We should enjoy your company. But if at some moment you could be terribly-terribly tactful and ... I don't know ... ask for half an hour of solutide to commune with Nature ... go collecting the local flora to press for your herbarium ...?"

"I quite understand, Mister Trotter. How exciting!"

"It is, indeed." He grinned. "It's just that no one, absolutely no one, is supposed to know of it. However, I'd guess the secret is safe with you?"

Tamsin nodded reassuringly and tried to look as understanding as possible.

"Do I intrude by any chance?"

They turned to see Daisy, walking briskly along the Esplanade toward them.

"Oh dear!" Tamsin murmured. "This is a friend of mine. Look! I'll walk to Newlyn and back with her and you two go off on your motor-jaunt as originally ..."

"Not at all." He also spoke in a murmur. "Two young men ... two pretty girls ... Coverley's right. What could be better? Introduce me, please!"

The maid was too close now for any further discussion. "Daisy!" Tamsin cried. "How nice to see you again! Allow me to present a friend, Mister Reginald Trotter, who is presently staying with us. Miss Daisy Dobbs."

Daisy shook hands with him like a patrician lady; her gratitude to Tamsin for *not* introducing her like a servant overflowed. "Were you thinking of going for a stroll somewhere?" she asked, jumping to obvious conclusions and supposing they would welcome a chaperon.

"Actually, Miss Dobbs, we were just talking of going for a spin to Land's End. We shall be back in time for tea. Would you care to join us?"

Daisy's eyes gleamed but she took care to get the nod from Tamsin before she accepted.

"Here he comes now ..." Trotter's voice trailed off as the first glimpses of the car, turning out of Morrab Road, resolved themselves into ... "One of the new Rolls-Royces!" he murmured.

"Rolls-what?" Tamsin asked. "Is that a motor car?"

"Not *a* motor car," he replied. "*The* motor car."

"D'you like her?" Standish Coverley drew to a halt in the middle of the road, forcing the drivers of lesser motors and dogcarts to edge around him as best they could. "Another bonny lass!" he added when he realized Daisy had joined the party. "How ducky! Hop aboard — we'll drive slowly and put on our motoring rags at the edge of town."

By now the throng of admirers around the car was so thick that all other traffic was forced to wait until the two ladies had settled in the back seat and Trotter had taken his place beside Coverley, in front. It was an open tourer so they felt like royalties, sitting there, the centre of all attention, gazing over the hats of the crowds and trying to look as if this were a regular afternoon outing and a bit of a bore, frankly.

There was a metallic snick as Coverley slipped into bottom gear. He pressed the rubber bulb and the hooter, which resembled those trumpets or shawms you see in Ancient Egyptian murals, gave out a melodious toot, rather like the posthorn on the old mail coaches, which they still parade at county fairs from time to time. The crowds parted in awe and the vehicle glided forward as smoothly and silently as an electric boat on mirror-calm waters.

"Is it electrical?" Tamsin asked. "It's so effortless."

"Well bred," Coverley replied. "She's identical to the one they call the Silver Ghost. Surely you've read of it? They're testing her non-stop, back-and-forth between London and Glasgow. By the end of next month she'll have done fifteen thousand miles non-stop — except for Sundays, of course, when they garage her under RAC guard. I got the next chassis off the line from Manchester and asked Barker's to build the identical body for her — white lacquered aluminium with silver-plated brass fittings. Except for the gear and brake levers, of course ..."

He leaned back to show them how one could change gear with a fingertip touch.

"These are nickel close-plated — not electro-plated, mark you. D'you know, they actually beat out sheets of nickel until it's only six-thou' thick and then they solder it onto the alloy levers ..." His incomprehensible praise of the vehicle's wonders continued thus until they reached the cross-roads at Stable Hobba, well outside the town. There, since they had to slow down anyway, he drew to a halt — once again on the crown of the road — and made Trotter get out. Those wonderful close-plated levers and the spare outer tube barred any exit on his side. From a box slung beneath the running board, he drew out dusters, to hold down the ladies' hats and keep their upper garments clean, motoring caps, for himself and Trotter, and goggles, for all four of them.

"Now we can do some serious motoring," he said.

"Does the engine start up automatically when you move those lever-things?" Tamsin asked.

He laughed. "She's running now."

The others strained their ears but could hear nothing — except for the cooing of a some pigeons and a cow lowing for her calf out in one of the fields.

"I'll show you." Coverley undid the snaps and lifted the bonnet. "There's proof."

Now they could hear the hiss of the carburettors and — only just — the deep rumble of the 40/50 horsepower engine.

"Watch this!" He took out a gold sovereign and balanced it on its edge on the top of the engine. It did not fall, even when he picked up a twig and prodded the throttle lever to make the engine race, or 'rev up,' as he called it. "Even if you coax her up to sixty," he added, "they say the noise of the motor is no louder than you'd get from a typical eight-day clock. Come on — let's go!" He snatched up the coin, refastened the bonnet snaps, and opened the door to the ladies' seats in the back, all with a showman's flourish.

"We're not going to try to reach sixty miles an hour, I hope?" Daisy said.

He replied that they'd have to go to Hayle Sands if they wished to do that because the roads around Land's End were too crooked and bumpy. "Watch!" he said. "She'll start in top gear without a complaint."

She did, too.

"Why are cars and ships always 'she'?" Daisy asked. "Can anyone tell me that?"

Trotter turned and winked at her. "Because they'd go all over the place without a man to control them."

"If you ask me," Tamsin replied, "it's because they can carry any number of good strong men but even the strongest men can't carry them. So there!"

Daisy looked at her askance; the two men stared rigidly ahead; she had the feeling they were struggling desperately not to laugh.

"What did I say?" she murmured to Daisy, whose only answer was to put a finger to her lips.

She felt mortified, without knowing why.

To anyone used to the rumble of even the most elegant carriage, with its wooden wheels and iron tyres, this beautiful motor seemed to glide along like something in a dream. It made forty miles an hour, which Coverley swore they were doing, seem more like twenty.

"It's a curious thing," Trotter said. "This part of Cornwall has more prehistoric antiquities, just about, than anywhere else in England. Yet you hardly get a glimpse of one of them from this particular road.

"Where are they?" Tamsin asked, glad of the new subject. "Could we see some?"

"Another day," Coverley promised. "The summer's not half done yet. How long are you staying, old bean?"

"As long as I want," Trotter replied.

Tamsin made a note to tell him that if he wanted the last three weeks in August, he'd better book soon, because the places were going fast.

"Good egg! And you two ladies?"

Tamsin explained that she lived in Penzance; Daisy said she'd be leaving next Saturday — turning toward Tamsin with an expression that said 'so-now-you-know.'

It was only eight miles from Penzance to Land's End, and in all that way they had done nothing but sit and occasionally clutch at their hats, not trusting the security provided by their dusters. And yet, when they pulled off the road by the gate where a track led down to the first and last cliff-promontory in England, they felt out of breath. And when they took off their goggles they had to laugh because the pale white patches around their eyes made them look like Christy's Minstrels.

But Coverley was equal to all occasions, it seemed, for another delve into the box below the running board produced a handful of small facecloths scented with rosewater.

Daisy and Tamsin went a little way off to wipe inside the hems of their blouses, where the dust had penetrated.

They put back the cloths and Coverley took out a couple of picnic rugs, oilcloth on one side, woollen plaid on the other, one of which he passed to Daisy. Then the four of them went down to the headland, past the little hôtel and the abandoned shepherd's hut. Tufts of sea pinks and a lush, tough grass whose blades were almost indistinguishable from sea-pink leaves made a springy pad underfoot, turning an ordinary walking pace into something like skipping.

"It's like a hundred-acre feather bed," Tamsin remarked. "Wouldn't it be fun if we were children and could just roll down over it!"

Coverley passed his hat and gloves to her and did a couple of somersaults downhill — of the handspring kind so that his alabaster-white clothes did not touch the green. Although he reached toward Tamsin to recover his hat and gloves, it was to Trotter that he looked for admiration.

They stood on the coastguard path at the cliff's edge and found the promontory to be just one among half a dozen, all of them pretty nearly identical; had it not been for a little cast-iron plaque, they would not have been entirely certain which one was the actual Land's End. They stared down at some seals, basking on the rocks, and a few of the creatures stared back at them. The sea was oily slick, which is rare in those waters where the Atlantic meets the Channel; there was not a breath of a breeze, either.

"I'd give two years of my life to swim now," Tamsin murmured, envying the seals. "D'you think ...?" Courage failed her.

"Go on," Coverley urged.

"Well ... I'm surprised there aren't more people about," she said. "Any people at all, actually — on a day like this."

"That's the Cornish sabbath," he told her. "No omnibuses. No cherry-bangs. I wonder how many tourists must complain before Mammon wins over the Nonconformist soul? But what were you going to suggest?"

"Well — if Miss Dobbs and I could find our way down to this cove and you two gentlemen could get down one on either side, we could disrobe modestly and swim out to meet at that point where the seals are basking. I'm sure they pose no danger."

The men accepted the suggestion without demur and stayed only to help the two ladies down a not very difficult path to the rocks below. Then they scrambled back up and over to the next inlet. "First to evict the seals!" Coverley called down the challenge to them.

"Come on!" Daisy urged. "We mustn't let them win."

But Tamsin just stood there, shaking her head, staring at the water. "I must have been mad," she said.

12 There was a reassuring overhang of rocks on the northern side of the cove — massive and thick, and not at all friable, like most of the cliffs near Penzance. There the two girls could undress safely out of sight from all but about twenty yards of the coastguard path above.

"What d'you make of them?" Daisy asked. "Our two fine feathered friends."

"They certainly outdress every other man in Penzance. And that Rolling Royce machine must be the finest car in the West. I didn't know such beautiful machines could exist. I say — d'you think they're interested in us?" She longed to tell Daisy about the secret society but honour forbade it.

Daisy shrugged. "Dunno. Usually you get a sort of feeling. But with these two … I don't know. We shan't offer them any encouragement, anyway. They certainly know how to dress well. There's a year's wages on their backs."

Tamsin turned her back to Daisy. "Can you just loosen the top lace? I didn't ask if you can swim — I'm sorry."

"Oh, I'd have sung out soon enough, don't worry." Daisy did as she was asked. "Anyway, there's a shallow bit there where a non-swimmer could stay in her depth."

She was naked now except for her shift and Tamsin noticed a silver locket hanging by a fine filigree chain around her neck.

"Hoo-hoo!" she challenged archly. "Is that a lover's portrait you carry next to your heart?"

Daisy removed it casually and hefted it in the palm of her hand. "Just a lock of hair," she answered casually. "For two pins I'd throw it out there as far as I could. And never go looking for it again, neither."

But she laid it delicately on top of her clothes and covered it with her shift. Then, suddenly, she seemed amused to notice how neatly Tamsin had piled her clothes. "Bet you weren't always so careful!" she teased. "Not when you had a maid to tidy up after you."

"That just shows how much you know!" She pouted playfully. "I always was neat and tidy." Then, more thoughtfully. "Perhaps I never was intended to be a lady of leisure. D'you envy them, Daisy — people with all the leisure in the world? D'you envy Mrs Thorne all her wealth and freedom?"

Daisy pulled a face. "Not often. 'Specially not when you see how she uses it. Come on — we're about as ready as ever we will be. And they did challenge us."

Naked at last they peeped out from under the rocky overhang and, though no spectators were in sight, they crept along beneath its protection until they reached a point where they could slip into the water without racing over open rocks — a quick one-two and a mighty splash.

"Here we come, Mister and Mrs Seal!" Tamsin called out just before the sea swallowed her.

It was the first time she had bathed in Cornish waters. The shock almost killed her — at least, that was the thought uppermost in her mind as she surfaced again with a scream: *I'll die! I'll surely die! I'll never be able to stand this!* She was too shocked to speak a word.

Heedless of how Daisy was faring in the same arctic grip, she struck out in her strongest trudgen-stroke for the rock from which she had so blithely jumped not five seconds earlier. But when she reached it and shook the water from her eyes she saw that an elderly couple were sauntering along the clifftop path and watching them with interest.

So she was trapped in the water. She could already feel its icy fingers gripping tight around every part of her, intent on strangling her circulation completely. It was only a matter of time, measured surely in minutes, before the last bit of life-sustaining warmth was sucked out of her.

And only now did she look about her to see how Daisy was managing to survive.

The girl was calmly treading water a dozen yards away, and grinning broadly. "Give it a minute or two, love," she said, "and you'll swear it's boiling. You scared off all the seals, anyway. Keep moving — that's best."

"If those people weren't watching, I'd move fast enough! I'd get out and never come back in."

"Don't let them bother you. With the water being this calm and clear, there's not much they can't see, anyway."

"Oh, Daisy!" To stop all her muscles freezing stiff she began a sort of dog-paddle out to join her friend, and as she drew near, she saw that it was, indeed, true. She could see all of the girl's body, even though it was in flickering, shivering images that kept breaking up and joining together again. There were her bosoms, her belly with the dark, reddish delta beneath it, and the white limbs that walked an invisible underwater treadmill. "It's true! Oh, lawks — what about the men?"

"What about them? See if I care!" Daisy laughed. "If a cat can look at a king, then I suppose a king may look at a cat, as well!" She set off at an easy breast-stroke toward the rock at the mouth of the narrow inlet, where the seals had been basking earlier. She breathed out an explosive spray that gave her a brief rainbow halo.

"We must keep splashing — that's all," Tamsin decided. "I hope you don't think — I mean, when I suggested this swim, I never thought the water would be so calm and transparent."

"Well ... if we drive them mad, that's their funeral. It could be fun. Come on!"

When she gained the rock she found a foothold and sprang from the water in another irridescent halo of spray, half-turning herself so that she landed sitting on its smooth edge, facing out to sea. "Beat you! Beat you!" she shouted toward the next cove northward, where, she presumed, the gentlemen were lurking still. Then she turned to Tamsin. "Are you coming out? This rock's lovely and warm from the sun."

She had a shapely figure and Tamsin, who had dabbled in art a little, admired the curvaceous pyramid of her hips as they tapered up into her slender waist. "But is it safe?" she asked, looking dubiously about them.

"Scared of sunburn?"

"No! You know very well what I mean." She trod water, glancing anxiously toward the next cove every so often. "Where did you learn to be so shameless, anyway?"

"A very good question!" Daisy said. She was suddenly quite serious. "My last lady, Mrs Ormesby, was a naturist. They had a tall yew hedge in the garden, all round a big square, where they could undress and lie in the sun or play tennis or they had a fountain where they could paddle and cool off. Brown as berries, they were, after every summer. She and the master used to go out there in winter, too, but the rest of the family wasn't so hardy. Or dedicated."

"You're right — it does feel quite warm after a while. And you mean to say they forced you servants to undress and go naked as well?" She prepared to offer sympathy.

"Not a bit. Only those who wanted to. Of course, it took me some time to see there was no shame in it. So when you called it shameless, you were more ..."

"And then you lay in the sun and played tennis with them?" Tamsin was incredulous.

"Oh yes, very likely, I must say! No, we stood as per usual — the few servants who took to naturism, that is. We'd stand around waiting to fetch balls from the long grass or lemonade from the ... there was a sort of changing hut where the other servants would bring the tea or wait for errands. And we were the go-betweens, sort of."

"Is that where you formed your low opinion of men?"

Daisy hesitated. "Yes," she said. "But that was ... something else. Nothing to do with the naturism side of it. Maybe I'll tell you one day."

"Talking of men — here they are." She laughed at the sight. Two dark heads on the shimmering water, their beautiful hair plastered slick against their skulls. "They look like a brace of sealions. Come back in, quickly!"

"No, I shan't," Daisy said truculently. She turned and shouted, "Beat you!" at them again. Then she added, "I forgot to mention I'm a naturist. D'you mind?"

They looked at each other and Coverley answered, "No. I've dabbled a bit myself, in fact."

Trotter added, "But perhaps Miss Harte would object?"

"To what?" Tamsin asked, hoping against hope that they were all just teasing her.

"Tamsin!" Daisy said despairingly.

"Object to our sitting on the rock like so many solemn Scandinavians, enjoying the sunshine?" Coverley replied.

They were right beside the rock now.

When he put it like that, making it sound so dull and innocent, how could she possibly object? But it annoyed her all the same to be forced into a corner by them. She looked daggers at Daisy, who had started it all.

"It's like the cold of the water, love," the girl replied, unabashed. "You think you can't bear it at the beginning but later you wonder what all the fuss was about. Come on — I'll help you up. There's a ledge here. Careful though. Don't kneel on it. There's millions of tiny barnacles."

"But none on the top." Trotter reached up and felt how smooth it was. "How odd."

"I expect the seals rubbed them all off," Coverley told him. "They bask here all year round."

While they sorted out the natural history, Tamsin took the first step into her own naturist history. She closed her eyes, put both feet on the barnacle-encrusted ledge, and let Daisy pull her out into the balmy sunshine.

She sat to Daisy's left, knees tight together, arms folded across her lap, and did not open her eyes again until the two men were seated as well; she was relieved to see they were a good yard beyond Daisy and on the farther side. She could not, however, resist a quick peep at Coverley, who, she discovered, had the body of a Greek athlete, as seen in all the best museums. She might have guessed it from the handspring somersaults he'd performed earlier; but guessing (and imagining) were one thing and seeing it with her own eyes was another.

She only took a quick peep, though.

"If one of those lonely men out there has a telescope," — Coverley pointed to the Longships lighthouse, just over a mile out to sea from where they were sitting — "he'll have a pretty eyeful this afternoon!"

They all laughed, a little nervously; now that the deed was done, the bullet bitten, they were all a little hesitant. And Tamsin discovered that Daisy was right, as always. There had been a few shocked moments as she died of shame — sitting there in a state of nature beside two handsome young fellows and a good-looking girl in the same scandalous state — and then the shame had withered even as the icy chill of the water had ceased to feel cold.

"No need to cringe and shrivel into a little ball like that," Daisy murmured to her.

Tamsin glanced at her and saw she was leaning back on rigid arms — so rigid, in fact, that they were bent a few degrees in the 'wrong' direction, as if she were double-jointed — and thrusting out her chest and lifting her chin to bare as much of herself to the sun as possible. "Some days can make up for months of misery," she said to no one in particular.

"Some days should go on for ever," Coverley murmured as he lay back upon the sun-warmed rock.

In fact, both men now stretched themselves full length and closed their eyes against the sun. Their feet were still in the water and every now and then they kicked idly, just to keep the circulation going.

Apart from paintings and statues, Tamsin had never before seen the undraped male body — and, since all the others had their eyes closed, she could not resist the temptation to make up for her ignorance now. Trotter was slightly podgy. Nothing that good tailoring couldn't hide but she could see each heartbeat make a tiny ripple down over his belly. He was also rather hairy, which was something you didn't see much of in marble statues.

Anyway, she wasted little time on him because his friend Coverley was quite the opposite — a flesh-coloured sculpture of Adonis, no less. She could not take her eyes off him.

Last year, before her father's death, she had enrolled part-time at Plymouth Art School, where her favourite pursuit had been clay modelling. She had done a quarter-size replica of the school's plaster cast of *Discobolo* — the famous Ancient Greek discus thrower with the tight, curly hair; the master said it was quite good. In art galleries she always wanted to touch the sculpture — to run her fingers over those marble hands and arms and shoulders and ribs and things; so it had been a great pleasure to have permission to do just that, even though it was only on a dusty old plaster cast that had seen better days.

But all that was as nothing compared with her present desire to touch that perfect body, stretched full out upon the rocks not a yard away from her. She did not think of it as having a name; it was not Standish Coverley; that would have made any sort of touching impossible — and even the *idea* of touching him, or, rather, it. *It* was not personal. It was a thing. An object of consummate beauty, as impersonal as Michelangelo's *David.*

David. The name stirred in her mind. Fisherman David. David Peters ... She pushed the thoughts away.

A thing of paramount beauty like this anonymous body at her side had something universal about it. Or did she mean immortal? Something that belonged to all the world, anyway. To all mankind, male and female alike.

Would she dare?

She could pretend. She reached out toward him, threading her arm between Daisy's double-jointed props. Daisy chose that moment to shake her wet hair, which incidentally moved her arms. In avoiding them, Tamsin touched Coverley on the shoulder. He opened his eyes and blinked in her direction.

"Sorry!" She laughed with embarrassment. "I was chasing away a fly and trying not to disturb you. You looked so ..."

But he did not wait to hear how he looked. He sprang to his feet and, all in the same movement, without a pause, did a pike into the water. His body arced through the seagreen fathoms in a streak of alabaster flesh and silver bubbles until he emerged again, a yard or so to her left and, still continuing the movement, burst from the sea, hands to the rock, shoulders rippling like the muscles on an Arab stallion, gymnast's spin on one hand ... and there he was, sitting beside her, knees bent, hugging them in his arms, head resting on them, looking at her with all the intensity those amazing, amethyst-blue eyes could muster. And not just looking at her, but looking her up and down, too.

She wanted to curl up with embarrassment but, to her utter astonishment, found that her body was doing quite the opposite — stretching out in the same way as Daisy, except that she kept her eyes open. She had no choice, in fact, for his now held hers in what seemed like a full-scale audit of her inner being.

"So, Miss Harte," he said, "tell me a little about yourself. Mister Trotter thinks you are one of the most admirable people he has ever met."

She swallowed hard. "Mister Trotter has no right to say such a thing." The answer was automatic but she could not think what else to say.

"A man has every right to speak the truth," Trotter drawled, sitting up and pulling his legs out of the water so as to adopt the same pose as his friend.

"I understand you went from wealth to relative poverty in the space of a few days and ..."

"It was a peculiar sort of poverty that allowed us to buy a substantial house in the most respectable part of Penzance and open it as ..."

"I did say *relative* poverty," he pointed out.

But she insisted. "It must happen to hundreds of people every day of the week. There's nothing very distinctive about it — especially if, like me, you discover you've landed on your feet and you actually enjoy the new life much better than the old. Setting aside my father's death, of course."

"Of course. But that's just what I find so interesting, you see: You enjoy managing the guest house more than ..."

"More than all those dreary balls and garden parties and playing tennis in long skirts and sitting in the butts admiring the men as they slaughter birds in their thousands? What d'you find so interesting in *that?*"

"Nothing. That was your former life. I'd much rather hear about what *you* find so interesting in your new situation. Unless, of course, you'd rather not talk about it?"

"Oh." Now she regretted her prickliness. "Well ... people, I suppose. The huge variety of people one meets. Actually, it's combination of that and the discovery that we can meet all their different needs. Food ... advice ... all sorts of things. I mean, when people say goodbye and tell you they've just enjoyed the best holiday in years and they'll certainly be back next year ... well, I can't remember anything in our old way of life that was half so satisfying."

"Good," he said. "That is marvellous. Well done! And what d'you mean by advice?"

"Which is the best beach — we just want to sit on the sands all day? Can you arrange for us to meet a fisherman and to go on a fishing trip with him? We're rather high-church, so where's the best place to worship?"

Trotter laughed. "Like looking for a needle in a hay *field* down here, I should think!"

"Breage-and-Germoe's fairly high," she told him. "We can even arrange a taxi for them. That parish was very Royalist in the Civil War, you know."

"The Civil War, eh? You're developing a memory as long as any Celt's!" he chided.

"There's other advice we get asked for, too," Tamsin said, more hesitantly now.

"For example?" Coverley urged.

"One woman asked me what food she could give her husband back home to help him lose a few inches. And husbands have asked if they could accompany me on a marketing trip so that I can help them buy some trinket for their wives. I've even been asked how to get rid of those pale brown spots you get in old books ..."

"Foxing," Daisy put in.

"That's it. People seem to think that because you've got a smattering of education *and* can manage a guest house without too many obvious disasters, you're the fount of all wisdom!"

"Ah me! Little do they know!" Daisy bared her teeth at her and winked.

Tamsin ignored the jibe. "Anyway, does that answer your question?" she asked Coverley.

"Admirably — and I'm grateful, Miss Harte." He rested his chin in the hollow between his knees and gazed out to sea. "Have you ever looked back through the very early volumes of *Punch?*" he asked.

"Who — me?" Tamsin said.

"Anybody. They're full of jokes about the *nouveaux riches* — not just the new-rich plutocrats but the new-rich middle class and, a bit later, the new-rich artisans and clerks — long before *The Diary of a Nobody* but people of that class. And you get the feeling that they're laughing at them because they think it's a temporary sort of fad and it'll go away in time. The basic thrust of *Punch's* humour, unlike almost all other satire, is that everything will get back to normal pretty soon and that nothing will ever, ever change. But, of course, it does ..."

"Has this got anything to do with Miss Harte?" Daisy asked rather sharply.

"Everything — and with you, too, Miss Dobbs. Those old jokes tell us they were living through a revolution, a social revolution — a very English social revolution — but they were only half aware of it. They imagined they could laugh it out of existence. Well, *Punch* still has the odd joke against the new rich but for every one of them there are dozens against the New Woman — the feminist, the suffragist, the respectable single business lady ... even those vast-bosomed headmistresses who cannot see without the aid of lorgnettes. It is, I believe, a sign that we're living through yet another very English social revolution and that, whatever *Punch* may think, it, too, will not fade away. Even our servants are part of it."

Daisy felt sure he was speaking of her though he did not so much as glance her way. "Really?" she said nervously.

"Yes, indeed," he continued, still giving the impression he was talking about remote third parties. "Two generations ago a servant would have stayed with his master and mistress for life. And even if he left them, it would have been for a similar position in some other household. But now, I expect, not a week goes by but the minds of half the servants in the land turn over other prospects? Do we doubt it?"

Daisy just shrugged, since her direct opinion did not seem to be called for. Perhaps he hadn't, after all, twigged that she was one of that class?

Realizing her difficulty, Tamsin sought to divert the conversation. "But why does *Punch* laugh at feminists and so on?" she asked. "That's surely the question?"

"Fear," he replied. "Oxford undergraduates yell and throw bread rolls at women who try to sit for degrees. They fear to discover that the women might equal them in any subject, or even outshine them. Eminent doctors will give you two dozen reasons why women are physically and mentally unsuited to positions of power — all very scientific. But, quite simply, they, too, fear that women will prove no better and no worse than men when it comes to pulling the levers of power."

"But you're a man," Tamsin objected. "Why don't you fear this competition from women, too?"

Coverley reached out and patted her hand. "That's another social revolution," he told her. "But it is one whose time has not yet come, I fear."

Not understanding a word of it, Tamsin felt patronized. And annoyed.

13 Tamsin turned over a dozen ways of making her point to Daisy and, in the end, she just came straight out with it: "You recall what you said about men yesterday? Hairy, bony, knobbly, et cetera? You certainly can't say that about Standish Coverley, can you!"

They were dressing once again, having sun-dried themselves on a secluded rock near the point of the promontory, where the only prying eye would have been in that distant lighthouse. Even their hair was dry, though slightly claggy from the salt.

Daisy sniffed but said nothing.

"Can you," Tamsin insisted.

"Do I have to give an opinion?" Daisy asked wearily.

"Well, *I* think he's ... pretty ... tremendous, anyway."

"Looks aren't everything."

"But they are in this case. I mean, that's all I'm talking about," Tamsin protested. "Good heavens! You don't think I mean" — she swallowed heavily — "something soppy and romantic, do you? It never occurred to me. I only mean he's pretty tremendous to *look* at. If you could cast his torso in plaster ... I mean, it would knock most Græco-Roman sculpture into a cocked hat."

Briefly she wondered what her mother would make of that ghastly expression. It made her realize she'd been farther from her mother that afternoon, both in statute miles and in spirit, than at any time since her father's death.

Daisy made a small, noncommittal murmur through her nose.

Tamsin thought she must be pretending her indifference. No one could be *that* uncaring about such a man. "Also, he's a jolly agreeable person — don't you think?" she added.

"You sure you're not getting ideas about him?"

"Of course not!" she exclaimed, and almost immediately wished she had not been quite so emphatic. "Though I don't see why not," she added. "You can't say he's completely devoid of interest in me."

"I didn't notice it much."

"What about all those questions he asked ... he was really interested in my replies. And you didn't see his eyes when he was talking to me." She shivered with remembered pleasure. "He seemed to look right inside me." Then, fearing she was just sounding silly and romantic, she sought to add a harder edge to her enthusiasm: "Also he's rich. And rich people are always interesting. He owns the Queen's Hôtel. He's got that marvellous motor car. And, most important of all in my case, he's got no prejudices against the new-poor!"

Daisy shrugged. "There's just something ... remote about him. About the pair of them. That's all."

She was thinking of social class, Tamsin supposed. In which case — from her point of view as a servant — she was quite right. It would, however, be unkind to point that out. Best to drop the matter entirely.

"Don't you feel it?" Daisy asked. "Like monks. Or no, not monks but members of a club and not much interested in anything that doesn't concern it. Something like that."

Again Tamsin almost blurted out what Trotter had told her. But how astute of Daisy to have spotted it anyway. She was certainly a bright, intelligent girl. It was a pity she'd be leaving Penzance so soon.

"Can you comb my hair out, there's a love?" Daisy asked. "I'll do yours after."

Tamsin took the offered comb and, sitting on the blanket behind Daisy, on a long, sloping shelf of rock, she began working away at the knotted ends all round, combing higher and higher up each tress as she went. "Anyway," she said, "whatever club you're thinking of, it's certainly not the usual kind. It's nice to meet men who aren't *men's* men. D'you know the sort I mean? Bluff, hearty creatures who live and breathe in yachting crews, rugby clubs, golf clubs ... those sorts of clubs. Men who go off and climb the Mountains of the Moon — all jolly chaps together. You have to allow that Messrs Trotter and Coverley aren't a bit like that — apart from his obsessive love of that Rolling-Royce. And even then, when you ride in it, you can quite understand him. If I had a car like that, I'd just drive and drive. Also, you couldn't talk music or art or things like that with *men's* men — not for more than two or three sentences. I've tried. I've probably got more experience of men's men than you have, actually. They try to turn the whole world into one vast boys' school where it's all 'Play up! Play up! And play the game!' You can't say Coverley and Trotter are like that." After a long pause she added, "Cat run off with your tongue, then?"

Daisy sighed. "I've said my say. We've both said our say. I can only repeat — they just seem a bit like ... I don't know — people training to be vicars or something. Anyway!" In quite a different tone she added, "Did you get that — what I said about leaving next Saturday and going back to Devon with the Thornes?"

"Yes." Tamsin sighed. "That's sad-making. For me, anyway. I suppose it's inevitable."

Daisy stiffened and then turned round. "What do you mean? Are you suggesting it needn't be or something?"

There was such an intensity in her eyes that Tamsin had to think back to what she *had* meant. In fact, she hadn't meant anything in particular — just what a pity it was in general that life was full of such inevitabilities. Friendships and partings. "Mean?" she echoed.

"Yes. I mean ... d'you think it's *not* inevitable?" She touched Tamsin's hand gingerly. "I'm not at all looking forward to saying goodbye, you know. I don't meet too many people I get on with so well, and so quickly."

"Nor me." Then the significance of Daisy's words struck her. "You mean you'd leave the Thornes — just like that?"

"Well, not 'just like that' — I mean, I'd give two weeks' proper notice. And then, by heavens, I'd give Madame Thorne a piece of my mind — but that's by the way. But it would depend on ... oh! Stop beating about the bush, girl! It would depend on *you*. Tell me straight — would there be any chance of a place for me at your guest house? There!" She let out a great sigh of relief. "That's the long and short of it."

"Gosh!" Tamsin stared out to sea; her mind seemed to have gone numb. Why hadn't the same thought occurred to her? The impossibility of finding the money for her wages, that's why. Especially for a lady's maid!

"Well, I wasn't expecting you to get up and dance!" Daisy sighed and turned her face away.

"It's not that," Tamsin assured her. "I'd just love it if it were only possible. Is it possible? I'd move heaven and earth to ... it's just that our particular bit of heaven-and-earth are so wretchedly small. And poor. How much ... I mean, what sort of wages ..."

"I'm getting thirty-five pounds a year at the moment."

"And 'the run of your teeth,' as Mrs Pascoe says."

"And one new uniform and shoes. What does Bridget get?"

"Thirty-five! I'm afraid ..."

"What does Bridget get?" Daisy asked again.

"Ten. Cornwall's a lot poorer than Devon, you know. We could never have afforded a house like ours around Exeter or Plymouth. And neither Mama nor I would have anything like thirty-five pounds to spend on ourselves in a year. Not even between us. Oh, I'm sorry, Daisy." She laughed with embarrassment. "We live in different worlds, obviously. You're rich. We're poor!" Desperate now to change the subject, she added, "Shall we go and see if the men are ready?"

"No!" Daisy grinned. "One thing I have learned is never make the running yourself. If *they* want something, make *them* sweat for it. If they don't, then running after them only panders to their vanity. Anyway you lose no face by sitting pretty. And apart from all that, don't you want me to comb your hair now? You've done a very good job on mine." She laughed. "Maybe *I* should take *you* on as my lady's maid!"

Their slightly forced laughter and the business of changing places allowed them to bury the topic.

But not for long. It was difficult to think of anything else to talk about.

"You're lucky your hair is so naturally oily," Daisy said as she ran the comb through Tamsin's locks in easy, graceful strokes. "The sea hardly touched it — and it's so glossy."

"It's murder on pillows, though. And it needs washing *every single* week."

The sun stole beneath the rock overhang, warm and kindly now that it had lost some of its noonday heat.

"Such a pity it burns one's skin brown and makes one look like a gipsy," Tamsin murmured, stretching her arms into its glow.

"My naturists said it's good for you. *Tanning,* they called it. It's all in the eye of the beholder."

"About what you said ..." Tamsin ventured.

"When?"

"You know — leaving the Thornes and coming to ..."

"Forget it. I shouldn't have asked."

"No. I shouldn't have said no like that."

Daisy popped her head over Tamsin's shoulder and grinned. "You didn't actually say no."

"I didn't exactly say yes, either!"

"Anyway, forget it." She returned to her combing.

"No, I shan't. I responded without thinking — or, at least, I only thought of the immediate situation. The way we manage things at this moment. But, if the business develops in the way I hope it will, well, I can't think of anyone I'd rather have — nor anyone more suited to be with us. I don't suppose you could stick it out another year with the Thornes?"

"What will change in a year's time, then?"

Tamsin described her plans for expanding the catering side of the business and for raising the general tone of their service so as to attract a higher class of guest.

"You see," she concluded, "just to give a specific example — Mrs Whyte brought me a pair of her husband's trousers last week. He'd sat in a spot of tar and she asked if we had anything to get it off. So Bridget said she always used butter to get tar off her skin, so we tried that, and ..."

"Aaaargh" Daisy gripped her by the shoulders and said, "No! Tell me you didn't!"

"We did! It got the tar out all right. Then I was up half the night trying to remove the butter. And poor Bridget went into hiding all next day whenever I was around."

"A threepenny bottle of benzine, which you can get from the chemist, was all you needed."

"You make my point, Daisy. You see, we don't have enough rooms to accommodate servants, not like the Queen's, so if we're going to attract ladies who are used to being waited on hand and foot, we'll have to offer that sort of service. You could do it blindfold. So can we keep in touch? Can I write to you and offer you a place — *if* we've managed to attract people of that class by next season?"

But Daisy, having enjoyed her Pisgah sight of the Promised Land, was reluctant to abandon it, even temporarily. While she wondered how to keep the way open, Tamsin added, "Even then, I doubt we could offer anything like your present wages.

But, on the other hand, you could easily make thirty in tips. Even Bridget and Catherine look set to make ten apiece — equalling their wages — before the season ends. And all they do is make beds, empty chamber pots, dust ... that sort of thing. They're very happy about it, anyway. So what d'you say?"

"How much ..." Daisy began. "I mean ... put it this way. You say you and your mother don't have as much as thirty-five pounds each out of the business in a year. Or even together. Well, forgive me for asking this, but how much would the sum be, then? I'm not just prying."

"Gosh! I'm only guessing, anyway, because the season's only just getting into full swing."

"A guess is better than nothing at all."

"Well ... there are our clothes, of course ... we no longer buy perfume, nor any cosmetics except Mama uses some face-powder ..."

"I didn't ask for every little detail!"

"No, but I'm trying to work it out. It's not something I've thought of much — though I should have, I suppose. There's also an occasional bottle of ordinary table wine. And our library subscriptions. And the *Ladies' Home Companion* ..."

"All right, all right! It must easily come to one pound, seven shillings, and threepence three farthings! I take your point."

"Well, I wouldn't think it came to more than fifteen pounds, dear. Eighteen at the very most. We haven't been poor through one whole winter yet, not really. Should we count doctors' bills and medicines, perhaps? No, because if any of the staff fell ill, we'd certainly pay for the ..."

"I'd come for fourteen!" Daisy blurted out. "You think you manage on fifteen quid a year. I'll accept fourteen. There!"

Stunned by this, Tamsin pulled away from her and sprang to her feet, edging even farther away so that she did not tower above her. "But why?" she asked. She felt a constriction in her throat and a prickling behind her eyelids. Daisy was so intense again, so frightened, almost.

"I don't know." Daisy rose and slipped the comb back into her handbag. "It just feels right. Or nothing else would feel *as* right. I've got savings put by — and it's not for getting married, as you may well believe! So I won't really feel the pinch. It's just that I suspect that, five years from now, I'll be saying it's the best decision I ever made." She laughed awkwardly. "And I'd hope you'd be saying the same — from your point of view, I mean."

"Oh, Daisy! Even now I don't have the slightest doubt about that, but ..."

"I mean," she interrupted, "sometimes in life you have to make these decisions, don't we. Something tells you this or that is absolutely the right choice for one and we just have to go along with it."

"Yes," Tamsin agreed. "But we do have a whole week ahead of us. There's no need to make a hard-and-fast decision just yet, is there? And, anyway, I really ought to discuss it with Mama — even though I know she'll agree ... in the end. So let's just say it's something we're both eager to do and we'll make a final decision toward the end of the week. Agreed?"

"Agreed," Daisy echoed, even though she had privately decided to hand in her notice that very evening.

"And now shall we go and see if the men are ..."

"No! Just be patient. Everyone thinks the hounds hunt the fox. But any hunting man will tell you — nine times out of ten it's the fox that leads the hounds. And a good time is had by all."

They shook the sand off the blanket and folded it up. "My turn to carry it," Tamsin said.

Daisy let her have her way.

As they approached the coastguard path, Tamsin paused and said, "Just one thing ..."

"What?"

"Your decision to leave the Thornes and come to us ..."

"Yes?"

"It's not ... I mean, it hasn't anything to do with ... you know what I mean?"

"I do not know. Spit it out!"

Tamsin laughed. "Mama is going to love your turn of phrase! What I mean is, it hasn't got anything to do with ... today? Or has it?"

"Today? What in particular?"

"You see — you're being evasive about it!"

"I am not! Just to say 'today' is pretty vague. Lots of things have happened today."

"But there's one thing in particular."

Daisy gazed at the sky and whistled a few bars of *Up in a balloon, boys.*

"You know very well what I'm talking about, Daisy — the biggest thing that happened today was meeting Standish Coverley." Now that Tamsin had managed to 'spit it out' at last, she gabbled the rest: "You're not just deciding to stay because of *him* I hope?"

Daisy just stared at the sky, fingered her locket, and said, "If only you knew!"

Part Two

Penzance from Newlyn
waiting for the fleet

The facts of life

14 Cicely Thorne noticed him the moment he entered the dining room at dinner that evening. By the time he was half-way across the floor, everyone was aware that someone of importance was among them. The headwaiter practically bowed him in, all the way from the entrance to the alcove half way down the long side of the salon, where his table was set. It had had no occupant all that week, and Cicely had noted that, too. Now she studied him through her lorgnettes, which, though they were furnished with plain glass, nonetheless helped her to see the (largely inferior) world around her in true perspective. Tonight she could wish they were opera glasses instead. "He *looks* distinguished, anyway," she murmured. "Find out who he is, dear."

"Go over to her and look for laundry marks, you mean?" her husband asked.

"He's a Mister Standish Coverley," Victor said.

His parents turned to him in surprise. "How d'you know?"

"He was on the seafront this afternoon, just before we went out for our promenade. I saw him from my window."

"I don't understand," Cicely said. "How do you come to know his name — you couldn't see that from your window?"

"He has a Rolls-Royce motor — a beautiful, gleaming white beast ..."

"He's not eating," Walter said. "He's not even ordering."

"He's waiting for someone," Charlotte put in.

"You all seem to know a great deal about him," Cicely snapped.

"There are three other places laid," Charlotte pointed out.

"We only know what we observe, Mama," Victor assured her. He did not tell her that he had also observed Tamsin Harte and Dobbs climbing into that same beautiful, gleaming white beast — along with an elegant but unknown gentleman. It had rankled with him ever since.

"Coverley?" Cicely mused. "Could it be *de* Coverley, I wonder? Wasn't there an admiral of that name ... sometime in history?"

"An admirable dancer, certainly," Victor offered. "Sir Roger de Coverley. He may have been an admiral, too, of course."

"Don't be facetious, dear," his mother said — though she had, in fact, been thinking of that same Sir Roger.

"Good God!" Walter exclaimed. "Just see *who* our man has been waiting for!"

Trying in vain to disguise their movements as no more than the result of random interest in all parts of the dining room, the whole family turned in unison toward the door, where the headwaiter, once again, was treating new arrivals like royalty. And the new arrivals were ...

"Miss Harte!" Cicely exploded in a barely contained whisper.

"And her mother, if I'm not very much mistaken," Charlotte added. "I wonder who the third party will be?"

They were certainly Coverley's expected guests for he had already risen from his place and was crossing the floor to welcome them.

Tamsin pretended to recognize the Thornes at that moment; she waggled her elegantly gloved fingers and called out, *"Bonsoir mes chèrs amis!"* just loud enough for them to catch. She murmured something to her mother, who then glanced toward the Thornes and dipped her head gravely.

Walter automatically returned the bow but his wife pinched his thigh under the table and hissed, "Fool!"

She then rounded on Victor and said, "If you know so much about him, why did you not make his acquaintance when you saw him this afternoon?"

"Well, Mama," he began, *"if* I were allowed out of doors all on my ownio, then perhaps ..."

But she had not finished. "Why isn't it Charlotte, your own poor sister, whom he is now helping into her seat instead of that ... that ...?" Polite words failed her. "You are the very epigraph of selfishness," she concluded.

"Epitome," Walter murmured.

"That's what I said — or meant to say. Does anybody know what Mister Standish Coverley *does?"*

"He owns this hôtel, madam," the waiter said. "Among other properties hereabouts."

She looked daggers at him. "Who asked you to butt in?"

His face frosted over. He bowed stiffly and withdrew, lips tight shut against other choice tidbits he might have divulged.

"Is there anyone you are *not* prepared to offend this evening, my dear?" Walter asked quietly.

"I'm not hungry," she snapped, rising to her feet. "I have a headache. I shall go to my bed. Where is Dobbs? I've hardly seen her all day."

She kept her husband and son standing.

"Could that be because it's her day off?" Victor suggested.

"She has no right to a day off — not when I'm feeling like this." She swept from the room. Walter tried to follow her but she sent him back, in full view of everyone, even before they reached the door.

"She's definitely getting worse," Victor murmured to his sister before their father returned. "Dobbs will hand in her notice if she continues like this — and who could blame her?"

"I wish *I* could hand in my notice," Charlotte replied. "And despite what dear Mama just said, I do *not* need you to go scouting for suitors on my behalf."

"D'you think I would?"

"I'm just warning you."

Coverley and his two guests had a waiter each; the other tables had one for each three or four diners. People notice such things — people like that, anyway.

"He's very handsome," Charlotte said as their father rejoined them; he had gone out of his way to talk to their waiter — to make it seem to the other diners as if that were why he had left the table in the first place.

"A bit of a dandy," Walter said. "Did you see his cummerbund as he passed?"

"Moiré silk," Victor replied. "It's quite fashionable. He was all in white this afternoon, with blue trim. That and his motor created quite a stir — mostly the motor, of course. You should get one, Pater. Perhaps we'd be granted one waiter each, then."

A commis-waiter removed their soup bowls and their waiter brought the main course — fat, juicy sea-trout served cold with salad and mayonnaise. The sommelier poured their wine, a crystal-clear Piesporter Kabinett, and left the half-full bottle in the ice bucket.

These rituals over, Walter leaned toward his son and daughter, lowered his voice, and said, "Perhaps one shouldn't be talking like this, but one is rather worried at your mother's present state of health."

Victor glanced at his sister. "D'you think it's our fault? For rebelling at the thought of yet another summer in a huntin'-shootin'-fishin' lodge in bonnie Scotland?"

He sighed. "Well ... Cornwall has turned into a bit of a disaster. It can't be denied."

"It's because she worries all the time about what people will think of us," Charlotte put in. "She's always looking over her shoulder. She can't ever relax."

"Listen," Walter said. "I think we all know the symptoms — without needing to dwell on them like this. It's remedies that seem scarce."

"Not Scotland again!" Victor said at once. "She wasn't particularly happy there, either, if you recall."

"Where *is* she happy?" Charlotte asked.

"Visiting the big shops," her brother said.

"She enjoys her charity afternoons, especially the MA."

The MA was the Mendicity Alliance, a national charity that gave its donors little printed cards that they could hand to street beggars instead of money — 'which they'd only spend on intoxicating liquor and horses.' On two afternoons a week the local MA committee, of which Cicely was the chairwoman, met at the parish-union workhouse and doled out cash in return for the cards — but only in deserving cases. That was the beauty of the scheme in its supporters' eyes. No one has time, when importuned for money in the street, to make exhaustive inquiries into the mendicant's circumstances, habits, attempts at self-help, and so forth; but Mrs Thorne and her committee had all the time in the world. Not until an applicant had bared every secret recess of his or her soul, in an interrogation that often reduced them to tears, would the MA part with a single brass farthing of its charity.

"Yes," Walter agreed despondently. "I suppose she's happiest of all there."

"Is there a local branch of the MA?" Charlotte wondered. "You know — she could go along, introduce herself, and ask if she might join their deliberations ... share information ... experiences ... that sort of thing."

"It could keep her occupied for an entire afternoon," Victor said cheerily.

"One must make inquiries," their father said.

Further discussion was curtailed because Cicely herself returned at that moment. Looking radiant, too. "I can't find that Dobbs anywhere," she said brightly. "But my headache has quite evaporated, so it's of no consequence." As husband and son jointly thrust her chair back beneath her, she added, "I think we have misjudged poor Miss Harte — or, rather, were led to misjudge her by those spiteful telegrams from ... well, never mind whom. But I shall have strong words with them when we return, I don't mind telling you."

"Ah! Here's our third party now," Charlotte cried. "What a very elegant young man!"

15 Standish Coverley smiled at Reginald Trotter and said, "I'm so sorry your mother was unable to join us this evening."

"Bishops take precedence," his friend replied. "Even retired ones. At least I managed to get away before the pudding. They didn't seem to mind."

"It's funny to think of bishops *retiring,*" Tamsin put in. "It's supposed to be more of a calling than a profession, I thought. After all, artists don't retire. Nor poets, nor writers."

"But that's the great thing about the Anglican Church," Coverley said. "It's a profession like any other. And it really *is* just for Sundays — even for their clergy. On the other six days of the week they can ride to hounds, ply the fly, dig up ancient tombs, prove that the Cornish are the Twelfth Lost Tribe of Israel ... whatever secular pursuit may take their fancy. Some of the finest agnostic minds in the country wear their collars back-to-front, you know."

While they laughed at his witty perversity, Trotter noticed that one particular party in the dining room was eyeing them with more than casual curiosity: a handsome young man of around twenty, his slightly younger sister, and their parents. They had finished their dinner some time earlier but were lingering over their coffees. Every sign of jollity from Coverley's table seemed of particular interest to them — in the way that the Little Match Girl was so poignantly interested in the feast she could never join; the mother, in particular, was quite pained at each round of laughter. At last he had to ask if anyone knew who they were.

"Guests," Coverley said in a tone that implied it was really all anyone needed to know — as one might say 'ants' or 'seagulls.'

"They are Mister Walter Thorne, his wife Cicely, their son Victor, and their daughter Charlotte," Harriet said. "They live at Peverill Hall, Clyst Saint Mary, just outside Exeter. They are seeking a good match for the daughter." She smiled at the two men. "I don't know if that is a warning to either of you? Or would it be an encouragement?"

"You are well informed, Mrs Harte," Coverley said with genuine admiration. "Do you happen to know the daughter's opinion in the matter?"

"Charlotte will make up her own mind," Tamsin said firmly.

"It's a habit daughters have these days," her mother added.

"We had noticed," Trotter said.

"Miss Dobbs is — or perhaps was — Charlotte's lady's maid," Tamsin added.

Coverley stared at her; his expression was suddenly cold. "Really?" he said. "I assumed she was a friend of yours."

"She's that, too," Tamsin assured him. "Now you're annoyed. You think I tricked you into entertaining a social inferior."

"Tamsin!" Her mother, being aware of their host's sudden frostiness, was shocked to hear her daughter spell out its cause. "You didn't!"

But Tamsin had been annoyed at Daisy's repeated hints that Coverley was more Stand-*off*-ish than Standish; she was determined to provoke him into some display of emotion, if only to see where it might lead. For, if Daisy were right, what had she to lose? "Of course I didn't," she replied, not taking her eyes off the man.

His nostrils flared; he would have contradicted her flatly if he had not been such a gentleman.

She continued: "I introduced her without comment — just as she was — and I left them to draw their own conclusions about her." She glanced from one to the other, challenging them to deny it. "You'd hardly believe it now," she added, "but at the time they seemed rather eager to have us accompany them on their jaunt."

"True, old bean," Trotter said.

Coverley looked at him, then at her; though still stony-faced, he seemed on the point of breaking into a smile, however unwilling. Harriet, who had been about to put her oar in, sensed the change in him and kept silent. But Tamsin decided to push him a little further.

"If Mister Coverley can show me that I've done him or his reputation or his business some harm," she said, "I will, of course, apologize."

These words, which she had spoken almost without thought — merely to challenge him to speak frankly — had the accidental effect of setting her to think in earnest.

What was it that annoyed him so much in learning he had entertained a servant as a social equal? Daisy had not *tried* to deceive him; she was a well-brought-up lass, enough, at least, to claim a place somewhere in the middle class — and she had not pretended to anything grander. He hadn't spotted it, that was all. Was he annoyed with himself for that?

Coverley suddenly broke into a broad smile. "You did the right thing, Miss Harte," he said, reaching across the table and giving her hand a squeeze. "You let us size Miss Dobbs up without prejudice and we found her acceptable. Therefore she *is* acceptable. A salutary lesson!" He turned to Trotter and added, "To us both."

"My dear chap!" Trotter replied. "I've knocked about the world so much I long ago lost all trace of social snobbery. Sartorial snobbery, mind you, is quite another thing. I'd cut any man who wore brown shoes in Town — or blue shoes anywhere."

Tamsin would have thrilled at that gentle squeeze of the hand — and she would have given her mother a tiny, superior smile of triumph, too — if she had not seen the glacial light that lingered on in Coverley's eyes. Daisy was right. The man *was* a cold fish. Beneath his urbane exterior, behind the polished wit, there lived a passionless man; perhaps even his obvious friendship for Trotter had something chill and manipulative at its core.

Her infatuation with him, kindled that afternoon and fanned to quite a fire by the time he issued his invitation to dine that evening, was suddenly extinguished — a six-hour wonder. Which was not to say she did not wish to continue their acquaintance; indeed, she even hoped it might ripen into friendship. But the special buzz of excitement that embellished her thoughts whenever they turned to him was silent now.

For no reason she could think of, she suddenly remembered David Peters — and, of course, the purchasing arrangements she hoped to make with him. If young Mr Peters could be furnished with a wardrobe as elegant as either of these two gentlemen's, he'd cut an even more dashing figure than both of them put together. Not that that was important — just rather amusing to contemplate, really. The important thing was that he enjoyed a universal reputation as one of the best fishermen in Newlyn, and he would certainly prove a reliable source of seafood of the finest quality. Yes, that was the important thing about him.

She fancied that Standish Coverley knew much more about the day-to-day running of his hôtel than he'd ever admit to. He'd probably pretend to be way above all that sort of thing but she had a shrewd idea that he'd know the thickness of each butter 'star' to a thirty-second of an inch and what the deposits on ginger-pop empties would return each week.

Daisy, who knew so much, might also know the secret of getting beneath that suave exterior to the man beneath.

The following morning she was awakened not by Bridget's gentle tap at her bedroom door but by the dainty clink of teacup and saucer on her bedside table. And the sounds of a suppressed giggling. And the rustle of a dress, as of someone sitting down.

She opened one bleary eye, for the day felt much too young for her to be woken up yet, and tried to focus. A moment later she opened both eyes and sat bolt upright in surprise. "Daisy!" she exclaimed.

"Guess what?" The maid giggled.

Tamsin groaned. "You gave in your notice?"

Daisy pouted. "You needn't sound quite so pleased."

"It's not that, my dear. It's just that you are rather jumping the starter's gun. I haven't even mentioned it to my mother yet."

"Then book me in as a guest for a couple of weeks. I don't mind. I got a nice little *bonne bouche* from the old dragon — which was a bit of a surprise, I don't mind telling you."

"Of course I shan't book you in as a guest. Not a paying guest, anyway. So I take it you did hand in your notice?"

"A bit of both, actually — me saying goodbye and her ladyship gently letting me go. I was just about to give her a right old piece of my mind when she asked me what I thought I'd do without a character from her. So I didn't see any harm in letting her know what's what."

"You told her you were coming to work here?"

"I told her it was one of several possibilities. I thought she'd catch fire but no! She suddenly turned all sweet and lovey-dovey. Gave me a good *bonne bouche,* as I said — and *this* for you." She produced an envelope and drew attention to its elaborate seal. "Be careful of that," she said. "Slip a hot knife under it to keep it intact."

"Why?" Tamsin took her seriously for a moment.

"Because — the way she goes on about it — it's probably worth a hundred guineas!"

Tamsin shattered the seal as they laughed. She read the note in silence, said, "Well, I'm jiggered!" and passed it over to Daisy, who read it aloud:

" 'Dear Miss Harte, We have absolutely fallen in love with Cornwall, and with dear little Penzance in particular. We only came down here to escape the smell of paint and the mess while the decorators carry out their annual business in our home. Now we hear that they will not be finished for at least a further week. But we are not *too* disappointed because, as I say, we are delighted with all we have experienced down here and long to discover more.

" 'One of my chief regrets is that we have not seen more of you this past week. From the moment of our amusing encounter on the beach last Monday, I confess I developed the warmest regard for you. And now it occurs to me to suggest that the remedy may be in our own hands. We must stay a further week and, though the Queen's Hôtel is all very congenial in its quaint, provincial way, we would much rather enjoy what I'm sure is the more genuine warmth of hospitality in your and your dear mother's establishment. (We had the pleasure of seeing her and you at Mr Coverley's table last night and took an immediate liking to her, as well.)

" 'Do please say you have three rooms vacant for us. I wait with eager ...' blah-blah." Daisy looked up. "What are you going to tell her?"

"Well done, Daisy!" Tamsin replied. "You managed to read it almost to the end without a single derogatory comment!"

"Have you got three rooms to spare?"

Tamsin nodded. "It so happens — if you don't mind sharing with Charlotte? I'll tell her it's the only way." She giggled. "We'll see how keen Madame Thorne is then!"

Daisy giggled, too, but she still pulled a face and said, "Definitely not the same bed."

"No, we've got two singles we can put in room eight."

Still the maid was unhappy. She pointed to Tamsin's fireplace. "We could put a single bed for me there," she suggested. "You won't be lighting a fire until November, I suppose."

Tamsin drained her cup of tea and kicked off the bedclothes. She shed her nightdress on the way to the washstand.

"Well?" Daisy asked.

"Don't rush me, dear," was the reply. "I'll still tell Madame that Charlotte will have to share. Just to see her response. Meanwhile, would you like to start singing for your supper — just a little?"

"How?" Daisy sprang to her feet and started symbolically rolling up her sleeves.

"No need for that," Tamsin assured her. "It's my turn to carry round the early-morning teas to all the bedrooms that ordered them. You could help by preparing the trays while I carry them round. That'll release Bridget to get on with blackleading the stove. And Catherine can whiten the front steps good and early. Oh, I do love Monday mornings, don't you!"

Daisy proved so efficient at preparing the trays that she quickly got ahead of Tamsin. So she decided to even things out by taking the double pot and two cups to room eleven herself. She knocked at the door and entered at the first sound, which was more like a groan than a 'come-in!'

The two young people, honeymooners by the look of them, were astonished to see her depositing the tray on their bedside table. But, quiet efficient servant that she was, she had gone before either of them could speak. Tamsin, coming toward her down the passage, said, "You didn't give him a pot?"

"Them," Daisy replied. "It was on your list — tea for Mister and Mrs Strong in room eleven."

"But they left yesterday. Tskoh! Bridget must have forgotten to put up the new list. It's supposed to be a Mister Wall in there — and his fiancée's in room twelve next door. Miss Roberts."

Daisy gasped and bit her lip, already more than half-guessing what had happened.

"I'll get it back," Tamsin said. And before Daisy could stop her she had opened the door to number eleven, stuck her head into the room, and said to the two frightened rabbits who sat up, clutching the sheets to them: "You didn't ask for early morning tea, did you?"

"N-n-no," the man stammered.

"I'll take it away then," she said, removing the tray again.

Back in the passageway she found Daisy cramming her fingers into her mouth in a vain attempt to stifle her laughter.

"What now?" Tamsin asked.

Daisy just beckoned her down the passage, back down the stairs, all the way to the kitchen before she explained. And even then she closed the door first. "Just think what it must look like to them," she said. "I carry the tray in. You go in immediately after and pluck it out again. They must think we arranged it between us to find out if they were two or one in the bed."

Tamsin joined her laughter, but not wholeheartedly.

"You still don't get it, do you," Daisy said. "Do you have any idea what those two have been up to all night?"

Tamsin shrugged awkwardly. "Practising at being married?"

"Yes — hallelujah! You know what it means, then?"

Tamsin gave what could have been either a nod or a shake of her head.

"You don't!" Daisy said. "Well, if you're going to make a go of this guest-house business, I reckon it's about time you did!"

She had just finished explaining when there was a peremptory *ding!* from the entrance hall. Tamsin went out to find Mr Wall and Miss Roberts standing there, fully dressed for the street and with their luggage already piled up by the front door. After that first glance, neither would look her in the eye. They had decided, he said, to move on ... yes, without breakfast ... would Miss Harte kindly produce their bill? No thank you, they would find their own taxi.

Watching them walk down the path to the front gate, Tamsin tried to imagine them doing It — what Daisy had just explained. It was difficult, of course, being so new to her. And yet it was as if some very secret part of her had always known it.

16 From the way Daisy had described It, Tamsin had no difficulty in understanding why Mr Wall and Miss Roberts had been so ashamed that they felt they had to leave before breakfast. How could people behave in such a horrid way? Especially people like those two, who had seemed so decent and well behaved when they arrived. And even more especially, how could a thoroughly genteel young lady like Miss Roberts, so well spoken and reserved, permit Mr Wall to ... words yielded to a shiver of distaste. And then the sheer hypocrisy of paying for two rooms and using only one of them — for, although Miss Roberts's bed had been turned down, it had not been slept in, nor even sat upon.

"She couldn't wait, see," Daisy said contemptuously when she pointed out this fact during their subsequent inspection of the two rooms. "Little minx! They're like polecats!"

Tamsin could see no particular similarity but, not wishing to appear the complete ignoramus yet again, she said nothing. Or, rather, she changed the subject — as she thought. "She *was* engaged to him, though," she said. "She showed me the ring last night. A solitaire diamond. A beauty."

Daisy was shivering by now, caught up in the toils of an emotion too powerful to contain. So much so that Tamsin began to fear for her.

"You mean he *bought* her," Daisy sneered. "Like this ... was it this sort of thing?"

Her trembling fingers struggled with the fasteners at her neck and then they pulled out the silver locket Tamsin had noticed yesterday at Land's End.

"This!" she repeated as she opened it to reveal ... not the lock of hair she had mentioned then but a silver ring, also with a solitaire diamond. More interesting still, however, was the photograph that accompanied it. And, even though Daisy snapped the locket shut before Tamsin could see much detail, what she had spied in that briefest of glimpses was vivid enough to burn an image in her mind's eye.

It was a photograph of a young man, or, rather, just his head, carefully cut out of a photo and pasted on a black background. It had then been embellished with devil's horns and long pointy ears, minutely painted in white gouache and indian ink. Tongues of red and yellow flames licked all around his neck, or where his neck would have been before the scissors had guillotined him.

This picture lingered in her mind, too shocking to be spoken of, while she examined the ring. "Yes," she said. "Pretty much that sort of thing."

Miss Roberts's diamond had, in fact, been almost twice the size of this.

"Yes!" Daisy was slightly calmer now, though still breathing hard. "They give you these things and then they think they own you. They think they can treat you like those ... those ..."

To Tamsin she seemed to be hearing her words slightly *after* she spoke them, so that she could not censor them in advance but had to wait until they were uttered. Now she put a hand to her mouth as if she wanted to stop their flow — in which case, she succeeded. "I'm sorry," she said in a small, dispirited voice. "They can't all be like that, of course. But there's more of them than you'd think out there — just waiting to pounce on us. So just you be warned, eh!"

She forced a smile and, stretching out her hand for her ring, said, "This will never break the back of the day, will it!" She held it up and eyed it sourly before popping it back inside the locket. "I was going to ram it down his throat and hope it'd choke him, but then I thought I could keep it as a warning — and sell it if ever I got in dire straits. Sell *it* rather than *me!*" She gave an awkward sort of laugh.

Tamsin laughed, too, though she did not really know why. "That young man ..." she tried.

"Don't!" Daisy turned the incriminating bedclothes up again, ready to be turned down for the next guest that evening.

After breakfast Tamsin sent Bridget round to the Queen's with a note to say that the Thornes would be welcome on the usual terms, which they would find printed on the back. There was no mention of Charlotte's having to share with Daisy. That had been a pleasant fantasy but, really, they did not want to risk an angry refusal. As Tamsin said to her mother, they were too curious to see what Mrs Thorne was up to.

"Up to?" Harriet echoed in distaste. "Never end a sentence with a single preposition, dear — let alone two. You could have said '... to see what Mrs Thorne may have it in her mind to do.' That would have been quite acceptable."

Daisy winked at Tamsin, unseen by the mother. Later, as they set out to do the day's marketing, she said, "You know just how to deflect your mother off the big decisions and onto the little ones, don't you. I wonder if she realizes it's you that runs this place, really."

Tamsin, reared in a tradition where certain things happened but were never talked about, felt awkward at this exposure — and even more awkward at the praise. She did not know what to say. In fact, she began to wonder if she'd been altogether wise in her haste to take Daisy in. Not that she wouldn't be useful in so many ways, to say nothing of being good fun in herself; it was just that their basic approach to life and its myriad daily problems was utterly different.

She had never consciously thought of such things before, but the maid was forcing her into it.

Just then they stopped at the greengrocer's in Alverton Street.

Daisy, sensing her reluctance, asked if she didn't agree.

"It's not whether or not I agree," she answered. "It's just that I was brought up to know that certain things are not always the way everyone pretends they were — but it isn't something to be spoken of."

"Like?"

"Like ... not all the grief you see at a funeral is genuine. Not all mayors, aldermen, and town councillors are selflessly dedicated, body and soul, to serving the populace. Not all marriages are made in heaven ..."

"Ha!"

No further examples were necessary; Tamsin had hit the perfect one. "But it just makes life easier all around if everyone agrees to pretend that the exceptions are few. And trivial. Cauliflower or red cabbage? Oh look — broad beans! I love them, don't you?"

"Why does it make life easier?" Daisy asked.

"We could have cauliflower and beans, and we can see if Oliver's has some neat's tongue." She lowered her voice and added, "It's a pity there's no fishing on Sundays. I'd love some whiting — or a nice piece of fresh cod."

"Why?" Daisy insisted, still sticking to her line.

But Tamsin appeared lost for a moment in her thoughts. And they had nothing to do with vegetables, either, for Mr Trevaskis, the greengrocer, stood patiently waiting for her to speak — which, eventually, she did.

They paid and set the bag aside to collect on their return. Daisy did not feel she could press her question yet again. They strolled on in easy silence, past Sargeant's, the fishmonger, where Tamsin stooped to gaze into the almost empty window.

Suddenly her entire demeanour changed — from relaxed to alert, from bent to bolt upright. "Talk of the devil!" she said, turning to Daisy and grinning from ear to ear.

"What?" She was bewildered, even slightly alarmed — understandably, when one considered the picture she carried next to her heart. "Which devil?"

"Look!" Tamsin tilted her head toward the dark interior of the shop.

But David Peters was already leaving. "Miss Harte," he said as he stepped outside.

"Mister Peters!" She held out her hand, which he shook with some slight surprise. "Not fishing today?"

He licked a finger and held it up into the dead calm air. "No," he agreed. "Too stormy."

"Silly of me — of course not."

"We had a smallish catch on Saturday, which missed the London train when the wind dropped. We have it on ice, of course, but I'm trying to see if we can get a better price locally."

"I see. That was a wonderful lobster, by the way. I meant to come and thank you but I gather you were at sea most of last week?" She hoped it was true.

He neither confirmed nor denied it. She glanced at Daisy, who nodded. "Allow me to present you to a friend of mine," she went on. "Miss Daisy Dobbs. Mister David Peters." They shook hands, too, while Tamsin added, "Miss Dobbs is going to be my right-hand man at the guest house."

In fact, the pair shook hands for rather longer than was usual. And their eyes lingered in each other's for quite a while, too — as if each were waiting for the other to speak.

It irked Tamsin but she passed no comment. "If you're going to deliver fish here," she said in a slightly more snappish tone than she intended, "you could drop some off on us in passing?"

"Whiting or a nice piece of fresh cod," Daisy added, letting his hand go at last.

"I have both," he replied. "You can choose when you see them. Are you ladies going toward Causeway Head? That's my next port of call. We could walk together?"

They waited for a heavy dray from Rosewarne's brewery to pass, then skipped between it and a motor delivery van.

"You see?" David pointed to the name along its side. "Warring's, the furniture shop, they've sold the old horse and cart and gone in for a motor. That's what we're doing — except we'll keep the sails, too, of course."

Tamsin paused briefly at the foot of Clarence Street to gaze at the Western Hôtel, which was only a third the size of the Queen's; she looked it up and down, with her head on one side, much as any other woman might run a critical eye over a new hat. Then she trotted to catch up with the other two.

"A fishing boat with a motor?" she asked as she pushed herself between them. "Won't it frighten off the fishes?"

"Seemingly not," he answered. "We can set the trawl or the line a good way astern."

"You should get a Rolls-Royce engine," Daisy said. "They're quieter than a whisper."

"Yes, I heard all about your outing yesterday," he said. His tone hinted at scandal.

Tamsin was cross at her for mentioning it anyway. And how dare he take that censorious attitude with her? What right had he to question her choice of companions? Or anything else, come to that?

Also she was worried, especially in the light of Daisy's revelations to her earlier that morning. She could not now believe that she had disported herself naked in front of Mr Coverley and Mr Trotter, two such gentlemen; never mind that they had not demurred. And how could Daisy have led her into doing such a thing — especially knowing all those horrid things about men and women and ... things? Could someone have spied on them? The lighthouse men ... a powerful telescope ... some semaphore to a passing coaster ... was it all over Newlyn by now? She cringed inwardly just to think of it, even though she had no choice now but to brave it out and pretend it never happened — just in case her fears were groundless.

As they turned into Causeway Head, she said, "Our guests sometimes ask us if we can arrange a fishing trip, Mister Peters. If you manage to outfit your boat with an engine, well, it would make such outings much safer and more reliable. In terms of getting back on time, I mean. Would you consider it, I wonder? And what sort of fee would be reasonable?"

"It's worth thinking about," he replied. "The *Saucy Sal* — trips to Saint Michael's Mount and back. First let me see what sort of motor we can get up at Smart's, the old blacksmith's. He was before your time, I suppose. But his son, George, has turned it into a motor shop. I'll get one as quiet and smooth as possible, then maybe you'll come out for a trip round the bay? Just to see what it's worth."

He was looking at Tamsin as he spoke but it was Daisy who answered: "Oh! Wouldn't that be fun!" A moment later she caught Tamsin's eye and added, hastily, "For *you,* I mean."

Tamsin was only partly mollified but at least it prevented an explosion. "Yes," she said to David. "That would be a good idea. Why not?"

"I'll bid 'ee good day, then." He touched his cap and left them, hastening away up the street.

Daisy fanned her face. "A narrow squeak!" she exclaimed. "Sorry, love — I didn't realize it was like that between you two."

Tamsin bristled. "Like what?"

"Like *that!*" She pounded her fist against her breast, hinting at a heart beating double.

"Don't be absurd!" Tamsin turned about and set off angrily for home, forgetting that Daisy had things to buy at the chemist's — toothbrush, dentifrice, soap ... that sort of thing.

"Come on!" Daisy ran after her and stood barring her way, staring into her face, trying to make her smile. "What did you mean back there when you said, 'Talk of the devil' — back there at that other shop?"

Tamsin shrugged impatiently. "What does anyone mean when they say that? I mean we'd just been talking about Mister Peters, hadn't we."

"But that's just the point — we hadn't. *You* had, I'm sure — up there." She touched Tamsin's forehead before she could draw back. "You said you wouldn't mind a bit of whiting or cod and then *pffft!* You vanished inside there." She grinned. "And now we know why."

Tamsin sighed and gazed over the rooftops opposite. "Go and get whatever you need," she said patiently. "I'll wait here."

Daisy, thinking it would be a good chance to let her simmer down, complied. But when she came back, Tamsin said, "You're a fine one to talk, anyway."

"I am?"

"Yes. All that ... that ... what's the opposite of misogyny? Where women hate men. Misandry? All that talk of yours, anyway, about how hateful men are — and then you go all dewy-eyed with the very first man I present to you, and ..."

"Is that what it looked like?" Daisy broke out laughing.

"You know very well. You could hardly bring yourself to let go of his hand."

"Dear God!" Daisy looked heavenward. "Strike me dead if I lie but I was waiting for him to ..."

"I don't wish to hear it." Tamsin turned homeward again and set off at a fair pace.

Daisy ran to catch up. Her words were oddly punctuated by her having to trot and skip at Tamsin's side. "I was waiting for him to *recognize* me, you ninny! I'm sure he did, too. I know I recognized him at once."

Yet again Tamsin stopped dead. "Recognized him? What d'you mean?" she snapped.

"Yes!" Daisy replied. "See what you miss when you jump to all the wrong conclusions, stop your ears against all the right ones, and flounce away like that!"

"I'm sorry!" She did not sound in the least contrite. "But what d'you mean — you *recognized* each other?"

"Just that. I had no idea you knew the man, or I'd have told you long before this. Honestly."

"So how d'you come to know him?" Tamsin was calmer now — and was beginning to feel ever so slightly ashamed of her earlier behaviour.

"Because ... what day did I bring you that note?"

"Last Tuesday."

"Well, the next morning, Wednesday, Miss Charlotte and Mister Victor, got me to accompany them on a stroll to Newlyn."

"No! What for? D'you mean to meet ..." She pointed vaguely in the direction David had taken. "But they didn't know him."

"Exactly! They had to go about the harbour side asking who the fisherman was who set his lobsterpots near the Wherry Rocks. No one would tell them, of course, because they're all tight as limpets down here. But finally they tried in the post office, where the woman said it could possibly be your friend Mister Peters. And ..."

"He's not particularly *my* friend."

"I believe you. Thousands wouldn't." Daisy winked. "Anyway, they caught up with him just as he was about to put to sea."

"And what did they talk about?"

"I don't know. Miss Charlotte took me away out of earshot. It was only Mister Victor who spoke with him. It could have been about arranging a fishing trip one day this week. Or — reading between the lines — maybe it was about nothing in particular. Just some errand that Victor made up so's he could ... how can I put it? Size up his ... *rival?*"

She grinned at Tamsin, who just tossed her head and said, "That's just ridiculous!"

"Yes — ridiculous. I quite agree."

"You can stop that at once, Daisy."

"Stop what? Didn't I say I agree with you?"

"I quite admit I'd like to know Mister Peters better. Even a great deal better — but only as a friend. He's one of the most honest, straightforward men you could ever ..."

"Certainly. I mean, look how he came straight out with it that we met each other last Tuesday!"

"That was different. He was waiting for you to mention it. And when you said nothing, he decided you had your own reasons for not speaking out, so he didn't go against your wishes. He's a natural gentleman, that's all." After a pause she added, "I didn't have a brother but if I had, I'd have wished him to be like David Peters. There! That puts it in a nutshell. I'd like him as a sort of proxy brother. And you can just wipe that superior smile off your lips because I know what I feel like and you don't. There! Oh, bother! Now you've made me go and forget the cauliflower and beans. We'll have to go back."

17 When the two young women returned with their various messages they found Harriet beside herself with excitement. "My dear!" she exclaimed, whisking Tamsin off to their private drawing room. "You'll never guess what! You'll remember Mrs Lock — Miriam Lock?"

"Denzil's mother?"

"Yes. Well, it seems that her husband, poor old Harold, was in Germany last month ..."

"The man we were never quite sure existed?"

"Well, that was your father's attempt at humour. Of course he existed. He was the life and soul of the golf club before ... that unfortunate incident. Anyway, never mind all that. The point is that Harold Lock was in some spa in Germany last month — Baden-Baden, I think — and he became friends with the Count and Countess de Ath. It seems that the count is dying — it's just a matter of time — and the Countess is quite ... 'reconciled' isn't quite the word ..."

"Resigned?"

"Of course — resigned. Oh dear me, I'm in such a fluster over this news!"

"You mean you *know* them both?"

"No, dear." Her face screwed up as if in pain. "Just don't interrupt all the time. It's bad enough that we have to keep it all under our hats. We mustn't breathe word of it to a soul — did I say that?"

"No, you didn't, as it happens. But anyway, I'm sorry. Let's go back to where you said she was quite *reconciled* to his death — and pretend I didn't butt in."

"Oh, you are such a vexing creature! You know that's not what I mean. Anyway, the long and short of it is that she will be coming here — to Penzance — to stay with *us* for an indefinite period. There now!"

After a pause, to make it clear she was not interrupting, Tamsin said, "I hesitate to ask this but ... you are speaking of the Countess? Not Miriam Lock?"

"Of course I mean the Countess. Isn't that what I said?"

"And why has she chosen to come to *us* — out of all the thousands of hôtels and boarding houses in England? D'you mean you *do* know them both?"

"Miriam must have written to Harold, or perhaps she was visiting him in Baden-Baden. Anyway, she must also have told him all about our misfortune. And Harold, out of the goodness of his heart, I suppose, is doing us this enormous favour. He must have praised us to the heavens ..."

"He must indeed! What on earth is she going to think when she actually ..."

"She'll come to us when the Count dies — which could be at any time or he could drag it ... I mean he could linger on until the autumn. The Countess has been abroad for some years and has completely lost touch with her friends in London, or so Harold says. And the strain of renewing old friendships in the midst of her bereavement ... well, you can just imagine it, I'm sure. I know I can. Anyway, there it is — sometime soon, or maybe not so soon, we shall number a *countess* among our guests! It's exactly the sort of good fortune we've been praying for. Where one ventures, others will surely follow! We shall give her special terms, of course, and ..."

"We most certainly will not!"

Mother and daughter attempted to stare each other out. Eventually the daughter said: "Ask Mister Coverley if he gives every unknown Lord and Lady Nonesuch 'special terms'! You'll get a very dusty answer, I'm sure. Anyway, if she's at Baden-Baden for an indefinite period, she's not short of shekels."

Harriet's nose curled in disgust at the phrase but Tamsin went on: "The cheapest place there costs over two guineas a day." She had no idea whether or not it was true, which is why she spoke the words with such conviction. "But if she and the count are staying at a first-class hôtel and taking the waters and all the other cures — to say nothing of concerts, the opera, *bals masques,* and all the other entertainments — not forgetting carriages and the casino — why, it could easily top twenty-five guineas a day! Do you think a reduction in our terms from twenty-one shillings to seventeen and sixpence is going to mean the slightest thing to a woman like that?"

"Not a woman, dear. A lady. A countess!"

But Tamsin, caught up in her own argument, was now having further thoughts. "Exactly," she said.

"What does that mean?" Harriet prepared to become exasperated all over again, even though she had been shaken by the force of her daughter's words.

"It means we should be rather careful about this whole idea. Before we hang out the bunting, let's make a few inquiries, eh?"

"I don't understand ..."

"Ask yourself — why is a woman, a *countess,* who is used to spending at the rate of twenty guineas a day ... why is she so keen to hide away here the moment her husband dies?"

"Hiding, dear? It's hardly that."

"Isn't it? She doesn't want us to tell a soul, and yet she's not hiding? What do you call it? Anyway, why *can't* she look up old friends in London? What better time could she possibly have than immediately after a bereavement? Or does she owe them money, perhaps? And does she owe money in Baden-Baden, too? Is that the sudden attraction Penzance seems to offer — the difficulties her creditors will have if they try to pursue her over here?"

Harriet was on the verge of tears by now. Her splendid bit of news, the answer to her nightly prayers, was shattered. Tamsin slipped her arms about her and gave her a reassuring hug. "Darling Mama!" she murmured. "I'm not saying it isn't marvellous. But let's remember *why* 'poor old Harold' Lock was 'the life and soul of the golf club' — and why he was found half-dead on one of the greens that afternoon — which is also why he's been an invalid ever since. The leopard can't change his spots, they say — and nor can the born practical joker. We must ask Mister Coverley how one can find out about people like this Count and Countess de Ath. Especially her. Could you ask Mrs Lock if she knows anything more about her background?"

She took out her notebook and scribbled '*Almanac de Gotha* — de Ath family? — try the library.'

"By the way, Mama," she added, making herself all bright and cheerful, "you know the Trotters? It seeems they're aptly named. They're real globe-trotters. Or Europe-trotters, anyway. They live by moving constantly between hôtels and guest houses — all around England in the summer and Italy and southern France in the winter."

"How nice for them." Harriet tried to sound enthusiastic.

"Yes, well, that's not really the point. The thing is, we could hardly hope to meet a more experienced pair when it comes to judging our humble little establishment — its good points and its shortcomings. Why not let's ask them to give us their candid opinion, eh? We'd be letting a golden opportunity slip by if we didn't do it sometime before they leave ..."

"Oh — talking of their leaving — I meant to tell you about that," Harriet put in. "This other news sent it right out of my mind. Anyway, it's not definite yet, but Mrs Trotter came to me this morning, just after you and Dobbs went out ..."

"Miss Dobbs, please."

Her mother pulled a face. "Very well. Just after you went out, Mrs Trotter told me she might be going on a retreat. She's Anglican — very High Church. She was talking to the bishop about it last night. It lasts a month, apparently — on some holy island up in Scotland."

"Iona?"

"She didn't say. Anyway, if she goes, she'd like her son to stay on here. I said that would be in order. It looked all right according to the bookings book. And he won't be any trouble. He sems to spend all his time playing billiards at the Queen's."

18 When David Peters had chosen the engine for *Merlin,* their fishing boat, he brought his father back to George Smart's garage for a second opinion. It was a Thorneycroft, eight-cylinder, side-valve, marine engine with electrical ignition. Electrical ignition was almost unheard of in English motor cars at that time, not simply because it was an American gadget but mainly because, as motor manufacturers told the American company that tried to sell them, 'Our car owners are gentlemen. They employ drivers to swing the handle for them.' The engine for the *Merlin* also had seawater cooling and was capable of developing fifty horsepower. "Which works out at ten bob per horse." George Smart said in his finest salesman's style. "If you mind to look at 'n that way."

These facts meant nothing to the Captain. "What good is a hundred hosses when you'm out o' sight o' land?" he asked facetiously. "If you mind to look at 'n *that* way?"

Smart came back at once. "When they'm all bottled up inside that lump o' cast iron, boss, they could push the *Merlin,* full-laden, back home at six to eight knots."

"And in a contrairy gale?" the Captain asked.

"They'd at least keep her head-up to the wind and waves and stop her swamping."

The Captain saw the weight of that argument, at least. He said they'd think it over, which his son took as a sign that he was wavering. His strongest objection, however, he reserved for their journey home in the pony and trap: "How the hell are we goin' to pay for 'n, then?"

"By a combination of this and that," David suggested.

"Oh yes?" His father eyed him coldly.

"I reckon young Smart'd let us have 'n for half down and five pound a month ..."

"That's still twenty-five down. And who's going to fit 'n?"

"I'll fit 'n, easy. It's no more than a bit of carpentry. The worst is to get the stuffing gland lined up true for the prop shaft. Harry would help us out with that."

"And the money?"

"I got fifteen now, to spare. And I needn't tell you where I could get the other ten. I could get double my fifteen in one moonless night."

"Our fifteen," the Captain said while he considered the suggestion. "New moon is the tenth — this Wednesday, so there's no moon tomorrow night, Tuesday. We could never make the arrangements in time."

"Oenone could send a telegram?"

The old man shook his head. "The Excise are now wise to that, so she says. They do get a copy of every cable to France from every port along the south coast. Betterfit you send a letter. The next moonless night'll be the eighth of August. That's a Thursday. You'll have to wait till then, boy."

"And miss half the summer season? Listen — if we had an engine, we could charge visitors four-and-six a go for a day's fishing along of us — and we could take half a dozen each time. Twenty-seven shilling a trip — come rain, come shine — come empty nets, come full! We shouldn't even notice five pound a month to George Smart."

"Thursday, August the eighth," the Captain repeated firmly. "Anything else is too risky."

But David did not give up that easily.

The very best brandy — superior old pale — retailed in England at around £8 a dozen. The same twelve bottles could be got in Brittany for £2 or less. The remaining £6 was, in the view of many a respectable Englishman (and just about *every* respectable Cornishman), a thoroughly iniquitous tax imposed by a grasping government through the Commissioners of Customs & Excise. Wherever there is an artificially raised price (and a tax is no more than that) there is room for enterprising men to make profits — £6 of room in the case of a case of superior old pale. Or 10s bottle. Or 1s 8d to the Brittany fisherman who dropped them off on a regular fishing trip in English waters, 5s to his Cornish counterpart, who 'tidied up' after him and ran the risk with the Excise, and 3s 4d to the purchaser, who had the added satisfaction of spitting in the eye of a greedy and oppressive government. Small wonder, then, that the verb 'to smuggle' did not carry the opprobrium among the Cornish populace that governments could have wished for

David had a plan. There was a particular Breton fisherman, Jean-Baptiste Clouet, who would supply the brandy. For £50 he'd bring over a cask, which could be bottled up and sold for £500. But first get your £50! For David's mere £15, however, he'd supply five dozen bottles of OSP; they had often cooperated along those lines in the past. He, David, would sell them for £30, thus doubling his outlay. Hence many jokes around the Newlyn taverns about 'double brandies' … 'doubling up with laughter — or over in pain' — depending on how astute the Excisemen had been.

And there was David's problem: to do it all under the noses of the Excise. If they were going to poke those same noses into every telegram to northern France from every south-coast fishing port, he would have to turn that fact to his advantage rather than theirs.

When he handed in his telegram to Cousin Oenone, she looked at him as if he were mad. The message wasn't even in code; it read, simply, *'60 croissants pour Peters.'*

Croissants is French for 'moonfish,' which, in turn, is a euphemism common among fishermen for the sort of 'fish' one might catch in the wake of a Frenchman on a moonless night.

"I do know what I'm doing," David assured her. "Just don't tell the old feller."

She agreed to hold her tongue but whether she'd stand by her word, he wasn't sure; if she just kept it until Thursday, all would be well.

He'd given Clouet little enough time to organize his end of the operation, so he had no way of knowing whether it could go ahead. He played his part, though, by placing fifteen sovereigns, securely sewn into a tube of sailcloth and tied inside one of his lobsterpots. But the night of the ninth was so perfectly moonless — and clouded over — that a hundred anxious scans of the inshore waters known as Gwavas Lake, chiefly between the Wherry and the Gear rocks, aided by a powerful telescope, had failed to reveal the smallest chink of light that might have been the Frenchman.

So far, so good. If he, knowing the time and place of the 'crime,' had failed to spot Clouet, the Excise couldn't possibly have managed it, either.

The following morning, Wednesday, he took a fine female cod over to the Morrab Guest House. When Tamsin saw his trap braked outside the tradesman's entrance she ran downstairs to see him. "What progress on fitting out your boat with an engine?" she asked breathlessly, smiling far more broadly than the question itself warranted.

"How important is it to you?" he asked in return.

"Well ..." The question startled her. "It would be ... how can I put it? Useful? A feather in our cap if we could offer fishing trips — genuine fishing trips with a genuine Cornish fisherman — to our guests. No one else can, as far as I know. Not even the mighty Queen's. Why?"

"So ... fitting the engine to *Merlin* sooner rather than later would help?"

"It would be a great help, Mister Peters. Why are you asking all these questions?"

"Because you could greatly assist me in bringing that day forward, Miss Harte."

"We don't have any money to spare," she told him at once.

He laughed. "May I invite you to accompany me on the round of my lobsterpots this afternoon?" he said.

She shook her head. "Don't change the subject. Let's deal with this other matter first. How may I help you bring the day forward — if not with money?"

"By accepting my invitation."

Now she was bewildered. "That's all?"

"You'll understand soon enough," he promised her. "It'll be low tide at two. I'll pick you up off the beach inside the Wherry Rocks then."

After he had gone, Daisy kept a straight enough face while she said, "I was afraid you'd break your neck running pell-mell like that to see him."

Tamsin did not deign to reply.

When David arrived back at Newlyn, he heard an ancient cry that would normally have set him dancing all the way way around the harbour wall: 'Hevva! Hevva!' It was immediately taken up by all who heard it — 'Hevva! Hevva!' until the whole town rang with the excitement of it. The word itself is a latter-day corruption of the old Cornish word *hesva,* a school of fish.

The crying of it up and down the streets meant that anything up to a million fish had just taken up lodgings somewhere in Gwavas Lake, just outside the harbour piers.

"What is it?" he asked one of the criers. "Pilchard or mullet?"

If the answer were 'pilchards,' he was safe enough. Pilchards are not usually fished before August, when they are at their fattest and oiliest. They would not be fished today, in any case, and that would leave his plans intact. But mullet were best taken as and when they arrived, for they had a habit of moving on as swiftly as they had arrived. A shoal of mullet now would ruin everything, for every able-bodied man, woman, and child in town would be expected to drop his own work, no matter what, until the last individual fish was dispatched or banked — a process that could take days.

"Mullet," came the happy reply.

Happy for everyone but David.

He was already wondering how he'd tell his father he had squandered the fifteen pounds with absolutely nothing to show for it. His only hope was that the Frenchman had not had time enough to bring the bottles over. He sauntered up to the harbour wall, the only glum man in town, to inspect the cause of his impending ruin.

To prevent himself from giving way entirely to his despair, he began to run through the mullet-catching operation in his mind, looking for any small opportunities it might still offer him.

The technique was the same for both mullet and pilchard. George Croom, the huer, or director of operations, would soon be standing silhouetted on the cliff above the town. In Captain Benny's young days, Croom's father had held a branch of furze in each hand; nowadays his son preferred a pair of clubs, with which he'd be semaphoring directions to the fishermen below. He, of course, had an eagle's-eye view of the entire shoal, which, to him, would seem like a single giant creature, the size of twenty whales, in the bay at his feet. It would be shimmering silver if mullet, or blood-red if pilchard.

Following his directions the seine boatmen — six rowers, a helm, and a payer — would gently make their way out, with muffled oars, out into the bay, until they drew near one end of the shoal. Behind them they'd trail a line, all the way back to the shore. It was, of course, attached to the beginning of the net.

David stood on tiptoe and saw they were already manhandling the seine boat down the slipway toward the water. With every minute that passed, his chances of retrieving his brandy unobserved — and unarrested — dwindled away.

When the seine boat finally reached the edge of the shoal, Croom would drop his arms and Johnny Harvey, the payer, would begin to 'shoot' or pay out the seine itself — a giant net curtain, over half a mile long, with floats at its top end and lead sinkers at its bottom. It was four fathoms deep, which was more than enough to brush the shallow sandy bottom in that part of the bay between the South Pier and Carn Gwavas, some three-quarters of a mile south of the harbour. Any shoal in that part of Gwavas Lake was as good as dead once the hevva cry went up.

Within five minutes, if all conditions were right — and certainly within fifteen — they'd shoot the entire seine net in a semicircle on the seaward side of the shoal, completing the operation by coming ashore with a line attached to its other end. There they'd join the dozens-strong shore party and begin the long, careful process of winding the capstans that hauled in the seine. Meanwhile the follower boat would be stretching the much shorter 'stop net' across the open ends of the seine, which by now would have the form of a narrowing U with its open end pointing toward the beach. Until the mouth was closed, they'd beat the water with their oars so as to frighten the fish into the back of the seine and prevent their escape — though the juvenile fry would, of course, wriggle through the mesh to live, breed, and fatten for another day.

Ideally, if the shoal proved quiet and not too skittish, they'd try to shoot the seine at low water and bring it ashore on the rising tide — in short, working with the flow rather than against the ebb. When they had it close to land, in water deep enough to keep the fish alive and trapped but shallow enough to allow the men to extract them bit by bit, the whole of Newlyn — himself included — would have but one objective: to get as much ashore in as marketable a condition as possible.

By now he had run the whole process through his mind and had still found no point that he could exploit for his own purposes. What he had been hoping — before this heller of a mullet shoal swam into the bay — was that the Excisemen, having read his telegram to Clouet, would conclude that he'd be out there tonight, lifting the brandy under cover of a darkness that would still be moonless until just before dawn. They'd never imagine he'd be rash enough to recover them and bring them ashore by daylight. In fact, that had been his plan, to retrieve the contraband while pretending to be taking a high-quarter lady on a little rowing trip about the bay. So their guard would have been down — and they might even have snatched a few hours' sleep so as to be sure of remaining alert all night. They had often done so in the past, and that was another thing he had been gambling on, too.

Suddenly he saw a little gleam of hope. In concentrating on the seine-netting side of the day's business, he'd overlooked what would be happening among those not immediately employed in shooting the net. Of course! Every man with lobsterpots in Gwavas Lake would be out there this afternoon, between low and three-fourths tide, lifting their pots while the seine-boat and its follower were encircling the shoal. And they wouldn't be resetting them, either, because the next few days would all be given over to packing, or salting and banking the mullet catch. So a couple of hundred lobsterpots would all be converging on Newlyn harbour at roughly the same time.

Or at *exactly* the same time, if he could orchestrate it properly. There were distinct possibilities here.

19 She was a fashion plate, standing there at the water's edge, waiting for him to round the Wherry Rocks and cross the low-tide pool to collect her. She wore a pale-blue dress in glazed cotton, discharge-printed with tiny flowers in yellow and red arrayed in bayadere stripes of an even paler blue. The same fabric covered her parasol and provided the ribbon that trimmed her straw hat. Her gloves were of white cotton lace, tinted with liberal use of the blue bag. On any normal lobster outing, such beautiful attire would have been ruined in the first five minutes; but, if all went according to plan, today would be very far from normal. He'd only be worrying about a couple of

pots — and neither of them would contain lobsters, unless Miss Harte wanted some for her table; nor would any pots be brought into the boat.

The keel grounded when he was still three or four paces from the edge. When he leaped into the shallow water, she floated again and he was able to get her a few feet closer — though still too far for Tamsin to jump.

He could have lifted the boat and dragged its prow right ashore. Instead he said, "I shall have to lift you," almost as if he were apologizing. He stooped to slip one outstretched arm behind her knees and to reach the other across her shoulder-blades. Before she could say a word, he had raised her as high as his chest. He made it seem no more strenuous than lifting an ostrich-feather boa.

She looked up at his face, considering it once again as a piece of artistic modelling. It was a good face, with strong lines and a firm contour. His straight, dark hair was rather long by current fashion, but it suited him well, framing his features and giving him the mein of a Celtic knight. Her romantic, artistic fancy could see such a man in his rightful place at King Arthur's Round Table.

He held her slightly away from him so that he could place his feet carefully among the rocks over the few paces between the shore and his boat. When he came to a halt, though, he let his arms relax a little, bringing the side of her chest tight against the front of his. He held her so awhile. It was a pleasant feeling and it made her realize how long it had been since anyone had given her even a mildly affectionate hug.

For a moment he stood there, gazing down into her face; his eyes had never seemed so intensely blue as now, catching as they did the light of the summer sky. For an awful part of that moment she imagined he was going to take the liberty of stealing a kiss. Her lips even prepared to receive it. And, when he set her upright, as light as thistledown, in the boat, she felt a surge of disappointment that he hadn't. But it was immediately followed by a more powerful wave of relief. That was *not* the sort of thing she wanted with David Peters. It was only some silly, schoolgirlish reflex, nurtured by Daisy's infantile teasing, that put such contrary ideas into her head at all.

"Take me to the horizon!" she said, stretching an imperious arm southward.

"You tell me how far it is and I'll take you there," he replied, putting a foot inboard, over the keel, and springing himself in. The boat grounded under their combined weight and he had to punt off with an oar.

"Oh!" She plucked a figure out of the air. "Twenty miles?"

He laughed. "How far is Saint Michael's Mount, then?" He took his seat and fitted the oars back in the rowlocks.

She turned her gaze eastward and exclaimed, "Goodness! It has sunk!"

"You're the one who has sunk, Miss Harte. Up there on the promenade you'd be what — fifteen ... twenty feet above sea level, counting in your own height? And then the horizon would be twice as far away — five or six miles. Down here it's only three, if that."

"You mean ..." She had a little difficulty with the idea. "The higher you go ... yes, I suppose that's logical. It just never struck me before."

"On Penlee headland, two hundred feet, you could see sixteen miles — across the bay to the Lizard. But you go up in a balloon — five or six thousand feet — and you could see a hundred miles or more — clear to Exeter!"

"My!" Her eyes gleamed at the very thought. "I'm going to do that one day. I'm going to do *everything* one day!"

"Beginning today?"

"Oh yes — today. Speaking of today, can you tell me now — how does my being here hasten the fitting of your engine?"

"Look beyond the rocks," he said. "What d'you see?"

They were moving swiftly over a calm sea by now, and just about to clear the eastern end of the Wherry group.

"Scores of other people tending their lobsterpots. How do you all know which ones are yours?"

"Look closer, just the far side of this nearest rock. What d'you see there?"

"Something floating — a bit of cork?"

"You'll notice something else when we get alongside."

"A coloured disk," she said as they closed the distance. "Red and white."

"That's mine, then. And there's nothing much wrong with your eyesight." He shipped oars and leaned out to grab the cork float as they passed.

He dropped it in the orlop and began hauling in the line attached to it.

"Clever," she said. "You all have different colours, I suppose."

"Here's the really clever bit," he told her as the pot loomed toward the surface. "See?"

"A lobster! Poor thing — I feel so sorry for them." Her mouth watered nonetheless and she wondered if she'd have to pay for it this time.

"Never mind him," he said. "What else?" He lifted it half out of the water. There was the muffled, submarine clinking of glass on glass.

She stared at what was rolling around in the bottom of the pot, then she turned great, searching eyes on him and broke into a slow, accusing sort of grin. "No!" she said in a hushed voice, barely above a whisper. "That's against the law!"

"There's an old Cornish saying," he replied. " 'Mining's gone scat. Farming's gone scat. Fishing's going scat. So 'tis back to wrecking, boys!' Well — morally speaking — this is better than wrecking, anyday."

She was still staring at the half-dozen bottles. He, meanwhile, was tying the pot fast to the thwart that formed his seat, so that it was just submerged, halfway along the port side. "How much ...?" she asked.

"For the lobster? It's yours." He dropped the creature in the orlop, too, and set off for his next pot.

"No! Thanks, of course, but you know very well what I mean. Is it brandy? They have the shape of brandy bottles."

"Superior old pale — the best. Three-and-fourpence in France. Five shillings to me, there in the pot. Ten bob to you, on your table. Thirteen and fourpence in the merchant's shop."

"Whew!" She fanned her face. "And to think that Papa used to buy it by the case!"

"And I'll wager it was at thirteen-and-fourpence, too. Unless he got it from someone like me at ten bob."

She licked her lips and eyed him shrewdly. "So ... there's five shillings ... Lordy!"

"Say it!" He nodded.

"Five shillings profit to you in every single bottle!" She looked around and about at all the bobbing corks and the lobstermen plying among them. "Is that what *everyone's* doing? Out here in the full light of day?"

"No!" He laughed again, though he also admired the speed with which she grasped the essentials. "At least I hope not."

"So it's only us? Won't we get caught?"

"It's possible. Are you afraid of that? I'll put you ashore again, if you prefer?"

"No." She shook her head defiantly. The lobster was edging toward her; she pushed it back with her foot. "If you're not afraid, why should I be? You're the one who'd go to prison for it. I'd tell them you kidnapped me."

"How kind! That would just about quadruple my sentence, you realize?"

"I'd bring you soup," she promised, blowing him an ironic kiss. "Every day."

"I'll take the kiss, instead," he risked saying.

For the first time she was at a loss for words.

He pressed home his advantage: "Only I wouldn't want it blown across the empty air like that. It might catch cold on the way, see."

She found her voice at that. "Mister Peters. Before we proceed any further, there's one thing I'd like you to understand." She was glad he was hauling up the next pot by then, so that she did not have to look him in the eyes.

"And what's that, Miss Harte?" he asked calmly.

"I do so very much hope that we can be *friends.*" She swallowed heavily, aware that she was sounding like one of those prim heroines in the sort of paper novels the servants liked to read — girls who do a lot of flouncing and who toss their curls in defiance at every imaginable threat to their virtue, from the Young Master who wishes to steal a kiss right down to the wicked scullery maid who suggests they share a sixpenny piece found under the drawing-room carpet. *I do so very much hope we can be friends!* She heard the echo of her words in her mind and cringed with embarrassment. But she could not think of other ways to put it.

She needn't have bothered. Those ten words, it seemed, were enough to stir him to amazement: "But that's *extraordinary!*" He stopped hauling for a moment and stared at her.

"What?" she asked, slightly alarmed.

"That's *exactly* how I feel, too!"

"Oh ... you!" She kicked him lightly on the shin — or, at least, she did not intend to kick him quite as hard as, in fact, she did.

It must have hurt him, for her toes were smarting, but he continued to clown — making his lips and eyelids tremble as if he were fighting back tears.

"I'm sorry," she blurted out. "All I meant to say was ..."

"I know," he interrupted her. And he was serious again — except, how could anyone be sure? "The very thought of any sort of romantic development between us is absolutely out of the question." He started hauling again.

"Well ..." She hesitated. "I wouldn't express it in quite those ... I mean, you put it very baldly. Lordy — more?"

"As well hang for a sheep as a lamb," he said as he tied this pot on the starboard side, balancing the first. "And there's another lobster going begging, too." He set it down beside the first.

"Six pounds!" she murmured, looking now left, now right.

"Only three — if you're talking about the profit."

"Still! Three quid! Just while rowing" — she stared back at the shore — "a couple of hundred yards!"

"About what you were saying ..." he began as he plied the oars again.

"The other lobstermen are all watching us," she replied, eager to get off that subject. "Do they know what you're really doing here?"

"Every man of them," he assured her. "But, er, about us being just friends, you and me — I completely agree."

"Yes, well, all right. I mean, we can take it as read ... and just drop the subject. All right?"

"Until you raised it, the thought never crossed my mind."

"Really? Well in that case I'm sorry I ever mentioned it."

"I thought, you see ..."

"Look! There's nothing to discuss, Mister Peters. We both find ourselves in complete agreement. Full stop! Are we going back now?"

"No, there's a few more pots to lift. We're in agreement, as you say, on the negative side of things — about what *isn't* going to happen. But I wonder if we're equally of one mind on the positive side?"

"Ah. There's a red-and-white marker, by the way."

"Well, thanks!" He had genuinely missed seeing it. "You'll earn your keep yet." He backed one oar until they were on the right course.

She realized how clever he was at not making splashes; she had been the victim of many an incompetent oarsman before. "My keep?" she echoed.

"It's just a saying." In three strong pulls they reached the next pot. He started hauling, speaking as he worked. "When we met on the shore last week, and you put the idea to me of a commercial arrangement to supply your kitchens, I was very happy."

"Oh! But it was only the very *germ* of an idea ..." She started to explain.

"I know that. I fully realize it may all come to nothing. But I hoped it wouldn't — shall I tell you why? Ah — here's another thirty shillings!"

Six more superior old pale bottles gleamed dully in the bottom of the pot, which also contained three lobsters, one of them small enough to throw back.

"Talk of being hanged for a sheep!" she murmured. "You're going for the entire flock!"

He laughed as he transferred the half dozen to the pot that was slung to starboard. "Here — Joe!" he called out to the nearest lobsterman. "Take that home for I, will 'ee?"

Joe pulled across and took the empty pot — empty, that is, except for the surviving pair of lobsters. His only 'comment' was a nod and a wink — the nod to Tamsin and the wink to David.

The pattern was starting to become clear to her. They were going to transfer all the brandy, however many bottles there were, to these two captive pots, leaving his friends to carry all the others back to harbour. She still wondered how he was going to slip the two full pots past the eyes of the Excisemen — assuming they even knew the first thing about it. "There's your next-nearest," she said, pointing out a red-white marker just four pulls away.

She expected him to pick up his interrupted explanation. Instead he began singing a shanty, more to himself than to her, though she could make out something about 'Lord Franklin' and 'one night on the deep.' He stopped when he began hauling in the line beneath the fourth marker.

"You were saying?" she prompted him.

"What?"

She glanced heavenward. "About supplying fish to us ... and ... all that."

"Oh yes. I was saying hoped we would become very close friends as time went by. But certainly nothing of a romantic nature — verily, no!"

She was a little miffed to hear him being quite so positive. "Good heavens!" she exclaimed. "Do you mean to say I'm as off-putting as all that?"

"N-o-o," he replied judiciously, as if he had to think about it for a second or two first. "No, no — not in the least. But — oh dear — I thought you'd understand. I mean, you were just as emphatic on the point as me. So I just assumed you must have some gentleman friend ... the same as me with Sarah ... well, never mind. I was wrong." He began hauling in once more. "Let's drop it."

For a moment she was too stunned by this most unexpected turn in the conversation to respond. Then she said, "Sarah? Who is Sarah?"

"It's of no consequence," he replied mildly. "She's not interested in me, either. Ho-ho! And here comes another thirty bob! Harvey, boy — here's a pot for 'ee! And as fine a cock-lobster as ever you seen!" He transferred the half dozen to the port pot and gave everthing else to another of his friends.

"As it happens," Tamsin said after pointing out their next 'pot-of-call,' as she named it, "there is no gentleman in my life at the moment, but ..."

"Ah, so I was wrong on all counts!" he cut in with cheerful self-reproach.

"My toe hurts where I kicked you," she said.

"Pull off your shoe and stick it in the water," he suggested.

She was on the point of following this advice when she realized it would mean showing him not just her ankle but quite a bit of her nether limb, to say nothing of sprawling with her limbs spread in front of him in a most unladylike manner. "Oh, it's not that bad," she lied.

A moment later it struck her as slightly unbalanced that she had sat naked as a babe on a rock with Messrs Coverley and Trotter, only three days ago, and yet now she shied away from exposing a few inches of one extremity, all of it well covered in a cotton stocking, to Mr Peters. It must indicate something but she could not imagine what.

"It's only temporary, anyway," he said soothingly.

"Mm-hmm," she agreed. She could bathe her toes in privacy when she got home again.

"An eyeable, doxy, high-quarter maid like you!"

"Pardon?"

"What you said — the lack of a gentleman in your life. It's only temporary. There'll be scats of them before long, surely? That Mister Thorne, for instance — he's more than a bit hurrisome for you, as they say." He started hauling in the fifth of his pots.

"I don't really wish to discuss him — or anyone else in that light," she announced, feeling once again like the sixpence-shocker heroine.

"Of course not," he agreed. "Even though that was ... well, what I hoped for. Another thirty bob! How much is that now?"

"Seven and a half quid," she replied at once. "If you're thinking only of the profit."

"Who isn't!" His grin, and his wink of approval, made her feel absurdly pleased — especially coming on the heels of those obscure compliments (she assumed) about her being 'eyeable and doxy.'

"What d'you mean — it was 'what you'd hoped for'?" she asked. "Why should you hope I'd have 'scats' of men friends? There's our next pot, by the way."

He spun the boat on a sixpence to face it in that direction. "I feel like some edjack, now," he said ruefully, "but I'll tell no lie, maid. I've got no sister to talk to, nor no cousin of an age to discuss such matters with, either. None who'd understand. So I did sort of hope that — you being so high-quarter and me being, well, no more'n a fisherman, and any sort of couranting carry-ons between us being out of the question, like you said — I did hope that ..." He ground to a halt, closed his eyes, and shook his head. "Never mind."

By now he was hauling in the next pot of gold.

"You hoped we'd become such good friends that we could talk about these matters with each other!" she exclaimed. "But that's extraordinary, Peter ... I mean *Mister* Peters! Silly of me!"

He leaped at once through the gap she had inadvertently opened. "It's David, if you're seeking the name," he said lightly. "Miss Harte."

"Er ... yes. I did know, actually. And your father is Benjamin."

"Benny, he prefers." He smiled expectantly.

"Oh ... it's Tamsin," she said.

"A good Cornish name. And here's *another* thirty bob!"

"Nine quid! It's dizzy-making. How many to go?"

"We'll stop at fifteen quid," he replied, as if he had the choice of going a lot further.

"Yes," she agreed grandly. "It's always best to leave something for another day."

"Are your parents Cornish, then?" he asked as they set off for the seventh pot.

"My father's from Falmouth — *was* from Falmouth, originally. He was apprenticed to a ship's chandler down there, which was where he learned the business. If only he'd stayed there, and taken it over in time ..." She shrugged. "Ah, well!" She had been about to say that he, David, wouldn't have considered the daughter of a small tradesman in Falmouth quite so far out of his reach; but then she realized it was not the sort of thought either of them wished to encourage. "Anyway," she went on, "I was about to say I have no brother, just like you with no sister. And I've often thought it would be so nice to have a man of around my own age, a man who was *just* a good friend. Nothing romantic. But someone I could share absolutely everything with — and who'd unburden all his cares and worries to me. I think that's what brothers and sisters can do ... sometimes, anyway. Don't you ... David?"

"Oh, Tamsin!" he exclaimed. "It's surely Fate that made me suggest this little outing this afternoon!"

"Don't get carried away now, David!" She laughed, partly out of embarrassment to admit, if only to herself, that to hear her name like that, on his rich, deep voice, was ridiculously pleasing. "We both know very well exactly what led you to suggest 'this little outing' — it was to disguise its true nature from the eyes of the Excisemen! D'you think they *are* watching us, by the way?"

He explained why he thought it not very likely — but why he was taking precautions nonetheless. When she heard about the excitement with the mullet shoal and the seine boat, she absolutely insisted on going back to Newlyn with him to see how they brought such a huge shoal ashore.

"And you can tell me all about your Sarah ... whatzername as we go," she added.

20 When they had thirty bottles of superior old pale in the port lobsterpot and thirty more to starboard, David put the two live lobsters back into one of the pots and gave a nod to Harry Peters, his second cousin, and 'Sonny' Sampson, a cousin by marriage. Together the three lobsterboats set off for the beach, making, it seemed to Tamsin, for the very spot where he had picked her up. For the first time she began to wonder about getting all five dozen bottles ashore — not in the sense of hiding the activity from the eyes of the law but the far simpler business of carrying them physically onto the land and then up the beach to ... wherever.

For, even though they were submerged in the water now, which helped reduce their weight by quite a bit, they were still a considerable drag on the buoyancy of the boat; she lay lower in the water by at least two strakes.

"Are you going to hide them somewhere?" she asked. "As soon as we get ashore, I mean?"

"That's the general idea," he agreed.

"Where?"

"Best you didn't know," he replied with an apologetic tilt of the head.

"We could hide them at the Morrab," she offered. "The Excise would never suspect such a respectable house."

"Respectable house, eh?" For some reason he found that highly amusing. "If you like, you can come with me when we distribute this bounty all around the district. You'll see quite a few 'respectable houses' then, I can promise you!"

They landed several yards higher up the beach, for the tide had advanced while they had been working. He asked if she'd mind guarding the three boats while they stowed the brandy. He promised it would not take above fifteen minutes.

"Guard them?" she asked sullenly. "Fight marauders off with my parasol, perhaps?"

"The very sight of you — standing there and looking so fierce as that — would be enough to see any marauders off," he assured her as he took the centre position between his two kinsmen and set out. The lobsterpots creaked ominously; they were so heavy they barely swung between the bearers. Over his shoulder he shouted, "We'll drop the two lobsters off on your mother, as well."

She ran after him and said, "You're not going to leave any of these bottles with her, though?"

"Oh? Here's a change of tune!" he replied.

"Not unless I come with you — that's what I meant when I offered. She could never cope. She's a hopeless liar."

He laughed and assured her it was not their intention, anyway.

She returned to the boats, only to discover an urchin holding the three painters. It was a moment or two before she recognized him as the one she had paid to throw sand at Charlotte Thorne — a lifetime ago, it now seemed.

"You nearly lost these, missiz," he said, handing her the lines and holding out his other hand expectantly.

"Oh no I didn't!" She took the ropes from him and put them back under the stone that had been pinning them down before he arrived.

"Don't want your money anyway," he said, sticking out his tongue. As he set off westward, beachcombing along the tidal zone of the sand, he added, "I can get all the money I want kaybin' mullet over Newlyn, see. So there!"

She was moving the ropes to another stone, higher up the shore in the face of the advancing tide, when she saw Victor Thorne sauntering down the beach to join her. "That's no job for one of Penzance's most elegant young ladies," he called out. "Allow me."

She set her foot upon the stone in the pose of a big-game hunter with his kill. "I thought you were moving over from the Queen's this afternoon," she replied.

"Then we were both suffering under a misapprehension," he said airily.

"Oh?"

"Yes. You see, I thought you'd be there to greet us."

"Oh!" she responded airily. "If only I'd known you cared so much!" She wondered what *her* misapprehension might be, but not strongly enough to make her want to ask him. Instead she said, "Anyway, what made your mother change her mind about us — Mama and me?"

"About *you*," he replied. "I don't imagine she had an opinion either way about your mater."

"From the moment she set eyes on me she took against me. And then, only a week later ... what has she learned in the meanwhile to change her mind?"

He sat on one of the gunwales, took out a gold cigarette case, and offered her one. "You'll find they're Virginia this side and Turkish on that."

A reflex from an earlier life made her look to see if his name were printed on them — in other words, whether he had them specially made up for himself by Alfred Dunhill or one of those London specialists. He hadn't. Maybe he would when he inherited all that money next year.

Given a choice she always went for Turkish. They were oval, which looked more interesting between one's fingers. They were perfumed, too, which always seemed more feminine. She took one and hung it nonchalantly between her lips, catching a whiff of its perfume.

"I prefer the Virginia," he said as he struck a match for her. "They're more manly."

"I'll bet Messrs Coverley and Trotter smoke Turkish," she said, taking her first puff.

His Virginia made him cough.

"Have you met Mister Trotter yet?" she asked. "He's in the room next to you."

"Really?" he said, looking at her slightly askance. "Is that some kind of warning or what?"

"It's not a warning at all," she protested. "You complain I wasn't there to greet you and, I presume, to make the introductions all round, so these are the things I would have said had I been there in person."

"I was only teasing," he said.

She saw a chance to tease him back. "Well, I only mentioned Mister Trotter because you both dress with such elegance. My days of following fashion are, as you well know, all behind me, but I vividly recall the fun we girls had in talking about *la mode*. So I just thought that two such proud peacocks as yourself and Reginald ..."

"Listen!" he shouted angrily, springing to his feet again. "I don't know what you've got into your pretty little head about me but I can assure you, I'm no peacock. I played in the first fifteen at school, you know. I'd have been captain, too, if it hadn't been for ... well, never mind all that. Just because a fellow dresses carefully ... one can't make you out at all," he grumbled.

"Obviously I've got the wrong end of the stick," she said. "The distinction between 'peacock' and careful dresser is evidently important to you though it escapes me entirely."

"You never spoke a truer word!" he said heavily. "For two pins I'd prove it, too."

"Well, I don't happen to have two pins about me," she replied, "but I could owe you."

He grinned. "I suppose I'll take that as an invitation," he said. "Come here."

"No. I'll get my feet wet. You come here."

"Now that *is* an invitation!" He leaned back on the boat and did a sort of gymnastic hand-vault forward, landing with his feet either side of hers. A split second later he was upright and they were touching each other from head to toe. And a split second after that his arms were about her and his lips were pressed hard against hers. She was too astonished to resist.

In fact, her first thought was that she mustn't burn his beautiful blazer with her cigarette — then that he mustn't accidentally burn her dress, either. And during those brief, fateful moments, the exquisite pleasure of being kissed by such a handsome, elegant young man of the world took control of her. A small, drowning voice within said it was her duty to resist ... that all the world was looking on ... that one simply did not behave in this fashion in public in the broad light of day.

And anyway, David would be returning soon.

Curiously enough, it was that thought, more than any of the others, which made her break off their kiss at last — that and the sudden, urgent need to breathe freely again.

"Satisfied now?" he asked.

But she was looking up toward the Esplanade — where she saw that David and his friends were already returning. Actually, David himself was standing at the top of the steps, leaning against the railing, staring at her ... as far as she could tell at such a distance. His friends were already walking across the sand, so he had probably been standing there for a good half-minute. How much had he seen, she wondered?

"Eh?" Victor prompted.

"What?" She tore her eyes away from David.

"I asked if you're satisfied?"

She smiled and gave him another kiss, a brief one this time, to show the world — and David — that it was all very insignificant. "Compleeeetely!" she purred. "Listen! I'll see you this evening. I'm going over to Newlyn now to see how they catch these mullet. You've heard about this huge shoal that appeared in the bay this morning?"

"Are you going with your fisherfolk pals?" he asked.

"Don't be silly."

"Silly?" He relit her cigarette, which had gone out. "What's silly about it?"

"Childish talk like that. David Peters is a good friend, that's all. He's probably the best friend I have down here. But, honestly, that's all."

"Really?"

"Cross my heart."

"Then chuck this jaunt to Newlyn, Tamsin. Let's hire a gig and go for a jaunt of our own somewhere! There's so much I want to talk about — you ... me ... *us!* We could even find some place to kiss again — in private — properly."

She was tempted, for it really had been ... well, quite nice to be kissed by him and to feel his body tight against her. It was excitingly alien, and with a hint of danger, too, especially after the things she had learned so recently from Daisy. Perhaps it was that which tilted the balance at last — that and the sight of David striding down the beach toward them, easily overtaking his two companions.

"Hallo!" he called out as soon as he was within hailing distance. Then, when he was a little closer, he added, "I was afraid you'd be bored, but I see I needn't have worried. Mister Thorne — good to meet you again."

He held out his hand, which Victor accepted with some reluctance; perhaps only Tamsin's taunt of 'Silly!' persuaded him to it.

"Again?" Tamsin pretended to be surprised.

"It was nothing," Victor assured her. "We just went over to Newlyn to inquire about makng a fishing trip." To David he added, "That's all." He turned back to Tamsin. "Well ... if you're sure?"

She darted forward and kissed him swiftly on the cheek. "*À bientôt, chérie!*" she murmured.

He nodded curtly at David and turned to make his way back up the beach.

"*À toute à l'heure, monsieur!*" David called after him.

He paused, briefly, but did not turn round.

"One in the eye for me!" Tamsin said as he punted them off again into the tideway.

"Yes. A great mistake — those education acts," he remarked. "Teaching the lower orders things they've no right to know."

"*Tu parles français, mon frère, hein?*" she asked.

"*Naturellement, ma petite soeur.*"

His French accent was as provincial as his Cornish accent was when he spoke English. "You've lived and worked in France," she said accusingly.

"Did I say otherwise? They have fishermen over there in Brittany, too, you know — and, as you've seen today, we cooperate over many things."

In calling her his 'little sister' he had reminded her of their earlier conversation. "What did Victor Thorne really want when he came over to Newlyn?" she asked.

"You heard what he said."

"Yes. And I also saw your expression when he said it."

"Well, he pretended to pick me out at random to ask about a fishing trip. What he didn't realize was that, when he went into the post office to ask where he could find David Peters, he was actually asking my aunt. So he came looking for me. It wasn't a casual meeting. I didn't really know why, though, until five minutes ago. Did he think I might be some kind of rival?"

She shrugged awkwardly.

"Sorry," he went on. "Isn't this exactly the sort of thing you wanted us to talk about — to be able to talk about?"

"Ye-es," she admitted reluctantly. Now that it was actually happening, it didn't seem half as wonderful as it had in her imagination. In fact, for some reason, she would far rather be talking with Victor about David. "What about your Sarah?" she went on.

"Oh, her!" He drew a deep breath and launched himself. "She's the daughter of a Saint Ives fisherman. That's more than half the trouble. There's no love lost between Saint Ives boats and Newlyn boats. I don't know how to get near her even." He gazed at her hopefully. "In a romantic sense, I mean."

"How often do you meet? No — start at the beginning. How did you meet first? How long ago?"

He gazed out to sea. "Promise you won't laugh?"

"As if I would!"

"D'you believe in love at first sight? D'you think a man can look at a maid and, before he could blink an eye, *know* she was the one he was going to marry?"

The intensity of his tone held her in thrall. She could only nod and beg him with her eyes to go on.

"No matter that she won't even let herself *think* of me in that way. I mean, she's perfectly friendly with me. In fact, if she *hated* me, I think I'd stand more chance. But there it is. I shall wed her one day — I know it." He let go an oar and tapped his breastbone. "In here. I'm as sure of it as ..." He gazed about them, at a loss for a comparison until, looking at her again, he said, "Well, as I'm sure of you sitting there now. And I knew all that the very moment I saw her. Thank you for not laughing, at least."

Laughing! Tamsin thought it the saddest, beautifullest, touchingest declaration she had ever heard — not that she had heard so many, mind. She thought this Sarah-maid must be one of the luckiest girls in Cornwall, to be the repository of such devotion. She must also be the stupidest, for spurning it aside. Or worse — for not even recognizing it.

"Does she have someone else?" she asked.

"That's what I suspected from the start," he replied, philosophical again. "And then lately I've had it confirmed. I've heard she's been seen couranting about with a young fellow from Carbis Bay."

"Next door to Saint Ives."

"Yes. A very *posh* little community. He's got money, of course."

"What does he do?"

"What do young men with money all do? Nothing!"

She felt his predicament so keenly now that she blurted out, "What a fool she must be! Is there anything *I* can do?"

He looked at her with new interest, hope even. "Like?"

"I don't know. You could take me somewhere where you're sure she's to be found ... introduce me ... leave us to talk? I'd be very discreet, I promise. I wouldn't say a word of your feelings unless I was utterly certain it'd do some good. But at the very least I could ... you know, 'size her up,' as they say. Get the measure of her."

"I don't know, Tamsin." He bit his lip and shook his head dubiously. "It'd be a risk. What if she saw through us, despite all the care you took? In affairs of the heart, one usually gets no more than a single chance, you know."

"Oh, David!" Her lip was trembling and there was a horrid lump in her throat.

"Oh, come on!" He laughed. "It'll work itself out in time. I'm even more sure of it now, especially after this talk with you."

"Me? I don't see how I've been of the slightest help."

"Well, you have — just take it from me. Now it's your turn in the confessional. Do you always choose the most public place in town for your spooning?"

She pulled a face. "I didn't ... I mean, that wasn't ... Oh dear! I've got to be honest with you, haven't I?"

He nodded sympathetically. "Otherwise there'd be no point."

"Quite. Well, if you were any other person in the world, man or woman, I'd never be able to admit to you that what you saw back there was the first kiss of my *life*. The first real kiss, I mean

— not like at party games. Nor like those quick pecks one used to snatch at dances and balls."

"But you must have given him the nod — if not in so many words, then ..."

"But I didn't. Or I didn't mean to. I don't know what I said but he took it as some kind of challenge that he had to prove he could kiss me. Anyway, it was very nice."

"For a first time."

"No. Just very nice." She giggled. "He didn't want me to come back to Newlyn with you. He wanted us to hire a gig and go off into the country somewhere."

"Why didn't you?"

"He's jealous of you, you know — until I told him you were just a friend."

"Ah! You told him that?"

"Probably the best friend I've got, I said."

"And he was happier then?"

She frowned. "I don't know, now that you mention it. Well, you saw the mood he was in when he left us — how would you describe it?"

He shook his head and smiled warily. "I never judge another man if there's a maid about to do it for me. You're so much better at it than us."

"That's true," she agreed. "Anyway, another reason I didn't go off with him is that no girl should ever fall in with all her young man's wishes all the time. What was it about Good Queen Bess — masterly procrastination? Something like that."

"Spin it out. A little goes a long way."

"Just so."

"No more kisses for a month."

"Oh no! That would be *really* spinning it out ... oh, you were joking. Beast!" She looked about them suddenly. "I say! We're almost there."

He looked over his shoulder and said, "Yes — we made good progress, maid."

21   When Victor regained the Esplanade, he turned and leaned against the railings, not knowing what else to do now. The lobster boats had formed into a flotilla, all headed home for Newlyn. Only one was not laden to the gunwales with lifted pots; but Tamsin would have been easy enough to distinguish, anyway — a dab of pale fabric in a cluster of sombre blacks, browns, and navy-blues. He waited for her to turn and wave. He waited until she was so far off that he probably wouldn't have been able to discern it if she had. He dropped his cigarette into the sand below and turned to face the town.

Life was not supposed to be like this for a rich young fellow without a care in the world. Jealousy was what you felt when some other chap picked the winner in the 2:30 at Sandown and your horse was so late it had to tiptoe back into the stables after dark; or when the chorus girl you were sure had winked at you walked off on the arm of your pal, who had been sitting at your side; or when that fellow you couldn't stand the sight of scored a century off the bowler who sent you back to the pavilion with a duck. Jealousy was for important, life-shaking events like that. It wasn't for thinking about a strange, wayward, strong-minded, infuriating, penniless girl, whom you hardly knew, anyway, sitting in a rowing boat with a common fisherman who probably couldn't shake more than a couple of tenners at the world.

He had intended going back to the Morrab and ... well, something would occur to him there. Perhaps Charlotte would like to join him in hiring a gig and going for a jaunt out into the country. Anything to escape from this dreary town for a while. She could dash off a water-colour and he could lie in the shade and engage in some serious thinking about his future. But he found himself unable to leave the seafront while that tiny pale spot still bobbed up and down out there on its slow progress toward Newlyn.

He lit another cigarette and sought the shade of the shelter. What was she, anyway, this Tamsin Harte, that she should so commandeer his thoughts? She was certainly NQOC. Her father, George Harte, had been no more than a chandler's apprentice who had made a few astute commercial decisions and ended up cock of the walk at Plymouth — until Nature balanced things out again by causing him to make a few *un*astute commercial decisions. No pedigree at all.

"Penny for them?" The mater's voice.

He sprang to his feet and turned toward her — or them, for he discovered both his parents standing at the other end of the shelter, staring at him with contrary expressions — his father's bored, his mother's concerned.

"Pater, dear," she said in a voice that did not expect any argument, "do go and see how late the Queen's serves those delicious cream teas."

He went without a word.

She joined her son in the shelter and turned to stare out to sea, following his gaze — or the gaze he had held while they watched him unawares.

"I see!" she said with a smile. She looked him up and down, the way a carter might gauge a draught horse to assess what weight it might pull. "Little Miss Harte is revelling in it now, of course. But, take it from me, darling — from one who knows, that is — she'll tire of it soon enough." She seated herself as she spoke. "She has bigger fish to fry." The metaphor was pleasing enough to make her laugh.

"How do you know?" he asked, remaining standing. He had meant the question to sound interested, conversational; but his morose humour came through in his tone.

"I know you think I'm just being fickle, don't you, darling ..." she began.

"I think you're punishing us for not wanting to gambol among the bonnie burns and braes this year. Have you seen my room? It's a broom cupboard!"

"It's perfectly adequate, but never mind that. If you suppose I'm just being wayward out of spite, then you understand nothing — and that worries me."

He shrugged and turned away from her as far as he dared. She always got him feeling like this — inadequate, incompetent, unfit for the great big grown-up world. "I don't see there's much to understand. You summed them up in one word — spelled n, q, o, c."

"Which was true as far as it went," she replied calmly. "But mature reflection showed it didn't go far enough. That's all. Sit down and let me explain. And please extinguish that cigarette. I know we're in the open air but it does annoy me so."

He flicked the offending butt across the Esplanade; it soared over the railings and fell somewhere upon the sand below.

"Have a care! Someone might be sitting there," his mother reprimanded him.

"More fool they," he replied, sitting down.

"Oh dear, you are in a bate! Was she really beastly to you? Never mind. It's much more important, just at this minute, for me to explain certain things. You may know that I am from a cadet branch of ..."

"... of the Duke of Radnor's family." He spoke in unison with her. "I believe I have heard it mentioned a time or two."

"There's no need to be sarcastic, dear. The same noble blood flows in your veins, too, in case you forget it. What I may not have told you *quite* so frequently is that our particular branch was not just thin and straggly and almost leafless — it was severed entirely from its parent tree and, to continue the metaphor, in danger of being carried off to some peasant cottage. In short, when your father met me, we had nothing left but our ancient pride. I was like Tess of the d'Urbervilles. In my situation, I mean — not at all in character or behaviour, I do assure you!"

"You mean ...?" Light was beginning to dawn on Victor — and he did not like what he thought it illuminated. "You and Miss Harte ...?"

"Oh, but we were much worse off than the Hartes. They aren't *renting* the Morrab Guest House, you know. They own it. But let's not go wandering off into precise comparisons. The point I'm trying to make is that no one knows better than me that fortunes can wane as well as wax. For Miss Harte they have both waxed and waned during the course of her still-young life. For us Cunninghams the decline went through three generations. We once owned over four hundred thousand acres, putting all our family holdings together. Twice we saved the dukedom itself from ruin — once in seventeen forty-six and again in eighteen oh-two."

"Such is gratitude!" Victor said, becoming interested now for he had never heard those wretched Cunninghams portrayed in quite this way before.

"Indeed. But *I* was the salvation of our particular branch of the family. I met your father, won his affection, married him, and, though I say it myself, it was I and I alone who put *his* family's affairs in order."

"Eh?" Victor sat up, all ears, at this.

"Oh yes! We like to give the impression that money is something distasteful, something we don't really wish to talk about, something that's always just *there,* like a well, to be dipped whenever we feel the need. In fact, we think of it very like a well, don't we! We take great care not to pollute the source and never to extract more than it can replace naturally. That would be your general view of our family's financial affairs, I suppose? Tell me if I'm wrong."

He shook his head and said, "But ... what?"

"Yes." She was pleased to see him following her line so closely. "It's a very big but, too. Because nothing in the world of finance is remotely equivalent to the rainfall that endlessly replenishes the groundwater and feeds the springs. So forget all thoughts of wells and concentrate instead on what really happens. Our income derives entirely from property, shares, and gilts — in other words, from rents and dividends — there's nothing God-given or automatic about any of it."

Victor stared at her in alarm. "You're not trying to work around to telling me ... I mean, this move from the Queen's to that crabby little guest house isn't because ..."

Her laughter cut him short. "Nothing of the kind. No. But it's all thanks to my constant vigilance, which means keeping a keen eye on the world, the way things are going ... trends here, there, and everywhere. And the trends are not good. Let's start with property. How did Lady Bracknell put it in that wickedly witty play by that dreadful man whose name we've all agreed to forget — 'What with the duties expected of one during one's life and the duties exacted of one when one is dead, there's neither pleasure in owning it nor profit in passing it on'? Something along those lines, anyway. And it's even more true now than it was then."

"So it's stocks and bonds?" he guessed. "Perhaps I should look for a place on the Stock Exchange? Get us a ringside seat, eh?" He imagined that was where this homily was leading.

And his mother went along with it, for the moment, anyway, rather than let her argument be diverted. "It's certainly worth considering, dear," she said. "However — in the long run — they may prove even less reliable than property. You're too young to recall the dreadful depression at the end of the last century, following the wars and revolutions of the seventies. And even now we are merely living through a sort of truce. The old rivalries are still going strong. There'll be another war in Europe at some time within the next ten years. Some say within the next five. And when it's over, it will leave us all impoverished, except for the shipbuilders and armaments manufacturers."

"I hope we have shares in them!" He tried a laugh.

"Naturally, darling. But that's not my point, either. It's much bigger than that. What I'm saying is that at the moment we have all our eggs in just two baskets. And, while that's better than having them in one, it's not as safe as having them in three. Or four. D'you see?"

He shrugged. "I see that, of course, now you've explained it. But I don't see how it relates to Tamsin Harte."

She leaned forward and peered into his face. "It's a curious thing about you, Victor. You're an astute observer of *people* — more acute than most women, even. But the more abstract things like this pass you by. Most odd. However, I can't accuse you of being unobservant in this case because it passed even me by until last Sunday evening. When I saw Mister Coverley greeting the Hartes as his guests, well, it was as if a veil was suddenly lifted from my eyes. I realized I'd been thinking, or concentrating my thoughts, much too closely on the mother and daughter. In other words — forgetting the importance of the late father."

"Now that *is* odd," he said. "I, too, was thinking about him at the moment you arrived."

"Good! Excellent, in fact. What exactly were your thoughts?"

"The man had no class," he replied. "He learned a clever trick or two as an apprentice, made a fortune, but there was no 'bottom' to him. I mean no ... *soundness*. No ..."

" 'Bottom' will do, dear. We all know what it means. Go on."

"Well, anyway, he lost it all again, didn't he! What was so special about Coverley entertaining the Hartes?"

"He's a self-made man, too. I know he inherited quite a bit ... and went to Oundle and all that. But he's turned a small fortune into something very much larger — so he's self-made to that extent. And *that* is what's missing from our family's affairs. I can put them in order but I can't manage that sort of multiplication. I'm a housekeeper not a capitalist."

Victor sighed. "I still don't *quite* see, you know, why Coverley's entertaining the Hartes ..."

"But of course you do!" she snapped. "You're just not thinking. She fascinates him. She has obviously inherited her father's commercial bent. If you could lift the lid and watch her brain-cogs working, I bet you'd be staggered at the vault of her ambitions. That girl is never going to remain a modest little guest-house keeper, or I'll eat all the wax fruits on this hat. And Coverley sees a kindred spirit in her. Apparently he took her and the Dobbs creature for a spin in his motor last Sunday ... which, incidentally, I'm surprised you didn't see fit to mention to your father and me when ..."

"You were hardly in the most receptive mood, mater — if you'll forgive me for pointing it out."

"Water under the bridge, dear. The point is, he must have recognized her qualities at some time during that jaunt — otherwise he'd hardly have invited them to his table that evening."

"So ... are you suggesting he's going to invest money in her or something like that?"

"*Someone* is going to. You may be absolutely sure of that. She has the begging bowl out. Not crudely, of course, but in her own subtle way. I don't think her meeting with us — when that urchin threw the sand at poor Charlotte — I don't think that was quite as accidental as it seemed."

For a moment he considered confirming her suspicions but then he decided she was already self-satisfied enough with her own astuteness. It would hardly do to say he'd known it all along.

"However," she continued, "even if I'm wrong, she has inherited her father's nose for investable money, and she'll get it by hook or by crook."

"For what purpose?"

"Oh, who knows — with a girl like that? At the moment she's in the hôtel-guest-house line, so it's probably an establishment to rival the Queen's. But if she were to become more interested in the fishing trade" — she eyed her son shrewdly as she put forward the suggestion — "it could turn into quite another ambition. To own the largest fleet in Mount's Bay, for instance. And why stop there? Or it could be something entirely different. People with that sort of nose for commerce don't get a calling to one particular trade. They see them all as interchangeable opportunities." She glanced over her shoulder, through the glass screen toward the hôtel. "Your father's taking an age. Shall we go over and join him?"

They rose and made to cross the road, but were delayed by a pony and trap that was racing toward them from the direction of Newlyn. The driver was tooting a horn to clear the way, which people did smartly enough. Like them, Victor and his mother assumed he was desperate to get his *enceinte* wife to hospital on time, following some complication that made a home birth impossible. Only as they drew close did they realize it was David Peters and Tamsin Harte. They swept past, grim of face, looking neither right nor left, and almost took a spill in rounding the corner into Morrab Road.

"Well!" Mrs Thorne exclaimed. "Here's some excitement! I think we shall leave your pater to his own devices and hasten back to the guest house, instead."

As they crossed the road, Victor, who hoped to tie up one or two loose ends, said, "Surely Coverley would never invest in a rival establishment?"

"Why not? Penzance is nowhere near its full development as a holiday resort. There are bound to be more hôtels to compete with the Queen's. What better than to own one of them! Two eggs — two baskets. I wouldn't put it past him to marry her, either — just to make sure."

He cleared his throat, being uncertain about her intentions again. Finally he said, "So ... are you suggesting that I should get in first?"

She laughed. "Of course not, darling. A foot in the door will do. Charm her but keep her dangling — and don't tell me you haven't had plenty of practice! Meanwhile we'll have a close-to chance to find out just what she's made of."

Victor accepted the commission with a nod even though he knew that, as a gentleman, he ought to confess he had already begun to lose his heart to Tamsin. His conscience was eased by a conviction that his mother, in turn, was holding back something of equal importance. He could not imagine what it might be; he had, in any case, long ago given up trying to follow his mother's thoughts and schemes through the labyrinths of her mind. But she was up to something even more devious than anything she had so far revealed — he was never more sure of anything.

22 Poor David! Not only was he eaten with the fear of losing half his haul of brandy, which, in turn, would undo all his moneymaking efforts of the past two days, but he was also having to divide his attention between whipping the pony to a gallop (without goading it to bolt) and trying to contain Tamsin's anger.

"But you *promised,*" she cried. "As good as promised, anyway. You said you had no intention of leaving any bottles at our place. Those were your last words on the subject."

"What happened was that we ..." was all he managed before she cut him short.

"Except you added you'd drop off the lobsters there. Only the lobsters. There was no mention of the bottles."

"The thing was ..."

"And I *told* you — I explained. My mother would be no good at lying if the Excisemen came to search the place. I told you that, didn't I."

"We got as far as ..."

"They've probably torn the house apart by now ..."

"We didn't leave it in the house," he managed to deliver an entire sentence at last. "We didn't go near the house — except, as I said, to go round to the kitchen door and give your cook those lobsters."

"So where did you leave it — we're talking about one of those lobsterpots full, I presume?"

"Yes. Two and a half dozen. The thing is, what happened was, we got as far as ... the other place, and ..."

"One of the lock-up garages behind the Queen's, I presume?"

The jerk of his hands almost checked the pony to a grateful halt. "I never told you that." He cracked the whip above the creature's head again, which almost jolted her backward, out of her seat.

"God, one can't even trust you to drive properly! I'll tell you one thing, David — you are *not* going to carry any of our guests out to sea. I don't care if you fit Roll-Royce engines to your boat. If one can't even rely on your word in a simple case like this ... oh, I am so *mad!*"

He thought it best to say nothing more for the moment; just concentrate on his driving.

"Where did you leave it, anyway?" she asked after a while.

By now they were cantering up toward the Esplanade, which had the usual throng of holiday-makers and promenaders. He put his hand to the hooter and began a monotonously urgent parp-parp-parp!

"You know that holly bush inside your gate?" he said.

"You hid it under that?" She was scandalized.

"Well under it."

"Listen! That bush is so small, there's only under or not-under. There's no such thing as *well* under. What possessed you?" She saw Victor and his mater standing at the kerb but she had no choice other than to ignore them.

"When we got to the first hiding place ... how did you know it was a garage behind the Queen's, anyway?"

"Out of the three thousand other likely places within ten minutes' walk of the beach, you mean? Oh, it took a lot of guesswork! What happened there, anyway?"

"Standish Coverley, he was waiting to take it in, as usual. And that Trotter fellow with him. It was Trotter suggested putting half there and half somewhere else — split the risk, see? For him and me."

"So you thought at once of the Morrab — naturally!"

"Well, it's not but a hundred paces farther on. How was I to know that Exciseman back there, old Sterne, was going to take such an interest in you and where you live?"

They almost overturned when taking the corner into Morrab Road, at which point the guest house itself came immediately into view.

The street was apparently empty. No police vans. Not a sign of a blue uniform. The sun was baking the pavements and splitting the trees.

"Don't slow down!" she cried as he started doing just that.

He ignored her. "They could be lying in wait," he warned. "We don't want to appear agitated now."

"But they couldn't have got here ahead of us — we'd have seen them."

"They could telephone the Penzance police. 'Tis *they* could be hiding in wait to catch us here." The pony was down to a welcome walk by now, which gave David time to prepare Tamsin for the coming ordeal. "Just to find a few bottles in someone's front garden isn't ..."

"A few!"

"Listen — I didn't finish! Just to *find* them there isn't good enough evidence for a conviction. Enemies could have left them, hoping to get you convicted — and a clever lawyer could get you off on that argument alone. So, if the police *are* in hiding, they'll wait for us to go to that bush and then they'll pounce. They may not even know it's there, in which case they'd be just waiting for us to lead them to it. Mind you, even then we might be able to buy them off with a couple of bottles."

Somewhat calmer now she said, "I still don't know what possessed you to leave it there."

"Tradition!" He laughed.

"Be serious!" She was cross again.

"I am," he assured her. "I once had two boxes of brandy buried under rhododendron leaves in Squire Blewitt's garden out to Madron, there. He's the local chairman of the bench."

"You were taking a risk!"

"Hardly. A dozen of those bottles were for him! He knew it was there. The police knew it was there, somewhere. They watched us both for four days — because they'd have needed a warrant to go in and search, see? And who is it that gives out the warrants, eh?"

"The magistrates?"

"Right. So we beat them that time. And, with a bit of luck, we'll beat them this time, too. Here we are now." He braked the trap in front of her gate. "We'll go directly up to the front door, and the last place you'll let your glance stray upon, please, is that there old holly bush!"

Guiltily she tore her eyes away from it. In turning to descend from the vehicle she looked back down Morrab Road. "Oh dear," she said. "Victor and his mater."

"The more the merrier," he replied, handing her down.

But Tamsin was thinking of the shame of being unmasked as a criminal — and with Victor looking on.

She intended tapping gently at the front door, so as not to disturb her mother, who was probably taking a nap upstairs. But Daisy was there, already waiting for them to arrive. She opened the door before they even reached the steps. "What? No more lobsters?" she asked, pretending to be disappointed.

"Have the police been here?" Tamsin replied, stepping past her and going into the guests' lounge, which had a bay window to the front of the house. She stood well back and began a careful survey of the street.

Daisy followed her and, coming right up behind, rested her chin playfully on her shoulder. "See the Anglican Convent there? Saint Breaca's? The laburnum in their garden?"

"Got them!" Even as she found the house in question she saw two fern leaves moving just above the garden fence. "Someone should tell them that ferns do not grow horizontally," she murmured. "D'you see them, David?"

Now that there was a defined enemy and they were all in it together, her rage had quite evaporated.

Daisy stood upright again and glanced at him, surprised to hear Tamsin use his first name.

He winked at her and said, "They should also understand that ferns don't waggle about in the wind when there isn't any wind. There's two more behind the stone pillar at Morrab Gardens entrance. And I saw another three on this side of the road as we drew up."

Tamsin looked at him accusingly. "You didn't say."

"I didn't want to startle you."

"I don't know what they're waiting for," Daisy said.

"I'll give you one guess," Tamsin responded glumly. But then she saw that the maid's face was split with a grin from ear to ear. "Daisy!" she said with mock severity. "What have you been and gone and done?"

"Nothing much," she answered. "Three careless men left a lobsterpot full of old bottles out there under the hollybush."

"They've decided to move!" David had not taken his eyes off them since he had them all located. "Quick!" he said to Daisy. "What did you do with them?"

"Brought the lot in here and hid them."

"Where?"

"In a place Mrs Pascoe showed me. No one would ever find them, not unless they knew."

The bell clanged.

"It's the two Thornes and the police together." David chuckled. "I don't know which of them is more suspicious of the other."

Mrs Harte came downstairs from her nap. "What on earth is going on?" she asked. "The garden is filled with policemen. Have we been burgled?"

"They think we're smugglers, Mama," Tamsin told her. "Don't distress yourself about it. Go back and finish your nap. I'll deal with them."

"You will not! This is *my* house. I will not have them upsetting our guests with this nonsense." She pushed past them and opened the door herself. "Smugglers, indeed!" she exclaimed. "I *beg* your pardon?"

"Not you, Mrs Thorne," Harriet assured her. "These gentlemen from the constabulary. Do come in." She stood aside to let the Thornes pass but immediately barred the way to the police, who had assumed the invitation included them. "Now, what is this nonsense? Who are you?"

She addressed the nearest constable, who immediately looked toward his superior. "Sergeant Hocken, ma'am, of the county constabulary. We have reason to believe that certain contraband items have been concealed upon these premises ..."

"What nonsense! Reason, you say? I should like to hear it."

"Sarge!" A constable came up the path holding the lobsterpot. "Empty," he said — which they might have guessed already from the way he dangled it by just two fingers.

"Where did you get that?" Harriet asked.

"Under that hollybush, ma'am," the constable said.

"Well, take it away. We don't want it." She looked half over her shoulder. "Mister Peters? Is this anything to do with you?"

David pushed his way to the front and pretended to examine the pot minutely. "It could very well be, missiz. We left you a brace of lobsters earlier this afternoon. My assistant might have forgotten the pot when we left."

"Very clever, Peters," the sergeant said. "Listen now!" He beckoned David aside, took him halfway down the garden path, and murmured, "A couple of bottles for me and my men and we'll see off the Excise for you."

Before they could come to any arrangement, however, the Excisemen themselves came thundering round the corner from the Esplanade in a van drawn by a pair of greys. The sergeant took off his helmet and mopped his brow. "We'll still do our best," he assured David as they rejoined the others.

Tamsin slipped her hand into Victor's and gave him a squeeze. "Exciting, eh?" she whispered before letting go again.

He took out his cigarette case and offered them around, but he himself was the only taker.

The two leading Excisemen hit the ground running. "Well?" the leader called out as they entered at the gate. He was Inspector Sterne, the one who had questioned Tamsin so closely — and so unexpectedly, according to David — when their boat tied up at Newlyn. He was well named, the fishermen all agreed.

Two further Excisemen descended from the van, of lowly rank, for they joined the two constables halfway up the path.

In reply to Sterne's question the sergeant pointed to the empty lobsterpot.

"Then they've hidden them," Sterne said at once. "Have you searched the garden?" Without waiting for a reply he motioned his men to begin. "It wouldn't be the first time certain persons have concealed certain items under bushes," he added, staring balefully at David.

"Stop that this minute!" Harriet's cry brought a sudden, complete hush. The Excisemen froze halfway across the little front lawn. "You will not search any part of these premises without a by-your-leave."

"We have a right to do it, ma'am," Sterne said. "And a duty, too. Mrs Harte is it?" He bowed stiffly. "Inspector Sterne, ma'am. I hope we'll enjoy your complete cooperation, for I shouldn't think you had any hand in smuggling dutiable goods. Nor," he added heavily, "would you wish to be tried and sentenced along with them as did it, I imagine." He stared directly at David and Tamsin.

But involving Tamsin was his mistake. Harriet would have gone only so far to protect David Peters; to protect her own daughter she would have gone to the ends of the earth. "If you wish to search any part of these premises," she said, "you will have to apply for a warrant."

"We can certainly do that, madam," he replied frostily. "If that is your wish." He took out his watch and consulted it ponderously. "We may not manage it today," he added — untruthfully — so I shall have to place a night-and-day picquet on your gate with instructions to search all who enter or leave. I don't think your guests will take too kindly to that, but, if that is your wish, so be it."

"What a detestable little man!" Cicely Thorne exclaimed suddenly. "Sterne, did you say? I shall have a word about you and this disgraceful behaviour with Sir Napier Redmond, one of your masters."

Sterne did not flinch. "I know very well who Sir Napier is, ma'am," he replied. "I also know that 'disgraceful behaviour' would be his judgement on smuggling, not on actions aimed at combating it." He turned back to Harriet. "Well, it's your choice, Mrs Harte. A guard on the gate and a search warrant tomorrow, or a by-your-leave search now."

"What does a search involve?" Tamsin asked. "Ripping up floorboards? Taking out window casings?"

His smile was calculated to chill. "Ah, Miss Harte," he replied. "Again! Let me assure you — if you were to go indoors now and lift a single floorboard and then put it back again — just one in the entire house — I and my men would find it inside five minutes. I promise you — we will lift nothing nor remove nothing that does not show clear signs of suffering the same treatment — by other hands" — and here he looked at David again — "within the past few hours. Is it a bargain?"

He was actually conceding nothing for he had already decided that if a friend of Sir Napier's was in the house, this investigation, unlike so many others, was going to be conducted strictly by the rules. "Oh, and one other thing," he added. "When we have inspected any particular room to our satisfaction, it will be locked, and remain locked, with the key in my keeping, until the entire search is complete. Contraband has a strange habit of wandering upstairs and downstairs behind our backs in any house we search."

"You may not search my room unless I am present," Cicely said.

"I would absolutely insist on it, Madam," he replied cheerfully. "Mrs Harte? You or some member of your staff will have to stand proxy while we search the rooms of guests who are out."

"I would insist on it, sir," she replied coldly.

"Then let us begin." He was more than eager by now, for he had seen one of the party (Daisy, though he did not then know her by name) slip quietly indoors and he was sure she was even now concealing the brandy. Or making its earlier concealment doubly sure. He nodded at his own three men, who sprang into action at once, moving round the party and into the house. "Sergeant?" He now turned to the police.

"Our orders are not to enter private premises without a warrant," Hocken replied, adding a delayed, "sir."

"Even with the consent of the owner of said premises?"

"I have no instructions as to that, sir, but I could send one of my boys to inquire."

Sterne knew he was lying, of course, and that the 'boy' would take longer than any conceivable search of the guest house. In his heart-of-hearts, he could not blame Sergeant Hocken. A bottle of brandy shared out among them was preferable by far to the hatred of every fisherman in the bay and their sullen refusal to cooperate in future police inquiries. He himself knew all about that hatred.

"Sir!" One of his men was calling him indoors.

He thanked Hocken with elaborate sarcasm for his offer of cooperation and went inside. He found the man standing at the kitchen door, his way being barred by a fierce-looking Bridget, wielding a mop. The floor was covered with a mixture of tealeaves and wet sawdust.

"Now then, what seems to be the trouble?" he asked in rule-book fashion.

"She says if we trample that stuff underfoot and carry it all over the house, there'll be blue murder, sir."

"Quite right, too," he told his astonished subordinate. "I should feel strongly about that myself, wouldn't you?" Then, to Bridget, "Obviously you're going to sweep it up, maid. How long will that take?"

She wondered how long she could spin it out. "Twenty minutes, sir?" she suggested.

The Exciseman expected his chief to explode and to order it to be finished within five — which would be generous enough. But, sweet as pie, he just smiled and promised to return then.

The sweetness soured, though, as room after room yielded nothing. It had to be in the kitchen, then. And, from the attention that maid had been lavishing upon the floor, he guessed the hoard would lie in a cavity under one of those big flagstones. How boring! he thought. Some people had no imagination.

He called off the search of the attics, where the cobwebs had obviously not been disturbed for days, or even weeks, and brought all three men down to the kitchen. There, to his annoyance, he found that, although Bridget had swept the stones themselves clean enough, the cracks between them, where there would be telltale signs of any recent disturbance, were still full of the sawdust-tealeaf mixture. The girl was now blackleading the kitchen range, a great brass and cast-iron monster that also heated all the water for the house.

He crossed the room, taking care to step only on the middle parts of the stones, and went out into the scullery. He returned with two yard brooms and the brush Bridget had used. Handing them to his men he told them to sweep out all the cracks, starting at the inside edges of the room and working toward the back door. He, meanwhile, got down on his hands and knees behind them and produced a large magnifying glass, with which he started to examine the cracks minutely.

"Mister Sherlock Sterne!" Victor quipped, "Where's your meerschaum, man? And the deerstalker?"

There were a few nervous laughs. Daisy had not had time to tell them where the bottles had been hidden but, like the inspector, they had concluded it must be there in the kitchen somewhere and that its discovery was now only a matter of time.

Where? Tamsin mouthed the word at Daisy, who responded with a tight little shake of the head.

David realized that, by crowding around the door like this, in such an anxious knot, they were only strengthening Sterne's conviction that he was close to his goal. Agonizing though it would be, he suggested that they should all leave the men to their doomed quest and repair to the lounge.

"For a cup of tea and some fairy cakes!" Tamsin added. "Mrs Pascoe — would that be possible?"

Mrs Pascoe said it would be entirely possible and went to take the simmering kettle off the stove.

The mention of 'fairy cakes' in present circumstances seemed hilarious to all of them.

Sterne gritted his teeth at their laughter and silently promised they'd pay for it the moment he'd found which flagstone to lift. Meanwhile he kept a surreptitious eye upon that maid who was blackleading the range — or pretending to. It was quite clear to him that she was just wasting time over there, watching him like a hawk and, no doubt, planning a diversion of some kind when he got too close to the hidey-hole.

The reward for his covert vigilance came at last — when he arrived at a particularly large stone right underneath the kitchen table. The moment he put his hands to it and discovered that it rocked, he saw the maid look across the room at the cook. He followed her glance and was just in time to see the woman give a terse little nod in reply. When she became aware that the gesture had been observed, she fixed him with a nervous smile and said, "A dish o' tay and a slice o' fuggan, inspector?"

"Thank'ee, ma'am," he replied, "but I'd be more obliged if you'd direct my men as to where to move this table? I'm sure it doesn't usually stand here, for it's the most inconvenient place in the whole kitchen. And you, maid" — he turned to Bridget — "you may go call your mistress to attend. I fancy our search is about to be rewarded."

He rose and dusted his hands. These moments were always sweet, and they quite made up for the daily cold bath of hatred from the rest of mankind.

As soon as they had reached the relative sanctuary of the lounge, and closed the door firmly behind them, everyone turned on Daisy with Tamsin's unvoiced question: *Where was the brandy hiding?*

But she put a finger to her lips and whispered, "It's best I don't tell anyone. You wouldn't believe me, anyway — because I didn't believe it myself until I saw it — and you'd have a job not to look that way to see if it was true."

And that had to serve for an answer until Bridget came with Inspector Sterne's triumphant message. "I'll stay here," Daisy said as they all trooped back to the kitchen. "Just in case."

"Where is there any sign of recent disturbance?" Harriet asked as soon as it became clear that Sterne intended raising one of the flagstones.

"Why, everywhere, ma'am!" The inspector pointed at random about the entire kitchen floor. "Disturbance of evidence!" He stood on the flag and made it wobble. "This one was lifted, I'll dare swear, but all evidence of it was disturbed by the sweeping of sawdust and tealeaves."

David leaned close to Tamsin and murmured in her ear, "I see what you mean about your mother's inability to cope."

She reached out a foot and trod hard on his boot — having forgotten her already bruised toes in all the excitement. She remembered them again now and winced.

One of Sterne's men had meanwhile brought a heavy shovel from the coalshed; another had a raker from the range. The captain nodded and they put their levers to each side of the wobbliest corner.

"Inspector," Mrs Pascoe said. "You'm wrong if you believe there's anything to interest 'ee under there."

He just laughed.

Tamsin's heart was beating so hard she could hear it pounding inside her head. Her hands were starting to shake uncontrollably. Victor slipped an arm about her waist and she felt that he was shivering, too. They were all hardly daring to breathe. Only David seemed above it all. He stood there with folded arms, watching dispassionately; and when he became aware that Tamsin was looking at him, he just winked and returned his gaze to the flagstone, on which all eyes were now fastened.

The levers slipped several times until the third Exciseman took the poker from the range and used it to wedge the flag between each pry. As soon as it was elevated enough for a man to get a grip, all three of them thrust their hands beneath it and lifted it without difficulty.

Everyone craned forward, leaning over the barrier of Sterne's outstretched arms. The cavity beneath the stone contained half-a-dozen bottles of ... ginger pop! They were instantly recognisable by the trapped marble in each bottle's neck.

"I don't believe it!" Sterne roared above the gales of laughter that suddenly filled the kitchen. "Rest that stone aside and pass us one."

It took two of them to 'walk' the stone to where it could be rested against a wall; the third reached into the cavity and withdrew one of the bottles, which he handed to his chief.

"It's some trick," Sterne mumbled. But when he put his thumb to the marble and pressed hard, it dropped from its rubber seat and there was a great eruption of ginger beer, which left his whole arm soused.

Mrs Pascoe passed him a dishcloth, saying, "Told 'ee!"

Tamsin was not alone in feeling almost sorry for the man. He was beaten and he knew it. As he did his best to dry his sleeve he looked about him wildly, " 'Tis here somewhere," he cried. "I know it."

"No you don't, Sterne," David said quietly.

The others stopped laughing and looked at him in surprise.

"You saw me and Harry and Sonny come ashore with lobsters for guest houses up and down Morrab Road — and a dozen for the Queen's — and you were so sure 'twas contraband that you never bothered to look in any of the other pots as were lifted in Gwavas Lake this afternoon."

They both knew that such an inspection would have been impossible — with forty men eager to get 'tucking' among the mullet and the whole of Newlyn depending on them, but it offered the inspector the smallest of fig-leaves, which he had little choice but to accept.

"You!" he cried, throwing the cloth into the sink and walking up to David with a single finger upraised, shaking with fury. He put it right below David's nose and growled, "You needn't think

I've done with you, boy! You may have the contraband put away somewhere — here or back home in Newlyn — but little good will it do you! The fine gentlemen of this district may nurse their thirst a while yet, for I'm your shadow, boy. From this day forth, I'll dog your steps until I catch you with it."

The threat was quite empty, of course. No one doubted that. Yet the man went up in the estimation of all for the dignity it allowed him to recover.

"My keys, if you please, Inspector!" Harriet held out her hand when it looked as if the man were about to depart without handing them over.

For a moment he seemed on the point of flinging them at her but then, perhaps remembering that friends of Sir Napier were present, he passed them over with a sickly smile.

When he had gone, taking his men with him, everyone crowded around Daisy, even though Mrs Pascoe or Bridget could have told them just as well; somehow the honour of revelation belonged to her.

She led them back to the kitchen and gave Bridget a nod. The maid opened a drawer, took out a small spanner, and went across to the range.

David's heart fell. "You never cooked it?" he cried.

For reply, Bridget undid the four nuts that secured a plate to one side of the range — the portion she had been blackleading while Sterne led himself up the garden path. The plate covered that part of the range where a buffer tank stored the hot water needed in the kitchen before passing on any excess to the tanks in the hot press upstairs.

But the bottles were not there, either — or not exactly. Daisy stood aside and gestured at a further cast-iron plate, deep within the cavity. It was beside the hot tank and in the wall of the cavity that was farthest from the range. "Mrs Pascoe can explain it best," she said.

The cook went over and patted the kitchen wall beside the open cavity. "There's an old bake-oven in there," she said. "The old range, the one as was there when they built the house, had an iron flue as went through 'n." She took off her pinafore and draped it over the hot-water tank. Then, kneeling down she slipped an arm inside. "And if you slide this here old plate back

… so! You can …" She grinned and pulled her arm out, clutching one of the brandy bottles, which she flourished so vigorously that David rushed forward to rescue it.

There was a loud, peremptory knock at the back door. Everyone stopped laughing and looked at the open hole in panic. With amazing speed, Mrs Pascoe popped the dismantled plate into the oven while Bridget placed the clothes-horse where it covered the open hole. David hid the bottle under his coat with a dexterity born of long practice. Daisy meanwhile opened the door.

It was Sergeant Hocken.

All he did was lick his lips and clear his throat.

David poked his head out of the door and glanced all about. Hocken smiled at him wearily, as if to say, 'D'you think I'd be standing here if there was any danger of being observed?'

David slipped him the bottle and he disappeared — and it all happened so fast that the others hardly believed their eyes.

"Well!" Cicely Thorne exclaimed. "Do you know — until this moment I've been feeling like the most wretched of criminals!"

Part Three

Maiden voyage

23 "We may all laugh about it now," Victor said the following day, "but I don't mind admitting my heart was in my mouth more than once."

He repeated the sentiment in different forms many times over the next few days. Tamsin, who could not disagree, nonetheless felt she had to stand up for David, who was, of course, the real, if unspecified, target of Victor's comments. "It was my fault — in a way," she would say (hoping the admission would never get back to David). "I did more or less suggest our house as a temporary hiding place."

She was more interested in the slight but unmistakable changes the episode had brought about among all who lived or worked at the Morrab. It would be too much to say that such a varied collection of people, brought together by chance and soon to disperse again, had been welded into a group of blood-brothers and -sisters, but there was a camaraderie, an informality that would not otherwise have existed. There were smiles when they passed one another on staircases where, before, there would have been formal nods and mumblings that might or might not have been actual words. Erstwhile 'Good-mornings' and grave 'Nice days' were replaced by cheery 'Hallos' and genuine inquiries after each other's health and untroubled sleep.

It caught on among the other holiday guests, too, even though all they were told of the incident was that the Excisemen had somehow got hold of the wrong end of the stick. They, too, caught the camaraderie infection. It was as if they had always wanted the chance to let their public faces show more of the private smile. Not too much, of course. The young man from Yorkshire who told another guest that he'd seen her 'hobnobbing' with one of the seafront photographers that morning was soon made to understand that such casual laxity of speech was not welcome — and it remained unwelcome even after the lady in question had had the actual meaning of the word explained to her. But, such unfortunate episodes aside, most of them said, as they paid their bills and left, that the Morrab Guest House was a real home-from-home.

Sterne's threat to dog David's shadow to the gates of Hell and back proved as empty as everyone had suspected it to be at the time he made it. Four skilled trackers, devoting their every waking hour to the job, could have kept one man under constant surveillance, given a large dose of luck. But what of his friends? And of all those people, spread throughout West Penwith, who had a financial or alcoholic interest in his success?

By the end of that second week in July every bottle had found a buyer. And David was working round the clock as a carpenter, building a sub-deck in the bowels of the *Merlyn* to take the engine housing. Meanwhile his cousin Harry was reaming out a precise hole through the sternpost to take the stuffing gland for the propshaft. They were so eager to try her out they were even discussing ways of beaching her round in some remote cove beyond Mousehole and continuing to fit her during the sabbath, though they both knew it was the dreamiest of pipedreams.

Meanwhile Victor, having no rival, was more and more in Tamsin's company during her free afternoon hours. Strolling up and down the Esplanade soon palled. They could not swim together because mixed bathing over the age of thirteen was not permitted on the town's beaches; the women had the bathing machines at the western end of the Esplanade while the men had the secluded cove between Battery Rocks and Chimney Rocks beyond the extreme eastern end of the beach. The curious thing about such rules was that any female who suffered from ignorance or felt the slightest curiosity about a man's anatomy could stroll along the unpatrolled shingle between Larrigan Rocks and Newlyn's North Pier, where gangs of beardless youths sported in the waves as naked as the day they were born — and there was no lady warden from the Watch Committee to sting their bottoms with her cane.

Victor soon took to hiring a gig and, with Charlotte for chaperon, they would drive out into the countryside, ostensibly to have their mind improved by visiting yet more of the dozens of Iron Age sites for which the Land's End peninsula is famous. Actually, Charlotte was their chaperon for the first outing only. It began with a rather dull drive to a chapel near Hea, where John Wesley once preached. Then on to just beyond Madron, where a half-mile walk brought them to a ruined chapel with a dried-up baptising well. Then to Lanyon Quoit — three massive upright slabs and a capstone, which, their guidebook said, had once been high enough for a horseman to ride beneath it. Maybe too many horsemen did just that because it fell in 1815 and when they rebuilt it they cut the uprights down to just over five feet high. Then to a field with three standing stones, about four foot high, one with a two-foot hole carved in it. Significance not merely unknown but entirely unguessable. The book said that if you shook hands on a bargain through the hole and then broke your word, the piskeys would get you; that must have worried a lot of people. Then along an old packhorse trail, across some open moorland, to the stone circle called Nine Maidens. Here the book spoke of twenty-two original stones but Victor and the girls could find only six standing and five toppled, the largest being just over seven foot long — "So where the Nine comes from is a mystery," Charlotte remarked. "Or the twenty-two."

Victor, who had suggested this outing and who therefore had done some preliminary reading, explained that nine was probably a magical number, since pagan practices had survived hereabout long after the coming of Christianity. The Christians had retaliated by spreading the tale that nine maidens had gone a-dancing on the sabbath and, for their sin, had been turned to stone by an early Cornish saint. The remaining two (or thirteen, if the book was right) were fiddlers, harpists, and spectators.

"We've looked at an awful lot of stones today," Tamsin said plaintively. "Are there many more to go?"

"Well …" He was reluctant to abandon what had seemed a splendid plan for an afternoon's jaunt. "We just walked straight past the remains of Ding Dong Mine, where they began digging for tin before Roman times …" he offered.

There were no takers.

"I'll go back to the gig and start making the tea," Charlotte offered, knowing well that such was the chaperon's role. "You two could hunt for more stones or … well, it'll be ready in about ten minutes, anyway."

Tamsin, unwilling to squander even ten seconds on coyness, ran to the lee of the nearest large stone and stood where none but choughs and hares could spy on them.

"Feeling cold?" Victor asked, thinking he'd tease her a little.

Her face soon disabused him of any such notion. He changed tack at once. "I thought this moment would nevermmm ..."

She had grabbed him by the sleeves and pulled him to her. Ever since he had kissed her on the beach that day, her heart had quickened and her lips had tingled as the memory of it returned to her, which was often. Now she was trembling all over and feeling decidedly weak at the knees; without the support of the stone she was sure she'd fall to the ground.

But would that be so awful, she wondered, half inclined to let it happen.

In the moment before their lips met once again, she opened her eyes wide and stared up into his. To her surprise he was gazing at her with a somewhat puzzled expression, as if he had not expected her to be so eager. But it didn't stop her. He could have looked at her with any expression he liked, or none at all, as long as he did not deny her the unbelievably sweet pressure of his lips and the crush of his arms about her and the dangerously exciting feel of his body straining against hers.

The pleasure was so exquisite it was almost beyond bearing. She seemed to have fallen deep into some dark void of passion — a well without walls — where everyday things and events, though still vaguely there around her, had become remote and hardly real. Far away she could both hear and feel that their breathing was shattered by the pounding of their hearts; indeed, several times when she tried to inhale, the turmoil within allowed no more than the briefest gasp, which was as likely to empty her lungs as fill them; vaguely she was aware that if she did not draw proper breath soon she would pass right out — but even that did not seem to matter. She was close to passing out from sheer ecstasy, anyway.

At last it was he who broke for breath. Yet, even as her breast snatched gratefully at the air, her lips were once again reaching for his, seeking more and yet more of that magical touch. "Oh, Victor!" she whispered desperately.

"Oh, Tamsin!" he moaned as he took her head between his hands, holding it like some priceless treasure as he closed the space between their mouths. Once again they strained to satisfy a hunger that seemed beyond all satisfying.

His fingernails began a gentle raking of her scalp, behind her ears and back around her neck, sending thrills and shivers through every part of her. Her fingers slipped up into his hair and did the same for him.

After that one brief kiss on the beach, she had thought that kissing alone must surely be the very pinnacle of courtship's joys; but this was as far beyond it as that had been beyond the sort of giggly, blushful kissing games she had experienced at adolescent birthday parties. What more could there be?

Strange things were happening in her stomach. It seemed to be hollowing out inside her. Or falling away, even deeper, into that same timeless void where the rest of her was floating in his arms. Or spinning slowly over and over. And, though she had never experienced such a sensation before, she knew at once what it must be — especially when it came all mixed up in the turmoil of those other delicious feelings: Love!

This was what love felt like. At last she knew it. This was that near-madness which drove poets to despair in their attempts to capture the precise nature of its … its … its *wonderfulnesses*. There — she was caught in the toils of that same creative inadequacy now! Why bother? Why try to speak the ineffable? Why not simply kiss and kiss and kiss her way across his cheek to the cavern of his ear and just whisper it: "Oh Victor, I do love you so!"

And, "Oh Tamsin!" he murmured into hers in return. "Oh Tamsin, Tamsin, Tamsin!"

Sweet though it was to hear her name murmnured so tenderly and across such an intimate distance, it had been sweeter still to hear those same three magic words from him.

"I love you and I love you and I love you …" she gasped, kissing the whorls of his ear and biting his lobe gently between the frantic outpouring of her words.

"I adore you, too," he whispered. "I worship every little stray hair of your head."

It was delightful to hear it, even when he left off his caresses for a moment to pull one or two of those worshipful strands out of his mouth; but it still wasn't the answer she desired to hear above all others from his lips. She wanted someone in this world to *love* her. And more than anyone else she wanted it to be

Victor — not just to love her as she now knew she loved him but to say so in what ought, surely, to be the three simplest words in all the world.

"The very thought of you when we're apart drives me to distraction," he said.

He tried to slip his hands down her back. She arched herself a little away from the stone and soon his fingernails were raking up and down her spine, bringing new and unexpected pleasures. He was obviously tiring of standing in the one position for he now moved his feet to a new position, to her right; then, finding that less of a relief than he expected, he moved them back again.

The resulting movement of his body against hers was yet another novel and delightful sensation.

Then, puzzlingly, he moved them back once more to the new position, only to return them to the former one yet again. When he repeated it twice more she realized he was not actually moving his feet at all — just the ... well, the middle portion of his ... of himself. Alarm bells began to ring — faint but clear. The pleasure it gave her put all the others into the shade; they had been located in lips, in fingers, cheeks, hair, neck, or spine — wherever the caress was also set; but this pleasure was everywhere within her, from the tingles in her scalp to the flutters in her feet. It threatened to take control of every nerve and fibre of her body, leaving her powerless in its grip. She had the first intimation that it was already starting to happen. Then, as someone standing at the edge of a crumbling scree and feeling it begin to slip and slide away beneath her will instinctively leap for the security of solid ground, so Tamsin now pushed him from her, held him at arm's length, and pleaded, "No! Please — no?"

His eyes could not hold her gaze. He hung his head and blushed. "I'm sorry," he murmured, taking her hands in his but still not looking at her. "Forgive me."

"No!" she cried, caausing him at last to look at her — in surprise. "I mean, it's not something to forgive. I'm just thankful you are a gentleman, Victor."

The words puzzled him but he did not ask her to explain them. "And I'm just thankful that you are *you,* Tamsin. Utterly unique. I've never known a girl like you and I'm sure I'll never meet another."

"You're embarrassing me now." She held out her hand and, when he linked his fingers with hers, turned and tugged him toward the dead chimney of Ding Dong. "Charlotte will be regretting her ten minutes of generosity, I fear."

On their way back to the gig he said, "Thinking back to last week — that Excise raid, and what a close-run thing it was ..."

"Victor ..." she began.

"It makes one realize how easy it is at times to stumble into criminality. What a narrow ..."

"I really think we've exhausted that topic, darling."

"Well, I was only going to say what a narrow dividing line it is. It also made me realize that poor people live close to that line all the time, day in day out. No wonder more of them end up in prison than people of our sort. I suppose one mustn't be too hard on young David Peters — for that reason. It's a timely warning to us, too, to stay well clear. That's all."

She said, "I've never been kissed before, you know — not like that. Are you shocked?"

"No!" He laughed in protest — and wondered if she'd listened to a single word.

"I mean — you don't think I'm just some silly *ingénue?*"

"Heavens, Tamsin! What is it you ..."

"What *do* you think of me, then?"

"I've told you — you're the most wonderful ..."

"Imagine you're in your club ... oh no, gentlemen don't discuss ladies in their clubs, do they. Or do they?"

"We try our best not to."

"Well then, imagine I'm a chum of yours and we're out here on a walking tour and you're trying to describe me to him, or what I mean to you — what do you say?"

"I say I've met this rather wonderful young girl. And then he sniggers and says, 'Oh yes?' because we chaps like to be manly about these things, don't-ye-know. And soft emotions tend to make us try to plait our toes. So he starts asking facetious and mildly indelicate questions. And I go all stiff and pompous and say, 'If you insist on discussing her in such terms, I would prefer not to speak at all.' And he says, 'Look! Isn't that a bog asphodel?' and for the rest of the afternoon we both indulge our botanical ignorance with enormous relief."

Behind his supercilious tone she detected something forlorn, a dirge for the prisoner trapped inside the cage of manly denial. She was still so emotionally overwrought that the perception brought a lump of pity to her throat. "Poor men!" she said, reaching up and brushing his cheek with her fingertips.

He caught it and carried it to his lips. "Oh, Tamsin," he said, kissing it fervently in the palm.

"Yes?"

"Nothing. Everything! Every moment alone with you is such joy, yet I fear it for it makes every minute apart such a torture."

"I was beginning to get worried," Charlotte called out from a hundred yards away.

Victor gave a start and tried to drop Tamsin's hand, but she held on tight to his and swung it demonstratively high as they walked, as children do when going along in crocodiles.

"Worried about what?" Victor asked his sister when they were nearer.

"That you might have been turned to stone, too, of course," she replied.

"Of all possible fates," he murmured to Tamsin, "that is the least likely, don't you think?"

She agreed; but her innermost thought at that moment — the one stirring in her heart-of-hearts — was that she was still pining to hear him say those three beautiful little words.

24 Despite the nonchalance that both Tamsin and Victor showed on their return to the gig, Charlotte sensed that more had passed between them than a bit of mild spooning behind one of those stones. She could not put it into so many words (and even if she could, she would probably not have wished to do so, anyway) but she insisted that the next time they went out on one of these afternoon jaunts, *she* should have a companion, too. Responsibility shared was responsibility halved. Obviously it could not be a man, for that sort of arrangement was considered worse than having no chaperon at all. Daisy was the obvious choice — indeed, the only one in their present circumstances, since the nearest friend of her own sort was over a hundred miles away.

Before that next outing took place, however, Harriet Harte made a surprise concession to her daughter's long-held wishes. Not that she put it quite like that. Indeed, to hear her talk, you'd have thought Tamsin had never spoken a word on the subject in all her life.

"I've had such an interesting conversation with young Mister Trotter," she said at dinner one evening. "While you were off counting stones the other afternoon, he invited me to tea at the Queen's. And no sooner had we sat down than that charming Mister Coverley joined us. Mister Trotter really is an extremely amiable man, too, mind. He'll make some lucky young gel an excellent husband one day — and so, I'm sure, will Mister Coverley, though, naturally, he is out of the running for you as long as Victor Thorne is around."

"Mama, dear!" Tamsin exclaimed. "What *are* you talking about? Is Mister Coverley now our wet-weather target, so to speak? Here you distract me with alternative quarry while I am dutifully shooting my arrows to pierce Victor Thorne through the heart — as directed by you!"

Charlotte was not alone in believing that a responsibility shared was thereby halved.

"Never mind all that!" Harriet waved the words away as if they were midges on the wing. "This is important. It is about the way we manage our ... oh, what was the word he used? Resources! Yes — how we manage our resources here at the guest house."

Tamsin was about to remind her that 'nice people like you and me' did not discuss money matters at the luncheon table either, but some instinct warned her that this was no time for such petty points-scoring. If her mother was about to break her strictest rule, then something important must be afoot. "Anything Mister Coverley might say on that subject would be well worth considering," she replied diplomatically.

"Just so, dear. He pointed out that a manufacturer who invested tens of thousands of pounds in factory machinery and then used it for only four hours a day would be wasting the other eighteen — which is a line of argument anyone of modest intellect can follow, I think."

"Especially if you said, 'the other *twenty*'."

"Yes, dear. But I was amazed when he went on to say that investment in a large hôtel or even a small guest house is no different in principle. The less use one makes of *any* investment, the more expensive it becomes when one does use it. I must confess that such a subtle argument had never even crossed my mind. And — correct me if I'm wrong — but I don't think it has occured to you, either?"

Tamsin bit her tongue rather than follow the invitation to correct her; the last thing she wanted was to get into an I-said-you-said sort of exchange. "It sounds all too obvious when one puts it like that," she replied. She could have added that she had, indeed, put it *exactly* like that in the car on the way home from that swim at Land's End; but bless Messrs Coverley and Trotter for not saying as much!

"So," Harriet continued, "we need to decide if we intend to remain open all year round. We haven't experienced a complete winter down here yet, but it cannot be so very different from what we had in Plymouth."

"We were here in January — and that was fairly mild, though stormy. Perhaps we should look into the cost of advertising in the medical and nursing journals? We should have had a word with Doctor Carlton, you know — before they left for home this morning. We could have sounded him out on the possibility."

"Sounded him out, dear?" Her mother frowned at the expression. "What possibility?"

"Convalescents," said Tamsin, who had already churned over every conceivable winter use of the Morrab and its *resources,* including putting up some of the artistes from Galligano's Circus, which had its winter quarters not far from Penzance. "People who are advised by their doctors to take a long holiday abroad, but who cannot face a Channel crossing in winter, nor the thought of all that greasy, garlicky foreign food which awaits their palates on the other side. They'd put up with a bit of rain and a few gales for the sake of our fresh sea air and mild temperatures. And Mrs Pascoe is such an excellent cook, we could even offer them their own simple diets — individual diets, I mean, as long as they really were simple. Steamed fish, coddled eggs, spinach ... that sort of thing. The point is — I don't think we could keep open through the winter if we just went in for holiday people. There aren't enough of them — and those who do come down here usually go in for hearty walking holidays from one guest house or inn to the next. We don't want to be laundering our sheets every day. But convalescents who stay three months would suit us very well."

Harriet was overwhelmed at the speed with which Tamsin had taken up *her* idea. But the girl had not nearly finished. "What's the name of that lady opposite — with the two adorbale children? Didn't someone say she used to be a nurse?"

"Mrs Bosinney — Frances Bosinney. Why?"

Tamsin had known the name very well but she wanted her mother to be the one to say it first, so that later she might imagine the whole idea had been hers, too. "She had to give up nursing when she got married, of course, but I'll bet she misses it. In which case, she might be quite agreeable to put on starched cuffs and a wimple again for a couple of hours a day, just to take care of the medical needs of convalescents. A bit of pin-money for her. And it would be a wonderful addition to our advertisement: 'A State Registered Nurse is a member of our daily staff and is experienced in all nursing requirements' — something vague but impressive like that."

"Dear me, Tamsin!" her mother sighed. "I believe that if I were to set paper and pencil before you now, you could write out all the daily rosters without even stopping to think."

"The thinking is already done, Mama. But listen — decisions on closing or staying open for the winter are a long way ahead. Also, we don't know how long your precious Countess de Ath will be staying. Until her creditors give up, I suspect. But *meanwhile*" — she raised her voice over her mother's protests — "there are other ways in which we could ... how would your factory owner put it? — make the most economical use of our existing resources."

"Name one!" her mother challenged, as if she did not believe Tamsin could.

"The resources in question comprise the guests' dining room, the kitchen, and, above all, dear Mrs Pascoe. Also ..." She eyed her mother cautiously here. "Let us not forget a certain fisherman over in Newlyn who now owes us a prodigious favour!"

"Eh?"

"Fish, Mama! Direct from ocean to table — and of prime quality, too. The glorious thing about such fish is that one does not need to mess it around in the Continental fashion with a lot of fancy sauces and things — whose real purpose, as any true Englishman knows, is to disguise the fact that they're hundreds of miles from the nearest fish quay. Straight, clean cooking with a few herbs and a simple white sauce is all it will require. And I know Mrs Pascoe will welcome the chance to make a few extra pounds before the season ends — even if we do stay open as a convalescent home in the coming winter."

"Pounds?" The word frightened Harriet.

"Look! The dining room can seat twenty in comfort. We can charge three shillings and sixpence for a *table d'hôte* with a limited choice … four and six with a good hock or chablis. If each seat were occupied twice over, we could be taking nine pounds a night — gross. Our outlay would be about two guineas. So our maximum profit will be the best part of seven pounds. And even if we have only twenty diners" — she avoided words like 'customer' out of deference to her mother's sensibilities — "we should still clear almost three pounds a night — which is the profit we presently make on six paying guests in an entire week."

Harriet sat down heavily. "Good heavens!" she exclaimed. "Goodness gracious me!"

"What now?"

"The speed with which you work these things out, dear! Scarcely have I broached the merest outlines of my idea and here you come with chapter and verse on every tiny detail! How do you do it? It was your father's gift, too, mind you — which is both comforting and frightening, remembering how it brought us down in the end!"

Tamsin walked past her to the window. Their conversation had suddenly entered tiger country. She must stalk her mother cautiously now or it would all come to nothing. "Forwarned is forearmed," she murmured, scratching idly at a tiny streak of dried paint beside one of the glazing bars.

"What does that mean?"

"Papa's gift for turning one guinea into two worked miracles when he confined the investment within the bounds of the expected return …"

"And what does *that* mean," her mother repeated herself more emphatically.

"Well, take this idea of ours for opening a fish restaurant. Even if only ten diners turn up, our investment would drop to one guinea or less — because we'd serve less fish, of course. And that would still be covered, just, by the profit on ten dinners. We start losing only if fewer then ten people turn up — which I'm sure will happen on one or two nights, but they will be more than balanced by nights when we'll have to turn people away." She crossed her fingers surreptitiously as she spoke those words. "In short, the investment is well within the bounds of the expected return. Papa's investments only began to fail when he forgot that golden rule — or so Mister Sampson told me."

"He had no right to say such things to you!" she exclaimed crossly. "A well brought up young lady has no need to know ..." She faltered, realizing where her unthinkingly conventional response was leading. In the same moment she also realized she had just conceded Tamsin's main argument by chasing after such an irrelevance.

Somewhat to her relief they were interrupted at that moment by a tap at the door. "Who is it?" she called out.

"Only me." Charlotte stuck her head into the room. "I do hope I'm not intruding?"

"Not at all. Do come in."

"Such excitement!" the girl said as Tamsin left the window and came to join them. "Mama has persuaded Victor to be more pleasant to Mister Trotter and, as a result, we are invited on a picnic to the Lizard this afternoon — in Mister Coverley's Rolling-Royce. All five of us." She nodded at Tamsin to show she was included. "And we're to bring our bathing suits!"

"Oh, Mama!" Tamsin turned delightedly to her mother.

But she was not giving leave just yet. "And did your mother not insist on taking a maidservant along with you?" she asked.

Charlotte shrugged awkwardly; she might well have responded by asking, 'What maidservant?'

"Well, I shall certainly insist upon it," Harriet continued. "My daughter may only join you if Miss Dobbs is also included. I realize it will make for some awkward seating arrangements in the car but that is my final word."

25 The long spell of settled sunshine looked as if it might be drawing to a close. When the car had wound its way uphill through the contortions of Marazion's main street and reached the crest, they could see how the sky over the Lizard faded to a hazy colour that might have been washed-out blue or even pale mauve, *nd it would have taken more than an amateur painter to have captured the merest suggestion of mighty cumulus towers floating within it. Out to sea it was still a cloudless azure overhead, but wherever the sluggish onshore breeze hit the coast it tended to form fluffy white cloudlets that wandered inland like flocks of drugged sheep. Whenever Standish halted to let them admire the view, the breeze did little or nothing to alleviate the oppressive humidity that had been building up all that day. They were glad of the motion of the car when they resumed their erratic progress toward the Lizard, which was still some twenty miles away — though only thirteen or so as a crow might fly directly across Mount's Bay.

"What does Lizard mean?" Charlotte asked the world in general. "Not that the place is crawling with the beastly little things, I hope."

Standish replied, "It's from *lis,* meaning 'enclosure' and *ard,* meaning 'high-up' — there must have been an enclosed settlement on one of the cliffs there at some time."

"Does every place name actually mean something?" Tamsin asked. "What's Marazion, for instance?"

Victor got in before Standish this time. "It must be related to Market Jew Street in Penzance," he said.

It annoyed her that he seemed to think that any general remark of hers needed funneling through him. Even the fact that she loved him to distraction did not give him the right to behave like that, she felt.

"How so?" Standish asked.

"Well ..." He explained it almost as one would to a child. *"Mara* must be 'market' and *zion* is quite obviously Jewish."

Standish offered an alternative: "The scholars claim that Market Jew is from *marghas yow* or 'market on Thursdays' —

which is what the old town charter allowed. Others say it's from *marghas byghan,* meaning 'little market'; still others hold it's from *marghas iou,* which translates as 'Joe's market' — take your pick." He glanced over his shoulder at Tamsin, who was sitting in the back between Charlotte and Daisy. "Four choices! Is that enough? One could think up a few more, I'm sure."

"Four is plenty!" she replied with feeling.

He continued, unabashed. "The advantage of a dead language, you see, is that nobody can prove that anyone else is wrong. This current attempt to revive Old Cornish is *carte blanche* for every crackpot scholar in the county. But let's not complain. While they're footling away with their glossaries they can't be out and about, doing actual harm to anyone."

Tamsin had no idea whether his etymologies for Marazion had been genuine or not; but the ease with which he produced them suggested a much greater familiarity with the Cornish revival than he seemed willing to admit. But why did he feel the need to mock it like that? Could it be that he was a far more serious person than he liked to pretend and so — as naval people put it — he 'made smoke' to disguise the fact?

He began to interest her more than ever. In the beginning, Daisy's confident assertion that he was a cold fish — with which she had, sometimes, to agree — made Standish more interesting, in the way that all forbidden, or unattainable, fruit has its own special fascination. Now, however, she was starting to realize that, if what Daisy said was true, then such a man would make an ideal surrogate brother of the kind she had hoped to find in David Peters. If Standish truly was incapable of developing a romantic interest in her as a woman — and yet was still interested in her as a person (which he showed every sign of being) ... well! He was ready-made for the part.

He stopped again at St Breaca's, the parish church of Breage, to show them some recently discovered frescoes, painted (quite obviously) in medieval times but covered over with limewash during the Civil War, to hide them from the Puritan iconoclasts, who went about England slighting all painted or graven images. There were a couple of bishops, or possibly saints, and a huge, twice-life-size painting of St. Christopher carrying a diminutive Christ on his shoulder.

They all thought Standish was going to make some further mock — and, indeed, perhaps he did. But if so, it was against them. For, as they stood there, ready to laugh and patronize these primitive daubs, he launched into paeans of praise for their vigour and strength. The boldness of the line ... the subtle strength of the colour ... the simple, direct expression of theme ... one would have thought that Michelangelo, Raphael, and Leonardo had all visited this little parish in some earlier, joint reincarnation and that God himself, recognizing creative competition when he saw it, had divided and diluted that single unknown artist into those three giants for their next cycle of life on earth.

"Every artist in England," Standish said, "should be brought here in fetters and locked inside this church on bread and water until he or she can see what they've been missing in their own feeble efforts."

On their way back to the car, Victor murmured to Tamsin, "If he starts foaming at the mouth, just get behind me, eh!"

"I think he makes a lot of sense," she replied.

His lips compressed to a thin, bloodless line and he stared rigidly ahead. How to make her understand that girls who did not agree with him soon fell into disfavour? If it wasn't for keeping his mother sweet, he'd start disentangling himself now.

She saw she had upset him and, fearing that reconciliations would eat up precious kissing time later, gave his arm a squeeze and said, "Sorry."

He smiled at her — not *too* affably, in case she should believe it was always going to be so easy — and said, "That's better."

She risked a tiny whisper: "I love you!"

"Me, too," he replied.

At the bottom of Breage Hill, where they could have gone directly onward to the top of Sithney Common Hill and so down into Helston, they turned instead toward the picturesque little fishing village of Porthleven. There they parked the car on the quay — well away from the coalyard, where a coal tramp was being unloaded, making enough dust to empty every washing line in sight — and strolled out to the end of the long stone jetty, which protected the harbour from the worst of any storm. Standish and Victor both brought their binoculars along, for the seabird life on the cliffs to the west of the harbour mouth was famous — being sustained by one of the busiest fishing quays in the entire bay.

"When the fleet returns," Standish said, training his glasses on the cliffs, "the sky is black with gulls of every kind."

Tamsin was watching Victor at the time. He was scanning the sea through his glasses; it seemed that, whatever Standish was doing, he would have to do something else. She was just about to make some quiet remark, to show him how petty she thought he was being, when she saw him give a little start and then peer intently, still looking directly out to sea.

Eventually he became aware that she was watching him. At once he offered her the glasses, saying "Porpoises." But he pointed well to the west of the point on which his own gaze had been trained. "Leaping like athletes."

She searched the sea where he had indicated but, finding nothing, swivelled round to look at the cliff instead. "Golly!" she exclaimed. "If one had a sardine, one could pop it right down their throats!"

She passed the glasses on to Daisy, since Standish had already passed his to Charlotte. Later, when Charlotte had finished looking, he offered them to Tamsin, saying, "See if they look as big with these."

"Every bit," she said after focusing. "Let's see if we can spot those porpoises!"

And now she swung back to where Victor had really been looking when he gave that little start — and almost at once she discovered why. For there, less than a mile out in the bay, was the *Merlyn,* with David Peters at the tiller and his cousin Harry at his side. The sails were up but were flapping in such a way that she could not believe they were urging the boat forward at such speed. So they must have fitted the new engine already — in which case, this outing was part of their trials. They were heading eastward, away from Newlyn.

A sudden, intense pang of disappointment made her realize how much she had wanted to be with him — with *them,* rather — on that great day. If only she'd realized how quickly they'd manage it, she'd have kept in better touch.

"Found them yet?" Victor asked anxiously.

"No," she replied calmly, passing the glasses back to Standish. She was determined not to show her disappointment to any of them. "Which way were they going? Toward Penzance?"

"That's right," he answered.

They stopped at the bottom of Helston to fill up with ethyl and to buy a couple of spare cans. The blacksmith was proud of his new pump, which had two large glass 'optics,' each of which held one gallon. He cranked the pump to fill the left-hand one with the pale, straw-coloured fuel, then flipped a valve to let it empty into the car's tank by gravity — during which time he continued to crank the pump to fill the right hand optic. It drained out so quickly that the flow of ethyl into the car tank was almost continuous.

"You can see you'm getting the full gallon, boss, and I'm not obliged to store a couple o' hundred gallon cans so close to the forge, see?"

He spoke to Reg, for Standish had taken Tamsin a little way back down the hill to point out the town's electricity works. "See that?" he said. "That was opened seven years ago by a remarkable woman — someone you ought to meet, I think. I'll try to arrange it, if you like."

"A woman?" Tamsin felt a little surge of excitement.

"Jessica Trelawney — Mrs Cornwallis Trelawney, that is — though back in those days she was Miss Jessica Kernow and barely twenty-one years of age, too. Indeed!" he added, seeing her eyes go wide. "A young woman of around your age did that — and in the teeth of local prejudice and her father's direct opposition. First they laughed at her, then, too late, they realized their mistake and tried to organize their own scheme to rival hers, but she licked the lot of them."

"Why are you telling me this, Mister Coverley?" she asked. "No, I mean why are you telling *me* this?"

"Because you're like a jumping squib in a barrel, Tamsin. D'you think we can dispense with the formalities, by the way? I'm Standish. And I think Mrs Trelawney could be the one to help you take the lid off your barrel and jump right out."

"Well, Standish, you flatter me much too much, I think. But I should certainly like to meet someone who can achieve anything half as grand as that!"

They returned to the blacksmith, where Standish paid for the ethyl and then started the car by running her off backwards, down the hill.

"What was the attraction?" Victor asked.

"The electrical generating station," she told him — not that he believed her.

As they left the town behind them, purring over Culdrose Downs, Standish said, "I've just realized that I'm driving through a completely different landscape from the rest of you. What you see is a smiling, fertile countryside complete with the customary farms and grand or grand*ish* houses. But I know that the man who farms there" — he pointed out one of the farms — "was the childhood sweetheart of the woman who lives in that house back there — with her husband and half-dozen children, I hasten to add. And that that same husband once erred and strayed like a lost sheep with a young widow who lived in that house there and who, in turn, was the wife's closest friend."

"I say, old chap," Victor protested. "D'you think this story is entirely suitable for ladies' ears?"

"Let's ask the ladies themselves, *old chap.*" Standish responded easily. "What's the vote?"

"Yes!" the three ladies chorused gleefully.

Victor said to Tamsin, "Well, I don't much care for *you* to hear such things, my dear."

"Now that *is* interesting," Standish said. "What does your solicitude imply, old chap?"

"I should have thought it quite obvious," Victor replied.

"On the face of it, yes. But look below the surface and nothing is clear. You obviously do not wish Tamsin to hear how husbands and wives and ex-sweethearts behave in real life. Yet ..."

"How *some* husbands and wives and ex-sweethearts behave — and very few, I should think."

"My dear old chap — you're talking to one who owns an hôtel, and at the posh end of the market, too. One week behind its genteel façade and you'd have to concede I'm talking about many if not *most* husbands, wives, and ex-sweethearts."

"What happened?" Tamsin cut across this sterile debate. "The farmer who was her childhood sweetheart — did he run off with her in the end?"

Standish laughed. "That would have been a true romance, wouldn't it! They would have lived in exile in France and the author would have made sure she soon died of consumption and he'd have gone off and become a lay missionary, teaching farming to the fuzzy-wuzzies. But no, alas. This is real life. He ended up marrying his housekeeper — a very pretty and determined young woman who had her sights on him from the moment they met. The widow married someone else — I don't remember who. And the husband and wife are reconciled and happy enough, I gather. It was just a storm that passed them by, you see. But that's *my* view of this landscape. Has it changed for you, too?"

They all agreed that it had.

All except Victor, who said, "There are *some* sorts of behaviour in real life that I should not like *anyone* to hear of."

"I quite agree, old boy," Standish drawled. "So let's all agree not to talk about them, eh!"

26 They did not actually reach Lizard Point that day — the southernmost cape on the British mainland. Standish said he had never swum there and could not recall if any of the nearby coves were even accessible, much less suitable. He did, however, know that Kynance Cove, a couple of miles short of it on the Mount's Bay shore, offered excellent possibilities at low tide, including a sandy beach and several caves, in any of which they could change in perfect seclusion. Also, many of the rocks had huge veins of pure serpentine and steatite, whose colours glowed quite magically, especially when wet. And to crown it all, there were two cottages where delicious cream teas could be obtained for very little money.

They parked on the verge at the beginning of a track that led half a mile, past the remains of yet another ancient settlement, to the edge of the cliff. The view from there was easily the most spectacular that Tamsin had seen since her arrival in Cornwall six months ago.

"*I* know why it's called the Lizard," she said. "See? Those rocks are just like a huge dragon's tail going out to sea. Which means we're standing on its body. Dragons are sort-of lizards, aren't they?"

"It's the most convincing explanation I've yet heard," Standish agreed solemnly. Then, in a different tone, "Oh dear! I see two people have already beaten us down to the sands. Cornwall is getting *so* crowded."

"Blame those hôteliers and guest-house keepers," Reg told him. "They make the place sound so attractive."

"Yes," Victor added. "And by the time the poor gullibles get here and discover the truth, they realize they're so far from home they might as well stay!"

The others conspired to take this as a joke and so, laughing, they wended their way down the path to the cove; around the half-way mark they reached a position where Rill Point, the headland to the northwest of Kynance, became visible — and, of course, all that part of Mount's Bay beyond it. And there, not quite a mile away, Tamsin once again spied the *Merlin* — she was sure it was the *Merlin* — apparently putting about and heading for home once more.

It was all she could do not to scream out at the top of her voice, and jump up and down, and wave, and do anything else she could think of to attract their attention — though nothing would actually have carried over so great a distance. Then she saw it put about again; and, a short while later, yet again. She realized then that they were conducting some sort of trial that involved going in tight circles and zigzags.

The others had continued on down to the beach, all except Victor, who said, "Did you tell him about this trip?"

She looked at him, then at the *Merlin,* then back at him. If ever there was a single moment when she decided to return to her original notion — that Victor Thorne was *just* a young man for kissing, in the same way that David Peters was *just* for serious and intimate conversation — that was it. "I can understand *why* you ask the question, Victor — though I must also say that I don't find it very admirable — but I can't for the life of me see *how* you can ask it. Just think — if you're any longer capable of it. *How* could I have told him? And *how* could I have guessed we'd be here at Kynance Cove, when it's clear that Standish himself only stopped here on a whim."

"I don't believe you should talk to me like that," he replied stiffly. "I am, after all, a paying guest of yours. Are you equally offensive to ..."

"Good!" she shouted as she turned to go. "If that's all you wish me to be, you'll soon discover I can play the part to ..."

"Oh, Tamsin!" He reached out and grabbed her hand. While she struggled to free it, he continued: "Darling! I'm so sorry! I didn't mean it, honestly. I don't know why I said it. Well, I do, actually. You've got me in such a lather. I've never met a girl like you. I'm in hell, I'm in heaven — a hundred times a day — all because of you."

She stopped struggling and let him keep her hand.

"I know I have no formal claim to your heart," he went on, "and yet, when I see you even looking at someone else, some other fellow, or laughing at his wit, I just get so insanely jealous."

His grip had relaxed enough to free her hand. She slipped that arm around him and, leaning her head against his shoulder, impelled him onward, down the path to join the others. "It's just so silly, darling," she began.

"There! You see! When you speak to me tenderly like that, my heart leaps up into the seventh heaven. And yet I know that the minute Coverley or Trotter says something to make you laugh, I'll see red again."

She realized that, since he was in somewhat of a confessional mood, she might as well press him a little. "Has it been the same with every other girl to whom you've taken a liking?" she asked. In fact, she already knew it had not been so, having been warned more than once by Daisy about his habit of 'toying with a girl's affections,' 'dangling her on a string,' 'taking his pleasure, his hat, and his leave' — and several other graphic descriptions of this young man and his ways.

He made several awkward noises and pretended that the steepness and unevenness of the path demanded all his attention.

"If so," she added, "one can understand your arrival in Penzance, unattached."

That goaded him into blurting out, "No! The very opposite. I deserve every moment of this torment for the way I've treated the girls who fell in love with me."

"But I fell in love with you," she objected.

If he noticed her use of the past-historic tense, he made no comment on it. "But you don't behave as they did," he replied.

"In what way am I so different, then?"

But that, apparently was one question he was not willing to answer. "The others are too close," he mumbled. "We must talk about this later."

As if she were not already wary enough, an alleged agony that could be turned on and off so speedily made her doubly so. It made her wonder, too, about the words with which he had begun this latest exchange, drawing attention to the *Merlin* and its occupants.

What would *she* have done if their positions had been reversed? What if she had seen him gazing after another girl, and not just any other girl but one for whom she suspected he already nursed some tenderness? She would surely have pointed in a different direction and murmured, 'Just look at that view!' Or, more subtly, she would have grabbed his arm and pressed it to her, saying, 'Let's slip away from the others once we're in the water — there are so many little secret inlets down there among all those rocks!' The very last thing she'd have done would have been to draw his attention to that other girl — much less start talking about her.

So was it just that Victor had not the first idea how to handle his own emotions — much less hers? Or was everything he did quite calculated — including his pretty convincing display of ecstasy and torment?

Behind these doubts lay one basic question: What had he to gain back there by behaving in such an apparently stupid and self-defeating way? To answer that — or even to think about it — she would have to put herself back into that frame of mind she had cast off so readily when Papa's death and bankruptcy had removed all the old protective wrapping and left her pleasantly exposed to the challenges of the real world. In short, how did an upper-middle-class young man, torn between head and heart — or, more accurately, between desire and purse — weigh up the pros and cons of a romance? David Peters, dear obliging man though he was, would not have the first idea when it came to navigating those treacherous waters. But Standish Coverley, who had a foot in both worlds and bestrode them with such elegance, would surely know all the answers. More than ever she needed some time alone to talk with him.

By now the sun was half hidden in its own heat haze, for which they were all grateful. It cast a rare silvery light upon the scene, giving it a strange, almost mythic quality that held them spellbound — even Victor. Tamsin's earlier remarks about dragons seemed even more apposite now. The nearest rocks were two ragged cones, thrusting upward out of the sand; even the smaller one dwarfed any human standing nearby. They were like shrouded giants, frozen in some ancient, pagan act — a vassal kneeling before his king, say, or an acolyte before an old arch-druid. Beyond them, as a dramatic backdrop, were three huge triangular rocks, their feet just in the water. In this eldritch light, they seemed part of some Arthurian legend — magic islands afloat in the mists of Time, all on a silvered sea that had no discernible horizon.

"*Merlin* ahoy!" Victor broke the spell, pointing toward the boat, which was just then rounding the islands and threading a careful way among the reefs at the other end of the little cove.

There he goes again! Tamsin thought.

"Engines and all," Standish added. "Courtesy of His Majesty's Customs and Excise! Just think how much the government could save in money *and* lives if it dished out subsidies directly to the fishermen! To buy engines, I mean."

"If they'd throw a line overboard," Reg said, "we could take turns to be towed through the water. Wouldn't that be joll!"

They hastened into the caves to change, so as to be in the water by the time the *Merlin* had worked its way into the middle of the cove, which seemed to be David's intention.

"Do you think your brother wants to go back to Penzance in the *Merlin?*" Tamsin asked Charlotte as they slipped out of their dresses.

"Good heavens!" she exclaimed. "Why?"

"It seems to fascinate him. He drew my attention to her when we were on the cliff path. And he was obviously just waiting for her to make an appearance round the point — the way he spotted her the moment she did."

Charlotte said she thought that a trip in the *Merlin* back across Mount's Bay was the last thing Victor would ever want.

Their costumes were, in effect, black trousers with black frilly legs beneath a black frilly knee-length skirt, and topped by a black blouse with black frilly epaulettes and more frills to disguise the contour of the bosom, and sleeves that finished below the elbow in yet more frills. And, of course, black frilly bonnets with a thin ribbon to tie them.

"D'you think this colour is *me?*" Tamsin wound the blue, one-eighth-inch-wide ribbon round her index finger and displayed it for the other two to judge.

Charlotte blushed and put a hand to her mouth, gazing from Tamsin to Daisy and back in a kind of amazement.

"What?" Tamsin asked. "It's just a bit of ribbon."

"No. Not that." She pointed to a hole through the cave wall. "That!"

"What about it?"

"I just saw someone's … you know … b-t-m through it. Mister Coverley's, I think!" She giggled.

Tamsin picked up a stalk of kelp and drew a serpentine line in the sand. "Was it like this?" she asked, hinting that it would be no novelty to her.

"You're *awful!*" Charlotte stamped on it and rubbed it out with her foot.

Then, laughing wildly, they ran out of their cave, down the beach, and, shedding their towels just below the high-tide mark, continued hand-in-hand into the sea. Though still cold, it was several degrees warmer than the oceanic waters at Land's End. Tamsin, now feeling quite the veteran, made no fuss, though it cost her all her will-power to stay silent. This time it was Charlotte who shrieked and just *knew* she was about to die, even as she started to wade ashore again. The other two grabbed her arms and dragged her without mercy into deeper waters until, at last, she had to agree it wasn't anything like as bad as it had seemed at first.

By then the men had joined them, manfully withholding their cries as their white flesh turned swiftly blue. Reg dived into a bed of kelp, visible on the surface at low tide, and sprang out upon a rock, clutching a handful, which he draped all around him, claiming to be the Old Man of the Sea.

The *Merlin* idled in among them, her engine shut down.

"Trouble?" Victor asked.

"In a way." David looked at them in turn, settling finally on Tamsin. "She drinks more petrol than we bargained for. Is there anywhere nearby that sells the stuff ashore?"

She grounded in the sand and he picked up two empty cans, ready to jump and wade the last few yards ashore.

Standish offered the two full cans of ethyl strapped to the running board of his car; he could refill the *Merlin's* two at Furber's in Mullion on the way home, he said. "And you can repay me in crab or lobster if you wish," he shouted after David as he went up the beach.

"Why don't you join us for a swim while you wait?" Tamsin asked Cousin Harry. "The water's lovely."

But he shook his head and said that wise fishermen forget how to swim when they turn fourteen. "Swimmin' for the likes o' we," he told her, "is just a longer form o' drownin'."

The bleak realism of his reply made her shiver.

"Last one to Gull Rock's a cad!" Reg challenged the other two men as he dived back in, giving himself a head start.

"Or a cadess!" Charlotte struck out after him, though doomed to failure by all those frills.

Tamsin tried to follow Reg's lead and cheat her way to the front by climbing out and running along the rocks at the foot of Asparagus Island, the first of the three that formed her fanciful 'dragon's tail.' But it was so deeply fissured, and so encrusted with tiny, razor-sharp limpets, that she even lost what advantage she'd had.

In the end the race was abandoned because Gull Rock proved to be farther out than the haze had made it seem and because the inlet between it and little Asparagus Island looked so inviting. To Tamsin, who had almost burst her heart and lungs in making up the lost ground — or water — a smooth, flat slab at the foot of Gull Rock looked more inviting still. But it was a little too high out of the water and there was no obliging ledge to give her a springboard onto it.

She was still struggling for some smaller foothold when she felt what she took to be a seal beneath her feet. Before she could even scream or kick out, it stood up, turned into Standish Coverley's shoulders, and raised her smoothly to her desired perch. He disappeared at once, below the surface again, only to re-emerge a moment later in a great eruption of spray and, with an athletic twist, land on the slab beside her.

"Pity those Thornes are here," he murmured as he wiped the water from his face and hair. "It was so much more pleasant to swim *au naturel,* don't you think, Tamsin?"

She agreed it had been pleasant — after the first shock.

"I do think young David Peters might have postponed the maiden voyage of the *Merlin* until you were free to join in," he went on.

"It would have been more thoughtful," she agreed.

"Especially after you saved his bacon — or, rather, his brandy — like that."

"Maybe he wanted to be sure she wouldn't leak after the refitting," she offered. "Or the engine wouldn't die suddenly out in the middle of the bay."

"Well, he must by now be pretty confident that neither of those things is going to happen. So, if you want to go back with him — as far as Porthleven, say — we can pick you up there on our way back."

The sudden gleam in her eyes was answer enough.

"Daisy!" he said — not needing to raise his voice too high, for she was swimming close by, eyeing them warily. "You're such a powerful swimmer, my darling — would you be an absolute angel and go and fetch Tamsin's clothes? Bundle them up well and pass them to Harry Peters there."

"Why?" Victor asked, for he was also treading water not too far away.

"Because I want to say I was on her maiden voyage," Tamsin told him. "As a motor trawler, anyway." As a sweetener she added, "Just as far as Porthleven."

"But that must be miles!"

"Nine, to be precise," Standish told him. "But there's a strong tide in their favour. They'll do it in an hour and we'll be there ourselves by then."

After that the only way he dared exhibit his displeasure was to swim away across the cove, as if to say he did not give a fig what she chose to do.

"He's a hard man to make out," Tamsin murmured.

"Really?" Standish seemed surprised.

"So hot one minute, so cold the next. Apologetic ... arrogant. Begging ... demanding. He keeps leaping between opposites."

"He's trying to protect you from me," he replied mildly. "But he'd hardly want to do that by putting you on a boat with young David Peters!"

"It's so silly!" she exclaimed.

"Are you in love with him?"

She was astonished. "That's not the sort of question a gentleman should ask a lady about another gentleman!"

"Well said!" He grinned. "I'd still like an answer, though."

She sighed. "I thought I was — until this afternoon. He's being so stupid."

"I'm still wondering why his mother moved the whole family out of the Queen's and into your place. It's certainly not the money. It's as if she suspects there's something afoot between you and me ... D'you mind my being so candid?"

She swallowed heavily. "No! Please go on."

"It's much harder for a guest at the Queen's to keep an eye on me than it would be for a guest at the Morrab to keep an eye on you. But *why* would she be so interested? Has she said anything to you? Hinted anything, even?"

Tamsin shook her head. "Nothing comes to mind."

"Well, maybe I'm completely barking up the wrong tree. But I can't think of anything else. Shall we try to force her hand? Force her out into the open?"

"How?" The very thought excited her for she, too, had felt that Mrs Thorne was hatching some plan; indeed, she seemed the sort of woman who couldn't watch two raindrops sliding down a windowpane without plotting to hinder one and help the other.

"Victor's going to go home a pretty disgruntled fellow today. At least, he will if I have anything to do with it! Which, incidentally, is why I had to know if you were in love with him. Perhaps that will be enough to goad his mama. If not, we shall just have to pour on a little more ethyl."

"He's changed his mind. He's coming back."

"While we're in the confessional, may I ask how you feel toward David Peters?"

She laughed. "While *we* are in the confessional," she echoed, "are you going to ask me how I feel about *you?*"

He dipped his head, conceding her point. "All right. How *do* you feel about me?"

She thought rapidly. She wanted to leave as many possibilities open as she could, but without seeming too forward just at the moment — or no more forward than she must already seem. Though he started it, so he could hardly complain now. "Feelings change," she replied. "So I'm only talking about now, this minute. Or this day. And just at the moment, I'd like to think of you as a friend to whom I could talk — as freely as we are talking now ... who would listen — as, indeed, you do ... who understands all the ins and outs of human behaviour much better than I do — which you've just proved."

"In short, you like things just the way they are?"

She grinned cheekily and stroked his forearm with the tip of one finger, lazily up and down, twice. "For the moment, yes."

27 David took one look at Tamsin's elegant dress and said, "You'd best put up a pair of dungarees, maid, and save those glad rags till we put in at Portlemm," by which he meant Porthleven. He found a cleanish pair and an oilskin jacket, which she put on (or put *up,* in the local dialect) in the lee of the wheelhouse — a glazed sort of sentry box just forward of the engine compartment. She changed in semidarkness for he had draped a sail over the housing for her privacy. When she had finished she could only half pull it off. Harry took it down completely and folded it away. "You might make a sailor, Miss Harte," he said, running an admiring eye over her figure in the dungarees, "but never a boy."

"Of all possible ambitions, Mister Peters," she replied, "you have chosen one that has never crossed my mind."

She waved at her companions in the water. Standish blew her a kiss. Daisy called out, "Bring us back a parrot and some coconuts, love!" Victor, sitting on a rock, hugging his knees, made no response.

The only furnishings in the wheelhouse were the helm itself, a compass, and a handle by which one could swivel a rubber squeegee against the outside of the glass windshield, to clear it in stormy weather.

She tapped the compass, which did not change its direction; she swivelled the squeegee, which dislodged nothing but a daddy-longlegs — or a 'tom taylor,' as Mrs Pascoe called it; and she spun the helm hard to both port and starboard. This produced a gurgling sound beneath the stern and sent two rings of slightly overlapping ripples outward.

"That's what I like to see," David told her as he screwed the cap back on the second spare can, which he had just emptied. "A volunteer. The place is yours, maid."

"No!" Tamsin cried, even as her hands sought the spokes of the wheel. "D'you think I dare?"

But he was already busy cranking up the flywheel. When he considered it had enough momentum he gave a nod and Harry released the exhaust lift. For a couple of revs she fired on one cylinder only, then two, then all four. With a sigh of relief he removed the starting handle and pushed it into its clips; everything was gleaming — the brass bright and the cast iron black and matt. The roar of the engine fell to a background hum when they closed the cowling.

"Is the propellor turning?" she asked, "because we don't seem to be moving much."

"It has a variable pitch," he explained. "She's set to feather at the moment. Now see that compass needle? As soon as we get under way, you steer until the needle's on two-two-five, and hold that course until I tell you otherwise."

"Due southwest abaft the lee quarter it is, sir," she replied, reading the verbal bearing off the compass circle as she took a firm grip on the wheel. "Brace the t'gallants and royals, Mister Midshipman Easy, let go fore and aft, and port the helm — or something like that!"

David and Harry stared at each other; David shrugged and pulled a humour-her-at-all-costs face as he increased both the throttle and the pitch on the propellor.

The deck vibrated under the sudden strain. As the *Merlin* lurched forward her exhaust came clear of the water for a moment and there was a satisfyingly deep throaty roar to send her off. Then the bows lifted a few degrees, enough to suggest an eager leap toward the open water. Amid a chorus of farewells which would have done a liner proud — from all but Victor — they motored out of the cove and into Mount's Bay.

Half a mile out, David shouted, "Starboard the helm to three-twenty, bosun!"

"Starboard to northwest and five, sir," she replied. But when the needle settled on the figure she peered dead ahead and added, "Why didn't you just tell me to steer toward Porthleven? I can see the Institute tower quite clearly."

He came into the deckhouse and, standing just behind her, leaned across and blocked out the glass with his jacket. "Now it's night time," he said. "Worse — there's a storm brewing and this is the first time you've ever done this line, Kynance to Portlemm, after dark. And every time you've done it by day, you just said 'point at the Institute tower.' So how are you going to know the compass course to steer, eh?"

"I see, yes. That's very good."

"And none of your 'north by west-north-west' navy talk, either. Leave that to Captain Marryat. Always take a compass bearing in full-circle degrees and learn it by heart." He took his jacket back and tousled her hair. "We'll make a full-ticket bosun of you yet, maid."

"What if I get seasick? We never thought of that."

He patted the wheel, as if that were the sovereign remedy.

She soon saw why he had accepted her aboard without a murmur. For most of the trip he and Harry performed a repeated series of dead-reckoning tests. They would first make a note of the throttle position and the propellor pitch and then they'd throw a glass float attached to a line into the water. As the float held its position among the waves, they would pay out the line, keeping it slack so as not to tug at the float. The line had much thinner bits of line tied around it in knots at regular intervals and they would count how many knots were payed out in a given time. Harry was the timekeeper, David the knot-counter. Then they hauled the float inboard, changed the throttle position, or the propellor pitch, and repeated the cycle.

"Now we know why we guzzled so much petrol on the way out," he said to Tamsin when they had finished. "At full throttle we only get one more knot out of her than we do at just under three-quarter throttle. The extra speed's not worth the extra petrol, see?"

Porthleven was now just over a mile off, still dead ahead. And he was right — her concentration on steering properly had kept her mind busy with other things than seasickness.

"So I have been of some use," she said.

"Couldn't have done it without you. You want to put up your glad rags now, do you? Harry! Come and hide your eyes until the maid is changed up."

He hung his jacket over the window again and steered by compass until Tamsin was back in her finery. She felt something of a wrench as she discarded the old dungarees, even though they smelled of fish and their coarseness had grated on her skin. On a day like this, she thought, a fisherman's life must be one of the best. Of course, one must not forget those other times, and the boats that never came back, and the young widows who went to the cliffs at sunset and scanned every aching, empty inch of ocean until they were sure that today was not that miracle day — again.

And yet, she suddenly realized, she could not think of David in that same category, the cast of the vulnerable. If the *Merlin* sank under him, far out to sea, he would somehow make it ashore and live to fish again. It was hard even to think of him ageing slowly and losing his faculties one by one.

This struck her as something so singular that she felt she had to tell him at once. She went back to the wheelhouse and took down his jacket.

"My!" he cried, looking her up and down. "You'm so pretty as a mabyer, maid!"

"Well!" She preened herself. "I hope a 'mabyer' is pretty, too — whatever it may be?"

" 'Tis a pullet. And I'd say you're prettier still than any pullet as ever I saw."

She bobbed a curtsy. "What would 'ugly' be in Cornwall? As ugly as a … what?"

The two men looked at each other in a way that suggested the obvious word would also be indelicate. "How about paddypaw?" Harry suggested.

David nodded. "So ugly as a paddypaw."

"What's that?"

"A toad." He offered her another one: "So quick as a witnick — that's a stoat, or a ferret, see."

"What would slow be, then?"

"So slow as a bulljink. That's a slug. Or as a bullgrannick. That's a snail."

" 'Course," Harry said, "you do know the famous one: So cold as a quilkin in a cundard. You heard that, surely?"

She shook her head.

David translated. "So cold as a frog in a drain." He laughed. "Us'll make a Cornishwoman of 'ee yet, maid."

"Can I go and stand right in the bows?" she asked.

He passed the wheel to Harry and accompanied her, standing immediately behind, one hand on each gunwale.

She leaned far out over the prow, lifting her head so that she could not see any part of the boat except the jib. "Whee!" she cried. "I'm a seagull, soaring over the briny, free as the wind!" Then she became aware how close he was; she looked over her shoulder and saw the protective semicircle of his arms. "What's that for?" she asked.

"To steady you if the pitching should throw you backward."

"Oh. And if it threw me forward? Would you jump in and save me from drowning?"

"A man who can't swim a yard to save his own life jumping overboard to save a maid who can swim a mile? That'd make a lot of sense! Who'd save who?"

"What *would* you do, then?"

"Put about and throw you a line."

"And what if I was your Sandra?" She deliberately misnamed the alleged love of his life because, thinking about it later, certain bits in his story, coupled with evasions in his telling of it, had led her to doubt the woman's existence entirely.

"My Sandra?" There was bewilderment in his voice but also, she thought, a tinge of panic; she guessed he was nine-tenths certain he had not named this (nonexistent?) young female Sandra but could not, on the spur of the moment, remember what name he had given her.

"I never told you about Sandra *as well,* did I?" he asked at long last.

Was he cleverly kicking for touch or had she, quite by chance, picked the name of some other *amour* of his?

"The daughter of the Saint Ives fisherman."

"Oh!" He laughed, but was it in relief that the name had just come back to him, or had she mistaken his genuine bewilderment for panic? "You mean Sarah! Sarah Rowe."

"So who is Sandra?" she asked quickly, not to give him time.

"She's the opposite case." He sighed. "She … I don't want to sound vain, now, but she set her cap at me when we were in the national school still, and she's never stopped since. Whenever we put to sea, she's there with a pasty for me. When we come home to Newlyn, she's there again, ready to unload. She won't take her eyes off me in chapel … knits me stockings and rollnecks in oiled wool … cooks niceys for me …"

"Poor man!" She laughed. "It must make your life a misery."

He ignored her sarcasm. "It does. I fear she'll get me in the end. One moment of human weakness and *snap!* She'll have me alongside of her at the altar."

"Still," Tamsin said, "since you cherish the same hopeless feelings for Miss Sarah Rowe, you must know exactly how wretched she feels."

"That's it," he agreed. "You hit 'n squarely. I can't turn her away, though I know 'twould be kindest in the long run. There's many a man would go down on his knees to her and make her a good husband, but she spurns them all."

"Perhaps you're the one who's being too choosy," she suggested. "Mooning after the unattainable Sarah. Shouldn't you cut your coat according to your cloth?"

"There's truth in that," he replied. "But 'Love is to all things blind, / Except to this — the wayward mind. / What it can have it will not see. / What it *must* have won't let it be.' So there!"

"That's neat," she said. "Who wrote it?" He did not reply. She turned at looked into his eyes. "You?"

He shrugged awkwardly. "I never wrote it down." Then, as if he thought he needed some kind of excuse: "There's not much to do, keeping the compass on just the one bearing — and no maid to talk to, only Harry and Sonny and some dead fish."

Harry cut the revs to half-throttle and came about to northeast as they lined up with Porthleven's outer harbour.

"No sign of our shore party yet," David remarked, scanning up and down the quayside. Then, seeing that his cousin was making for the iron ladder below the Institute, which Tamsin could never have scaled in her dress, he pointed instead to the steps in the middle harbour, on the eastern or Sithney side.

Harry nodded and altered course slightly.

"They probably delayed over their cream tea," Tamsin said.

He caught a note of wistfulness in her voice and offered a slice of fuggan cake or of saffron bread — all he had left.

"And which of them was baked by the poor, lovelorn Sandra?" she asked.

"Neither," he admitted.

"Listen!" She flapped her hands at him. "If there are two more hapless females who cherish an unrequited love for you — and who foolishly believe the way to your heart is through your belly — I simply don't want to hear of it. I'm sure I can get a cream tea in one of those cottages on the harbour front — if you'll just drop me off here and go your ways."

But he wouldn't dream of it. As the *Merlin* nosed into the alcove that held the broad granite steps, he leaped off ahead of her and held out his hands to help her make the small leap after him. The narrowing of the harbour had the effect of turning a barely perceptible two-foot ocean swell into six-foot waves, which could drop the boat right out from under you if, like Tamsin, you had only one foot ashore at the time. David grabbed both her arms and pulled her hard, making no allowance for her own efforts in the same direction. The impact of her body thrust him a couple of paces back against the inner wall of the recess — and impelled her from his arm's-length grip into his embrace.

She struggled for all of half a second and then surrendered. Or, rather, it was not she who surrendered but her unthinking body, which found the crush of his arms and the hard contact of his strong, lean frame impossible to resist. His earlier words — 'one moment of human weakness' — echoed vaguely somewhere in her mind but they were distant and she was no longer there to heed them. She was in her bones, her sinews, her nerves — in every living part of her flesh — rejoicing.

But her self-control did not entirely desert her — only to the extent that she did nothing to break off this rapturous, if accidental, embrace. She pressed her head against his chest, knowing that if she looked up at him, he would kiss her. And though at that particular moment she could not think of anything more pleasant in all the world, she knew it would change everything between them utterly. It would upset the delicate relationships of her world and play havoc with their carefully chosen purpose in her life.

It lasted no more than ten seconds — but for seven of them they were perfectly stable on the granite steps and in no need of mutual propping up. In the end it was David who pushed her away — he being unable to move, with his back to the massive stone wall. His hands shivered, his arms shook, as if the muscles were at war throughout his body. "Let's see about that cream tea," he said. Over her shoulder he pointed at Harry, who was grinning and making crudely encouraging gestures, and then toward the inner harbour.

Harry grasped his meaning and, pausing only to throw the bundle containing her towel and bathing things up the steps ahead of them, set off for the narrow mouth that helped protect Porthleven's fleet from storms and their mountainous seas.

"Mister Victor Thorne did not seem too pleased when you came along of us." David picked up the bundle and moved to her seaward side — there being no handrail to the steps. He took her gently by the elbow.

"Mister Victor Thorne is not too pleased with most aspects of his life at the moment," she replied, taking his hand and wrapping it firmly around the crook of her arm.

Now that he was no longer holding her, the intensity of her feelings only a moment or two earlier seemed inexplicable. But they had left her shaken — and not just as a figure of speech but quite literally, too. There was a sort of shivery weakness running right through her — the same as she could feel in him.

She went on: "Mister Victor Thorne has too much money, too much time on his hands, and not enough to occupy him — that's my opinion. He has no inner resources."

"And would you say the same of Standish Coverley?" he asked as they reached the top of the steps.

She noticed he did not accord Standish an ironic 'Mister.'

"Would you?" she responded.

"There's something of the same lack about that man," he said. "Not that he's idle. But he plays with things. He's a bit like a monkey — picks things up, plays with them a bit, then puts them down and picks up something else."

She grinned at him. "Is that a warning for me?"

"No, no. Not people. Things. When he bought the Queen's and turned it into the first class hôtel it is, why, he hardly slept o'nights and ..."

"Really? I thought it was a family inheritance. How long ago was this?"

"Half a dozen years. Round the turn of the century. He bought it off of his uncle, so it was in the family before. But then, like I said, he was heart-and-soul into it. Now he's hardly there but two days a week. He'll be looking for something new afore too long — you'll see."

"Maybe a coachbuilding works for posh motors?" she suggested, thinking of his obsession with his car.

"Or mebbe he needs a good woman to keep him steady."

"Not this woman — if that's what you're thinking," she said. A moment later she wondered why. Then, to make her comment seem more general, she added, "I don't think he wants that sort of complication in his life — just at the moment, anyway."

"What a person *wants* and what that person *needs* are rarely the same thing." He pointed along the harbourside road, where the white Rolls-Royce was inching and bouncing along. "He's now coming. We shall have to have that cream tea another day."

The coal tramp had discharged her cargo and was now waiting for the evening tide to float her.

"Tomorrow?" she suggested eagerly.

He shook his head. "I shall be at sea these next few days. If this slack breeze holds, I can fish where others can't."

"Good luck, then," she said. "And oh, by the way, what's the Cornish saying for 'warm'? I know 'so cold as a quilkin in a cundard' but it'd be 'so warm as ...' what?"

"So warm as a peach," he replied.

"That doesn't make sense."

He laughed as he walked away. "It would if you knew what 'peach' can also mean. See'ee again, maid. I'm glad you were on the maiden trip after all. It felt incomplete without you."

28 Ten days after the jaunt to Kynance, Tamsin came of age. She awoke early, wished herself a *Happy Birthday!* (silently, to avoid waking Daisy in her bed by the fireplace) and began a thorough inventory of body, mind, and spirit to see if she could detect any difference. It ought to be possible, she felt. The wise lawmakers who decreed that yesterday she was unfit to own a bank account, run up debts, or marry without parental consent, whereas today she was fully capable of all three, must have had their reasons. Mind you, those same wise lawmakers also decreed that she was unfit to vote, to sit on a jury, to fight for her country, or to work above the most menial levels of the Civil Service, so perhaps 'reason' was not their strongest suit. All the same, a twenty-first birthday was one of life's big gateways — the portal where one shed all childish things and put on the mantle of maturity.

And what mature decisions now awaited her?

Well, for a start, she told herself, she must try to distinguish ambitions from pipedreams and desires from real needs. She really must. It was urgent. And she must go beyond that, too. She must start taking account of the way ambitions and real needs interact. For example, if it truly was her ambition to turn the guest house into a small hôtel by ploughing back every penny of profit, it would mean years of skimping and saving and very little money for spending on fun.

Could she tolerate that, especially since fun had started coming back into her life lately?

Don't answer yet, she advised. Continue the line of thought to its logical end. That would be the mature, responsible way of doing things. Take plenty of time about it. Be thorough. Think everything through.

Because even the small hôtel was only a way-station in the unfolding of her full ambition. The idea would be to trade it at some time for a medium-size hôtel. And then — how many years later? — to graduate to something as grand as the Queen's. Or even grander! Why not? Ambitions are but guiding stars, and even the Three Kings never actually reached theirs. They just let it guide them to their real goal.

It would mean not marrying, of course. No husband, no children, no ordinary domestic life. And no love — except that hopeless kind which never got closer than three pews away. There would be no one in all the world who thought you were the most wonderful, most special person ever — and no one of whom you could say the same in return. None of that. She'd be a spinster ... an old maid. A *sour* old maid. One of those quavering voices that filled a third of the church each Sunday. Those whiskered women in black and clerical grey, with their creaking bones in their withered shanks. Would the wealth and power that went with the ownership of a place like the Queen's be compensation enough for that?

Oh dear — choices! They were wonderful things when you had them all set out before you, like so many birthday presents all wrapped in gaudy paper. The trouble was, the moment you opened one of them and said, 'Mine!' the others just shrivelled and blew away. Perhaps that was what maturity meant — making your one true choice and kissing the others goodbye. 'Forsaking all others, keep thee only unto him or her' ... it was the same thing.

The trouble was, she really did *desire* Victor and it clouded her every attempt to think calmly and rationally about all the other choices in her present life. She knew very well that he was a spoiled and selfish ... well, *child* was not too harsh a word. It made no difference to her wanting him. That he adored her — if only for the present — was obvious. And his talk of being alternately in heaven and hell, all because of her, was nothing more than his vanity fighting against that feeling of being trapped by his love; he loved her insanely and he hated her for having that enslaving effect on him.

For her part, she now doubted she loved him in the smallest degree; but that made her desire to be kissed and held by him all the more naked, since she could not cloak it in the gentle blush of romance. Now that she knew all about It — the thing that adult men and women did together — thanks to Daisy's disgusted but vivid description, she realized only too well that kissing and hugging were not ends in themselves but mere overtures to something dark and hot, powerful and dangerous, repellent and yet enticing.

As a child she had loved to be frightened — when Papa got into a dark cupboard with her and did *Fee-fi-fo-fum* or stuck his finger in a mousehole and shouted and roared, pretending it was being bitten to the bone by rats. Was her obsession for Victor just a subtler, older version of that same basic need for fear? Put it another way — was she ever going to change, or would she just find more and more adult ways of satisfying the same endless, elemental urges?

She sat up and looked over toward Daisy's bed, to see if she was awake yet. To her surprise it was empty. Daisy was not an eager riser in the mornings; and on this particular Tuesday, the last day in July, she would have been even more loath than usual, since no guests were due to arrive or depart. It was, by the standards of the high season, a slack day.

Tamsin's bewilderment did not last long. She was just sitting up and struggling into her dressing gown — for it was now seven o'clock and past her own usual time for rising — when Daisy pushed open the door with her foot and advanced to the bedside carrying a breakfast tray and singing, *Rah, rah, rah for the birthday girl!*

Tamsin's surprise was doubled when she saw her mother, right behind Daisy and carrying a vase of deep-red roses. "Has my clock stopped?" she asked as she smoothed out the bedlinen to accept the tray.

"Don't be rude, dear," Harriet answered with a smile. "I'm quite capable of rising early if the circumstances warrant it. Guess who these are from!"

"You mean 'from whom these are,' don't you? I was going to guess *you?*"

Her mother set the vase down upon the tray and tweaked a miniature envelope out from among the stems. "Read it," she said, stooping to exchange a kiss.

The envelope was mauve with scalloped edges embossed in glossy purple ink. So was the card inside. Both smelled of attar of roses.

"No *two* guesses, now!" Daisy warned.

"As if!" Tamsin replied.

The card read: 'Many happy returns and congrats — let the motley begin! Warmest regards, Standish.'

"You must keep this for your album," Harriet said, plucking it from between her daughter's fingers and tucking it back inside its envelope. "It's a pity the perfume will fade." As she left she added, "I have a little present for you downstairs, darling. D'you feel any different?"

"Heaps," Tamsin replied.

"I've got one for you, too," Daisy said, producing a plain envelope from her pocket. "No scents, just good sense."

Inside was a simple white card on which Daisy had written in three different coloured inks:

A WISE WORD FROM THE WISE TO THE WISE
    16 nods = 1 smile
    16 smiles = 1 word
    28 words = 1 tryst
    4 trysts = 1 kiss
    20 kisses = 1 proposal
    2 proposals = 1 engagement
    1 engagement = 3 times cried in chapel
    3 times cried in chapel = 1 marriage
    1 marriage = 50 years' misery
    50 years misery = 1 funeral
    1 funeral = the happiest day in a woman's life

To Tamsin Harte from her sincere friend Daisy Dobbs.

"Oh, Daisy!" Tamsin's laugh was half humorous, half despairing. "There's something amiss with your arithmetic, anyway. I'm far beyond twenty kisses … and still no proposal in sight."

"The currency is debased, then," Daisy answered primly.

"Nothing from Victor? What has my mother gone and got for me, I wonder?"

"Eat your toast while it's still warm."

"Tell me, then."

"No. I'm not going to spoil the surprise."

"Why not?" Tamsin buttered a slice and spread it with marmalade. "You've already ruined the surprise of marriage for me. What's the spoiling of one little birthday treat! Is it something I ought to know about?"

"I don't know about *ought,*" Daisy replied warily.

"Mmmm! You're an angel for this." She ate with relish. "Is it something I should be prepared to grin my head off at — but which might make my face fall if I wasn't forewarned?"

"I don't know, I'm sure." Daisy was growing more uncomfortable by the minute, which did nothing for Tamsin's confidence.

"But you do know what it is?"

"I saw it before she covered it with a cloth, yes."

"Is it something you'd want for yourself?"

"It would be too expensive for me," Daisy assured her. "It's more what you'd call an heirloom."

"Oh no!" Half way through buttering a second slice she dropped the knife and covered her face with her hands.

"What?" Daisy asked.

"I have a horrible feeling, that's all. Is it made of wood, with four ugly, ornate legs, about so high, and plastered all over with brass and ivory inlay?" She could tell from Daisy's face that the shot was a bullseye.

"How did you know?" the girl asked. "She went to such pains to keep it secret. It's been hidden in five rooms in this house over the past two weeks to my certain knowledge. Inspector Sterne himself would never have found it."

"It was my great-aunt Biddy's sewing box ..."

"There's enough in it to make a tapestry fit for a royal palace."

"You don't need to tell me! When we put it in the auction, Mama wept and I had to pretend to be sad, too. In fact, I had to get up at midnight and dance three times round the tennis court to work off my glee. But when I tried to find out which unfortunate soul had bought it, the auctioneer's list just said 'A .N . OTHER — cash paid.' I had a certain foreboding then, but, when it didn't turn up here, I thought we were spared. Oh dear! This is going to call for all my thespian skills — and you, Daisy, did absolutely the right thing to blurt it out like that."

Daisy drew back her fist and then laughed. "You're absolutely incorrigible, you know."

"I'm twenty-one! What did you do on your twenty-first?"

"Went through all Mrs Ormesby's furs looking for signs of moth and then replaced the camphor balls. Shall I go on? There's more."

"My father used to make little paper boats that were driven by camphor balls. It's true! You put a camphor ball at the stern and it'll go forward by magic. What d'you make of Standish, eh? A dozen red roses and a rose-scented note!"

Daisy shrugged. "I can't make him out. Hot one minute, cold the next. Turn your teacup upside down and I'll tell your fortune in the leaves."

Tamsin did as she was told, saying, "That never works for me. All I ever get is dogs — blobs of leaves that couldn't be anything other than dogs. See — it's done it again! Oh, and look — now there's a cat as well!"

Daisy took the cup from her. "Dogs and cats!" she said scornfully. "Look at that! What d'you see there?"

"A letter U? Victor's going to give me an umbrella? I'm going to go *Up* in the world? I know — you're about to Utter nonsense! And it will be Utter nonsense."

"And if we turn it this way up?" Daisy asked patiently.

"Oh, how clever! It's turned into an upside-down U."

"Nonsense. It's a crown — a royal crown."

"Oh yes!" Tamsin laughed in fascination. "You didn't twiddle the leaves about a bit, did you?"

"Certainly not! Who wears a crown like that? Not a king. Theirs have those bulgy bits."

"A queen!" Tamsin giggled. "It's saying I'm to be the queen of someone's heart!"

Daisy clenched her eyes tight and gritted her teeth. "I obviously have to lead you every step of the way. *You're* supposed to see these things, not me! If it's not the king's crown then it's …? Fill in the missing word."

"The queen's!"

"Allelulia! Perhaps the name rings a bell?"

"The Queen's! Oh, my!" Tamsin stuffed her fingers into her mouth and stared at Daisy wide-eyed. "D'you think …?"

"Destiny!"

"It can't be. How can it be? It can't — we both know that."

"Well …" Daisy pulled a reluctant face. "I *thought* I did. But the tealeaves never lie — as long as you know how to read them." She stared critically at the pattern in the cup. "Yep! It's a crown all right. And it's the Queen's for you."

29 Harriet eyed her newly adult daughter nervously as the girl ran exploring fingers over the dustsheet. "I do hope it's the right thing, dear," she said.

Tamsin, postponing the moment when, as she had said, all her thespian skills would be needed, stared in apparent fascination at the cloth, which came down all the way to the ground on all four sides. "You've probably disguised it," she mused. "So this isn't its true shape. But what could it be? A bicycle? You've bought me a bicycle so that I can get through the marketing in half the time!"

"Oh dear!" Harriet said. "Is that what you'd have preferred?"

"So it's not a bicycle. Is it a badminton set for the beach?"

"Unveil it, darling. Just tug the cloth away. There's no need for all this guessing. I'm quite sure you're going to love it. I remember how ... well, never mind. I'll tell you when you've ... oh go on, do!"

Unable to postpone the dreaded moment any longer, Tamsin gripped the cloth and swirled it away with a magician's flourish. Later she rather thought she overdid the delighted surprise but her mother accepted every squeal and sigh as genuine. "Great Aunt Biddy's sewing box!" she cried. "Oh, Mama — you utter utter *angel!*"

"I remember how you wept when it had to go into the auction, so I secretly bought it out again and kept it for this day. You are pleased, aren't you?"

"Pleased? *Pleased?* The word just isn't strong enough." She opened the lid and ran her eye over a good half-acre of bobbins displaying every known colour in the universe; silk, art silk, cellulose acetate, wool, cotton, twist, button thread, cobbler's thread, sailmaker's twine ... if someone made it and dyed it, anywhere in the civilized world, Great Aunt Biddy had sent for a mile of it and found room for it here. The thing was a portable museum of the seamstress's art — and that was only the top shelf. On the one below were needles of every shape and size — for milliners, embroiderers, tapestry weavers, boot makers, upholsterers ... name the trade and its practitioners would find their tools here. There were semicircular needles, ribbon-threading bodkins, gold-eyed stitchers, blunt-nosed darners, and triangular-sided things that looked like sabres for Tom Thumb — or so they had seemed to Tamsin as a little girl. And, of course, thimbles; thimbles from Dresden and Sèvres for looking at; thimbles from Sheffield for use. On mining even deeper into this chest of treasures one came upon shears and scissors of every kind, hole punches, hammers and anvils for eyelets, balls of wax, liners of soap and chalk, darning frames, embroidery harnesses, and two whole compartments for knitting needles and crochet hooks. Finally, there was an ornamented box-within-a-box full of bobbins, pins, hooks, and a well-stabbed cushion for lace-making.

It was, indeed, an heirloom. Daisy could not have picked a word more apt. Objectively, Tamsin knew she was being given something her grandchildren (if she ever took the first step toward begetting them) would probably drool over; but oh! the weariness that weighed her soul at the very sight of it now. Some Biddys are made to ply the needle like wizards, and some Tamsins are not. She would rather pull a cartload of weeds from a virgin garden than crochet a single doily for a cream jug — though, given the choice, she'd rather go for a ride in a Rolling-Royce than either. Or a sea trip in the *Merlin* even.

So it was no mean theatrical feat to sustain her outward joy in the face of her mother's anxious scrutiny.

Harriet, satisfied at last that her kindness was well received, relaxed and said, *"Now* let anyone who dares try to say you are not suitable!"

This was such a gnomic utterance that Tamsin, half against her better instincts, had to ask for an explanation.

"Well, dear," her mother replied. "Try to see yourself as others must see you — a well brought up girl without a dowry. You are familiar with Good Society. You are *au fait* with all its rules. You are at ease in the highest sort of company. And, in helping to manage this guest house, you demonstrate that no household, however large, will ever get the better of you. Why else d'you think I have allowed you such a free hand here, if not to make that plain? These assets half make up for your lack of a dowry. There is no household in the kingdom you could not manage. You could hold your own with duchesses and American heiresses and ..."

"Mama!"

"No. Hear me out. This is important. I have much to tell you on this important day — indeed, it could well prove to be the most important day in your entire life. Come and sit down here by the window. I have given orders we shall not be disturbed."

With sinking heart Tamsin followed her to the settee in the bay window; at least there would be the whole fascinating panorama of Morrab Road to distract her.

Her mother resumed the homily. "Your character and capabilities, as I said, amount to half your assets — and a very considerable half they are, too. And this sewing chest of Great Aunt Biddy's will, if properly used, add a further quarter."

"I have to *use* it?" Tamsin could not help blurting out.

But, if her mother noticed this sudden change in tone, she did not react to it. She was too eager to press her own argument home. "I know you have not inherited Great Aunt Biddy's skill with the needle along with her chest, dear, but you might have a little embroidery on the go — something you can pick up and stab away at when you are entertaining gentleman callers."

Gentleman callers? Tamsin felt the rational world beginning to dissolve around her. Was her mother going ever so slightly dottissima? "D'you mean Victor Thorne?" she asked.

"For one," her mother conceded.

"A rather lonely one at the moment — and I can't think of anything more calculated to make him come all unglued than to see me stabbing furiously, not at the embroidery but more likely at my own fingertips and bleeding all over his ..."

"Yes-yes, dear. Very vivid. But not at all helpful. The point is, Mister Thorne is no longer your sole gentleman caller. How can you have forgotten that lovely bunch of roses already!"

"Standish Coverley?" she said.

"Oh good — you haven't forgotten! Yes, Mister Standish Coverley. I know he's in trade, but then so are we — for the moment. And anyway, he hardly bothers himself with the sordid details of the hôtel and his other commercial properties and interests. So it's almost like owning land and stocks and things. You would make a very suitable young wife for such a wealthy man. An ornament. A jewel in his crown. And, since he seems interested in you — to put it no higher — well ... now you have *two* eager suitors, which is not just twice as good as one, it is two *thousand* times better. Besides, you needn't worry about producing an impressive bit of embroidery. I can do that for you after the whole house has gone to bed." She smiled magnanimously, already forgiving her daughter for her lack of needlework skills — as long as she could use the ammo provided by this family heirloom to conquer her man.

Tamsin decided that, whether or not her mother's mind was 'coming unglued,' she had better assume it so. How on earth did Great Aunt Biddy's sewing chest provide a further quarter of her 'assets' in the marriage stakes? (And what constituted the other quarter? — though she would not pursue that question until this sewing-chest business was sorted out.)

Harriet, seeing her daughter's perplexity, smiled graciously and said, "I can see you have not entirely grasped my purpose in giving you this sewing chest, darling. Let me explain. The way you manage the day-to-day affairs of the Morrab Guest House ... your quiet, calm proficiency ..."

"You don't hear me in the kitchen every now and then!"

"I do, dear, but the others don't. So, as far as the world is concerned, it doesn't happen. But, as I was saying, your proficiency might suggest to a gentleman caller that you are a domineering sort of female who must have her way at all costs."

"Well, to be quite honest ..."

"Do stop interrupting, dear. We are not talking about honesty here. Honesty doesn't come into it. We're discussing appearances. And you might *appear* to be a sort of termagant once you get inside your own front door. So — don't you see? — the sight of you with your sweet, pretty head bent over an embroidery frame will help redress the balance. A flawless mistress of the domestic staff but a submissive and happy little embroiderer in her leisure hours — with no wider ambitions that might challenge a gentleman in his own manly world. Why, soon you will have not two suitors but *twenty*-two!"

"Steady the Buffs, Mama dear!" Tamsin forced a laugh. Her mother clearly *was* losing a hinge. However, there was no point in arguing, so all she said was, "But I do what you mean."

"Twenty-two is a bit of an exaggeration, I know. But if you can manage to project such a rounded picture of the perfect wife for a gentleman, well ... it is certain to attract more to your side than the current two!"

"It's certainly worth a try." Tamsin was already thinking in terms of scalded fingers, sprained wrists ... anything to avoid picking up a needle. And did Penzance have a choral society, a debating club, a philately group — anything to occupy time that might otherwise be spent in bending her pretty little head over an embroidery frame. At least in a group of stamp collectors she'd be mingling with people who were only *half* mad.

"Of course it is," her mother agreed. "I know that needlework is not your most congenial hobby. I did think of other feminine accomplishments. Water-colours, for instance. But down here in Cornwall, painting is such a *professional* business. Last Saturday one could hardly walk through Newlyn without tripping over sketching easels — and female artists showing much too much ankle to be ladies. So, all in all, a little light embroidery will be best, I think."

"So that takes care of three-fourths of my ... *assets* in the marital stakes. Whence cometh the fourth fourth?"

To Tamsin's surprise her mother blushed slightly and looked away, out into the street. Unfortunately for her, just at that moment, three dogs and a bitch were preparing to do what they so often do in the street — and three impudent boys were gathered to watch them, waiting to laugh.

To Tamsin's further surprise, her mother did not twitch the curtain to hide the distressing incident from view. "Perhaps it is a blessing in diguise," she murmured, still uncomfortable but now with the slightly martyred air of one who cannot escape a distasteful duty. Pointing toward the dogs but keeping her eyes fixed on her daughter, she said, "You know all about *that* sort of thing, I suppose?"

Tamsin swallowed hard and tried to seem nonchalant, though her heart stopped a moment and then came back with a thump. "A little, I think," she said. "The dogs are *serving* the bitch and in due course she'll produce a litter of puppies."

"Good." Her mother was shaking a bit, too. "And humans ... men and women ..."

"Engage in something a little more civilized but essentially the same. Didn't girls at school talk about such things in your day?" She took charge of this conversation, although it made her want to knit her toes, because she didn't want her mother to get anywhere near discovering Daisy's role in her enlightenment. In fact, older girls at her school *had* whispered furtively (and grossly inaccurately) about such things, but it had passed right over Tamsin's head at the time.

"I was educated at home," Harriet replied. "D'you mean they *did* at Bishops Cheriton?"

Tamsin nodded and smiled apologetically. "Not that I understood much of it, mind."

"Well, I'm overjoyed to hear it. But ..."

"So you see — if you find it difficult to talk about, there's no need!" She smiled, happy that it was over.

Her mother did not smile back; it was not over. "It *is* difficult, precious," she admitted, "but not half as difficult as the things I really have to tell you now. Merely to understand the ... the *biology*" — she produced the word with elegant distaste — "does not get one to the heart of the matter. Not even close. The thing is ... um ... how can I put it? Perhaps an analogy will serve. We all know it is wicked and wrong to use cosmetics — and yet we all do it when the occasion demands. Whenever you hear a grand matron bleating about 'painted Jezebels' and the like, you may be sure she has discreetly reddened her own cheeks and lips or darkened her eyelashes or put laudanum drops into her eyes to make the pupils go big and dark and mysterious. We've all done it."

"Discreetly," Tamsin added, hoping to hurry her mother away from the analogy and toward the point.

"Quite so, dear — discreetly. You take the very word out of my mouth. Now the purpose of marriage — one of its purposes, anyway — is to take, er, *that* sort of thing" — again she waved a hand toward the dogs without so much as a glance in their direction — "and regularize it. Confine it to hearth and home ... well, not even the hearth, actually. To the bedroom."

By now, Tamsin was starting to wonder where the analogy with cosmetics fitted in. "Is it nice?" she asked. "You know what I mean — is it a pleasure?"

Her mother gazed at the ceiling ... into the empty grate ... at the hand-coloured photograph of St. Michael's Mount ... at a cinder burn in the hearthrug. "Perhaps not all that smutty schoolgirl talk passed over your head, eh?" she murmured.

"But is it?"

"Yes, dear." She spoke as if defeated in some way. "With the right person it is. With the man you love it is a pleasure almost too sweet to bear. I hope I'm doing right to tell you this. I hope I don't need to add that it should not be attempted, not even with the man you love — and no matter how desperate that love may be — unless that man has put both a diamond and a golden ring upon your hand. Anything else is wrong, wrong, wrong." Then she closed her eyes and added, "However ..."

Tamsin sat up, all ears suddenly. Here at last was the real nub of her mother's homily on this, the most significant day of her life so far. "Yes?" she said encouragingly.

"You remember what I said about painting and powdering one's features? How, even though we all agree it is wrong, we all do it discreetly? Just a little bit. We don't paint ourselves up like clowns or Jezebels. We don't 'go the whole hog,' as the saying has it. Just a little bit, you see — a discreet little bit."

"Like kissing?"

"A little bit more than that, dear." Her hand strayed toward her bosom and then lost courage.

But Tamsin nodded to show she understood.

Harriet, glad at last to be over the summit of this particular talk, continued: "One can't lay down hard and fast rules — thus far but no further. But the principle is that you must always remain in control of the situation."

"Was this so in your day?" Tamsin asked. "Or is it something new, for nowadays?"

"I suspect it has always been so, darling. We think of some ages as being notoriously licentious and others as being impossibly puritanical, but I suspect that what I'm talking about has always gone on, regardless of the tides of public opinion on the matter. Perhaps it is a little more necessary these days. There are so many seemingly confirmed bachelors around — all of them rich and quite contented to remain idle and free of domestic hindrance in their selfish pursuit of pleasure. And, I'm afraid I have to say, there are also too many women of the wrong sort to assist them in that purpose!"

"The ones we don't look at down around the harbour?"

Tamsin had never come within miles of such a frank, grown-up discussion with her mother before; now at last she felt that the unnoticed stroke of midnight last night had truly marked a great divide in her life.

"Not quite so degraded as those creatures, darling — or not so conspicuously degraded, anyway. In fact, you could pass them in the street and not be able to tell them from rich and respectable misses. So you see — with such competition out there — we have to break the rules a little, both in the business of cosmetics and, er, the seemly rituals of respectable courtship. But never lose control, as I say, and never permit anything that involves lifting the hem of your skirt."

Tamsin wondered where swimming and sunbathing in a state of nature came in her mother's scale of things, but she was not so foolish as to ask. Instead she said, "Do you miss it, Mama? D'you miss Papa in that way, too?"

Harriet was surprised almost out of her skin to think that this conversation had reached a point where the girl could ask such a question. She was even more shocked to hear herself answer it: "More than I can tell you, dear. After twenty-odd years you think it's just a habit. Then it goes away and you realize how much it really meant. Still ..." She forced herself to be bright. "Let's get you settled first. Then I'll do something about me."

30 It was as well that no party had been planned for Tamsin's twenty-first; just a bit of a spread at teatime, including a birthday cake with twenty-one candles. That very afternoon a telegram arrived from Baden-Baden to say that Count de Ath had died in his sleep the previous night and that the Countess would be returning to England immediately after the funeral, which was to take place quietly on the first of August; she expected to arrive on the third, which was the coming Saturday. That left only three whole days (plus two half days) in which to prepare to receive this grand old lady; if Harriet had had to cope with a coming-of-age party as well, and

on the day this news arrived, she was sure her mind would have snapped. Especially as every room in the house was already fully booked for the entire fortnight.

Tamsin tried pointing out that Saturday was their regular change-over day, when around half their PGs left and a new half arrived to take their places. "And since 'half,' in our case, amounts to no more than six families," she added, "fitting in an extra one person is hardly going to break our backs."

"But that's the whole point!" Harriet shrieked, pointing at the bookings ledger.

"Shush!"

"I will not shush! Don't you understand — *we have no room available!* Unless someone cancels ..." Her voice trailed away and a crafty look stole into her eyes. "Or unless *we* cancel *someone!* Who's farthest away?" She turned the ledger toward her. "Mister and Mrs Macrae, Edinburgh. They'll do. If we say we've got scarlet fever or something here — the truth will never reach them. Anyway, it may even be true. It must be. There must be a case of scarlet fever somewhere in Penzance, surely? And I'm certain there are *lovely* seaside places in Scotland where they'd be much happier ..."

"Mo-ther!" Tamsin only called her *mo-ther* — in two admonitory syllables like that — when she was about to lose all patience with her.

"What now? We must send a telegram at once."

"No telegrams will be sent to the Macraes." She rotated the ledger back toward her so that her mother could not read the address. "We shall not turn away any of our custom — especially if it is merely to oblige a highly dubious lady, with a foreign title, who may end up doing a midnight flit on us."

"We're not turning her down!"

"No, we're not turning her down, either. She may have your room. You can have my bed and I'll play sardines with Daisy." Her mother did at least appear to consider the proposal. "Or," Tamsin went on, "perhaps Chynoweth next door has a vacancy. Or a cancellation. If so, you could take a room with Mister Vissick and compare notes."

"Darling! I hardly know the man," she objected.

Such mild reluctance meant the idea appealed to her.

"Hardly know him? Why, you only spend ten minutes hob-nobbing with him every time your paths happen to cross — which is just about every day."

"Hobnobbing!" she sneered. "I do no such thing. What a disgraceful expression. Mister Vissick and I engage in civilized conversation, that is all."

"Pop next door and ask him now. I'll give you ten to one he says yes. He's got his eye on you — you know he has."

She had wanted to say as much earlier, at the end of that morning's embarrassing conversation in the bay window; but it had not seemed quite the right moment for a little gentle teasing. In fact, it was so gentle that she was surprised to see the tips of her mother's ears, which she always prided for their delicate, alabaster quality, turn a decided shade of pink.

"Such nonsense!" she exclaimed, though she was already reaching for a notepad to draft a reply to the Countess.

Tamsin pressed it further. "He *has* got his eye on you — and you know it. Anyone can see that. He has dynastic ambitions to amalgamate the two properties and, perhaps, run them as a small temperance hôtel."

She did not add that Bill Vissick was quite a handsome eyeful in himself. A tall, wiry man with a mane of wavy hair, beetling brows, dark and deepset eyes, chiselled lips, and a rugged chin … always in command of himself and the situation … never sly, never flustered … he was the cause of many a hopeful sigh among the spinsters and widows of the town.

But none of them owned a successful boarding house right next door! *Owned,* mark you. That was her mother's trump card and maybe this was the moment to play it — from every point of view. For the girl could not help thinking that a mother who was caught up in affairs of her own heart would have less time to worry about those in which her daughter might be engaged — and would, in any case, be on lower moral ground than otherwise when it came to dishing out the crits.

"Do it now before you think better of it," she advised her mother. "Because there isn't actually any 'better' for you to think — is there!"

It required half an hour's preparation and a complete change of clothes before Harriet felt able to walk the dozen yards that

separated the Morrab from Chynoweth. And, notwithstanding
the extreme urgency of the situation — considering that they
only had about ninety-five hours left in which to make up a bed
for the Countess and, er, well, make up her bed — it seemingly
required a further thirty-five minutes to ascertain whether
Mr Vissick had a room free.

He had — and it would, indeed, be *free* to Mrs Harte. And
why wait till Saturday when the room was empty now? Mrs Harte
said she'd think about it, thought about it, and accepted.

And so the Countess's room was ready and waiting before
they even sat down to Tamsin's slightly delayed birthday tea.
Charlotte came, with an invitation from her brother for Tamsin
to dine with him that night at the Queen's. Her parents, she
announced, had taken the early-morning train home to Exeter
to inspect the recent progress on the refurbishment of Peveril
Hall; they were not expected to return until tomorrow.

"What is Victor doing at the moment?" Tamsin asked.

"Playing billiards with Reg Trotter and Standish Coverley at
the Queen's, I think. And smoking like a chimney, I know."

"He seems to be spending more and more time with them
lately," Harriet commented as she carried the taper from candle
to candle on her daughter's cake.

"I know!" Charlotte pulled a glum face.

Harriet missed the expression but caught the tone of voice.
"You sound as if you don't approve?"

"No. I think it's just so silly, Mrs Harte. I know I should be
grateful and all that rot. And I know that all mothers have their
daughters' best interests at heart always and for ever. But I still
think it's silly."

"There! All with one match — thanks to a little cheating."
Harriet blew out the taper and surveyed the cake with pride,
though she had done nothing beyond sticking it with twenty-one
candles. "What d'you think is silly, dear?"

"Oh! The only reason Victor's spending so much time with
those two is to humour this whim of our mother's." She went on
to explain Cicely Thorne's quaint ideas about the effeteness of
rich families and how they need to renew their capitalist spirit
every so often by marrying outside the narrow caste of people
with inherited wealth.

Harriet, whose nimble mind raced ahead of the girl's diffident rehash of her mother's ideas, thought she now understood why the Thornes had left the Queen's and come to the Morrab. If anyone had possessed the capitalist spirit, and in goodly measure, too, it was Tamsin's father. So Victor was under maternal pressure to propose to the sprig of that worthy stock!

This happy thought rang so loud in her mind that she almost missed Charlotte's conclusion: "So poor Victor is having to ingratiate himself with Mister Coverley in the hopes that it might bring him closer to *me!*"

"No!" Daisy, Tamsin, and Harriet all cried out simultaneously — and then stared at each other, abashed at their sudden unanimity.

It surprised Charlotte, too. She turned to Tamsin and asked why her denial was so vehement.

"I just ... well, he strikes me as the sort of bachelor who's having much too much fun *being* a bachelor to even think of marriage." She waited for her mother to say something about splitting infinitives but no word came.

Instead, Harriet asked Charlotte what her feelings in the matter might be.

The girl leaned forward and lowered her voice. "I don't really want to marry anyone just yet. Mister Coverley's very nice but there are lots more fish in the sea."

"Good for you!" Harriet cried — to Tamsin's astonishment.

Meanwhile, Tamsin realized, she now had part of the answer to Standish's question: why had the Thornes moved from the Queen's to the Morrab?

Charlotte continued: "I don't see why bachelors should have all the fun of being single. I want to go to art school and have some fun myself."

"Be a bachelor-*girl!*" Tamsin suggested.

"Spinster, dear," her mother said abstractedly.

The three young women exchanged smiles: 'spinster' and 'bachelor-girl' were not synonyms.

Harriet, meanwhile, was busy putting the best possible construction on this revelation: Victor's true purpose — *and* Mrs Thorne's true purpose, since Victor was partly her agent — was to distract young Coverley with thoughts of Charlotte, leaving the way to Tamsin's heart clear for himself. After all, why should the Thornes wish to import this so-called 'capitalist blood' into the *female* line? The offspring of any union with Charlotte would be Coverleys, not Thornes. No! Preposterous though that woman's fanciful notions might be, the 'capitalist blood' was in Tamsin, just as she, Harriet, had assumed on first hearing of it. And the offspring of her marriage with Victor would be Thornes.

"Just think how different all our social arrangements and calculations would be if surnames followed down the female line instead of the male!" she said brightly.

This apparent non-sequitur silenced them for a moment and then there seemed no point in picking the subject up again. In any case, Bridget came in at that moment to say that David Peters was at the kitchen door with 'something for Miss Tamsin.'

In rushing to her feet Tamsin almost bowled her chair over; and the speed with which she raced out back made Charlotte and Daisy giggle — until Mrs Harte told them she saw nothing amusing in such unpolished behaviour.

"David!" Tamsin cried, throwing her arms about his neck and giving him a hasty kiss on the cheek. "The only man who cared to turn up to my birthday tea in person! Come on in."

" 'Twas only to bring these," he replied, waving a bottle of champagne from which the sea had washed the label, and as fine a brace of sea-trout as ever came ashore at Newlyn. "I can't stay, no more'n a minute."

"Nonsense! Of course you can. You must." She gave him another peck and let him go. "Come on in and have some of my cake. No one will mind how you're dressed. We're just four old maids longing for some manly company."

Even then she had to drag him up the passage and into the dining room. "A chair, Daisy," she cried, "for the guest of honour. I'll get some glasses."

He had left the fish with Mrs Pascoe but he still had the champagne in his hand. "Bollinger," he said, putting it down beside the cake, where the candles had almost burned down to the sugar roses that held them.

"Leave the glasses, darling," her mother cried urgently. "The candles are nearly dead. It's time to make your wish."

"My wish! Golly!" She hadn't thought. There were so many possibilities. Wishes for herself. For her mother. For their joint prosperity. For ...

She bent over the table, bringing her lips as near the cake as she dared, and drew the deepest breath she could manage. At the last moment she looked up and saw David's eyes upon her. Then, with all the world to wish for, all she could think of was: *I wish David and I will always be ... will be ...* Her mind hovered over the word. She knew it so well, and yet it stubbornly refused to be thought.

She could hold her breath no longer, so she blew and blew, this way and that. *Friends!* That was the word. *Just* friends. How stupid! Twenty candles smoked; one guttered and sprang back to life — after she was sure she'd blown it out. And she had no breath left. So the wish wasn't going to come true, anyway. Despondently she drew a second breath, but David reached out his great, work-toughened hand and pinched the flame out. "No one saw that, did they?" he asked innocently.

"I'm not sure, Mister Peters ..." Harriet began.

"Act of friendship," he said.

An uncommon sympathy of minds? she wondered. Or could it be pure coincidence?

Everyone agreed that the cake was another of Mrs Pascoe's minor miracles; they had two slices each. And that made it necessary to have two glasses of champagne each, as well. And so they all became a little giggly — except for Harriet, who, even then, was racking her brains for ways of keeping David Peters away from the house while the Countess was under their roof.

After tea, David said he really did have to leave now. He was due to go on a three-day trip to the mid-Channel, where there were rumours of a mighty cod shoal and he could earn enough to buy the *Merlin's* engine outright.

Tamsin remarked that she could do with a breath of fresh air and suggested accompanying him — with Daisy and Charlotte along for company, if they wished.

Harriet said it didn't matter what *they* wished, she, Tamsin, wasn't going unless they went along, too.

Out in the hall, while the girls were changing into outdoor boots, she managed to murmur a few more instructions in her daughter's ear — namely that she was not to dine at the Queen's that night without having first listened to a few more words of advice and wisdom. "And dear little Charlotte," she whispered, "charming gel though she is ... we have to kill any idea of a liaison between her and Mister Coverley stone dead. I'm sure it's nothing serious — that is, I'm sure it's a feint on the part of Mrs Thorne, but these tricks have a way of going horribly wrong, so ..."

"May I go, please?" Tamsin asked.

There were dust devils in the road outside, scurrying along at random like upside-down monks, spinning on their pointed cowls. A hot, dry, fitful wind stirred through the gardens, making a clatter among the palm trees and rattling the gates.

"There's a change on the way," David told Tamsin.

Charlotte and Daisy were walking a discreet four or five paces behind them.

"A storm?" she asked anxiously.

"Heavy weather, anyway."

"And you'll still go to sea? Is it safe? You won't wait for it to blow over?"

"It's a question of whether the cod will wait. Anyway, we've fitted double tanks for this voyage. Also, mid-Channel's the best place to be when the weather closes in. You're out of the shipping lanes and the waves are longer and not so high."

"Well, just be careful," she said, feeling helpless.

"I'm always that. But if I'm numbered to go, then I'm numbered to go. And that's all about it."

She shivered and grabbed his arm. "Just don't talk about it." Then a new thought struck her. "Perhaps you'd better give me Sarah's Rowe's exact address — so that if anything does happen, I could let her know?"

"Her!" He gave a sardonic laugh. "She wouldn't want to know, anyway."

"Or Sandra whatzername's, then?"

"She'll know soon enough — before you do, in fact."

"Oh, I just hate it when people are so fatalistic! If I offered you money not to go to sea tonight, would you accept? I can't, mind, because I haven't got any, but would you?"

"Why is it so important, Tamsin?"

His words had the form of a question but they sounded more like a challenge to her. She became more cautious at once. "I don't know," she answered. "Maybe it's not important at all — except ..."

"Yes?"

"Well, I'd just feel ... I mean, this place just wouldn't be the same if you weren't there any more. That's all I'm saying."

He gave a baffled laugh. "We don't hardly meet more than once a week — if that. So I can't see as *I* make much difference."

"Its just nice to know you're *there,* that's all. Look — don't force me to make a big song and dance about it. Let's just drop the subject."

"That's all right by me."

After twenty or so paces in silence she said, "That was superb champagne. I can still feel the tickle. Have you been sending more messages to Brittany lately?"

"No." He sighed. "I've had that bottle nearly two years now. I thought I might as well dedicate it to a happy occasion as see it there, under the slates, mouldering away."

"Champagne doesn't moulder away. It gets better with age."

"So they say."

"Well then! You could have left it to improve — still, I'm glad you didn't."

She suspected he had put it aside against his eventual wedding day with Sarah Rowe — *if* she existed at all. Either way, he was trying to fix that thought in her mind without so much as a single direct word about it.

"Have you got any more?" she asked. "Or was that the last?"

"There's naught but one bottle to go," he said with a smile. "Such is hope, eh?"

31 Victor fretted in the lounge at the Morrab, waiting for Tamsin to be ready. Eventually Harriet sent Daisy to tell him to go on ahead and make sure of the table as the dear gel would be some time yet.

"He'll get his own back for that," Tamsin warned. "He'll sit near the entrance and then pretend not to notice me when I arrive. He's so childish, you know — I can read his every move."

"Then you'll not only be ready for him, you'll also astound him with your beauty." She eyed her daughter critically, head on one side. "Try pinching your cheeks."

When that didn't work, she locked the door, opened the secret drawer in her dressing table, and took out a pot of terracotta dust and a hare's foot. Also an eyebrow pencil. Also a box of powder and a puff.

"You'll make me look like an old woman of forty," Tamsin complained. Then, remembering that her mother was exactly that age, added, "I mean forty-five."

"Neither age could be called old these days," Harriet replied grimly. "Besides, we shall use these aids to beauty *very* discreetly."

"Discreet! That's the watchword for today."

"And so it should be. Why d'you think it's called 'reaching the age of discretion'?"

Tamsin surveyed the result of using the hare's foot *very* discreetly and was actually quite pleased. But she still kept up her complaint. "Victor sees me every single day with my face shining like a pearl and my lips as pale as raw mackerel. *This* won't deceive him one bit."

"Our purpose is not to deceive, darling. It is to show him — and, incidentally Mister Coverley, if he's there — it's to show each gentleman the sort of lady who might be standing by his side, greeting their guests at the entrance to some grand soirée. A wife is not merely a support, a helpmeet, a mother, a nurse in times of sickness, and … the other thing, you know. She is also an ornament for her husband to show off with pride. That's what this is all about. Of course he knows what you look like every day. This is to show him how you could look on a *special* day — and how he could be getting so much more for just a teeny little extra effort. Sit still or it'll smudge."

Tamsin surveyed the latest stage in her transformation and could not deny that her mother's subtle use of terracotta on her cheeks, pencil on her eyebrows, and *Bois de rose* cream on her lips had achieved a startling effect. "If only I could be sure of looking like this first thing every morning," she said, "I think I'd rise an hour earlier."

There was a further tussle between them when it came to deciding the degree of her décolletage. Harriet kept pulling it down an inch and Tamsin would hitch it up again. In the end, since Harriet realized that the girl could place it wherever she wanted the moment she left the house, she settled for an artistic solution, instead. She drew an eyebrow-pencil down the midline of her daughter's cleavage and feathered it outward on both sides with her thumb to accentuate the shadow; then a little pale powder on the most prominent parts of each bosom — and the effect was as good as the one she had wished for with a lower line to the bodice. The ultimate touch was an oriental jacket of the finest, most transparent gauze, embroidered with gold thread in Arabic sort of patterns, and all so feather-light that Tamsin hardly knew she was wearing it.

Harriet looked her up and down and saw that she had achieved precisely what she had set out to achieve: the dignity of the grand actress combined with the seductiveness of the ingénue chorus girl.

"We should have your likeness taken in this," she said. "it would be something to show your grandchildren."

"Yes, I could say, 'But for this gown, my darlings, you might not even exist, for this is the one that brought your grandad to his knees'!"

"You young gels don't know how lucky you are — the *freedom* you enjoy nowadays. When I was your age it would have been absolutely unthinkable for a single girl to dine out alone with a man — except, perhaps, in the very final weeks of a long engagement. Heaven alone knows where all this freedom is going to end."

On the way out Tamsin's last words to her mother were, "You know — the more I contemplate remaining a spinster, the more desperately do I feel I must find someone to marry. And yet the more I contemplate marriage, the more attractive it seems to remain single!"

"Go on with you!" Harriet said. "You're not the first young girl to have had such thoughts. They evaporate almost entirely once there's the sparkle of gold on that particular finger."

"*Almost* entirely?"

Her mother made sure the carriage was waiting before giving her a final push. "The few misgivings which remain after that are best dismissed as the *mystery* of marriage."

Tamsin had forgotten the discomforts of travelling inside a carriage — the rumble of the iron tyres and the excessive bounciness of the springs on seemingly level ground, contrasted with their obstinate stiffness when lurching over potholes. How different it was when those same springs were applied to a couple of tons of wrought steel, driven by an engine as silent as a ghost! It was such a pity that Standish Coverley, so warm in friendship, was so cool on romance; if she had to find some husband for sound commercial reasons, he was worth ten of Victor Thorne. If he were in the hôtel tonight — and saw her looking like this — perhaps he'd change his mind. The image that had faced her in the looking glass came back to her now: herself transformed. Herself and yet not herself. Herself almost as a third person. A property up for bids. That was it, really. Tonight she was a desirable property, launched into the oldest market on earth.

The idea that she was *desirable* sent a strange, thrilling kind of tremble all through her. That image of oneself as a third person, a semi-stranger staring back at one ... there must be something in every mature woman that allows her to inspect herself in that way, to see herself as a man might see her. To see desirable features as a man might see them — the blush on the cheeks, the gleam in the hair, the rose-red lips, the swanlike neck, the swelling bosom.

She shivered with a curious mixture of excitement and fear. Half of her wanted to turn about and scuttle home and wipe all these powders and pigments away and curl up with a good book; the other half could not wait to cry 'On with the motley!'

There were a few spots of rain on the wind — and quite a boisterous wind it was, too, out there on the exposed Esplanade — as she huddled into herself beneath the doorman's umbrella and trotted across the pavement to the hôtel entrance. She thought briefly of David, somewhere out there, and then pushed him from her mind. David was this afternoon; the evening was Victor's. And, who knows, Standish's, too?

Victor was waiting for her in the lobby — waiting in the sense that she had predicted. He was lying almost to attention in a chesterfield armchair, pretending to be engrossed in one of the Plymouth evening papers. Colonel Hill, the craggy old gentleman with eyebrows like furze bushes, who had lately become a permanent resident and who now considered that particular chair to be his by right of custom, sat erect in an identical chair a little way off and trained upon the oblivious young man a glare that had reduced new subalterns to a month's voluntary silence in the mess. But that was in better days — far, far better days than these.

Tamsin fixed him with something that could almost have been a smile and started to walk across the lobby toward him. At first he surveyed her with manly interest, admiring just about everything he saw, except for that ridiculous hat, which looked like a hussar's shako after an accident with a cock pheasant. But his interest swiftly turned to alarm when it seemed she was intent on forcing him to offer up his seat. Him! Colonel of the 52nd of Foot — the Oxfordshires! Hero of the relief of Kimberley and the battle of Paardeburg in the late war! The man who had risked his life in far-flung lands for whippersnappers like this insolent young lounge lizard basking in *his* chair! He had just begun a plaintively awkward rise from his present, temporary seat when the tottie in the gauze jacket breezed past him with a smile and kicked the lizard on the shin, saying, "If you haven't smoked yourself to exhaustion, Victor, you could propel me vaguely in the direction of some grub. I could eat a horse, I ought to warn you."

The person she called Victor looked up over his paper, said, "Righty-oh" and rolled lazily upright, half supporting himself on her outstretched arm, adding, "You look pretty edible yourself, you know."

And she, the minx, appeared to take it as a compliment!

This caused the colonel an even greater apoplexy than had the thought of vacating his seat. If he had ever been so remiss in his social duty at the age of this Victor person, he would have locked himself in his room with a loaded revolver and done the decent thing. And to crown it all, he raced out of that temporary chair and into his rightful one with such force that he cricked his neck — the neck that had gone through the Indian Mutiny without a murmur.

"Happy birthday, by the way," Victor said. "D'you feel any different now?"

"Curiously enough — yes," she replied as they glided across the dining- room carpet. "When I woke up this morning I realized at once that some enormous change had occured during the night."

"Goodness!" He let the waiter deal with her chair. "Does it hurt? Is it curable?"

"I realized that my standards had just about doubled in height. You will find me much more demanding now that I have put away childish things."

"Well, I'm more than aware that you've put away your childish *dresses*. Am I allowed to say that that is quite a spiffing gown?"

"No, but I'll permit it on this occasion — on condition that you do not imspect it quite so blatantly for more than a few seconds each minute. Otherwise you will make me so self-conscious that I shall feel obliged to retire."

By now he could not have withdrawn his gaze from her face even if he had wanted to. This was a Tamsin he had never seen before — in fact, a Tamsin he had never even *met* before. So poised, so ready with her repartee ... and so subtly and inex-pressibly beautiful. Some of it must be artificial, of course, but by candlelight he was damned if he could tell where Nature stopped and the apothecary took over.

He held the menu well up into his field of view to prevent his gaze from slipping down to that astonishing revelation of a bosom which, like her standards, seemed to have doubled in size overnight.

Had Dobbs achieved this transformation of face and torso? If so, his mother had let a jewel pass out of her hands. This was precisely the transformation Charlotte needed if she was to raise her sights beyond the few rural boors who were currently on the *qui-vive* around Peveril Hall. That and a few lessons in repartee from this extraordinary young lady.

It occurred to him that, since she seemed to be in such a worldly mood tonight, he might try nudging his luck a little further out along the scales of licence. "I'm interested to hear you say you'll permit such-and-such *on this occasion,* Tamsin. Do you believe that *all* permissions are nowadays conditional upon their occasion, then? Have we left the age of inflexible and unvarying rules behind?"

"Mock turtle soup and cold tongue with the vegetable compôte, please," she said. "You only need inflexible rules if you think that most people are determined to break them, and will do so at every opportunity. The more you can *trust* people to behave sensibly, the more flexibile you can afford to be."

He ordered a dozen oysters and steak and kidney pudding with mashed potatoes and peas.

"And champagne," he added, raising a finger to the sommelier.

"It had better outshine a Bollinger," she said airily. "If that's at all possible."

"The old widow — a Veuve-Clicquot — is just as good, I think," he replied. "Why?"

"David Peters brought a bottle of Bollinger to my tea party this afternoon. It was wonderful. So you see — even my standards in champagne have leapt up overnight."

"The devil he did," Victor muttered. "Bollinger, eh? We'll go for a vintage, then."

"Look who's here!" she exclaimed. And when he did not follow her gaze she added, "Standish Coverley and Reg Trotter — but who's that lady with them?"

He still did not turn around. "Shortish woman?" he asked. "Dark? Rather bonny?"

She was gratified to see that Standish did not (could not?) take his eyes off her all the way across the floor. "Yes. You know her? Shh! They're coming here."

Victor sprang to his feet.

The woman said, "Oh, please don't get up." But he was already up so he didn't sit down again.

Reg gave Tamsin a passing nod and a smile and continued on to their regular table in the alcove, where he stood waiting for the other two.

"We shan't disturb you," Standish said. He turned to Tamsin, who at once thanked him for the roses.

" 'Not so much honouring thee,' " he replied. " 'As in the hope that in thy house, they might not withered be.' " He gave a little bow. "But now — allow me to present you to Mrs Cornwallis Trelawney. You may remember my mentioning her when we were looking at the Helston generating station. This is Miss Tamsin Harte."

"Oh yes — magnificent!" Tamsin said as they shook hands. "I do admire you."

She shook hands with Victor, too, apparently with no need for introductions. Meanwhile Standish continued: "She and her husband are singing in the Penzance Operatic Society's production of — what else? — *The Pirates* of that ilk. And most beautifully they do it, too."

Mrs Trelawney bobbed him an ironic curtsy. "Perhaps we can all meet up over coffee in the lounge later?" she suggested.

And so it was arranged.

"You and she have already met?" Tamsin asked.

"This afternoon," Victor said as he resumed his seat. "She popped in to pow-wow with Coverley between rehearsals. I think they're in quite a few enterprises together. From what he told me this afternoon, she had a Gog-and-Magog of all battles with her father when she was struggling to set up the generating company. He accepted her in the end — in fact, they now trade rather endearingly as 'Kernow and Daughter.' Kernow's her maiden name. But she's never trusted him fully, so she and her husband have formed business alliances elsewhere, including some with Standish, I gather. She may even be a partner here in the Queen's Hôtel."

On hearing this Tamsin clenched her fists and uttered a strangled, "Aaargh!"

"What now?" he asked in surprise.

"To have part-ownership of a hotel and just turn up for the occasional eats! If it were me, I'd want to spend every waking hour here."

"Well — that's enough about them," he said. "We'll get more of it over coffee, I'm sure." He preferred the nonchalant, sardonic young lady to this zealous fantasist.

She sensed it and, for the rest of the dinner, obliged him — this was, after all, *his* dinner in *her* honour. Throughout the meal his own attempts at nonchalance grew thinner and thinner, revealing a deeper excitement. At first it pricked her curiosity but that soon gave way to unease and, finally, to alarm. For it suddenly struck her that he was showing every sign of a man trying to work his way round to a proposal. Not that she had ever faced a man in that condition before, but the same instinct which tells a gazelle she is being stalked now warned Tamsin that a proposal was in the offing.

She tried not to panic. She would say no, of course, but the question was, how? She dismissed at once the first and most childish response, which would be to plead a call of nature the moment his intention became clear. Not only was that infantile, it merely prolonged the dilemma by five or ten minutes. But the etiquette-book response — that she was sensible of the honour, blah-blah, and would think it over most seriously — was no different in essence; indeed, it was worse, for it prolonged the dilemma by five or ten *days*. What she needed was some kindly way of saying a very cruel thing.

Here was a man — a fellow member of the human race, a decent, kindly, well-meaning fellow, even if he had not yet quite grown up — who was about to bare his innermost feelings, to pledge himself like a knight of old to serve and honour her unto death, and she had to find some amiable way of saying, 'No thanks, Victor. I'm waiting for something better to come along'!

It was impossible.

And ohmigod — he was about to begin!

She felt the blood drain from her face — indeed, from her entire head, for the room began to sway uneasily, like the deck of a boat on a mild sea. Paralyzed with panic she could only sit and watch as he gave their waiter a conspiratorial nod. Then he leaned forward and smiled at her — rather as her mother had smiled that morning when leading her to the unveiling of that dreaded sewing chest. Until this moment, though, she had not imagined that any birthday present could be less welcome than that monstrosity.

The waiter brought a box, a cube of about three inches, all wrapped in gaudy paper and tied with a gold thread.

"For you, my dearest," Victor murmured, taking it from the man and passing it immediately to her.

"For me?" She was amazed at how excited she managed to sound, considering how miserable she actually was. "Oh, Victor, I don't know that I'm ..."

"Just open it!" He was quite literally sitting on the edge of his seat, performing what was indelicately called a buttock-jig and breathing like a runner after a hard sprint.

Her fingers, allies to her fear, fumbled with the knot. "I don't know why you should think I'm ...."

"Open it!" The words were loud enough to attract amused attention from several nearby tables.

Only when he reached across and threatened to open it for her did her fingers stop tripping each other up and do what they could have done in half a second at any other time. She slipped a nail under the edge of the paper and tore the glue spots apart. The wrapping fell open to reveal a distinguished-looking box, flocked in black to resemble velvet and embossed in gold with the copperplate legend: *F. Wearne, Goldsmith, Silversmith, and Jeweler — Causeway Head, Penzance.*

"I popped out and snapped it up today," Victor said, back in nonchalant mode now that it only remained for her to lift the lid.

Tamsin's heart fell yet further, which was another thing she would have said was impossible until that moment came. If this was the modern sort of engagement ring — that is, with a diamond setting rather than the simple gold band of their parents' generation — then he must have bought something the size of the Koh-i-Noor, the 'Mountain of Light.'

Her trembling fingers closed around the lid. She looked up, into his eyes, and whispered, "I'm scared!"

"No need, old thing." He laughed, now as overnonchalant as he had, moments earlier, been undernonchalant. "It's just an antique bauble."

Again it was his reaching across to perform the opening ceremony that galvanized her to act. She lifted the lid and, just for a moment, had no idea what she was looking at. She had been so direfully certain of finding an engagement ring inside that the gigantic blue-green blur meant nothing to her.

"Like it?" he asked eagerly, buttock-jigging once again.

Like it? What *was* it? Slowly, as she emerged from her daze, the gigantic blue-green blur resolved itself into the largest turquoise she had ever seen. "Oh, Victor!" The delight with which she now gazed at him was entirely due to the fact that here was no engagement ring, but he was not to know that.

"You do like it!" he exclaimed. "I knew you would. It's exactly the colour of your eyes — that's why I chose it. Here, let me put it on." He rose and came round the table.

"Oh, but ..." A sense of reality came flooding back. She clapped her hand over the open box. "I couldn't possibly ..." She was going to say, 'accept this,' but then realized it would be almost as cruel as the kindly kiss of death that had eluded her earlier. "... wear it with, er, this jacket. It would clash."

"Nonsense!" he replied. "You're just being modest. You'd never pick anything that clashed with the colour of your eyes."

It was too persuasive a point for her to be able to resist his fingers as they removed her hand and lifted out the gem.

There were gasps of admiration and envy from those same nearby tables. Tamsin surrendered to the inevitable. There was now no form of kindly rejection that would not also be a public humiliation for him.

"It was a brooch when I spotted it," he said, "but I had them remake it as a gold necklace."

As he leaned over her, lowering it slowly before her eyes, she became aware that he must be staring down into her cleavage. To her amazement, instead of doing the girlish thing and trying surreptitiously to shrink into herself, she breathed in deeply and leaned an almost imperceptible degree or two backward. In some obscure way, which she did not even want to think about, she knew she was instinctively rewarding him for this costly and quite unexpected gift. And the instinct was somewhere 'down there' in her sinews, not at all in her mind; indeed, if she had contemplated it for a moment, she would have remained as paralyzed as before.

This was a continuation of her thoughts on the way here; in fact, they had prepared her for this revelation. There was something in her veins that wanted, quite automatically, to gratify the male fascination and something in her mind that would equally robustly deny it and take refuge in her feminine modesty. Both felt quite natural, and both were at war inside her, but she had never felt the clash of them so strongly before. With some sense of irony, she also realized that, even without the embarrassing little homily that morning, she would instinctively have discovered that *discreet* relaxation of the moral code which her mother had urged upon her.

Victor clicked the two halves of the clasp together, checked that they held, and then gave their waiter another little nod.

Like a magician, the man produced a mock-tortoiseshell hand mirror from somewhere on his trolley.

"Oh, but I couldn't *possibly* look at myself in public!" Tamsin exclaimed. "It just isn't done."

"Of course it is!" He lifted the wing of his tail coat and made a symbolic protective curtain, smiling jocularly all around. The nearby diners, amused at the antics of Young Love, pretended to look away — that is, they *did* look away but only until Tamsin yielded and glanced at herself in the glass.

Glanced?

Gazed!

If her mother's discreet modifications had earlier amazed her, the addition of this magnificent gemstone — which was, indeed, precisely the colour of her eyes — was something quite transcendent. The mirror revealed a beautiful, refined, mature young lady who seemed to be offering an Alice-Through-the-Looking-Glass invitation to leave the stale old world behind and join her in there, in that exciting new order.

She had at last been transformed into that object of desire which can make men hollow-eyed and sleepless. More — she could feel that desire within her, too, fluttering, palpitating ... a lust for herself. In future, whenever she saw that hooded, enigmatic plea in a man's eye, she would know it for what it was, not as something alien, but as an echo in herself. She would become a fellow conspirator in his enhungered craving, too.

She turned from herself with a shiver. She closed her eyes and breathed deeply until it passed over.

She relinquished the glass at last and looked around. Mrs Trelawney was talking to Standish but he was gazing at her, Tamsin. He smiled at her and only then returned his attention to Mrs T. For some reason she now felt much more comfortable about accepting this gift from Victor.

He, meanwhile, had let his coat resume its natural, figure-hugging shape and the nearby diners were once more watching with amused, tender, undisguised interest. The women smiled encouragingly at her while the men divided their admiration between her and Victor. She knew well enough — now — what they were thinking: *Well done, you lucky beggar! You're on your way to the Great Reward.*

"I'm overwhelmed, Victor," she said as he resumed his seat. "And also a little ashamed."

"Ashamed? For heaven's sake — why?"

"Because I feel I've given you so little — certainly nothing that deserves this."

"But you have!" he insisted. "You've given me the most precious thing a girl can give a chap."

"What?"

"Hope, of course."

"Oh," she answered bleakly. "In a way, that's what I meant."

32 Mrs Trelawney and the two gentlemen were already in the lounge by the time Victor and Tamsin joined them. They had all witnessed the drama of the turqoise necklet and Mrs Trelawney mentioned it at once, begging to be allowed to see and touch it. Observing her now in a rather stronger light, Tamsin thought she looked rather young for a woman who had already achieved so much — under thirty, even. She held up the stone and at once noticed its perfect match with Tamsin's eyes. "You are so lucky, Miss Harte," she said. "The only thing that matches *my* eyes is amber — and I won't wear it because I can't bear the thought of all those teeny prehistoric insects being trapped like that."

Laughing, they all sat down again, and the woman went on: "We were playing a little parlour game just before you arrived — something like that one where you look at a tray full of random objects for ten seconds and then hide your eyes and see how many you can remember. Only we were playing it with real live people."

"The people in the dining room," Standish added. "I made a list of them all, so I'm referee. These two have to see how many of them they can remember."

"How *few!*" Reg corrected him.

"Quite," Mrs Trelawney concluded. "We are thoroughly ashamed of ourselves."

"Care to play?" Standish invited the newcomers.

"I'm afraid Tamsin and I only had eyes for each other," Victor announced grandly.

"Speak for yourself, sir!" Tamsin rejoined. "I think I could tell you most of them."

"Easily said," Standish challenged.

She took up the gauntlet. "All right! Fire away — where d'you want me to begin?"

"Clockwise from the alcove where we were sitting." He consulted his list. "The fat jolly couple at table thirteen."

She eyed him suspiciously. "Have you changed all the table numbers, then?"

He grinned as if she had caught him out — which, indeed, she had. "Why d'you ask?"

"Because you don't even have a table thirteen. The table you mentioned is table six, I'm almost sure."

His grin broadened to a laugh. "That's amazing. How d'you happen to know that? You've only been in the dining room once before tonight, and that was when you and your mother dined with me and Reginald. I didn't see you going round all the tables on that occasion."

He glanced inquiringly at Victor, who said, "Nor tonight, either, old chap."

They all turned again to Tamsin, wondering how she would explain it. She gave a guilty smile and admitted she had actually visited the dining room before either occasion. "It was immediately after we moved to Penzance," she said. "The week before we opened at the Morrab. I wanted to see how the premier hôtel in town laid their tables — because I was determined we'd be equal to them at least. So I sneaked in before the dinner service began and took notes."

Mrs Trelawney clapped her hands and cried, "Capital! And you remembered all the table numbers from that one visit?"

"It's not too difficult," Tamsin assured her. "It starts at table one in the corner farthest from the big window and goes round clockwise in a sort of spiral, except for number thirteen. Our table tonight, by the way, was twenty-one — appropriately enough!" She turned again to Standish. "And there was no fat couple at table six, only a pair of middle-aged gentlemen as thin as rakes. My guess is that they're on a walking holiday around the coast — from the way they both limped and tried to disguise it from each other. I hope you offered them a mustard bath?"

Mrs Trelawney was even more delighted at this and encouraged her to continue.

After she had described the occupants of the next three tables in equally sharp detail, it became clear that she could have gone on to dispatch all twenty-four. Then Standish challenged her to a few more tables chosen at random, by number. And when she managed that, he tore the list in two and said, "You're the outright champion, Tamsin. The rest of the field may retire."

"Then I claim a reward," she replied swiftly, before he could suggest something boring of his own. "A kiss from the umpire, if you please." And she pointed her left cheek at him.

Standish did the thing properly, going down on his knees and making such a production that even Victor was amused. And he kissed her in that ambiguous area between the corner of her lips and her cheek proper. In the circumstances, and with all that melodramatic build-up, she found it not nearly as exciting as she might have done; indeed, it was not exciting at all. He must have had the steak au poivre, she decided.

Still, it was an ice-breaker of sorts. Next time would be easier. And different.

"Tell them how you remember my name," Reg said when Standish was seated again. "She's the Memory Lady!"

Two waiters poured their coffees in demitasses and left a full carafe to keep hot over a low candle.

"Oh, Reg!" She gave an embarrased laugh. "I don't need to do that any more, not in your case."

"I know that. But you still do it with the names of all the new guests. Tell them how you did it with mine when Mama and I first came."

"I've even forgotten," she said. "Did I imagine you mashing a plate of cabbage with a pig's foot?"

"What?" cried a fascinated Mrs Trelawney.

"No!" Reg replied. "The principle's the same but it was much funnier." He turned to the other two. "She imagined my frizzy hair was a cauliflower head ..."

"No need to *imagine* it," Victor put in.

Reg made a fist at him and warned him that he didn't yet know how she remembered 'Victor Thorne.' "Anyway," he went on, "she imagined me holding a pig's foot in my mouth and my hair turned into a cauliflower head."

Mrs Trelawney frowned in bewilderment at Tamsin, who explained: "Cauliflower gives me veg. Veg — Reg. And pig's foot — Trotter."

"She never gets them wrong, either," Reg added.

"I do," Tamsin admitted. "There was a dreadful moment when I called a Mrs Hastings, 'Mrs Battle'."

"What about Trelawney, then?" the woman challenged.

"Easy," Tamsin told her. "The moment we were introduced — that's always the best moment for this memory trick — I made myself picture you up a ladder, in the branches of a dead tree, sticking patches of green turf all over it. Making the *tree* '*lawny*' you see? When I started with this trick I would just have thought of a tree, a lawn, and a knee — in your case. But it doesn't work. I don't know why. The image will only stick in your mind if it's utterly ludicrous."

"Now Coverley," Standish challenged.

"I pictured you lying in a meadow — a lea — and I mean *in* it, so that it covered you. Like a tumulus."

"Gruesome!" Reg exclaimed.

"Don't leave me out, please," Victor begged.

She'd been waiting for it ever since Reg had returned the sneer. "I needed no assistance to remember your name, my dear," she replied. "From the moment our eyes met, you were the *victor* over my heart."

"Oooaah!" the others chorused, slightly embarrassed because she actually seemed to mean it.

"And the Thorne part?" he persisted.

"Where would love be without its thorns? — one of which, I must warn everybody, is about to begin, this very minute, unless you can manage to change the subject! In my opinion, little twenty-one-year-old girls should be seen and not heard!"

Victor turned to Mrs Trelawney, "Do tell us about this Gilbert and Sullivan production. Where is it to be? Can we take a box and bring all our friends?"

And so, for the rest of the hour they passed in each other's company, the conversation moved from one generality to the next. Toward the end Tamsin went to the ladies' room, where she was joined a moment later by Mrs Trelawney. As they stood in front of the looking glasses, scrutinizing their appearances before rejoining the men, the woman said, "Forgive me if I trespass, Miss Harte, but from the moment Mister Thorne produced that jeweler's box in the dining room, I could not take my eyes off you. It's none of my business, of course, but I assure you I do not ask out of idle curiosity. I had the impression you were expecting it to contain something quite different — an engagement ring, perhaps?"

The woman was so pleasant, her whole attitude so unthreatening, that Tamsin found it impossible to take offence at this intrusion; in fact, it hardly seemed like intrusion, at all.

"Bullseye!" she pulled a face. "I assure you things have not progressed so far between Mister Thorne and me, but he is so ... well ... what can I call it?"

"Mercurial? Impetuous?"

"To put it kindly. In fact, he has no right, really, even to give me this pendant. I don't know how I'm going to be able to accept it. But I couldn't turn it down on the spot — it would have been so humiliating for him. I just wish he hadn't done it, that's all. Have you any suggestions?"

She smiled. "If it should ever come to a clash of wills between the two of you ..."

"Oh it will!" Tamsin assured her.

"Then, if it's of any comfort to you, I don't think *your* will is ever going to experience the slightest difficulty in prevailing over his. And in the meantime I shouldn't worry too much about that turquoise. After all, the decision to buy it was his alone — and it was obviously *made* for you, with those eyes!" She touched Tamsin's cheek gently, taking care to avoid the terra cotta portion. "Do forgive my impertinence but I did just wonder if wedding bells were in the offing."

"Not with Mister Thorne, rest assured!"

Mrs Trelawney caught the hint of an unspoken 'but ...' behind her reply. "Then with someone else?" she dared to ask.

Tamsin blushed. "I'd rather not say."

The moment she spoke the words she regretted it — especially when she saw the look of intense disappointment that passed across Mrs Trelawney's face.

"I mean," she added, *"he* hasn't the faintest idea of my feelings about him. And — to be honest — I'm still in two minds about the man myself."

"Enough said!"

On their way back up the corridor Tamsin said, "I wonder if Standish will ever tie the knot?"

Mrs Trelawney halted and stared at her. "Is that idle curiosity, or …?" She did not name an alternative.

"Idle curiosity," Tamsin assured her. "I probably won't get the chance tonight, but you will. You could let him know I have at least part of the answer to a question he once asked me — if you'd be so kind?"

"Gladly!" Her eyes danced with amusement. "Perhaps he'll explain it to me, too?"

Tamsin nodded, ignoring the blatant invitation. "That would be his prerogative, not mine."

Just before they re-entered the lounge, Mrs Trelawney said, "There's something my husband once said to me before we were married, and I've never forgotten it. Perhaps you won't mind if I pass it on now?"

"Please do." Tamsin waited eagerly.

"It was when I was working day and night to beat my father at his own game. Just because he wouldn't take me seriously and tried to freeze me out. And Cornwallis — he's my husband now, but at that time he was my appallingly neglected fiancé — he advised me to be very careful when I compiled my list of wishes, 'because,' he said, 'strong-minded people like you have a way of persuading Fate to grant them all.'"

"And you think the same applies to me?" Tamsin asked.

"What I think is neither here nor there. It's what you think that matters. If you think the advice might apply to you, there's no harm in heeding it."

It was by then close to midnight and Tamsin said she had to go home, otherwise she'd be turned back into a pumpkin. Standish insisted on accompanying them to the cloakroom, then to the door. There he kissed Tamsin's hand, rather theatrically, and, referring back to her spying mission in his dining room, asked her casually if the Queen's had any other department she would care to investigate.

She was on the point of telling him what Charlotte had blurted out that afternoon; but she realized it would take far too long — and Victor was already chafing, probably. Besides, Mrs Trelawney would tell him, and that would make him very keen to see her again — unencumbered by other social obligations. So, although she realized he was just being facetious with his offer to inspect other departments of the Queen's, she also saw it was too good a chance to pass by. *"Every* department," she replied firmly.

It took him by surprise, of course, but he was too good a hôtelier to let it show; in fact, he even pretended to be pleased. "Shall we say this Friday, then?" he suggested. "Come to luncheon and I'll show you around afterwards." He bowed and was gone.

A full gale was blowing outside. Tamsin felt guilty that she had not given a moment's thought to poor David, somewhere out there, since the moment they had entered the hôtel, about four hours earlier. She asked the driver of their carriage if he thought any of the fleet had put out from Newlyn and he replied that Newlyn men were all mad but none was mad enough to do that. She wondered if common sense had kept David in port after all, even though he had seemed so determined to test the *Merlin's* new engines to the limit against this deterioration in the weather. If Victor had not been there, she would have directed the coach to Newlyn first, just to set her mind at rest.

In the carriage on their brief journey home, Victor took her in his arms and kissed her with a barely controlled passion. Physically she found it as pleasing as ever but her worries about David made it impossible for her to yield as completely as she usually did — indeed, as she would have liked to do.

His left arm crushed her to him, leaving his right hand free to caress her face, her cheek, her neck ... So much was by now part of their established ritual. But tonight he added something new. The thumb and three fingers of his right hand stayed above her collarbone, but the little finger began straying just below, into territory that was usually well covered up and scarcely available to fingers, big or little.

When the incursion met with no immediate protest a second finger slipped down into that hitherto inviolable space. She held her breath. It wasn't unpleasant — quite the opposite. And this was, after all, something along the lines her mother had exhorted her to encourage …

But no! That was to help a man decide that you were the only girl in the world — and she was pretty sure that Victor was there already. So if she continued to permit his fingers to stray, it was merely to satisfy her own curiosity. That was all right as long as it was clearly understood. By her, anyway.

It wasn't many seconds before a third finger joined the two already there — then a fourth and finally the thumb

By now the space between her collarbone and the hem of her bodice was tingling with stray fingers. She felt an answering tingle in her nipples, even though his fingertips were still inches away from them; all the same, she knew they wanted to feel his touch there, too.

And yet the moment his little finger, the smallest and boldest pioneer of the five, touched her there (and, to be fair, it could have been an accident, caused by the sudden jolt of the carriage as it drew up outside the Morrab) something inside her head cried *Stop!* so loudly that she felt sure he must have heard it, too. She had not the heart to push his hand roughly away, so, instead, she folded her entire body inward, toward his, and pressed herself tight against him until only an oyster knife could have parted them again. She made it seem like a sudden rush of overpowering passion, so that he wouldn't feel rejected. Tonight of all nights she owed him that.

And tomorrow could take care of itself.

33 When Cicely and Walter Thorne returned from Peveril Hall the following day, and heard what Victor had done, they were furious. Cicely, seeking a private place for her inquisition, made him accompany her out onto the Esplanade, where it was still blowing a full sou'—westerly gale. Unable to converse above its roar, they walked toward town and, near Battery Point, found a deserted café where they were welcomed like rescuers. Cicely chose a seat by the window, where the moaning of the wind would mask from other ears what she knew would be a frank and painful conversation.

"What did I tell you?" she demanded as soon as the waitress had taken their order. "What did I say was our purpose in moving out of the Queen's and into that poky little boarding house of theirs?"

"Block Tamsin. Spotlight Charlotte," he replied laconically.

"That is a crude pastiche of what I actually said. I told you to steer the narrowest path between the courtship of Miss Harte on the one hand and mere friendly association with her on the other. I said you were to remain cooler than the first but warmer than the second. The whole idea, as I'm sure I made quite clear at the time, was to place a temporary obstacle — a *very* temporary obstacle — between dear Mister Coverley and the Harte girl while simultaneously opening the way for the man to see what a catch Charlotte would be, especially as she was no longer a guest under his roof. I'm sure you recall it all now?"

"Just so," Victor agreed. "Block one, spotlight t'other. Isn't that what I said?"

The waitress brought their tea and Bath buns.

And the Mater was waiting for a proper answer. He could hardly tell her the truth — that he had adopted her absurd 'plan' in the first place because he was bored with Penzance and Tamsin was the only interesting feature in the entire county — that he knew Charlotte had her mind set on other things, anyway — that, from being merely fascinated with Tamsin, he had become obsessed with her — that he was now fighting to cure himself of that obsession as fiercely as any dope fiend might fight to abstain from the fatal poppy — and that last night's *tête-à-tête* with the darling girl had been as irresistible as an opium pipe to the same poor slave.

"How much did this turquoise cost, anyway?" his mother asked — still waiting for her son's defence.

"It was a brooch in the shilling tray in a rag-and-bone man's shop," he lied. "The fellow thought it was a piece of coloured glass. It cost me more to get it changed to a pendant with a gold chain and patent clasp."

"How much more?"

"Ten bob — and you're the only person who knows it. So if word should reach Tamsin's ear, I'll know how. And, more important, by whom."

She bristled. "How dare you threaten me! I shall, of course, consider what you have told me and, *if I so decide,* I shall tell Miss Harte everything. You speak of confidence? Let me tell you — your father and I have lost all confidence in you and your sense of judgement. You were entrusted with the simplest of tasks — *two* simple tasks — and, as far as anyone can tell, you have failed at both. The fact that *you* paid a mere song for this expensive turquoise is really neither here nor there. You have obviously allowed Miss Harte to believe you gave full value for it — and it *is* a valuable stone, am I not right?"

He just managed to stop himself from replying that its value was not one millionth part of a millionth part of the preciousness of her who received it. "It's just a lump of cupro-aluminium phosphate," he replied. "But I suppose they'd ask a fair bit for it in Bond Street."

Neither his sarcasm nor his admission that the stone was valuable pleased her. " You're so impetuous," she said. "You just don't think ahead at all. When a man gives a lady jewelry of any kind, she is bound to see a link between its value in the world and her value in his esteem. A gem of any kind would have misled Miss Harte into supposing you are in love with her. To give her such a large and costly stone is as good as saying that she, too, is most precious and your love is equally large. Well, the harm's done now — though no actual promises were made, I hope?"

"What sort of promises? I say, these are good buns, what?"

"Don't be deliberately obtuse, dear. I know you too well. You have not made a proposal of marriage?"

"No."

"And I trust you have not spoken those three fatal words, 'I love you' yet?"

He shrugged awkwardly. "Not just those three, no."

"What *have* you said, then?"

"Well, she's spoken them to me ..."

"That's neither here nor there. Nobody's going to sue *her* for breach of promise!" She laughed.

He saw a way of nudging her onto a related but less awkward topic — from his point of view. "Ah, yes — but what about *her* feelings, though?"

"What about them? They're her business, not ours. If you had only acted throughout in the way I directed, you would have captured her affections on nothing more than the promise of a light-hearted summer romance at the seaside. If she had chosen to take your playful advances seriously, then that would have been her bad luck. One could have told her not to be so trusting the next time some handsome young *flâneur* winks at her along the Esplanade. But this costly gift makes *that* escape a little difficult." She vanished into her own thoughts for a moment and then added, "I wonder if there's not some way of getting it back from her?"

"Absolutely not!" he exclaimed.

"I'm not talking about your attempting it," she said. "Obviously *I* would have to arrange it all."

"Steal into her room at night?" he sneered.

"No," she replied calmly. "Just explain what sort of a romantic, hot-headed idiot you are and tell her to expect nothing to come of it in the end. She might even accept money for it, then. Yes! She wouldn't dare sue for breach of promise if it could be shown she was as mercenary as all that!"

He peered out of the window, watching huge breakers smash against the sea wall of the Esplanade — sudden vertical sheets of white, and whiter than any laundry would dare to promise. If David Peters had been fool enough to put to sea in the teeth of this gale, he thought, the man deserved everything Old Father Neptune threw at him.

"As for Mister Coverley," she went on, "I begin to fear that he is a broken reed."

"It would be news to him, I'm sure."

"I wonder …?" she mused.

He caught a certain sharp edge to her tone and became alert at once. "You know something," he said.

"I heard a whisper or two. Well-connected friends in Exeter — never mind who. I think there may be trouble brewing for Mister Coverley."

"What? Do tell?" This was the best news of the season.

She eyed him coldly a long while, making him shiver. At length she said, "I think we'll leave it at that for the moment. I only tell you this much in order to explain why I've changed my mind about him. It may all blow over — or he may be the innocent dupe of ... of an extremely cunning plot. It's really no concern of ours. But for the moment, all attempts to — how did you express it — *spotlight* Charlotte are to cease. We shall cut our losses and return home as soon as possible."

"Today?" he asked in dismay.

"Of course not. Such haste would arouse suspicions if this expected trouble does befall Mister Coverley — suspicions that we were implicated in some way. No. We shall give due notice and leave at the agreed time."

"Well, if I'm to have no more to do with Miss Harte," he said, "we can't leave soon enough for me!" He was thinking that, with his parents and sister out of the way, he could return to Penzance and enjoy a clear field. True, he hadn't the income as yet to support himself independently — and almost all his savings had gone on that turquoise for Tamsin — but the moneylenders would fall over themselves to let him have whatever he wanted against next year's inheritance.

She was at once suspicious of his eagerness, but all she said was, "I'm glad you agree. In fact, but for one thing, I'd tell Mrs Harte we'll be leaving this Saturday."

"What's that?"

"This Countess de Ath. I'm intrigued. What do we know about her? And why should she pick an obscure little boarding house at the tail end of England for her bereavement? Our library shelves were still under the dust sheets or I should have hunted for the *Almanac de Gotha* yesterday."

"No need for any of that," he assured her. "Tamsin has already looked her up — in the public library at the top of Morrab Road."

"Well!" His mother was obviously impressed but — equally obviously — unwilling to say so. "The *public* library!" she said. "It would never have crossed my mind. What does 'Mrs Lock the turnkey's wife' or 'Tom Tallow the candlestick maker' want with a reference book on the aristocracy of Europe? Never mind, though — what did she learn?"

"That the said Countess must be well into her eighties, for she married the Count in the eighteen-forties ..."

"What was her maiden name?"

"The Count turned ninety-two last month. Her maiden name was Esterhazy."

"One of the grand families of Europe! Curiouser and curiouser! Any issue?"

"None listed. Of course, there could be a few on the wrong side of the blanket. But the title will have died with him."

"So — barring a few no doubt trivial bequests to illegitimates — she will inherit the lot. How many addresses were given, did Miss Harte say?"

"Not to me. But you can go to the library yourself and ..."

"Me? Go into one of those places? How *could* you! They're full of smelly tramps secretly drinking methylated spirits while they pretend to be reading leaders in the *Morning Post.* I've heard all about them at Mendicity Alliance meetings. But you could do it for me, dear ... please?"

"If it means I'm forgiven?"

"It would mean you've taken the first *teeny* step toward forgiveness." She became thoughtful again. "There's still the mystery as to why an octogenarian countess from one of the noblest families in Europe should arrange to spend her period of mourning in a modest boarding house as far from Europe as you can possibly get — without going to Ireland, of course."

"Tamsin says some friends of theirs called Lock — Harold and Miriam Lock, I think — met her in Baden and puffed the place up no end."

"Even so ... it's pretty odd. Especially as she made the preliminary arrangements even before he died — or so I hear."

"Oh, that's true. She did. Tamsin thinks they may have spent themselves out. They may have run up substantial debts and so the Countess is coming here to hide from her creditors. She says they're going to ask her for some payment in advance."

When his mother made no response to this he said, "What are you thinking now?"

"Miss Harte," she said. "That girl is too shrewd for her own good. At twenty-one a girl should be innocent, trusting, naïve, ingenuous, and charming ... unsullied by the world and its ways — like your dear sister. But Miss Harte at twenty-one is already what she should not become until she has been thirty-nine for some years at least. What will she be like then!"

Still your daughter-in-law, I hope! he replied in the silence of his thoughts.

"However," his mother continued, "if her speculation is correct, then I do not see how we can possibly leave Penzance without witnessing the Countess's arrival and her settling in. If she should turn out to be a lively sort of eighty-year-old — and I have met many who become so in the months after widowhood turns their hair gold with grief — without children of her own — and with or without a goodly fortune ... who knows? She might quite like to take Charlotte under her wing and help bring her out in the world. Such patronage can lead to an extremely advantageous marriage. In fact, if she were broke, she might be glad of a little honorarium in return."

The furious mother who had entered the café not half an hour earlier had completely gone; in her place was a smiling, dedicated woman with a new sense of purpose. Indeed, she was so ecstatic at the prospects for the week ahead that she mistook a silver sixpence in her purse for the fractionally smaller silver threepenny bit and so tipped the waitress twice what she considered the girl to be worth.

But what unquestionably revealed her excitement was that fact that, once she discovered her error, she did not return to the café and ask the girl for threepence back.

34 Tamsin fretted through her work on the morning after her coming-of-age celebration at the Queen's. She did not even dare look at the turquoise Victor had given her; heavy though it was as a gem, it lay heavier still on her conscience. She thought of a thousand ways of returning it to him, but none that would not also hurt him where he was most vulnerable — in his pride. However, if the best antidote to worry is an even greater worry, she had that, too — the worry of not knowing whether David had put out from Newlyn the previous night.

She lingered over her marketing in the town that morning, calling at every fishmonger and asking if they had news of any boat sailing from the port last night. The answer was a double no — no one in his right mind would have done so, but no, they had no personal knowledge of the matter, one way or the other.

So, having forced herself to eat a hearty lunch — for she did not know what sort of afternoon now faced her and she did not want the distractions of hunger on top of everything else — she set off to walk around the shore to Newlyn. Never had one statute English mile seemed so long. Bent almost double against the gale, she had to thrust herself step by step into its steady blast. Running was impossible. Even walking over the level ground seemed more like climbing a steep slope. Time and again she had to stop and fight for breath; and the muscles down the front of her legs, beside her shinbones, seemed perpetually on the verge of cramp. Thank heavens the rain had at least passed over.

In fact, the sun put in a fitful appearance when she was halfway there — or, rather, half a dozen fitful appearances as gaps in the cloud opened up. It showed itself in searchlight beams that played fitfully across the bay, highlighting at random the white horses that stretched as far as the eye could see — which, as she knew from David's little talk on the subject, on a much happier day than this, was not actually very far.

Curiously enough, that knowledge was a comfort to her now. To know that 'the far-distant horizon' of the poet's imagination was, in fact, no more than eight miles away from her present elevation meant that David could, even now, be a mere nine miles from port and yet be out of sight. And nine miles was the distance she had steered between Kynance and 'Portlemm.' He might even have put to sea, realized how foolhardy he had been, and run before the gale into that very harbour. If so, a telegram from Porthleven would surely be waiting to set her mind at rest the moment she arrived at the Peterses' little cottage on the harbour front.

'No fishing' does not mean a day of rest for fishermen. At every loft the doors were open and men sat or squatted about, mending nets, repairing sails, inspecting long lines of vicious-looking fishhooks, or making good the ravages of time and tide — and brandy — upon their lobsterpots. Most were one floor up. She stopped by the first one she found at ground level and peered inside. It reeked of tar, chewing tobacco, and fish. At first she could see nothing, for they worked without candlelight, making do with whatever daylight filtered in through the open door — half of which was now occupied by her. Soon, however, she made out one dim figure, nearest her, sitting cross-legged to splice a rope around a metal eye. She asked him if anyone had put to sea the previous evening.

"He did, Miss Harte," the man replied — for, of course, the whole village knew of her and of David's interest. "Step inside if you mind." He rose and came to join her at the door — a short, muscular man with the rolling gait of a sailor. "Stop out the wind a bit."

"And has he ..."

But his face answered her before she could finish the question.

"Could he have put in at Portlemm?" she asked. "And if so, would he have sent a telegram or something?"

The man poked his head out into the wind and then caught hold of her arm, propelling her half out again. "See that there woman — with the dark-brown skirt and the black shawl — goin' 'long by th'old quay there?"

'Drab skirt and drab shawl' described just about every woman in Newlyn, but, fortunately, only one of them was passing the stub of the old quay at that moment. "Yes," she said.

"Well, that's Oenone Peters, the postmistress. David's aunty. Her could tell 'ee more'n anyone else here. 'Specially if there's been a telegram."

She turned to thank him but he pushed her onward, saying, "Run, maid, and you'll catch she up. Her's now gwin up with that basket to Penlee Point, to old Benny Peters, see."

Tamsin caught up with the woman at the edge of town, where the coastal lane leads on to Mousehole, the next fishing village, a mile or so to the south. "Mrs Peters!" she called out with her last gasp of breath.

The woman turned round. "Miss Harte?"

She nodded, being too busy getting her breath back to speak.

"I said you'd come. Old Benny said you wouldn't. He said you'd just send to find out."

"Has there been any word?" she managed to ask at last.

"No, my lover. The old man's been there since sunrise. I'm now taking a bit croust and tay for 'n." She lifted a corner of the cloth that covered her basket and Tamsin caught the whiff of hot pasty.

"Can I take it up to him for you?" she asked. "Or were you going there anyway?"

The woman hesitated. "Well," she said. "Tell 'ee what — I'll take 'ee so far as the path that do go up Penlee Head. That's some climb for these old bones."

Tamsin took this as a hint to relieve her of the basket. She wondered if, when she reached her early forties, she, too, might be talking of 'old bones' to youngsters half her age.

Talk was desultory even though they were now in the lee of the hill, which reduced the force of the gale considerably. But she did manage to establish that the entire Peters family — indeed, the whole of Newlyn — was angry at David and Harry for tempting fate by putting to sea last night. The so-called engine test over calm seas, in full sunlight, inside the bay had proved nothing. It only needed the spark to fail once and the gale would drive them bare-masted onto the rocks.

"Why did they do it, then?" Tamsin asked. "Surely they understand that as well as anyone?"

"Well now ..." Oenone stopped to catch her breath. Selling stamps and writing out telegrams did little for a person's fitness. "That's a question, see. You do know, I s'pose, he lost two brothers — Harvey and Jacko — backalong a while. Nineteen-oh-three it was. In the Fall. November time. The eighth as I recall — the sabbath. They should ought to of been back the day before, by rights." They set off again. "David wasn't but twenty then but he always said as if he'd been aboard, they wouldn't never of foundered. He's always been the last to put back to port in bad weather — like he's got to prove it, see?"

They were nearing the headland now, which reduced their shelter from the wind. About a hundred paces short of it they came to a stile beside the road and, beyond it, a path that wound in a zigzag up the slope.

"Now, my lover," Oenone said. "That's the path as many a widow has trod! When you do get up top there, you'll see a coastguard shelter and the old man leaning fore'nenst it to steady his spyglass, I'm sure — if he's not inside."

Tamsin thanked her and set off up the path. There were places where the strong and fit had shunned the zigzag and gone directly up the slope. She tried the first few and then settled for the longer but gentler path for the rest of the way. It was a climb of two hundred and fifty feet in only a quarter of a mile. And, as David himself had told her on the day they had lifted the brandy, the view from the top was over eighteen miles.

The Captain, as she still liked to call him, saw her when she was just a head and shoulders, cut off by the edge of the hill. "You come when you could then, maid," he called out, his voice carrying to her downwind. "I said 'ee would."

She was too puffed to reply. She had to push hard down on her thighs with her free hand, like a pistons, to make the last few yards. He came back along the path to meet her and relieve her of the basket.

"Meet Oenone, did 'ee?" he asked. "Her'll be some glad she never had to make that climb!"

"Believe ... you ..." she panted.

He put an arm around her shoulders and pressed her forward into the shelter of the lookout. "Coastguard'll be here four o'clock," he said. "Us'll have to get out then." He laughed. "We met first in one shelter and now we meet in another!"

With eager hands he disinterred the pasty from the cloth, broke it in two, and offered half to her. "Eat 'n fitty-like," he said. "There's no knives nor forks."

She thanked him and explained that she had already had a good lunch — for this very purpose. The pasty did smell delicious, though. Perhaps she and Mrs Pascoe should look out some old Cornish recipes and offer them alongside a purely fish menu? "No sign of the *Merlin,* I suppose?" she asked.

"She'll come back when her hold is full," he replied.

So he wasn't going to admit to her that David was in any danger; the good news he was so anxiously waiting for up here was merely of a full hold, not of the safe return of his last remaining son from the storm.

She had to admit that, from this height, the sea did not look nearly as ominous as it did from the shore. The white horses that dotted its surface were fathered by the wind, acting on ripples. The waves that made up the underlying swell were much farther apart — several boat lengths, in fact. They did not seem menacing until they reached the shallows, inshore, where they reared up suddenly and fell upon the beaches and rocks with a thunderous roar. All around this end of Mount's Bay, as far as Cudden Point, six miles away to the east, she could see the sudden stabs or streaks of white as the waves boiled and foamed in their death throes against the land.

Porthleven was hidden behind Trewarvas Head. In fact, the next part of the coast she could see from there was the blue-grey streak of the Lizard Peninsula, lost in the haze that hid the entire horizon.

"We can see what? Eighteen miles?" she asked.

He could only nod, his mouth being full of beef, potato, and turnip. "You'll share a dish o' tay, maid?" he asked when he had swallowed it. He took a pint lemonade bottle, full of sweet, milky tea, from the basket and filled a black enamel mug. "This'll be my side, that's yours," he said, offering it to her first.

She sipped and then drank gratefully. Normally she'd rather drink ice-cold seawater than sweet tea but somehow her exertions and the buffeting she had endured turned it into an elixir. He topped up the mug and drank from it in turns with bites of pasty — 'cement mixing,' as her father had called it. But, she supposed, it was something one simply had to do if one had lost a lot of back teeth.

Since he was pretending that nothing was really amiss, she decided to challenge him head-on. "Your sister-in-law says it's a stubborn streak in David that drives him to do reckless things like this," she said as soon as the last of the pasty had been washed down with the last of the tea.

"Stubborn?" He nodded. " 'Es, stubborn." His tone was ambiguous; she could not tell whether he was proud or critical.

He put a spyglass to his eye, resting its other end against the stone that fringed the open doorway, and scanned the sea from west to east; she said nothing to distract him, though she longed to know what he really thought of David's chances against last night's storm. After three sweeps he handed the glass to her, saying, "See if they young eyes of yourn can do better."

She took it from him with trembling fingers. The wind had filled her eyes with water and she had to wipe them, too. *Please, please, please let him be there!* she prayed silently, though whether it was to God or to some more primitive arbiter of human destiny she was unclear. She raised the glass to her eye.

She copied the Captain, sweeping from west to east, beginning at the horizon and working closer with each successive sweep. There were plenty of steamboats and tall-masted sailing ships out there — well out, for the Cornish coast is a notorious graveyard of the hundreds that have sought its shelter. But she saw no sign of a small mast and a trapezoid sail. Or ought she to be looking for the flotsam of a wreck? She did not ask it aloud.

For the next hour they took turn and turn about to scan the bay. Often, in the act of handing over the glasses, he would pause and start a conversation. One time he admitted that when he'd agreed to buy the engine for the *Merlin,* he'd intended it to make normal fishing trips safer, not to encourage his son to put to sea when no sane man without an engine would set his nose beyond the harbour wall. But he spoke in such an offhand way — as if to say, 'Just my luck!' — that she could not give *her* true opinion of his folly.

However, if he was trying to buck Fate, or whistle down the wind, with all this seeming nonchalance, it was a bad decision, for he could not keep his true feelings back forever. She, for her part, had simply tried to match his mood and seem equally unconcerned. So, she wondered, was either of them deceiving the other any longer?

" 'Twas good of 'ee to come all this way, maid," he said on another of those occasions.

And she pooh-poohed any claim to goodness ... she had been going for a walk anyway ... happened to meet his sister-in-law ... volunteered to carry his basket of croust. That was all.

"Shall I tell the boy you did come all the way out here to see was he safe or no?" he asked another time.

"If you don't," she replied lightly, "I'm sure Mrs Oenone will, so where's the harm?"

At other times he tried to disguise his fears by telling the sort of tales any Cornishman will tell another at any sort of meeting at all — at a bus stop, by the hearth, sharing a mile ... anywhere at all. He told her, for instance, of a farmer who had the land on the far side of the valley from where they were standing — over toward the hamlet of Sheffield, above Mousehole. "Stanley Roseveare, he'm called. And when he's out ploughing or harving he won't stop for man nor beast, see. His missiz can stand by the headland and baal her head off and he won't pay she no more heed than he'd pay a mother-marget on his coat ..."

"What's that?"

He thought a moment and said, "A bluebottle. So then one day when she had her mind set to stop 'n, out she goes to the field with a basket on her arm and a cloth over the basket. Nothin' in the basket, o' course, but he don't know that, see? And ole Roseveare, he dropped the hames, left the horse stood where 'twas, an come running like ... like ..."

"So quick as a witnick?" she offered.

"'Es!" He laughed delightedly. "You got 'n — so quick as a witnick! My soul! Us'll have 'ee Cornished yet, maid!"

But all the stories and all the good-humoured banter in the world did nothing to disguise his anxiety for his son.

She wished there was something she could say, some sign she could make, to let him know that she, too, cared more than she was admitting.

She tried an oblique approach in the end. "I wonder if Sarah Rowe would be here if she knew he'd put out to sea last night."

"Sarah *Rowe!*" he exclaimed. "Why she's dead these thirty years. He never told 'ee about she?"

Tamsin was on the point of explaining that it must be a different Sarah Rowe when the old man added, "Why, I courted she for years — or tried to — afore I settled for th'old woman I got. Saint Ives people they were. Lot of actions, they had."

"Actions?"

"Lawdydaw folk. Her wouldn't so much as look at I. A Newlyn boy!" He spat down the wind and laughed.

"Was she the one who married some fine fellow up Carbis Bay?" she asked.

"That's the one! Henry Noy — son of Cap'n Noy, who retired from the East India trade and ran the ferry between Lelant and Hayle. Much good it did her, too. He never could fix no babby in her. And then she died of a malignancy. Weel!" He looked at her with new interest. "So David has told 'ee all about that, then, has he? He must be some hurrisome for *thee,* maid — that's all I can say."

She wanted to explain that David had, in fact, merely purloined the story in order to ... well what? To put her off, she supposed.

Well, she didn't need any putting off, thank you! All she ever wanted to be with him was friends. However, it was getting too complicated to explain, so she just let it go and went back to scanning the bay, with or without his spyglass. And always, before each sweep, she repeated that same silent prayer — *Please let him be there this time!*

She tried to picture the map of Mount's Bay and let her mind's eye roam this way and that, north to south, east to west, until something inside her cried, *There!* — a sort of mystical, mental dowsing. Then she would sweep that area minutely through the glass, feeling sure that this time her intuition had borne fruit.

It was all to no avail. By four o'clock, when the coastguard ought to have arrived and kicked them out, she felt she could draw from memory every rock on every cliff from Marazion to Cudden Point, to say nothing of the dozens of reefs and shoals that ringed the shore, each one a hazard for the unwary.

She was just about to tell the Captain that she had to be getting back to Penzance when he nudged her with his elbow and, passing over the glass, murmured, "I hope these eyes do not deceive me now."

She followed his pointing finger, almost due south, and at once saw ... no, that could not be it — a two-masted sailing ship right on the horizon. A sloop? A brig? A barquentine? She almost laughed — here was a matter of life and death and she was worrying about naval correctitude! "That two-masted ship," she said, "which way from that? If you imagine that's the centre of a clock face?"

He took the glass back from her, hunted around, and handed it back, saying, "Seven o'clock." His attitude was subtly different this time — much more sure of himself and thus much less dependent on her confirmation.

This time! she prayed yet again.

And this time she found him. It was the *Merlin,* all right, running with a reefed sail before the wind. The glass shivered and clouded over. She did not realize, until the Captain took it from her and wiped it, that she was weeping. She turned from him and tried to bury her face between two stones in the rough wall of the shelter.

He touched her gingerly on one shoulder. "Shall I tell 'n you come looking out for 'n, then, maid?" he asked, repeating one of his earlier questions.

"Tell him anything you like," she cried. "Tell him I'll kill him next time I see him!" She wrenched herself away and stumbled, half blind, outside. "You tell him that," she added as she strode away, wiping her cheeks on her sleeves. "Tell him to keep away from me if he knows what's good for him."

Part Four

'Portlemm'

An outing to France

35 By Friday morning Tamsin was doing her best to forget the entire episode. Shame at her sudden and unexpected weakness had made her shout out those ridiculous threats to the Captain on Penlee lookout; and now she felt doubly ashamed that she had allowed her emotions to boil over like that. If anyone deserved punishment, it was herself. It wasn't as if David meant anything to her. He was just a friend. There was absolutely no reason why her happiness at his safe homecoming should not have turned to tears like that. And if she had simply laughed at her own weakness and dried her eyes, no one would have thought any more about it. All her outburst had achieved was to give everyone the wrong impression and make things awkward for the future.

She resolved then to stay away from David, have nothing to do with him, make no inquiries about his ordeal at sea — if, indeed, it had been an ordeal at all ... in short, to cut him out of her life as far as the world was concerned. For how long? Well, there was no need to decide that now. For a good long time, anyway — at least until people could see for themselves that she had no feelings for him beyond plain and simple friendship.

She would miss him of course ...

She shook her head angrily. There was no point in thinking about that now. The damage was done and it had to be repaired first. Friendship could wait.

Whenever anyone asked her — Daisy, Charlotte, her mother ... everyone except Victor — how David had fared, she replied offhandedly that she knew very little more than they did. She had gone for a simple afternoon stroll (to Newlyn, as it happened) and she had heard that someone had spied him from some lookout or other. Near Mousehole, they said. And the *Merlin* appeared to be sound — which was good news, wasn't it, but excuse her please as she had work to do before taking luncheon with Mr Coverley at the Queen's. Also the Countess would be arriving by the afternoon train tomorrow — in case they'd all forgotten it.

Busy or not, Cicely Thorne found occasion that Friday morning to beg a moment of her time. Tamsin suggested the guests' lounge. Cicely said she didn't wish to take up precious minutes and offered instead to accompany her on her regular outing to the shops.

"Presumably you'd rather Daisy did not accompany us?" Tamsin said.

"Quite so," Cicely agreed.

"Only she usually helps me carry things, you see."

Tamsin thought that would put a stop to this unwelcome suggestion, for she was quite sure the woman would rather be seen dead than walk abroad carrying bags or parcels. And, indeed, it looked that way for a moment; but then Cicely brightened. "I know," she said. "Let us do it in proper style. We'll take a motor cab from the rank on the Esplanade and make the shopkeepers come out to serve us."

Tamsin, whose limbs were still weary from a walk that had seemed more like a climb, and a climb that had seemed more like a vertical ascent, accepted the first part of this offer but insisted that she would have to alight from the cab herself and choose the produce, as the shopkeepers of Penzance were not used to the *grande dame* style of marketing and would certainly palm off inferior goods on anyone who tried it.

There was a slight altercation at the cab rank when Cicely passed by the first three cabs and picked the fourth. The man refused to accept them until she explained that his was the first cab in the line that had a glass partition between passengers and chauffeur, and she wished to have a private conversation with her young friend.

Tamsin dircted him to Oliver's, the butcher, first.

"Now," Cicely said as soon as they set off, "I've just heard that my silly little boy gave you a rather splendid coming-of-age present last Tuesday?"

Had it not been for her upset over David, Tamsin might have taken a completely different line in answer to this opening sally. She really did not want to keep the turquoise, notwithstanding Jessica Trelawney's advice; she did not wish to feel under any obligation to Victor nor do anything which might seem to acknowledge that his undoubted love for her gave him any rights. And, she realized, that was still much the most sensible attitude for her to take. Unfortunately, something deep inside her, not amenable to logical calculations of best and worst interests, refused to adopt it. Instead she would punish herself by doing the opposite — and, in some obscure way, which she would have been ashamed to explain in so many words, it would also show David where he stood.

So she replied, "Yes! 'Silly little boy' is just right! But he's utterly adorable, too."

"If you say so." Her tone was distant. "Of course, I have not actually seen it yet — a turquoise, was it?" She was colder now that she suspected she was in for a long haul.

"Yes, the biggest one I ever saw. And beautifully polished and set, too. Flawless. I was brought up never to wear jewelry before evening." Here she glanced for the merest fraction of a reluctant second at the pearl brooch and ruby ring the woman was wearing. "Otherwise I could show it to you now."

"Well, I'm looking forward to seeing it — whenever you can find time. He told me of his extraordinary luck in finding it in the … well, in the place where it was. I suppose he told you, too?"

"He told me so many things that evening, Mrs Thorne. We got on famously. Actually" — she glanced all about and lowered her voice dramatically — "I don't mind admitting it to *you,* but I was in a blue funk when he produced the box and I saw the jeweler's name upon it. For one awful moment, I thought it would turn out to hold an engagement ring!"

Surprise at this unexpectedly frank admission caused the woman's mask to slip. Tamsin saw that she had achieved her purpose — to put Cicely Thorne in a blue funk, as a punishment for daring to interfere with *her* decisions about *her* life.

"My dear Miss Harte," she replied. "I confess I'm glad to hear you speak of a possible betrothal in such terms. It would, of course, be absurd and out of the question. But tell me — have things progressed so far between you that such fears could …"

"Time!" Tamsin interrupted airily. "What is time to those in love! They say love laughs at locksmiths. I believe clockmakers and calendar printers should be added to the list."

"Well, dear, I regret to say that you force me to speak quite bluntly. I hope you understand that time is not of the essence here — in any case. No matter how long the friendship between you and my son may endure — and, of course, one hopes it will endure a lifetime — there can *never* be any question of a betrothal between you. Much less of a permanent union."

"Really?" Tamsin said icily. "Since we are both of age, I don't quite see how ..."

"Oliver's, ladies!" The driver called through the glass partition.

"Shall I come with you?" Cicely asked, knowing not only that Tamsin would refuse the offer but also that it would give her a few precious minutes alone in which to think.

Tamsin did, naturally, refuse the offer, adding that she'd be as quick as she could.

Cicely knew very well that the girl was trying to hurt her. She knew Victor was an unreliable mixture of the sentimental, the bull-headed, and the impetuous, but she doubted that even he would go so far as to engage himself after so short an acquaintance. However, Victor was not the problem here. Tamsin was. And it would be useless to lay down the law or to appeal to the conventions to *that* young miss. She would have to show her that marriage to Victor would threaten her *own* ambitions.

It would, of course, be helpful if she knew what Tamsin's ambitions were. She did not doubt that the girl was consumed with them. You only needed to watch her make her selections, in there with the butcher, poor man. She made him turn every piece over; she looked into every corner to see whether a better cut had not been set aside for a more favoured customer ... and when it came to price, no doubt she'd shave every halfpenny to a farthing. Here was a young woman determined to beat all challengers and emerge on top. What was that, if not ambition?

On her return Tamsin left the wrapped meat in the taxi's luggage space beside the driver and directed him next to Trevaskis, the greengrocer. Normally she'd have got the butcher to deliver but she remembered saying that Daisy usually helped her carry things.

"About what you were saying," she began as she climbed back into the cab.

Cicely laid a soothing hand on her arm. "Let me first explain my point a little more fully — to save us both from pursuing the wrong hare. I know what you're thinking — and also, I suspect, what you're *not* thinking. You probably imagine that when I say marriage is out of the question, I'm referring to the reduced circumstances in which you and your dear Mama find yourselves. Nothing could be further from the truth. It would be ridiculous to think of you as fortune hunters. And in any case, I trust Mister Thorne and I are above such snobbery."

"If that is true, Mrs Thorne, I'm sure you won't mind my asking what else could induce you to lay down such ..."

"You may certainly *ask*, my dear, but I should think that, of all the people in the world, the one most qualified to answer the question is *yourself!*"

"Me?"

"Indeed. Who knows you better than yourself? Who knows your dreams and ambitions down to the last detail — and I'm sure you have both in abundance! Believe me, I am not 'fishing,' as they say, to discover what they may be. But I'm sure that marriage to a wealthy husband would go a great way toward achieving them. However, I wonder if you have pictured yourself trying to achieve them if *Victor* were that husband? He is very fond of having his own way, you know. He will never tolerate a dilettante mother. No hobbyist home-maker for him! And he will expect a family — a large one, if I know him. And families do have a way of interfering with one's own grand schemes! So let me rephrase the question you were about to ask: How closely do his expectations connect with yours?"

When Tamsin did not reply, she added: "And so was I not right to say that any betrothal between you and Victor would be impossible — by which I meant that it would be a cruel deception of a man whose heart has temporarily outpaced his brain?"

The girl's thoughtful silence implied that she did, indeed, have ambitions as big as a barn — and that Victor's expectations would do as much to frustrate them as his money would do to foster them. An irresistible force had met an immovable object.

"Am I not right, dear?" she prompted.

Still the girl did not reply.

"I hope I am," Cicely continued. "Because in so many ways you would make him an excellent wife. But I have watched you about the Morrab and I could almost think some guardian angel arranged for your straitened circumstances. *Not*, I hasten to add, for your father's death! That would be too crass. But for the chances that brought you to that guest house. I could almost think you had managed a much grander place in a past existence. Am I getting warm?"

Tamsin nodded — and even managed a tight little smile. Trevaskis opened the door at that moment, giving her time to consider how to continue this discussion now that the woman had so completely turned the tables on her.

As if to emphasize her victory, Cicely added as Tamsin got out: "And I'm sure your hopes are not something you'd relinquish in order to conform to my son's expectations of a good little wife — not for all the wealth in Lombardy."

When her business with the greengrocer was done, Tamsin put the vegetables she had bought directly into his messenger boy's basket, together with the meat from Oliver's, and saw him on his way.

"You could have done the same at the butcher's," Cicely commented. "I've seen his messenger boy about the town."

"Except that he switched cuts on me once when I let him do that, so now I always carry it," Tamsin explained — wishing she could find as easy an escape from Mrs Thorne's other arguments. She directed the cab back to the Morrab.

"Shall we lay all our cards on the table now?" Cicely proposed. "It's less exciting to play with open hands, I know, but in this case it might prove more profitable to both of us. Shall I begin?" She smiled. "I'm probably more used to it than you are!"

"I don't know." Tamsin shrugged. "Everything's happening at once. It's like cramming spring, summer, autumn, and winter all into one day."

"When I saw that Victor was taking an interest in you, I knew he must be making secret plans to return to Penzance after we had left — assuming we had left when we originally intended. So I wrote to our steward, Mister Merrick, and asked him to carry out certain refurbishments to Peveril Hall — which I knew he'd been eager to do for some time. Then we moved into the Morrab. One way or another, I knew that would bring matters to a head — as, indeed, it has."

"I must admit," Tamsin put in, "the same thought had occurred to me — that Victor might return, I mean."

"And you were looking forward to it?"

She shrugged.

"Well, I shall not press you for a decision now, my dear. You are a mature and sensible young woman, I know. But you will require a little time to think these matters over. You are taking luncheon with Mister Coverley, I hear?"

"At the Queen's, yes. He is going to show me how a great establishment like that is run."

"Is he, indeed!"

Her knowing tone surprised Tamsin. "D'you think that's extraordinary? The Morrab is hardly any competition to him."

The woman smiled. "Perhaps that's the last thing on his mind — just at the moment." She looked Tamsin up and down. "Do you think you could manage a big place like that?"

"What an extraordinary question!" she exclaimed. "If we're talking about 'the last thing on his mind,' I'm sure that is it."

"You're probably right, dear. We shall see what we shall see."

36 The luncheon was to be served in a private room. Tamsin was wary of this arrangement until she heard that she was not to enjoy the *tête-à-tête* she had expected; both Reg Trotter and Mrs Trelawney were to be there, too. Wariness then gave way to disappointment. It crossed her mind that one very good way of getting all the girls in town interested in you would be to behave as if you were interested in none of them!

Mrs Trelawney was so relaxed and so poised. Tamsin saw what wealth could do for a woman, especially wealth she had created for herself. True, Mr Trelawney had not exactly been poor, but — or so it was said — she had been able to match him pound for pound on the day they were wed. And his was family wealth whereas she'd made hers all by herself.

The conversation ranged over many topics — the meaning-behind-the-meaning of *The Pirates of Penzance* ... Mata Hari, the new Hindoo dance sensation in Paris ... what the accidental drowning of the bishop of Hong Kong had revealed of God's will ... the anti-infidel riots in Casablanca ... Galsworthy's latest novel of the Forsytes, *A Man of Property* ... and whether Penzance should build an open-air salt-water swimming pool at Battery Point. Tamsin soon realized that the other three expected her to have an opinion on each and every topic, no matter how little it related to her life or theirs. In the circumstances she thought she did well enough not to have annoyed any of them by making a point that, quite accidentally, ran contrary to one or other's strongly held beliefs.

Why people should concern themselves with such things when there was so much work to be done and money to be made was a mystery to her, but she supposed it was the sort of thing they could indulge in once they were secure and could afford to enjoy their leisure. As far as she was concerned, though, it was a bit of a bore and she had to call on all her self-discipline not to let it show. Still, the wine flowed freely — a Montrachet followed by a deliciously sweet Barsac — so she could not really complain.

Toward the end of their meal, when she felt she'd had enough of world gossip, she asked Standish how he was finding the season so far. There was a little frisson of embarrassment around the table. Clearly one did not talk shop on such an occasion; but she was past caring by then. She had a clock ticking in her head, even if the others couldn't hear it.

"Not bad," he said. "We've had better. Middling, I'd say. How about you?"

"Well, we've no previous years to compare it with but I'll say that future years will find it hard to beat this one. We're fully booked right through to the first week in September. Mama has even had to take a room at Chynoweth, next door, where they still have vacancies — to make room for this Countess de Ath, who's arriving tomorrow and leaving God knows when."

When that had been explained, and the excitement had died down, Standish said, "That's a marvellous achievement for your opening season, you know."

"Well," she gushed, "we thought at first it was going to be a disaster. We opened the doors at Easter and for weeks we couldn't get beyond half full."

"Half full!" Standish chuckled. "Most of us would give our eye teeth to be as busy as that in spring! Anyway, what brought about the change?"

"I think it was word of mouth. Most of the guests we're getting now say something like, 'We're so looking forward to this holiday — we've heard all about you from our friends the

Snoddys'... or some such name. And, it turns out, the Snoddys, or whoever, were guests of ours earlier in the season. Also about half of them are already booking to come back next summer — which is very gratifying."

After that, Standish took her on the promised guided tour of the Queen's, which was as fascinating to her as a tour of a railway works would be to most little boys. He covered everything, from the servants' quarters, where the live-in maids slept four to a room in bunks, to the cellar-within-a-cellar, where the rarest wines and finest brandies were kept. Half a dozen of the latter looked rather familiar.

"Where are the other six?" she asked.

He laid a finger against the side of his nose and winked.

Suddenly she realized they were all alone, here, in what was probably the most private place in the whole of Penzance. If there was a better moment to test his interest in her, she could not imagine it. *Now!* she told herself. *Before you get cold feet.*

"Just a mo ..." She peered at his face in the flatteringly golden light of the single candle he was carrying — one of the most rugged, attractive, manly faces she had ever seen. Especially as close as this.

"Eh?" he responded.

Her heart began to race; it hammered in the back of her neck, near the base of her skull. Surely he could hear it, too? "You've collected a cobweb," she said. He had, too — a rolled-up skein of silk, heavy with dust. She reached out and peeled it off his collar, lifting it where he could see she wasn't playing games.

"Don't move yet!"

"More?" he asked.

"It's left a mark." She had to go very close to him to brush off the smear. Even though they were not touching — except where her hand brushed his collar — she could feel the whole of her body glowing at the nearness of him.

"You hate disorder," he murmured.

Oh, if he could only sense the disorder inside her!

"I admire order," she agreed. "I admire the people who bring it about, too." She looked up into his eyes. "I admire you, Standish, for what you've achieved here. In fact, I think you're a pretty wonderful person all round."

He swallowed heavily but, for once, seemed tonguetied.

Committed now, she sprang on tiptoes and kissed him quickly on the corner of his mouth.

His whole body went rigid — surely not with distaste? Please let it be anything but that!

"You don't mind?" she asked, rocking back on her heels.

"Mind? Of course not!"

"Kiss me, then."

He set the candle down behind her and, for one delirious moment, he took her head between his hands. And then he kissed her on the forehead. Her throat tightened. Tears sprang to her eyes. She would have shed them, too, if he had not added, "You are in such a hurry, Tamsin — my dear girl. But there's no need. Just slow down, eh?"

The tears turned to laughter, equally hysterical but much easier to bear. She blew out the candle, grabbed his arm, and said, "Lead me back to the light!"

She had meant it as a challenge, to see how well he knew his way around his own hôtel. But what had been pitch dark when the candle went out was already turning to a paler shade of black and, by the time they reached the end of the bins, the exit door was easy to discern.

Before they went back upstairs, however, he caught her by the arm and said, "I had a particular reason for bringing you down here. *Not,* I regret to say, the one you may have suspected."

"You mean you don't find me attractive?" she blurted out — determined to make him come down off the fence for once and for all.

"On the contrary!" he exclaimed fervently. "I've been well aware of a growing mutual interest between us. But there are things you do not know."

"Obstacles?"

"Yes. You see ..."

"You're married already!"

"No. Just listen, and you'll understand why I've seemed so lukewarm. I've brought you down here because it's the one place I can be sure of not being overheard. Some years ago I entered into a very foolish partnership — not a marriage — a commercial partnership, with a man who ... well, he seemed to have the Midas touch. Without going into all the gory details, I'll just say I lost a lot of money. Not everything — obviously — but a fair few shekels. I put it down to experience and dissolved the partnership. I can warn you now that, if ever anyone should offer you the chance to buy into a hundred-percent, copper-bottomed, sure-fire money-making scheme that will return your investment many times over, and hustles you into a quick decision before the shutters come down — just thank him for thinking of you and walk away. It's what I should have done. The only reason I'm telling you this, Tamsin, is that my erstwhile partner, a man called Marcus Mitchell, has continued with his swindling ways — of course — but, in an attempt to cover his tracks, he has fabricated a number of documents, dating them back to the time of our partnership, and he has forged my signature upon them. So, you see ..."

"Oh, Standish!" More than ever now she wanted to hug him, to comfort him, to ask how she could help, no matter how small or trivial the way. "How long has this been going on?"

"You mean when did I first hear of it? About this time last year. I just laughed at first, becuase I thought nothing would be easier than to prove they were forgeries. But Mitchell's a lot cleverer than I bargained for and, though the wheels of the law grin exceeding slow, they are relentless. Just lately it has become a great deal more serious. So you will surely understand that any sort of romantic entanglement at this time would be the height of dishonour on my part."

"If I can help in any way ...?" she stammered.

"You can!" He rubbed his hands briskly. "I'm not beaten yet — not by any means. And meanwhile I have this hôtel to run. So, if you wish to help me right now" — he took her arm and started back upstairs — "you could tell me why you're so interested in our operations here. So few people take any interest in what goes on behind the scenes — though they soon let you know if anything goes wrong out in front!"

She confessed then, that it had been her passion from the moment the Morrab was just a gleam in the eye — and she went on to tell him about her fantasies of managing a great liner.

"Well," he replied, "if it's confession time, I must admit that I feel I've run into a brick wall here. The place is a success. It has developed its own set ways — and because they work, no one wants to change them, including me. But I know that can be fatal. Traditions will kill you unless you continually adapt them to the ever-changing situation. You remember what you said at lunch when Mrs Trelawney told us she'd just bought the piano transcription to Elgar's new 'Pomp and Circumstance March'?"

"No. I was completely out of my depth during most of those conversations, I hope you realize."

"Go on with you! You said, 'The trouble with England is too much pomp and not enough circumstance.' I thought it was the best comment anyone made throughout the entire meal."

"Really? It's just the way I feel."

"Anyway — it shows you understand the need to keep old traditions on their toes. So come on — put your penny on the drum: What changes would you make if you were me?"

"I wouldn't wear a white blazer down into the cellars," she replied. "Look at you!"

He laughed.

They had reached the cloakroom by now, where he helped her back into her cape and retrieved her parasol. Then he saw her to the door — and beyond. Another place beyond the reach of eavesdroppers.

"I'm serious," he said, leading her across the Esplanade to the railings overlooking the beach. "If you owned the Queen's, what changes would you make?"

"I'd have a different menu every day for fourteen days," she replied at once.

"Why?"

"You have a seven-day rotation at the moment, right?"

"Yes."

"Which is probably all right in the winter, when most of your custom must be from travelling salesmen and people on blustery walking holidays. But for people who stay a full fortnight in the summer it means they get the same menu again each Monday, Tuesday … and so on. It was one of the first things Mrs Thorne commented on when she moved in when she moved in at the Morrab — not a single breakfast menu has been repeated." She laughed. "She'll get a shock next week, mind. It will be day after day of 'dayja vu'!"

"Any other changes?" he asked.

"I'd offer special cheap Saturday luncheons for boarding-house landladies — and gentlemen. There are dozens of them all around you — as you surely know. I'd do it even at no profit. Let me tell you — Saturday mornings are hell in boarding-house land. It's when half your house empties first thing in the morning so that they can catch the early trains back up country. Then you have all the rooms to turn out and get ready. Then there's this ghastly pause when you're too exhausted to make a meal ..."

"Wait! What about the cook?"

"It's the best day for her to take off — because most of the breakfasts are early and she can go for an early start. Anyway, then there's a new rush when the up-country trains start arriving around three o'clock in the afternoon. And it goes on until quite late in the evening. So if someone said, come and have a cheap lunch at the Queen's ... we'd all leap at it."

"I'm sure you would — but what's in it for us?"

"Us? We wouldn't rest. We'd go from table to table, showing them our menus, asking their opinions ... flattering them ... making them feel we're all in it together — this wonderful business of catering for visitors. So when their bed-and-breakfast guests ask where to go for lunch or dinner — as ours do all the time — what will they tell them? We could even send them away with little cards saying, 'For first-class cuisine, including many local Cornish specialities, all at prices that won't give you indigestion ...' you know — something like that. However, d'you know what I think you *really* ought to do?"

He eyed her warily. She laughed and said, "If you can afford it, I think you should buy the Mount's Bay next door, knock it down, and extend the Queen's in the same grand style ... double the size of your ballroom, and ..."

"Stop!" He put his fingers demonstratively in his ears. Then, "You haven't just thought of all this on the spur of the moment, have you! You've been mulling it over for some time."

"Not just about the Queen's," she replied.

"Oh?" He was wary again. "Where else, then?"

"It doesn't matter. It's just a pipe-dream." All the same, she could not help glancing down the Esplanade at the empty space opposite the bath house.

He saw it, followed her gaze, then turned slowly back to her. "Dear God!" he murmured.

"Of course," she said jovially. "If you'd rather spend the money on *that* ..."

"Get thee behind me!" he cried.

She told him she really had to go — if only to stop her mother from having a fit over the arrival of the Countess tomorrow.

On her way home she remembered she still hadn't told him about Charlotte's outburst on the afternoon of her birthday party. However, in view of what he had just revealed, none of that seemed to matter any more.

37 When Bridget discovered that carnauba-wax polish does not lie down very well over freshly shone beeswax, Harriet Harte threw her fifteenth panic-tantrum of the morning. Tamsin bore it as long as she could before remembering an urgent errand, which allowed her to escape.

"Don't go in there," she warned Daisy, just outside the door. "Honestly! If there is ever to be another morning in my life quite like this, then please someone give me enough warning so I can lay in a stock of ether, laudanum, cask-strength whisky ... *anything* to keep me mercifully oblivious to it!"

Daisy pulled a sympathetic face.

Tamsin, finding it a great relief to let off steam, took her arm and led her away to safety. "She's being *utterly* insufferable," she said. "As if we didn't have enough to do already, what with half our regular rooms turning over this morning. She knows very well how much extra work that means, but, no, everything must yield to making the wretched old Countess de Ath feel as if she were coming home to her palace — or whatever grand *loge* might be her habitual residence."

"I was totting up the bills for the departing guests," Daisy said, almost apologizing for not taking her share of the agony.

"Yes, bless you! I'd stay out of the way among the ledgers, if I were you. Tot them all up again. *Someone* here has to maintain her sanity."

"What's this smell?"

"*Perfume,* please! It's quadruple strength lavender beeswax. Poor Bridget and Catherine have polished every surface in the Countess's room *three times* already this morning. Then dear Mama remembered that carnauba wax is more durable and gives a deeper shine. So Bridget must go out into the town to wake up the nearest colourman and get some from him. Oh! I know what the *rest* of the stench is — turpentine. Bridget had to boil some up to dissolve the carnauba wax — plus, of course, gallons more oil of lavender."

"And doesn't it work?"

They were passing through the kitchen by now. Mrs Pascoe raised her eyes but made no spoken comment.

"We're just going out for a bit of fresh air," Tamsin told her. Safely in the back garden she answered Daisy's question. "It works perfectly well — provided you haven't already put down three layers of soft beeswax first. Then the carnauba wax just pushes it into streaks. And what d'you think will bring back the shine then? Apart from elbow grease? Silk? No, not silk. Cotton, then? No, not cotton, either. Linen? No — positively not. We've tried all of these. And if the wax won't wash out, we have a heap of what was once good clothing and is now only fit for the rag-and-bone man."

"Didn't you try wool?"

"Oh, Daisy — we should have asked you first. Yes — lambswool works a treat." She sighed. "I just hope the Countess has always wanted to die of lavender poisoning — if there is such a thing. Otherwise, she is not going to appreciate the gallons of the stuff that we've poured into every crevice in her room."

A window above shrieked open. "*There* you are!" Harriet cried. "How dare you skulk out there while there's so much to do?"

"We're trying to organize the day calmly," Tamsin replied. "Daisy has the bills all ready to present." Then — foolishly, but in the hope of deflecting her mother's thoughts — she added, "I was just saying that I hope the Countess *likes* the smell of lavender. We haven't given her much choice in the matter."

"Mis-ta-ake!" Daisy murmured.

And a moment later, Tamsin could only agree, for her mother immediately flew into a fresh panic over how to get rid of the smell of lavender.

Tamsin, kicking herself, ran back indoors and up the stairs. "Mo-ther!" she cried breathlessly. "I wasn't serious. The woman must be in her eighties. She's probably blind, and she'll have as much sense of smell as a tailor's mannequin."

It was to no avail. Bridget was already putting up her bonnet for her second errand of the morning, this time to buy as many carnations as her arms could carry.

Tamsin gave up and turned instead to the normal business of a Saturday morning — serving the early breakfasts for those with trains to catch and making sure the bills were paid.

Daisy took her turn at keeping Harriet as calm as possible.

When the Countess's room was filled with all the carnations Bridget brought home, the combination of the two perfumes was so overpowering that even a tailor's mannequin would have turned pale.

"What do you think?" Harriet asked Daisy.

"Perhaps four bunches would be enough?" she suggested. "And if both windows were left wide open ...? After all, she isn't due for another six hours. It might clear by then."

So all but four bunches of carnations were removed and distributed through the house.

Down in the dining room an elderly lady who had spent the entire past week on the clifftops, potting seagulls with an air gun, asked if a dog had been sick.

Tamsin assured her there was no dog in the house and that the smell was, in fact, carnations.

"I know that perfectly well, you stupid girl!" she replied. "Carnations mask the smell of dog vomit — didn't you know?"

Tamsin thought it was not a helpful comment to be made out loud in the breakfast room, but she said nothing.

As the morning lurched on from one panic to the next, Tamsin had to assure herself, several times, that this was not a nightmare — it was all actually happening *sub specie æternitatis*. Even more frequently she had to pacify poor Bridget and Catherine and assure them that the day would end, as all days must, and that everything would be different once the Countess was settled in. "After all," ran her trump card, "her ladyship would not have chosen to stay at a small guest house if she was expecting the sort of service she'd get in a first class hôtel." Like lick and brown paper when the glue has run out, it just about held them together.

The high point of fantasy came when, around two o'clock, she found herself taking part in a curtsying class for the two maids and Daisy, and, of course, herself. By then she had realized that any objection she made only served to screw her mother's panic to a new pitch — besides inducing rebellion among the maids. By two-fifteen, no ballerina ever curtsied more elegantly than those four young females; unfortunately, Harriet herself was in such an excitable state that she went down as if her limbs were broken in several places.

At two-twenty, dressed as if for a state wedding, mother and daughter were about to climb into a taxi (ordered four days ago and confirmed twice a day since then) for the five-minute drive to the station when there was a shawm-like hoot from down Morrab Road and they saw Standish Coverley milking the steering wheel of his Rolls-Royce as it glided out of the mews behind the Queen's. Reg Trotter was at his side.

"Thought you'd like to greet the old dowager in style," Standish said as they both leaped nimbly out — Reg to help the two ladies climb in, Standish to settle some minor compensation with the cabbie before setting off. "Knew you'd want to be good and early," he added.

Harriet was too overawed to speak until they reached the Esplanade. Then the thanks simply poured out of her in a stream of consciousness that slowly turned dark, revealing all her old fears about this momentous occasion.

"Where will her ladyship sit?" she asked, looking about her and finding no extra room. Ladies' dresses were so ample.

"Trotter can take a cab back and supervise her luggage," Standish assured her. "Then Tamsin can sit in front by me and you can take care of the Countess in the back."

"Is it 'Your Grace' for a Countess? No — stupid! Your *Ladyship!* These foreign titles are so confusing. Would she sit above or below an English countess?"

"I doubt that'll be much of a problem, Mo-ther," Tamsin said heavily. "But if you really want to know, the Congress of Vienna decided that a count and countess will rank as a duke in those countries that ..."

"A duke?" Harriet almost shrieked. "She ranks as a *duchess?* Heavens, child! Why did you not tell me before?"

"Because the way you are behaving now is sufficient answer to that! Listen! They will rank as a duke and duchess *in those countries whose peerages have no dukes or marquises.* The English court has never accepted the ruling and in England they rank with the eldest son of the equivalent English rank — in the Countess's case she would rank as the *daughter* of an earl and countess rather than as a countess in her own right."

"I say!" Standish glanced briefly over his shoulder at her as they took the corner into the commercial harbour. "How d'you know all that?"

"Because I went to the library and mugged it up the moment she confirmed her booking."

"Mugged it up!" Harriet muttered distastefully. "Please avoid such locutions when her ladyship is present." Then, looking all about her with horror, she added, "We must not bring her back *this* way!"

"No, certainly not. I thought we'd go out through Market Jew Street, past the statue of Sir Humphrey Davy, which is quite imposing, and the Old Town Hall, out to Stable Hobba, then back by way of the Esplanade …"

"That would give time," Tamsin cut in, "for Reg to get back to the Morrab with her bags — which would impress her."

"Two minds with but a single thought!" Standish remarked as he drew up on the station forecourt — or, rather, sidecourt.

The usual crowd of fishporters, urchins, and idlers gathered around to admire the car. Standish went over to the kiosk where the beach photographers, Collett & Trevarton, displayed and sold prints to departing holidaymakers; the salesman there agreed to keep an eye on the car.

"Can you trust him?" Harriet asked as they entered station.

"They use one of our old stables behind the Queen's as a darkroom every summer," he replied. Then, turning to Tamsin, "Which reminds me — seeing you in all your finery the other night, I thought it deserved a photo."

"Photo*graph,*" Harriet said.

"I can thoroughly recommend Jim Collett — a real artist with the camera."

"Please!" Harriet said anxiously. "We have no time to think of such things now."

It wasn't true. They had nearly half an hour, for, as one of the station officials told them, the train was just leaving Camborne, about fifteen miles up the line, with further stops at Gwinear Road, for Helston, and St. Erth, for St. Ives.

Reg suggested a cup of tea at the buffet.

Harriet said, "How could you!"

So, after buying platform tickets they drifted back outside. Harriet objected until Tamsin pointed out that the station, a vast, arched barn open to the sky only at its eastern end, was full of smuts and they didn't want to look like colliers when her ladyship arrived, did they.

They went down to the harbour wall, where most of the fishing fleet was already tied up, ready for the sabbath tomorrow — a third of a square mile, filled with bare masts, nodding on the gentle swell. A couple of smacks were still unloading their catches at the fish quay, beside the ice house. The system was quite different from Newlyn, where the fishwives waded out to the boats and carried great creels of fish ashore. Here the creels were loaded in the holds by the crew and winched ashore by derricks, directly into the open-sided sheds, where men and fishwives gutted the fish as fast as the eye could follow them. Then, sorted into boxes and packed in ice, they were hauled on trolleys to the railway goods yard. There a marshalled line of wagons stood, dripping meltwater that reeked of dead fish, ready to depart within the hour.

"Swimming free in Mount's Bay this morning," Standish mused. "Dead on a marble slab in Billingsgate by two o'clock tonight! What a fabulous civilization!"

"What a dreadful smell to greet our visitors!" Harriet responded. "Why couldn't they have moved the harbour a little way up the line?"

Reg drew breath to explain but Tamsin silenced him with a shake of her head; economic geography and stark social terror did not mix.

They remained outside the station until five minutes before the train was due, when, smuts or no smuts, Harriet could tarry no longer. On re-entering the station they were surprised to see

Cicely Thorne at the newsagent's stall — and even more surprised to discover her concealed behind a display of picture postcards, apparently trying to make her choice in the darkest area.

"It does rotate, Mrs Thorne," an amused Standish pointed out, demonstrating the facility with the flick of a finger.

The woman froze. Her eyes looked straight through him and she said, "Dear Mrs Harte — and Tamsin! No need to ask why you're here, though I doubt you fête *all* your PGs thus."

"I say, are you cutting me?" Standish asked.

She ignored him and returned to her choice of postcards, now from the well-lighted side.

"You are!" Standish laughed. "I say, Reginald, old boy. We are being cut."

"Oh dear, oh dear, oh dear ..." Harriet wrung her hands in misery. "At a time like this ... such a thing to ... I can't ..." Her voice broke, her lips trembled.

"Mo-ther!" Tamsin put an arm around her and looked daggers at Cicely Thorne. "How *could* you!" she spat. "Come away, Mama. Pay her no heed. She's obviously got some new bee in her bonnet — silly woman!"

A shocked silence followed this denunciation; even the pigeons ceased their cooing, though that was no doubt coincidental.

"Mister Coverley!" Cicely rapped out as they moved toward the arrivals platform.

He stopped but did not turn to face her.

"You have less friends than you may think."

"Fewer," Harriet said.

He turned to her then. "It's a brave woman who dares count *her* friends aloud and in public, ma'am," he replied.

Tamsin alone saw the smile on Cicely's face as the others turned away. So she must have discovered something more concrete than the vague rumours she had hinted at yesterday — God, was it only yesterday! She must warn Standish that his troubles with that Mitchell man were more widely known than he believed. All the same, she thought it rash for a woman who was sixty miles away from all her influential friends — and all of them in another county, at that — to threaten a man as well established and popular as Standish Coverley, here in his own back yard.

However, the ticket collector, whose ears could detect sounds that were meaningless to others, told them that the London train was now steaming through Longrock, a couple of miles out from he terminus, so they gave him their platform tickets and went through. The first class compartments would be at the rear of the train, he added, between the dining carriage and the guard's van.

"I love the guard's van, don't you?" Tamsin said to the two men as they made their way up the platform, out into the sunlight once again, for the platforms were twice as long as the covered portion. "A dear little caravan on wheels, with its own stove where you can fry eggs and bacon and brew tea, and the observation platform at the back. If I were a man, that's what I'd be — a train guard."

He was not as amused or relaxed as she expected. He, too, must have worked out the implications of Cicely Thorne's absurd insults.

"How can your head be full of such scribble at a time like this?" Harriet asked crossly.

"How can it *not!*" Tamsin replied robustly. The train was in sight by now, less than half a mile up the track. "Is the world going mad? What with Mrs Thorne off on some lunatic tack of her own, and you going completely overboard about ..."

"About the honour of entertaining Ivy, the Dowager Countess de Ath beneath our roof. You don't seem to understand ..."

"Ladies!" Standish intervened. The train was approaching so fast that he feared it would run into the buffers.

But Tamsin was not going to let her mother have the last word. "What *you* don't seem to understand is that an old woman of eighty is no asset to a boarding house like ours, dowager or not. She belongs in a nursing home. What if she kicks the bucket *beneath our roof?*"

"Oh! Aah! I can't breathe!" Harriet gasped and fumbled with the hooks and eyes at her throat.

"Now then, Mrs Harte!" Standish put an arm about her and hugged her tight — which seemed to rally her remarkably. It was his turn to look daggers, now at Tamsin. "Your daughter has very little sense of occasion, I fear. We must all do our best to educate her. Now here's the train, so take long, deep breaths —

long and deep, long and deep. That's it. Can I let you go now —
before the Countess gets the wrong impression?"

"Oh God! Is she here?" Harriet opened her eyes and blinked
at the watery blur before them.

"She soon will be. I think we're in the perfect position."

He let go and turned to frown once more at Tamsin, who was
stuffing a handkerchief into her mouth to avoid hysterics. He
turned his fist into a symbolic pistol and shot her dead between
the eyes.

"Perfect!" Reg said as the first of the three doors on the first-
class carriage came to a screeching halt directly in front of them.

Harriet had passed from deep breathing to hyperventilation.
Her head swam. She felt herself going. It was all too much. Only
a curtsy would save her ... get her close to the ground.

With a creaking and cracking in her knees she sank, her body
leaned forward ... one set of knuckles casually but oh so
necessarily touched the tarmacadam ... and ...

"Cor lummie!" cried a cultivated voice — cultivated well
within the sound of Bow Bells, that is — "Here's a welcome
party then!"

The other three stood with their jaws agape. If Ivy, the Dowager
Countess de Ath, could be considered so much as twenty-three
years old, it would be more thanks to cosmetics than to the
calendar. She was in black from head to foot, of course — but
what a silken, glossy, figure-hugging black it was. And what a
head! What a foot! What an everything-in-between!

She writhed wickedly, like a knowing snake, as she descended
to the platform. From her shoulders to her hobbled knees her
dress clung to every subtle nuance of all her ample curves; from
her hobbled knees down to her ankles it burst into a froth of
black tulle at the front, through which the high-booted outlines
of her shins, calves, and ankles could easily be glimpsed. Even
the extremities of her boots looked more like dainty black feet
than anything a cobbler might have made.

"You must be Miss Tamsin Harte." She offered her hand.

Standish became aware that Harriet was about to tumble. He
and Reg took an arm each and raised her again.

"Yes, your ladyship," Tamsin said meanwhile. "Are you ..."
She could not think how to phrase it.

"You were expecting a *real* dowager, eh?" She laughed. "That was poor old Josie, God rest her. Lovely lady. She passed away, very sadly, just the week before Christmas last — and now the dear old Count has gone to join her."

"But you *are* ..." Again she fought shy of the actual words.

"Oh yes, pet — I most certainly am! We got married Christmas Day!" And she stretched forth a right hand on which every finger was crusted with jewels — among them, by inference, rings that symbolized betrothal and matrimony in the Continental manner. "And Mrs Harte!" She swivelled the hand round and offered it, not for a kiss but to be shaken. "It's so kind of you to meet me. I wasn't expecting such a thing."

Harriet made a few noises in her throat, shook the hand, told herself to stop staring — and found that she was quite unable to obey the command.

"And who may these fine gentlemen be?" She turned her huge, blue, limpid eyes upon Standish and Reg. "Do please present them to me!"

Standish, more accustomed to an all-sorts world than the others, was the first to recover. "Standish Coverley, Countess," he said, kissing that same hand. "Penzance is suddenly brighter."

"Oooh!" she said on a rising-falling tone. "I think I have to agree, Mister Coverley."

"And may I present my very good friend, Reginald Trotter."

Reg, too, kissed her hand and told her they were fellow guests at the Morrab, where he was looking forward to her company.

"Oh, really?" she replied, looking again at Standish with a raised eyebrow.

He shook his head. "I, too, shall look forward to your company, Countess, but not at the Morrab. I'm connected to a rival Penzance establishment."

"Mister Coverley owns the Queen's Hôtel," Tamsin put in. "The biggest and best in Cornwall."

"Hardly!" Standish murmured, pleased, all the same.

"I see." The Countess's eyes scanned rapidly between the two of them. Her brain was obviously working double-tides, for why else would a handsome young man turn out to greet a rival's honoured guest — unless said rival was a remarkably good-looking young woman?

"Where is your ladyship's lady's maid?" Harriet asked, anxious again and peering up and down the platform. Two porters were unloading what eventually amounted to a dozen portmanteaux and travelling wardrobes from the luggage van, but there was no sign of the valet, groom, or lady's maid who would normally be keeping a tally.

"I dismissed the lot," she sneered. "Snooty Continentals — I can't abide them. Quack-quack — all that French. I thought I might pick up a good old English one down here."

"We can offer all the services of a lady's maid at the Morrab," Tamsin said.

Her mother plucked her sleeve. "Say 'your ladyship'!" she tried to whisper.

"Oh, forget all that!" The Countess dismissed the injunction with a wave of her hand. " 'Countess' will do till we get on better terms. Or nothing at all."

"Are those all your boxes, Countess?" Reg asked.

"I only need the two purple ones," she replied. "They've got my weeds. The rest they can stop here till we find a repository."

Reg went to instruct the porters. The others started to walk down the platform. Tamsin asked if she had been to Penzance before. She said no, and that was one reason why she chose it.

"Well," Tamsin went on, "talking of *choosing* places, we know you met our friends the Locks at Baden-Baden, but … I hope you realize — the Morrab is a very modest establishment."

"Can't you guess why I'm here? Now you've met me and seen what a common little Cockney blowsabella I am — you still can't make a guess?"

Tamsin shook her head. "And anyway," she said, "I don't think you do yourself justice."

"If yoo cahn't even guess," she said in a parody of upper-class speech, "then ay shall just hev too tell yooo."

The inspector accepted her ticket without looking at it, because he was unable to take his eyes off her — even after she had passed beyond him into the concourse.

Standish saw Cicely Thorne, still rooted near the newsagent's stall. He turned to the Countess and asked if he might buy her a guide book to the town and locality. She accepted, slightly baffled — as, indeed, were the others.

"Come and choose," he said.

Cicely made those small, flustered movements people make when they are about to meet royalty or anyone of social prominence, but Standish led the Countess straight past her, bought a shilling copy of the official guide (published under the direction of the mayor and corporation), presented it to her, and led her back to join the others, who were outside by then. He did not so much as glance at Cicely, though he passed within inches of her.

"Who was that woman staring at us," the Countess asked. "She seemed to know you."

"Mrs Thorne — Cicely Thorne of Peveril Hall, near Exeter. She knows me very well but she cut me dead on our way into the station, about ten minutes ago."

"I see," the Countess said coldly. "You just used me, then!"

"Her only purpose here was to inspect you — and, if possible, carry back some scandal or gossip."

"Yet she cut *you* — even knowing you were going to meet me off of the train. That sounds serious. D'you know what you've done to offend her?"

"I suspect she has heard certain rumours about me — quite untrue, I assure you, but they have alarmed her."

The Countess's eyes raked the skies — or the dirty glass overhead. "And all I wanted was some peace and quiet!"

38 Even the two purple portmanteaux were so heavy that they would need the Great Western delivery dray, and the company's burly delivery men, rather than Reg and a taxi, to get them to the Morrab. So Standish's plan for their seating was abandoned. Besides, the Countess took charge at once.

She went into raptures the moment she saw the car — and forgave, or forgot, his use of her to revenge himself on that woman in there. "Crikey!" she shouted, running at the hobble ahead of them, and with such sinuous movements that none could take their eyes off her, especially not the fishporters and idlers. "You've got one of *these!*" She turned excitedly back to Standish. "I've seen one in Baden. The archduke of whatsizname has one … what's the place called? That little country. Sneeze and you miss it. Anyway, he's got one, only it's nothing like so good as what this one is."

She ran admiring hands over the white lacquer and touched the polished metal with delicate, black-gloved fingertips, as if she could not believe anything could be so smooth and shiny.

"I'll stand on the running board," Reg offered.

"You will not!" she insisted. "Come on, Mrs Harte, dear — you in the front. Then you, pet." She nodded at Tamsin. "In the back with you. And Mister T between us. No fighting, eh!"

And so the day's honoured guest ended up being the last to enter the car, but all at her own behest. She did not seem to notice that Harriet Harte was being rather cool and withdrawn. In fact, none of the others *seemed* to notice it, either — though, of course, all of them did. And then, in that way people have when one of the company has made an embarrassing fool of him-or her-self, they became extra-jolly in the hope that their heartiness would cover up the silent one's embarrassment and encourage it to vanish.

Standish tossed a coin to the man who had swung the starting handle and, with a wave of thanks to the attendant in the photographer's kiosk, pulled out into Station Road.

"So this is Penzance, eh," the Countess went on as they left the station yard. Her eye scanned the hundred and more fishing smacks at anchor in the harbour. "Just count those boats! I'm surprised there's a fish left within a hundred miles. Though my nose tells me there is!" She laughed.

"You were going to explain why you chose the Morrab," Tamsin said as they turned away from the quayside, up Albert Street toward the bottom of Market Jew.

"Come on!" the Countess chided. "Surely a bright girl like you can work it out?" She adopted an exaggerrated Cockney — or perhaps it was her original speech. "'Ere's me, common as could be but with oodles of oof, and you and your Mum, down on your uppers but with class coming out of your ears." Then, back in her more refined speech, though still with an unmistakable East End overtone: "Market Jew Street! That's a funny name! Anyway, do you get it now, pet?"

"Sort of, I suppose," Tamsin replied.

"Toot court — can you make a silk purse out of this sow's ear? That's what it boils down to. I got along all right on 'Le Continong,' see, because they don't know Mile End from Mayfair. And table manners and visiting cards don't trouble me no more — *any* more. But here in England — where I'd much rather be living — it's a different story. One word out of my mouth and I can hear sniggers all around. So — before I resume my noble career — I want to buy a touch of class, see? On the outside, anyway. And the moment the Locks told me your sad tale, I thought we could each do the other some good. Of course, if you'd rather not ..."

"No, no!" Tamsin cried, for she had already taken a great liking to this strange and strangely endearing young woman. "Given five years, I think we might manage something."

"Tamsin!" Harriet exclaimed.

The Countess reached behind Reg, who obligingly leaned forward to let her give Tamsin a gentle pinch on the arm. "It's six months or my money back," she said. Then, to Harriet, "I hope your daughter speaks for you, too, Mrs Harte?"

"I'm not sure, Countess." She only half turned as she replied, so that she avoided looking the woman in the eye without seeming to do so deliberately. "It's not something one can decide within five minutes of first meeting, I think."

"Good," the Countess said in a disappointed tone. "As long as it's not out of the question from the start." Half to herself she added, "The Locks seemed to think you'd leap at it. *They* didn't think me unsuitable."

Tamsin tapped her on the shoulder and made a soothing gesture. Meanwhile her mother was saying, "It's not a question of being unsuitable ... oh dear!"

But, of course, it was precisely that.

"You mentioned a 'noble career' just now, Countess," Standish said. "What would that be?"

"Who's that noble-looking fellow? And what's he holding?"

"That's Sir Humphrey Davy, Penzance's most famous son. He invented the miner's safety lamp — which is what he's holding. And this is our old town hall."

"Blocks the traffic a bit, what? Anyway — my noble career. My career ... I suppose if I've got to *prove* my suitability, I shall have to tell you the lot." She rolled her eyes upward, pulled a

face, and then looked all about her, especially at Tamsin.
"We're all grown up here, I hope? We all know how one and
one can make three?"

"I really think ..." Harriet began in alarm. "I mean I hope ..."

But there was no stopping the Countess now. "Cards on the
table," she said. "Penny on the drum. My noble career, you
might say, began at the age of sixteen when I had the honour to
become Lady Summers, the second wife of Sir Morgan Summers
of South Audley Street, Mayfair — which I remained until I
reached the age of twenty, when Sir Morgan passed over. Then,
last Christmas, at the age of twenty-two, I married Hugo de Ath,
Comte d'Aumer, and, of course, became his countess. That was
in Paris. He, too passed away — as you know — last week. No —
this week. Aiee! Is it still only this week?"

She knew what they were all thinking: *These statements are
verifiable in the public record. Would she make them if it were all a
pack of lies?*

"Hard to credit, eh?" she went on, "but I'm not ashamed of
marrying two rich men in their declining years. I'd do it again ...
because I don't think a woman all alone in the world can have
too many friends at the bank, do you? What's that?"

"The hospital," Standish told her. "And the new town hall."

"Lovely. Anyway. Like I was saying, both gentlemen said I
gave them the happiest years of their lives, and ..."

"Years?" Harriet queried. In her innocence she supposed
that she had caught the woman out. "Pardon me, but didn't you
say you married the Count only last Christmas?"

"Yes, but it wasn't no whirlwind romance, Mrs Harte. The
then Countess had been ailing for many years. It was she who
introduced me to her husband — not long after I was widowed.
And she encouraged our friendship until the day she died,
which was only four days before the Count married me. She
gave us her blessing. She was a saint. Almost her last act on
earth was to wrap her grandmother's lace shawl as a wedding
gift to me ..." Her voice broke on these last words.

"Well ... well ..." Harriet was mortified that she had unintent-
ionally pushed the poor woman to this.

The Countess sniffed deeply and said, "There now — no
bones broken. So now you know — that's my noble career in a

nutshell. Here! Where are we off to? I thought the Morrab Guest House was *in* Penzance?"

"So it is," Standish assured her, swinging the car around toward the bay. "This is Stable Hobba. We'll be going back along the seafront."

"Oh good. Anyway, like I said, I'm not ashamed of ..."

"*As* I said." Harriet just had to correct her. "Not 'like I said'."

"Bless you!" she replied, taking it as some kind of acceptance of her tale. "You've started work already and we haven't even agreed a rate for the job!"

"Sir Morgan's first wife," Tamsin said. "Did he and she ... forgive me for asking, but ..."

The Countess laughed. "You're quick, pet! Yes — they had two sons. Harry and John. Harry inherited the baronetcy but nothing else. They were a very fiery family — always quarreling, always making it up again. But then there was one quarrel they couldn't make up. No prizes for guessing what about. Or *who* it was about."

Harriet's lips mimed *whom* but she held her tongue this time.

"And, to save you asking, the Count had no issue — or none as he'd own up to."

"Up to which he'd own," Tamsin said, watching to see if her mother reacted.

"Eh?" the Countess exclaimed.

"Only joking," the girl assured her.

"Only teasing me!" her mother added.

"So!" the Countess concluded. "Though I know it's bad form to speak of one's money, I am the heiress to two fortunes. But I'm sure you'll forgive me for mentioning it — especially seeing as it was the whole purpose of your question!"

"Never mind that," Reg said. "It's a fascinating story."

"I'll tell you something more — I kept both of those fine gentlemen happier than that Consuela Vanderbilt managed with her duke. What d'you think of her, anyway? If the daughter of a Yankee millionaire marries into a near-bankrupt English dukedom — her for the sake of his title, him for the sake of her dollars — is that better or worse than my own noble career? Much worse, I'd say, because instead of keeping her duke happy, she went and divorced him."

"Perhaps the dollars were all he needed to keep him happy," Tamsin suggested.

She laughed. "Yes, well, you may have a point there. No flies on *you!* But listen — one thing I want to make clear. The way it was between me and the Count, while his first wife was still alive … I mean, I *was* a widow then. It's different for a widow, don't you think? Anyway, it *wasn't* like that between me and Sir Morgan, despite all his tricks. None of that while *his* first wife still lived — nor for a good while after, neither. Not till he put that ring on my finger. Ah, here we are, back at the sea."

"And that's the Queen's Hôtel," Reg told her. "The big building up ahead. Mister Coverley's place, you remember."

She looked admiringly at the hôtel, but all she said was, "Can we get out and go for a stroll? I've been cooped up all day and I'm sure they can't have delivered my bags yet."

"Spiffing!" Reg said.

"I'll go home," Harriet said. "They'll be along with those portmanteaux and someone must be there to receive them."

"I'll take you there," Standish said. "Then, Countess, I'm afraid I have some urgent affairs to attend to — so have you, Reginald, in case you've forgotten."

"Eh? What?"

Standish glanced at him briefly, over his shoulder — after which he said a not-very-convincing, "Oh yes, of course! Silly me! I did forget."

Standish set them down opposite the entrance to the Queen's.

"There's a man in some sort of trouble," the Countess murmured as she and Tamsin stood on the Esplanade, watching the car take the corner into Morrab Road.

Well! Tamsin thought. *No flies on this Countess, either!*

She led the woman a few paces more, until she could point out the guest house.

"All I've got is cash and jewels and clothes," the Countess said. "It must be funny to have very little cash and yet to own a *house,* Tamsin. May I call you Tamsin? I'm Ivy, by the way." She chuckled. "Not the most aristocratic name in the world!"

"Surely you owned that house in South Audley Street?" Tamsin replied. "After Sir Morgan died, I mean. Or didn't you inherit that as well?"

"Oh, I inherited, all right. But I turned it into cash as soon as I could, before the sons, Harry and John, could come down on me with a ton of writs — which they did. But that money's all in Monaco where they can't touch it." She took Tamsin's arm. "I'll tell you one good thing about cash, love. Gold, that is. It's portable. An English judge, faced with a choice between Sir Harry Summers, Baronet, deprived of his inheritance, and little Ivy, the servant girl from Mile End who twisted the master into marrying her, is going to make his mind up before she even opens her common mouth — isn't he. But put everything into cash and send it all abroad, beyond the reach of English so-called justice, and it's only amazing how the best legal minds in London lose all interest in the case! Still — enough about me. Tell me all about you and Penzance — the exciting bits. Where's all the fun when the sun's gone down?"

"Oh, there's so much!" Tamsin replied. "Where shall I begin? D'you like embroidery? Amateur piano playing? Would you swoon at the prospect of a lantern lecture from an explorer who climbed two-thirds of the way up Mount Everest before throwing in the towel? Or how about a returned missionary with several amusing fuzzy-wuzzy anecdotes including how he nearly got cooked for their supper, and how he came across a ruined hut where Doctor Livingstone once spent the night?"

"Ohmigawd!" Ivy groaned. "As bad as that?"

"I won't tell you my best fun lately."

"That means you're going to — sooner or later, so why not get it over with now?"

"D'you want to go down on the sands?"

Ivy shook her head and waited.

"You won't laugh? Most people think I'm a bit cracked."

"Go on!"

"My best fun lately was being shown over the Queen's by Standish Coverley himself. In person! He showed me everything."

"And?"

"That's it."

"And that's fun?"

"Oh yes! I'd just love to own a big hôtel. I think they're the most fascinating places in all the world."

Ivy, watching her face light up, did not doubt a word of it.

"Does his nibs know?" she asked, tilting her head in the direction of the Queen's.

"Of course. I can't seem to keep it a secret." She smiled ruefully. "As you have just discovered."

"Hmm!" Ivy was thoughtful. "I'm just beginning to wonder if he has the same problem? Secrets, I mean — leaking out?" She peered intently into Tamsin's eyes. "D'you know what I'm talking about, pet?"

Tamsin shook her head.

Ivy shrugged. "No business of mine, I suppose. He uses me — me, who he's only just met — to score points off of that Mrs Thorne, but no, it's no business of mine!"

She glanced at Tamsin and saw her weakening.

She went on, "He told me certain ugly rumours were circulating about him but they're all lies."

"They are!"

"They are circulating or they are lies?"

"Both."

"About him and Mister Trotter?"

"No! A man called Mitchell. Marcus Mitchell."

"That name rings a bell. Was he in the papers lately?"

"I shouldn't be surprised. He's a professional swindler. I might as well tell you all I know — which isn't much — seeing that Mister Coverley told you the gist of it anyway. Mitchell has forged some papers that incriminate Mister Coverley in something illegal. Mister Coverley's been fighting the accusations on and off for the past year but ... I don't know. All I do know is that it seems to be getting very serious."

The Countess stretched and yawned. " 'Scuse me! It's all this sea air after beeing cooped up in that compartment all day. Shall we go home? I wouldn't worry too much about Mister Coverley if I was you. He strikes me as a man who can take very good care of number one."

39 On their way back to the Morrab, Tamsin and Ivy saw Victor coming toward them, or, rather, coming in their direction, for he clearly did not notice them — nor anyone else for that matter.

"Here's a young fellow with the cares of the world about him," Ivy said. "Not a bad looker, either!"

"He's Victor Thorne, son of that Mrs Thorne at the station," Tamsin replied. "One of your fellow guests under our roof."

Ivy, aware that Tamsin was being just a shade too nonchalant, said, "You get the pick of them, don't you!" and was rewarded with a blush. "Is he rich?"

"He will be next year. Or soon. I don't know exactly."

When he was still a dozen paces away, Ivy stepped into his path — a movement that caught his attention for the first time. He halted, still a few yards off, and stared in confusion, seeing an elegant young lady in deep mourning and, yes, Tamsin, his own beloved. Understanding followed a fraction of a second later for, until that moment, he had been a hundred miles away.

"Countess," Tamsin said. "Allow me to present Mister Victor Thorne of Peveril Hall, near Exeter. Ivy, Countess de Ath."

She offered her hand for a kiss. While he lowered his head Tamsin saw his eyes conduct a lightning audit of her person, from the neck down; again, as far as she could tell, he, too, liked what he saw — as who would not? "Allow me to express my sincere condolences, Countess."

"Ah well," she replied. "These things happen. He had eighty good years and four *very* good ones."

He started in surprise at her accent, though he still lingered over releasing her hand.

She winked at Tamsin and said, "See!"

"Forgive me for not noticing you." He released her hand at last and turned to Tamsin. "I've had a bit of a blow, to tell the truth. The Mater and Pater are determined to leave tonight."

"Oh!" Tamsin glanced toward the Morrab, almost as if she expected to see them coming down the path. She relaxed a little when she recalled that her mother and Daisy were at home; neither would let the Thornes go without settling.

"It's all right," he said. "The train's not until half-past eight — though how we'll manage the fifteen miles from Exeter to the Hall is anybody's guess."

"Do *you* have to go, too?" Tamsin asked.

"I'm sorry, Countess," he said. "This must be very tedious to you, especially after such a long train journey."

"Don't stand bareheaded in this sun, please," she replied.

"Walk back with us," Tamsin suggested. "Unless you were on some particular errand?"

"No, no," he replied lugubriously. "I was just going to drown myself or something. I'll come part-way." He turned and took the gentlemanly position nearest the kerb but Tamsin stepped beyond him and sandwiched him between them.

"If you insist," he said. "The thing is, you see, I do, more or less, have to go back with them — finding myself a little short of steam at the moment. I was actually on my way to touch old Coverley for a few quid, if you really want to know — because the last place on earth *I* want to be at the moment ..."

"Gambling?" Tamsin guessed.

He gave her a wry smile. "In a way. You could call it that."

She realized he was talking about the turquoise necklace. "Would you borrow from me instead?" she suggested.

"From a *lady?*" He was horrified, or made it seem so. They halted and formed a triangular group again.

"Fair exchange is no robbery," she said. "And the pawnbroker in Jennings Street is very discreet, I'm told. Ladies can approach him through the milliner's next door."

"Well ... at the risk of sounding churlish, may I just say I'll keep your kind offer in mind, but I'll first see if Coverley's in a generous mood. That's where I'm actually heading — because, as it happens, I'm in a position to do him a big favour, too."

He tipped his hat and was about to continue on his way to the Queen's when Tamsin said, "Just a mo! Why are your parents in such a rush? Is it something *we've* said? Or done?"

"No." The reply was awkward. "They just don't want to be in Penzance tomorrow morning."

"For any particular reason?"

"Nothing you've done, anyway — you and your mother. But it's why I have to see Coverley now — rather urgently. So, if you'll excuse me ...?"

"You didn't tell me about *these* excitements," Ivy said as they resumed their homeward stroll. "Is Penzance always like this?"

"Not at all. But rather a lot seems to be happening lately. David Peters being almost drowned at sea ... the brandy smuggling ... there's a lot to tell you, Ivy."

"David Peters?" she said.

"Oh ... just a fisherman I know. He works from Newlyn, which is ... no, you can't see it from here. But it's a mile or so that way. You can see it from my bedroom window."

"Ah!" Ivy said knowingly. "Just a fisherman you ... *know?*"

"It's nothing like that," Tamsin assured her. And she went on to explain about the seafood restaurant and David's role.

Ivy paid less attention to the words than to the animation that showed in the face of her new-found friend.

"Mmm-hmm," was her only comment. Then: "I like the look of your Mister Victor Thorne, though. Did I gather just now that he's cleaned himself out in buying some present for you?"

Tamsin explained about the turquoise, and then all the reasons Cicely Thorne had given for not marrying him — which were utter common sense, really. "So," she concluded, "I think I'll ask Daisy to slip out tonight and pawn it — and give him the money and the pledge. I've been racking my brains for days how to return the present without hurting him. This is ideal, and it'll be one less weight on my mind. What d'you think?"

After a silence, during which they arrived at the front gate, Ivy said, "If it's a good turquoise ..."

"Oh, it is. The best I ever saw."

"The colour of your eyes?"

"That's why he bought it — so he said."

"Well, if it's as good as all that, you could pawn it with me, instead — only don't let him know."

"Really? You're not just being kind?"

"Kind to myself, if anything. I don't imagine this town is bristling with handsome, rich young *boolevardiers* like him?"

"Certainly not! Standish and Reg are the only other two I know of."

"Point taken! So it would be a kindness to me, above all, if he was free to remain here — at least until I've had a chance to size him up."

Tamsin paused inside the gate. There was one question she just had to ask this woman of the world and it would be impossible if others were around. "D'you think it's wrong for a woman to be mercenary, Ivy?" she asked.

"Like me?" She laughed.

"I'm thinking more of myself. I mean, if a rich man asked me to marry him — and I don't mean one who's young and handsome, like Victor, though of course that would be ideal — but any rich man — fat, old, ugly ... anyone — and if he said I could have as much of his money as I wanted so I could build my hôtel, well ... I don't think I'd hesitate too long. Is that awful?"

"How would you treat him?" she asked. "Would you keep your side of the bargain — spoken or unspoken? Make sure he dies with that certain smile on his lips? Know what I mean?"

"No, I think I might be more like Consuela Vanderbilt," Tamsin admitted.

"Then it would be wrong, pet. Very wrong."

40 It is curious how life can bubble along quite merrily for years and then suddenly, in the space of half an hour, everything can change. It happened to Tamsin the following morning, the first Sunday in August, and it came without warning out of a clear blue sky — or, more precisely, a grey and threatening sky. On Sundays, breakfasts were served an hour later than usual, so Tamsin had the chance of a well-deserved lie-in. She would have indulged herself, too, if her restless spirit had not woken her even earlier than her usual time.

She rose and dressed without disturbing Daisy and went downstairs, thinking she might as well go to early Communion — and would God mind if she had a ginger faring and a glass of milk first? She was surprised to find Victor and Ivy already in the kitchen, rather sheepishly helping themselves to bread and marmalade. They, too, had the Communion service in mind, mainly because, duty done, they'd have the rest of the day free.

"Your parents left some books behind," Tamsin told him. "A Wilkie Collins and a couple of Sherlock Holmes yarns."

"Put them in your bookshelf," he said. "They bought them down here and, somehow, I don't think they'll be wanting too many souvenirs of Penzance!"

They left together and walked down Morrab Road to the seafront. It had been a fine, warm night but they could now see the last of the blue sky vanishing over the Lizard. Overhead was a mass of pale grey cloud that seemed curiously upside-down. Usually the lowest part of a cloud is flat bottomed and dark; here it hung down in bulbous clumps, each one of which seemed to be lighted powerfully from within by flares of sulphur. Victor remarked that it was like a giant cauliflower, daubed grey and yellow, and hung upside-down overhead. They all hoped it did not mean that the fine weather of the past two days was breaking up yet again.

Then, just after they had crossed the road to walk along the seaward side of the Esplanade, the doorman from the Queen's came hurrying after them.

"Miss Harte!" he called out when he was still some way off. They stopped and turned to face him.

"Sorry!" he panted as he drew near. "It's just Miss Harte, really. The boss sends his compliments and asks would you join him for breakfast, miss?"

"Really?" She was astounded. "But why?"

"It's urgent, miss. That's all I know."

She glanced at Ivy, who said, "I think you should ought to go, pet. We'll make your apologies for you!" She raised her eyes toward that huge upside-down cauliflower above.

Mystified, Tamsin followed the man back to the hôtel. There a waiter took over and guided her upstairs. Her bewilderment turned to mild alarm when she saw she was expected to dine alone in one of the bedrooms with Standish; and the bed wasn't even made.

"Where's Reg?" she asked.

"He's gone ahead of me to France," he replied. She had never seen him so agitated.

"To France?"

"Sit down, Tamsin — please. And loosen anything that might impede the flow of blood to your brain, because you're going to have to think as you've never thought before in all your life." To the waiter he said, "That's all, George, thank you."

He followed the man to the door and locked it behind him. "Don't be alarmed," he said, pocketing the key. "It's just a pre-caution. What can we offer you?" He went over to the dressing table, which had been turned into a makeshift buffet. "Kipper, haddock, fish kedgeree, devilled kidneys, scramblers, bacon ..."

"What are you having?"

"I couldn't touch a thing, love."

"Standish!" She touched his arm gently. "What's happening?"

"What's happening is that that devil Mitchell has won. This round, anyway. I have to get out of the country, if I'm to stand a chance of continuing the fight to prove my innocence. And I have to get out toot sweep! I may already have left it too late. Unless ..." He eyed her uncertainly.

"Unless what?"

"Unless you help me. Sure you don't want to eat anything?"

"Not until I know what's what. How on earth can I help you?"

"Do sit down — please." He held a chair expectantly, more or less forcing her to obey.

He seated himself opposite her and spoke to a point somewhere just in front of her empty plate. "Please consider what I'm about to ask you very carefully," he said. He spoke slowly, as if he had rehearsed his words many times — which, she soon suspected, was indeed the case.

"I'm going to ask you to commit an illegal act ..."

She missed the next few words — perhaps even a sentence or two — because her mind was reeling and her fingers were automatically loosening the hooks in her bodice, at her throat.

"... assured me I would have time," he was saying when the dizziness passed.

"I'm sorry," she blurted out.

"Don't say no yet," he pleaded. "Just hear ..."

"No, no — it's not that. I didn't catch everything you said ... something about not being pursued."

"Oh. I was just explaining that the chief constable is an old family friend and he says he can hold the hounds at bay but only until this evening."

"Standish, have you ..." She paused and then thought better of it. "No. You go on. I won't interrupt."

"I'm actually going to ask you *two* huge favours. One of them is going to sound like a bribe to induce you to ... to carry out the other. But here goes. I would like you to consider taking over the management of this hôtel in my absence."

She gasped. In her confusion, the only thing she could think of asking was, "Is that an illegal act?"

He laughed, with little humour. "No. It's the bribe — though the offer stands even if you do not wish to do me the other favour, the illegal one. You undertand that? You'll be manageress here, come what may — whether I'm in gaol or France."

"France! You're going to France as well?"

"That's the idea. Reginald is being absolutely marvellous. He knows a hundred pensions and so on where I'll be safe — and meanwhile he'll be free to pop back and forth across the Channel, tend to his mama, collect papers, brief lawyers and private inquiry agents ... all that sort of thing. I do not deserve such friends. Even young Victor ..." He seemed lost in thought.

"We met him last night, the Countess and I. He talked of doing you a favour, too."

"And so he did — an enormous one." He smiled ruefully. "I wish we'd worked out earlier what his mother's intentions were when she moved from here to your place. I wouldn't have made such an enemy of her — and then I might have had another month or so to order my affairs here."

Guilty that she had said nothing when she had known everything, Tamsin asked, "How has she brought it all about, then?"

"It's more a question of *why,*" he replied. "I had a long, enjoyable chat with Charlotte, who told me all about her ambitions to become a professional artist. And I rather encouraged her, I'm afraid. I should have realized that if a mother like Mrs Thorne allows her daughter an hour of unchaperoned intercourse with a gentleman, she has hopes of a certain outcome. And if that gentleman then encourages the daughter to strike out on her own" — he smiled wanly — "he's asking for trouble. And I certainly got it!"

Tamsin frowned. "Even so, how could she ..."

"Don't ask me! I can only assume that Devon is crammed with retired legal bigwigs who can still bend an ear and twist an arm up in London — and that many of them are friends of the Thornes. Anyway, that's what Victor came to warn me of last night. So — can we come back to my offer of the management of the Queen's? You would have complete day-to-day control of the entire business."

He went to the window and peeped out at the street through a crack between the curtains.

"Oh!" She felt that swimming feeling come over her again. "But I'm not ..."

He interrupted her as he returned to the table. "Time's short, Tamsin. If I'm wrong about you, then it's my responsibility. But I'm sure I'm not wrong. Indeed, I've never been so sure of anything in my life. Also, Jessica Trelawney agrees — and she's nobody's fool when it comes to judging character and ability. Listen! The farmers hereabout have a saying — 'The best dung is the master's boot,' meaning that you can spread all the artificial fertilizer you like on the land but if the master takes no interest, it's not going to do much good."

"But Standish! To expect me to run an hôtel the size of the Queen's! *You* may have confidence in me, but I don't."

"I'm only talking about day-to-day running. Jessica will retain control of all financial affairs and will remain the ultimate authority. Think of yourself as the public face of the Queen's — the hostess who stamps her personality upon the place — and heaven knows it needs such a person. And that person is you, is you, is you! Especially with Jessica standing discreetly in the wings to support you. She's full of admiration for you, you know. So am I, of course. And, believe me, *I'm* not likely to interfere with your management from somewhere deep in the Gironde or the Dordogne!"

She could feel her doubts crumbling inside her. She decided to gamble everything. "What if we got married, Standish?" she asked. "That would make it ..."

"Married!" he exclaimed.

"Is it such an outlandish idea? I could so easily love you — I think. The difference between love and what I feel for you already is so fine ..."

"Oh no it isn't, Tamsin. If you think that, then you're not even close to loving anyone — yet. Believe me, I'm not insensible of the honour you do me, but an hôtelier sees enough of loveless marriages to know what hell-on-earth they are."

"But it could so easily *become* love," she insisted.

"How can I make you understand?" He closed his eyes a moment and then began again. "When your father died — forgive me if it's still painful — but didn't something deep inside you simply refuse to believe it?"

She nodded. She had been close enough to tears before he spoke his latest words; now she was afraid he'd drive her over the edge.

"And didn't you go around for days, looking for him, almost expecting the very intensity of your grief to bring him back?"

"Yes," she whispered.

"And ... I don't know — was he a sailing man?"

She shook her head. "He said he had enough of the sea at his work. He liked walking."

"Well then, suppose he'd gone walking up on Dartmoor and didn't come back when you expected. Got lost in the mist or a storm or something. Wouldn't you have gone racing up, on foot, on pony, any way you could, and stood on some tor up there, scanning every acre of bog and heath for some sign of him?"

"Yes." She laughed.

Surprised, he said, "It wouldn't be so funny at the time."

"No ... I was just thinking ... it doesn't matter."

"What?"

"Well, only last Wednesday I was standing at the lookout above Penlee Point, alongside old Benny Peters, scanning every part of Mount's Bay and the Channel for some sign of David, who had gone out in that tropical storm or whatever it was — the idiot!"

"And he came back, surely? The whole town would have ..."

"Yes. Calm as you like — I could have hit him! I would have, too, if I'd stayed until he made landfall. Sorry, but it doesn't exactly support *your* point, does it!"

"You did all *that?* As soon as you heard he was missing?"

"No, I waited until the afternoon. It was stupid of me."

He hesitated, as if he would say more, but then he just shrugged and said, "If you say so. My main point, however, is that what I was describing ... what I was trying to evoke in recalling your own love for your father ..."

"Oh, but you were right there. That *does* support what you were saying."

"Well," he said simply. "Until you feel with that sort of intensity ..." He let a shrug complete the thought. "Now let's talk about your salary — a proper salary. A thousand pounds a year, I'd suggest — if that's acceptable to you?"

He misinterpreted her shock as some kind of doubt. "Plus ... what shall we say? Ten percent of any increase in profits at the end of each year? No, ten is niggardly — because we're only talking about the *increase.* Say, twenty-five? A quarter of any increase in profits? You'd deserve it. Anyway, you're quite right not to say yes and not to say no just at the moment. We can come to some arrangement later. The main thing is for me to get to France as soon as maybe and without getting myself arrested." He glanced nervously toward the window again.

"Was that the other favour?" she asked, already having a good idea of the details.

He nodded and gave a nervous smile. "And, as I said, it's not conditional on your becoming manageress. The other way round, I mean."

She smiled and said, "Would you mind terribly if you arrived in Brittany smelling of fish?"

41 If Tamsin hadn't known Cornwall so well by now, she'd have assumed that someone of importance to the whole community of Newlyn had died. Black was the sabbath colour there. So black was the colour of most people's only good clothes. So black was the keynote of galas, fêtes, festivals, and holidays, too — not that today was any of those. The entire harbour was ringed with black-clad men and black-garbed women, ostentatiously honouring the day of rest. Finding David was going to be like looking for one redcoat in an entire army.

The skies were sombre as well, as if to match their mood. People were predicting rain — and maybe winds to go with it, but certainly rain in abundance.

Offhand, too, one would have said that Ivy, in widow's weeds from head to toe, would not have looked out of place in such a throng. But no woman of that village, who from a distance and collectively resembled so many black beehives, could ever have been mistaken for her. Today, in yet another figure-clinging outfit of shimmering black silk, she had all the sinuous grace of a wet otter at play. Men gazed after her with hooded eyes as she passed and they thought of the hour, that afternoon, when the children would all be safely out of the house at Sunday School.

She, for her part, seemed oblivious to it all, being much more interested in hearing about Tamsin's interview with Standish that morning; she spent most of their walk to Newlyn talking about it, picking it to pieces, analyzing it, and putting it back in every possible way. "I still think you should hold out for marriage, pet," she finally concluded.

"Possibly. But the important thing, just at the moment, is to get the poor man safely away to France."

"Right, I can see that. But *then* you can ... aren't you going to ask any of these people where your friend is?"

"I don't think so." Tamsin spoke softly in case her words carried. "I'm going to ask him to put to sea on the sabbath — which is like social death here."

"I can imagine!" She gazed around at a sea of dour, suspicious faces. "Anyway, once he's safely in France — assuming you get him there — I think you shouldn't waste much time in making it clear that this manageress idea is just for the time being."

"I don't really think it's *that* important, do you?"

"Not important? Listen! What if he meets and marries some other bit of skirt over there, some French mott. And then suppose that something nasty should happen to him, which God forbid, but she'd become the owner and you could be out on your ear. Take it from one who knows — nothing beats that little gold band just *there!*" She stretched out her right hand and admired it. "Well, of course, it's on the other hand in England but you know what I mean."

"It certainly is a point," Tamsin had to agree. She kept on scanning the crowds, looking either for Cousin Harry or for David himself.

"It's not *a* point, pet. It's *the* point — the only one. The Married Women's Property Act beats any contract of employment into a cocked hat — especially a verbal one. It's as good as any title deed."

"There he is." Tamsin nodded toward the end of the South Pier, where David was standing alone, staring out to sea.

A moment later they met Harry. After introductions and a few solemn pleasantries, Tamsin asked him what he thought the chances were that David might put to sea in the *Merlin,* either that afternoon or early that evening.

"As close to nothing as do make no odds," he replied. "You heard, then?"

"Heard what?"

He became suspicious. "How are you asking about me putting to sea if you haven't heard?"

"I've got my own reasons. Heard what?"

He refused to say more. Her eyes took in the situation — David standing alone at the pier's end ... the rest of the village gathered around the inner-harbour wall. She made a leap: "You mean he *wants* to go out — himself — anyway?" She turned to Ivy. "That's good news!"

"I doubt it is," Harry said. "If he goes, he'll go alone — which even he's not edjack enough to risk. I shan't go with 'n. Nor will any other man — or none he'd trust. So I reckon as he's stuck here till tomorrow, anyway."

"Come on," Tamsin said to Ivy when Harry had moved away. "Let's hear what the man himself has to say.

There was an exciting tingle in her spine as they set off along the stone road of the pier. Like a child, suddenly, she walked along the shiny rails of the narrow-gauge line used by the fish drams that unloaded catches from the larger trawlers, the ones that could not come to the fishwives inshore. Judging by what Harry had said, it would seem that David had some urgent reason to put to sea quite soon — before midnight, anyway — and that no other fisherman was willing to breach the sabbath and go with him. Or maybe they had some other reason — like not wanting to put to sea in a small boat skippered by a lunatic?

Ivy was silent, too, for once. All she did was keep a close eye on Tamsin, all the way.

"And the same to you!" David called out the moment he spied them approaching.

"I was about to say you look as miserable as that fisherman who lifted a lobsterpot and found nothing inside it apart from only a dozen huge lobsters."

He laughed, almost against his will, it seemed. And he soon became morose again. "You hit the nail on the head, fair and square," he sighed.

They were close enough now for introductions. He was not greatly awed by Ivy's title.

"Is that the *Merlin?*" she asked with a nod toward the boat Tamsin had pointed out to her as soon as they came in sight of the harbour.

"Yes," he agreed. "For all the use she is to me!"

"We met Harry," Tamsin said. "He seemed to think you wanted to go fishing on the sabbath."

"The sabbath!" he said wearily. "It'll be over, well over, by the time I reach the grounds I'd want to be fishing tonight." He stretched an impressive arm southward. "Over the harrizen, as Edward John used to call it."

"It must be some fine shoal of fish to make you want to risk it."

"Fish be damned," he replied. "Pardon my French, Countess. It's a shoal of a different order. A shoal worth ..." He hesitated.

"You can trust the Countess," Tamsin assured him.

He looked all around and, lowering his voice to a purr, said, "One hundred and twenty-five pound!"

Ivy whistled and looked at him with a new respect.

"Two hundred and fifty bottles?" Tamsin asked, almost in a whisper. "Where will you fit them all?" She gazed again at the *Merlin*. "And how will you bring them back past old Sterne?"

She had told Ivy all about her encounter with the Excise during their walk to Newlyn.

"How many gallons in that many bottles?" David asked. "I'll save you the bother — forty-two."

"Ah — it's a barrel, then! Or a firkin?" As the future manageress of the Queen's, she thought it best to get such things right.

"One barrel," he agreed. "The French equivalent."

"Even so," she went on, "how are you going to ... oh, never mind. That's your problem. Mine is that I want to help Standish Coverley get to France tonight without anyone knowing. D'you think our two problems might have something in common?"

"What's it worth to him?" David said at once.

"No, David." She shook her head firmly. "What's it worth to you? What will you pay him to crew for you?"

Ivy laughed but he was not amused. "And what about coming back?" he asked. "Never thought about that, did you!"

"No, it completely slipped my mind," she said, unruffled. "Well, I thought I'd just be coming along to enjoy the ride, but I can see I shall have to roll up my sleeves and get stuck in, too."

This time Ivy not only laughed, she spun a full circle and slapped Tamsin on the back, saying, "My! Ain't you the gel!"

Tamsin knew at once that David was going to agree, just as she knew he was going to hold out against the suggestion until the last possible moment. Then, suddenly, the hair bristled on her neck and she knew why he had risked putting to sea in that storm three days ago — it would have been worth five hundred pounds. Somehow he had missed the rendezvous when the Frenchman was on the way out to ... wherever. Biscay or the South Irish Sea. Tonight was his only chance to pick them up during their return up the Channel. If he didn't make a meeting tonight, a hundred and twenty-five pound's worth of brandy would go all the way home again to Brittany!

Then she knew not only that she had him but also the why of it — which made her position impregnable.

42 The chief constable had given Standish twenty-four hours to settle his affairs. He could explain it away as a ruse to net any accomplices Standish might have in this sorry business. Standish would not be arrested if he left the hôtel during that time but he would be followed — with all the resulting scandal. He was more sorry than he could say but that was the best he could promise.

The first plan to thwart these arrangements was for Victor to dress in some of Standish's clothes and, wrapping himslf in mufflers and goggles, drive the Rolls-Royce out toward Longrock — drawing the police away while Standish and Tamsin went off in a gig in the opposite direction, toward Mousehole, where they were to rendezvous with David at five that evening. But when they found that an extra constable had been stationed in the mews, as well as the one they already knew about on the Esplanade, they had to abandon that arrangement.

"What about the car, anyway," Victor asked.

"You can drive it up to Plymouth and bring it over to me anytime you like," Standish told him. "Only for God's sake choose dry days. The hide stinks after rain. Otherwise," he added, "Reginald can collect it on one of his visits."

After that setback, their actual escape owed more to the appalling weather than to any cunning plan on their part. The curiously bulbous, sulphur-yellow clouds continued to hang overhead throughout the day. Around four o'clock that after-noon, half an hour before their deadline for leaving the hôtel, sheet lightning began to play somewhere above them, giving the effect of arc lights, flickering in a pale yellow jelly; there was no accompanying thunder, which somehow made the effect even more uncanny. Everyone was jittery — including, they hoped, the man on watch along the Esplanade.

At half-past four, when their timing was getting pretty critical, the heavens opened at last — and not just in ordinary summer rain but in a flood such as Tamsin could not remember at any time in her life. The man on the Esplanade ran for the shelter, where he could continue to watch the entrance through the glass, though how much he could actually make out through that cascade of stair-rods was anybody's guess. It was still more than three hours to sunset but the eerily bright daylight, combined with the rain, did more to hinder visibility than to help it.

A motor cab drew up to let a couple alight. The commissionaire shielded them as best he could with his umbrella and asked the driver to wait.

"Now or never," Tamsin said, peering out of the front lobby.

A chain of signals brought Standish running from the manager's office, out onto the pavement, where, again sheltered (and hidden) by that capacious umbrella, they made it safely into the cab. The commissionaire thrust the umbrella in after them.

"Where to, Mister Coverley, sir?" the man asked, adding that he was surprised anyone wanted to go out on such a night.

They directed him to Mousehole.

"When are you going to change?" Standish asked Tamsin as soon as they were off.

"Why not now?" she replied. "Good idea."

They were both already wearing fishermen's oilskin jackets and hoods. Now she pulled on a pair of Victor's cricket flannels, loaned for the occasion, before unhooking her skirt, which she folded up neatly and placed in the carpet bag. Fortunately, the cabbie only had eyes for the road ahead, or what he could see of it through the vertical river from above.

"You've got your passport?" she asked.

He patted his pocket. "Plus enough francs to bribe my way out of any little difficulty. Also I *am* going to pay David Peters. I wouldn't dream of not doing so — whatever you say."

When they arrived at the tiny fishing village, no one was abroad, for the rain was as heavy as ever; they could not even see to the end of the harbour wall. Though David had selected this cove for no better reason than that it lay nearest his route between Newlyn and his meeting with Jean-Baptiste Clouet, his Breton fisherman-accomplice, the choice was nonetheless perfect for such a venture. The long, narrow, crooked valley, studded with houses that seemed more to hang in space than to perch on those impossibly steep sides, seemed to close around them in a protective scrum; and the tiny, oval harbour — a sea puddle, really — between the towering bastions of Penlee and Halwyn was invisible from Newlyn, Penzance, Marazion ... from any place, in fact, where authority might lurk. To see *into* it from outside, even on a good day with the rising sun behind you, you'd need to be on a clifftop miles across the bay with a good pair of glasses — and even then it would be little more than a grey blur on the wide green sprawl of the Land's End peninsula. The two runaways felt safe the moment the cab began whining its way down in low gear from St. Paul.

They told the driver to take the carpet bag back to the hôtel and then, huddled beneath the wide umbrella, they made their way toward the deserted quay. The rain thundered down upon the fabric like a hundred drummers all out of time. It took less than a dozen paces for them to decide it was futile to try to avoid puddles; the place was one giant lake and the slipway, where David was to pick them up, was a torrent.

"No sign of him yet." Standish took out his watch. "Five minutes to go — at least he won't be able to say we held him up."

"That won't stop him!"

"You're pretty hard on him, aren't you," he remarked.

"Am I?" The thought had not occurred to her.

It was weird to be standing there amid all those shuttered houses, in a deluge of biblical proportions ... they could have been the last two people in the world. She wondered what he'd do if they were. It was an ancient daydream — castaways, alone on a tropic island. Would the old injunction, *Go forth and multiply,* seize him then, and would he love and cherish her as the only love possible?

Standish interrupted her thoughts. "If there's any doubt, he never seems to get the benefit of it from you," he said.

"Perhaps he doesn't deserve it," she replied. "I don't know. He just annoys me. He's such a *liar.*" The sudden vehemence of this denunciation surprised even her. "Well ..."

She started to retract a little but he was already responding. "Strong stuff, Tamsin! Why doth the lady protest so much? Doth the lady herself even know? Or perhaps I mean: Doth the lady even *know herself?*"

So now she had to justify her outburst instead. "He thinks he's so clever. Inventing things. And just look at the risks he takes! For what? He doesn't think of the people he'd be leaving behind. His poor father, who's already lost two sons to the sea."

"I see. So when you say 'liar' ..."

"Yes! He tells stupid lies, which wouldn't even deceive a child. About ... well, it doesn't matter."

"Lies to the Customs and Excise?" he suggested.

"No! Lies about ... you know — girls."

"Not about you, I hope?"

"About a girl who died years ago — a girl his *father* loved and lost. He just made it up ... I know very well why he did it and it was just ... *stupid!* Can't we talk about something else?"

"Yes, of course," he said in a considerate tone. "Obviously it upset you dreadfully. I'm sorry I pursued it."

"It didn't upset me at all!" she almost shouted. "He's not ... he won't win. He's not ... he's not ... *suitable!* That's all I've got to say. He's not suitable. Why are we wasting time on him? Here he is, anyway. He's just a ferryman as far as I'm concerned. We ought to be talking about important things like the Queen's."

"Yes, you're quite right," he said briskly. "Still, we've got several hours ahead of us if this meeting is to take place somewhere near mid-Channel."

The deep rumble of the *Merlin's* engines rose to a roar as David reversed the pitch and threw the tiller hard over, yawing the boat to a momentary halt parallel to and only a foot away from the sheer wall of the slipway. He'd become a dreadful show-off since he'd fitted that engine — throwing the boat around like that ... putting to sea in any sort of weather ...

"Jump!" he cried as the stern swung round. "I'm not stopping to tie up."

Standish just had time to collapse the umbrella before they both made their leap, side by side; the umbrella opened again, like a parachute, and clicked fast as they hit the deck, which had been about three feet below them — but wet and slippery. More by luck than anything, they landed on a falling swell, which absorbed something of their impact. Even so, they sprawled in an ungainly heap from which it took several seconds to extricate themselves, during which time, of course, their trouser legs became soaked to the skin.

"What with perspiring inside the oilskins and getting soused outside them," Tamsin said, "there's not much point in wearing clothes at all."

"All hands to the pump!" David shouted as he hit the throttle and set the pitch to forward once again. He had rigged an extra shelter of canvas aft, between the wheelhouse and the stern.

"Where?" Standish called back.

He pointed to a handle amidships, for the back-and-forth type of pump. Standish seized it and set to with vigour.

"You, maid, come and take the wheel."

"Aye *aye,* Cap'n," she replied with a sarcasm that was completely lost on him.

He piloted the *Merlin* through the narrow harbour mouth and on out through the gap between St. Clement's Isle and the Merlyn Rock — the 'Mousehole' that gives the village its name. But once they were safely into open water he set the course to 180° — due south — and handed the wheel to her.

"Aren't you glad to see us?" she asked.

But he was still smarting at the way she had cheated him (as he saw it) out of a fee for carrying Standish Coverley to safety. "I could have done it alone," he replied, "what with this wind."

True or not, a wind had, indeed, sprung up even in the short while since they had left Penzance. Or, perhaps, since it blew from the north, they had been sheltered from it, both there and in Mousehole harbour. Out here on open water, however, it was good and strong.

With Standish's help he set all the canvas she could carry — a jib, which he left loose as a spinnaker, a foresail, and a main. The tarpaulin over the stern was not one of the sails, being there to keep the rain off the engine housing, but, as they were running before the wind, it, too had some effect. Soon they were making enough way to allow David to cut the engine.

"Can we afford to do that?" she asked.

"Do I try and tell you how to run the Morrab?" he replied.

She wanted to tell him she was about to 'run' something much grander than the Morrab and so he could put that in his pipe and smoke it; but she realized she would merely be descending to his level of childishness, or churlishness, so she just maintained a dignified silence — and a course of 180°.

David next relieved Standish at the pump. He came aft, flapping his arms with relief, like a bird in slowed-down motion. "I've just realized how long it's been since I did any really hard labour," he said.

"But 'hard labour' is supposed to be what you're fleeing from," she pointed out.

He laughed. "It might have done me good — my health if not my reputation. Anyway, let's talk about the Queen's."

And so he told her what she'd need to know in order to start at the job. The chef, he said, would run the kitchen and still room entirely; he'd take orders of a general nature but would not tolerate the slightest interference in day-to-day matters.

"And suppose I just walk through the kitchen and see … I don't know — flies on exposed meat … or a chef-de-rang picking his nose. What then?"

"You tell me."

"I'd give them a ticking off. What would you do?"

"Frankly, I'd never venture into the kitchen at all. You'd be horrified at what goes on, even in the best hôtels in the world."

"Well, they're not going to go on inside the Queen's. I'll tell you that now — while you can still change your mind."

He laughed, rather bleakly, and said, "I shan't interfere but be prepared for a clash of wills. And I wouldn't start in the kitchens, if I were you. Start with the chambermaids and the standards of cleanliness in the bedrooms and other public places. Establish yourself as undisputed mistress there and then move on to the porters, pageboys, and bar. The bar is not going to be easy, either. There are so many ways to cheat customers who are already half sozzled anyway."

"Dip your finger in gin and wipe it round the rim of the glass — that sort of thing?"

He leaned over her shoulder and peered into her face. "Don't tell me you haven't worked in hôtels somewhere, sometime!"

"All right," she replied. "I won't."

"Anyway, there's the strategy I'd follow if I were you. Get every other department squirming under your rod of iron before you even stick your nose inside the kitchen door. Let your dragon-reputation go before you, breathing fire."

They continued in this way for more than an hour, hardly noticing that David had long since stopped pumping the bilge, nor even that the rain had fallen to a mere pitter-patter on the tarpaulin above their heads. Tamsin was left feeling even more daunted at the thought of all that lay ahead of her, and yet her confidence was all the greater because Standish never doubted for a moment that she could do it.

She did not really become aware of their surroundings until David came aft and, standing just outside the wheelhouse, shading his eyes while he peered into the gloom where she stood, said, "Have you noticed this wet stuff all around us, maid? It's what we call the sea! I only mention it because every now and then much bigger boats than this one make use of it, too — so it's not a bad idea to keep what we call 'a weather eye' out for them. And talking of the weather ..."

"Ha ha, very funny!" she shouted back. "If I'm just a little fool, then all my weather eye can see at this moment is a much bigger one. And he's blocking the view completely."

"Shall I get out and walk?" Standish offered, stepping out from behind the wheelhouse to a position halfway between them, still under the awning. "I say!" He stretched a hand out into the open. "It's stopped raining completely. And the cloud's gone over, too — it's nothing but clear sky behind. I wondered why it wasn't getting much darker."

A few moments later the trailing edge of the cloud passed clear of the sun, which was now within a few minutes of setting. As yet it showed but a thin section of its disc, but immediately everything was outlined in gold — the mast, the jib, the gunwales, the frames of the wheelhouse ... and David's head. The transformation took her unawares. As the cloud moved on and the light strengthened, so, too, did that magical aura of gold that now bathed him. How long that moment lasted was of no consequence; it was, in any case, snatched from normal Time. For that brief eternity their eyes dwelled deep, each in the other's, and something passed between them that could never be put in words — indeed, it was deeper even than thoughts, something visceral and merciless.

In a panic she tore her gaze away and turned for help to Standish. Since he was still in the shade of the awning, his eyes were hard to read. But his gesture was unambiguous. He shrugged and spread his hands with their palms toward her, as if to say, 'This is what I told you about. What can anyone do?'

No!

She was not going to let it happen. Not to her.

"David!" she called out. "Come and take the wheel. I'm tired of this."

Again he took her by surprise, placing his huge, salt-browned hands over hers, which she removed as if they were scalded.

Fighting tears of rage — or outrage, perhaps — she made her way forrard to the prow, where she caught hold of both gunwales and leaned out as far as she could. Her body spilled wind off the spinnaker, which began to flap. Far away to her right the sea was now swallowing the huge crimson orb of the sun, as oval as a rugby football.

He came and stood behind her. "Go away," she said.

"He sent me to catch you if you fell." It was not David but Standish.

"Oh, I'm sorry." She turned and gave him a brief, wan smile.

They stood thus awhile in the silence of wind and ocean, and the mewing of the single gull that had followed them thus far.

"Now you know," he said at length.

"No, I do not," she replied. "It was just a trick of the light. He's the least suitable man for me in all Cornwall. I don't have time for any of that. There's no place ... no place for ..." Her voice trailed off into a single, exasperated sigh.

"The best of luck, then," he said.

43 How David managed to make a rendezvous at dead of night, on a completely featureless ocean, with a fleet whose movements he could only guess at from long experience, was both mystery and miracle. He frequently checked the stars, but what could they tell him of the Breton fleet's movements? And several times he dipped an enamel mug into the sea, sipping it and spitting it out like a winetaster; and once or twice he poured it out where the wheelhouse light would shine through it — all of which might have told him something about the tides and the currents, or the fish that might inhabit them; but, again, how would that have led him to the French boats?

And yet, at two o'clock that night, drifting bare-masted and silent, they saw a dozen masthead lights way off to the west; and it was well within the hour when he had predicted their meeting.

"Not bad, eh!" he said to Tamsin as he hoisted a signal light and prepared to send up a maroon.

"If I'd known you were so wonderful, I wouldn't have bothered myself over you at all last week," she replied.

She had intended the words to be cutting but, somehow, they didn't emerge like that.

He rubbed the 'slatch,' as he called it, against the self-igniting fuse and stood back. There was a mighty whoosh and a shower of sparks. The well of the deck filled with smoke and the acrid tang of burned sulphur and saltpetre. They held their breaths as it drifted away, watching, meanwhile, the fiery parabola of the maroon, which burst into stars of descending crimson immediately after reaching its peak.

The Frenchmen gave an answering hoot on a klaxon, which carried faintly to them across the water.

David hoisted the mainsail again and set off in their direction. The wind had dropped considerably by now.

To Tamsin they were just so many dimly glimpsed boats, locatable only by their lights, but David seemed to know by instinct which one was Jean-Baptiste's. There was a hasty conference in a dialect she found impossible to follow beyond the occasional word, some of them none too edifying. *"Comme la vache qui pisse!"* she heard distinctly.

At one stage tots of brandy were offered all round. She declined. Eventually a price for carrying Standish was agreed. He parted with some of his francs, then turned and held out his arms to her. "It's *au revoir,* little face," he said, hugging her tight, "not goodbye."

"I wish it could be you, Standish," she said. "Not him." David must have heard but she didn't care.

"No you don't," he chided.

"I do. It would make so much more sense all round."

"Yes, well, *sense* is what aristocrats marry for. That's why their lines all become extinct. Just thank God that hot blood rules the rest of us — or those who dare follow where it leads!"

When he was aboard the lugger that was to take him to France, he called back across the ever-widening divide, "That wasn't what I meant to say at all. What I really wanted to say was that there are some people of fifty who couldn't order a daily newspaper with any conviction — and some youngsters of twenty who could order an army into battle and win. You're in that second group!"

"But I'm twenty-*one!"* she called back.

"See!" His voice only just carried to her by now. "You're ahead already!"

The tears were running down her cheeks by then, though, thankfully, she was not sobbing; she would have hated David to discover such weakness in her.

"Come-us on, maid!" he said, rubbing his hands briskly. "That's only the easy part over."

"Just tell me what to do, then," she snapped as she returned to the wheelhouse.

He was already handling the mainsail boom sheets. "Bring her about and try and steer fine to forty-five degrees. Tell me when we're there — or how near you can get. If she loses headway, ease off the helm until she picks up again."

She had to 'ease off on the helm' a couple of times before the needle settled at $45°$; each time he adjusted the sheets to change the angle of the mainsail.

"And now?" she asked.

"Just hold her steady for the next four hours."

"What!"

"Sing out if you see any sort of light."

"What if it's a lighthouse?"

"It won't be — or if you see one, you'll see two. The Longships and the Wolf Rock — in which case we'll be very late into port."

"Four *hours,* you said?"

"Watch the bearing, maid. You'm too close to the wind."

She glanced down and saw that the needle had, indeed, moved; she swung the helm until the alignment was back at 45°.

"What are *you* doing?" she asked. Having to keep her eye on the lighted compass ruined her night vision. All she could see was that he was up forrard, near the reserve fuel tank.

"Working," he replied.

After a while she called out again. "Can't we start the engine?"

"No," he replied. "We're short of petrol."

"What? You've got two forty-five-gallon tanks and you haven't used any yet — except for the bit from Newlyn to Mousehole."

He appeared at her side suddenly. "How do you know we've got *two* tanks?"

"Because, when you stowed the tarpaulin, I saw a copper pipe running from the main tank, here under my feet, to somewhere up there. Doesn't it go to a spare tank, then?"

"Quite right," he said casually. "Just wondered how you knew."

"Did you get your barrel of brandy?"

"That's what I was now hiding. Listen, I was joking when I said four hours. There's a pile of nets up forrard. That'd be the softest place now. You go put your head down if you mind to." When she seemed about to argue he added, "Gusson with you! We may yet need your quick wits, so it's best you were rested."

The nets were damp and reeked of tar and barking; the deck pitched endlessly beneath her; and yet, to her amazement, she fell asleep at once and did not wake until he nudged her at just after six the following morning. "There's a cup of tea and some saffron bread aft," he said.

It was half an hour before sunrise but the sky was already a horrid shade of acid pink.

"Oh, I must look *awful!*" she cried, sitting up stiffly, yawning, and rubbing bricks of sleep from her eyes.

"You do," he agreed, "but it's nothing a good tot of brandy won't cure."

"Who's to drink it — me or you?"

He laughed and returned to the wheelhouse.

As she followed him she saw he'd rigged up a sort of tarpaulin curtain, diagonally across part of the stern. "There's a bucket there to wash your face and hands and that," he said. "And for calls of nature what you do is you slip this noose around you, under your arms, and you hold fast this sheet, and you sit as far back over the gunwale as you need."

The Cornish coast — the Land's End peninsula, she hoped — almost filled the northern horizon. She could just see occasional breakers — the high ones, she assumed, so they must be less than four miles from land.

Ten minutes later a different Tamsin joined him in the wheelhouse, ready to take on the world. Saffron bread tasted good at any time but never so good as then. And as for hot tea, sweet-sweet-sweetened with condensed milk ... it was the finest beverage in all the world.

"You need a shave, David," she said, rubbing her knuckles up and down the stubble of his jaw. The alien feel of it sent shivers through her.

"If it's shaves you want, there's a close one now coming up," he replied, not taking his eye off the water ahead. "Three and a half miles out — they weren't taking any chances."

She followed his gaze and saw two long, sleek boats, navy blue in colour, patrolling back and forth, each counter to the other. Her stomach seemed to fall away inside her.

"Steam launches from Falmouth," he added with a laugh. "No expense spared!"

"How can you laugh?" she cried. "We can't possibly escape."

"They can't touch us beyond the three-mile line," he said.

"And we can't stay outside it for ever."

"No," he conceded laconically. "That's the truth. Take the wheel. It's time to start the engine."

First he struck the mainsail and then, leaving the boat to drift for a moment, he got her to hold the exhaust lift while he swung the flywheel 'up to revs.' After several goes the engine coughed into life, wavered, picked up, and then roared away.

"Right," he said, fitting the cover back in place. "A little cat and mouse before we let them catch us!"

He throttled up to maximum revs and headed straight for the nearest Customs boat, steering to follow it wherever it went. The other launch turned about and came steaming in at full power to the rescue. The first launch soon found itself in a narrowing pincer movement — unwilling to turn to port, toward the *Merlin*, being uncertain of how reckless David was prepared to be, and unable to turn to starboard because of the 'help' steaming in from that quarter.

At the last minute, its helmsman realized he had no choice but to turn away from the *Merlin*, which seemed hell-bent on self-destruction, taking them along, too. By a miracle of seamanship it just managed to avoid its 'rescuer' though seamen aboard each vessel must have had a rare glance down the funnel of the other. The *Merlin* passed close enough astern of the second launch to see the whites of Inspector Sterne's eyes — the terrified whites of his eyes.

"What dreadful seamanship, Mister Sterne!" David mocked, turning a cheeky circle before speeding off again. "You don't belong to go to sea enough — that's your trouble!"

The wild, exultant gleam in his eye frightened Tamsin — and yet it thrilled her, too. She understood now how some men could lead others into any sort of danger, even into certain death. She felt it at that moment and knew she would follow him to the end of this 'cat-and-mouse' game, as he called it, no matter where it led.

"Wheeee!" she cried suddenly, surprising herself and startling him into leaving a hairpin of a wobble in their wake. "Ram them properly next time!" she added.

"Aye-aye, Cap'n!" He came about and pushed up to full throttle once more, this time making for the second launch, with Sterne aboard.

"No!" Tamsin yelled in his ear. "I was joking."

"Too late now!" he replied. "Hold on to your hat!"

But this time it was the *Merlin* that veered at the last moment, after which David cut the engine to idle and set the propellor pitch to feather.

"Enough of this fun!" he called out to the two launches. "You're welcome aboard to search — since that's what you seem to want."

Sterne's launch came gently alongside. A couple of seamen leaped aboard the *Merlin* and tied the two boats fast. When the Inspector made to come aboard, David even leaned over and considerately helped him — something the man did not welcome.

"What's all this?" he asked testily, shaking David's hand away.

"Just a bit of fun, sir," came the reply. "No harm done."

"Fun?" the man asked. "Call that fun?"

"Well, let's just say I had my reasons."

Their eyes met and held each other's. Sterne blinked first. "Get aboard you men, you know what to do."

The men certainly knew what to do. In fact, they found the brandy barrel before the first minute was up.

"Oh, horror!" David cried, holding up his hands like the worst sort of strolling actor. "Who could have put that there, I wonder."

Sterne paid him no heed. "Bring it aboard," he said. "Six men! Lifting party!"

But the man who found it already had the bung out. "It's seawater, sir," he said.

"All of it?" The inspector sighed. "Tip it out."

At that moment Tamsin had an idea. David's game of cat-and-mouse had been simple high spirits, she was sure of it. But she now saw a way to make it seem part of a plan. His enigmatic words, 'I had my reasons' had put the idea into her head.

She pretended to lose interest in Sterne and his activities. "You don't mind if I get on with the washing up?" she said. And she went to the wheelhouse to take out the mugs and dip them in the sea. While she did so, she stared in what she hoped was a surreptitious manner toward the coast — toward Lamorna or Porthgwarra, if she had her bearings right. Eventually she had been at the simple chore of washing two cups for so long that the ever-suspicious Sterne came to see what she was really up to. She 'noticed' him then with a guilty start and hastily took her eyes off the distant coast.

Then, seeing that she hadn't fooled him, she said, "Very beautiful in the dawn, isn't it."

"Take a good hard look, Miss Harte," he replied. "Because when I find what I'm looking for — and I shall — there's many a dawn you'll see only on the ceiling of a prison cell. And how are you in man's trousers, anyway?"

"D'you think they'd agree to send me to a man's prison, then?" she asked.

He returned to his work without a further word.

The barrel was filled with seawater to the last drop.

"What's this, sir?" One of the men had the engine cowling up. He had noticed the pipe to the reserve fuel tank, the same one Tamsin had spotted.

"Reserve fuel," David explained. "Up forrard, for ballast, see."

He started to lead them to it but Sterne barked, "Stop him! I'll find it, don't you fear!"

"There's no trick," David said. "Just lift that decking."

They did as he directed and there, indeed, was the reserve tank — the twin of the main tank, which they had already discovered and dipped. And found to be nearly empty.

"It's got to be in there!" Sterne said delightedly. "We've looked everywhere else."

Tamsin agreed. Despite David's insouciance, she felt sure their game was now up — and jokes about prison no longer seemed quite so hilarious. Desperately clinging on to her decoy-idea, she caught hold of the mast, stepped up on the coaming of the fish-hold, and, shielding her eyes (even though the sun was rising behind her), peered even more intently toward the land.

One of the officers unscrewed the cap of the tank. Another brought forward a dipstick, a twisted strand of quarter-inch copper wire with a piece of lint trapped at the bottom.

Sterne leaned forward, ready to pounce.

David glanced anxiously at Tamsin, wondering what she was playing at.

The officer made several stabs at pushing the dipstick into the tank, thwarted by the rocking of the boat.

Sterne shouted at him and told him to get a grip of himself.

David was still far more concerned for Tamsin than the dipping of the tank.

Sterne noticed it and followed his eyes, only to discover Tamsin once again staring at the land, almost as if she expected some sort of rescue to come from that quarter.

"Got it!" The officer slipped the long rod down into the tank.

"All the way!" Sterne shouted. "We know all about tanks with false bottoms!"

His underling tapped it twice on the bottom of the tank. He pinched his finger and thumb to mark the position of the top of the filler neck and then cautiously withdrew it.

Sterne snatched at the lower end, where the lint was held, and brought it up to his nose. "Petrol!" he said in disgust. "Measure the depth."

The officer, who still had the position marked, held it level with the top of the tank and four or five heads went down to see if the end of the stick was level with the bottom of the tank.

Which, of course, it was.

They dipped it again to make sure.

But Sterne already knew he had lost — for not only was young Thorne completely unconcerned with what they were doing, he was far more interested in the antics of the Harte woman.

What *was* she doing there?

He sprang to his feet and turned to look at her properly. But at that moment she leaped lightly down from the coaming, and, with an air look of immense relief, gave David a nod. And then at last she turned a broad, triumphant smile upon the Inspector.

"Quick, lads!" he shouted. " Drop all that! Step lively now — back aboard. We've been decoyed out here but, by God, we s'll catch 'em ashore!"

As he waited for his men to cross back onto the launch he said to David, "All right, young Peters. What were you doing last night? A whole tank of fuel used and nothing in the hold to show for it?"

"You should have asked me that first," David told him. "It seemed that Mister Standish Coverley had an urgent need to get to France last night. I helped him on his way, that's all."

The man frowned. "Mister Coverley — a fugitive from justice?"

"I didn't say that. I merely said he had an urgent need to get to France — just like you've got an urgent need to get to Lamorna. Oops!" He clapped his hand over his mouth and looked guilty.

"Right, cox'n! Porthgwarra it is!" He leaped back aboard the launch — this time with no offer of help. "Full speed ahead!"

David and Tamsin waited until they were well away before giving vent to cries of victory. Then she took him by the arms and danced him round and round in a wild jig on the hatch cover of the fish hold.

Louder and louder was their exultation, wilder and wilder grew their steps, until — inevitably — she stumbled and fell backward. And he, trying to hold her, fell also, half upon her, half at her side.

And there they lay, fighting for breath, their hearts beating much faster than even their exertions would warrant, their eyes locked in a full-scale audit of each other.

"All right then!" she cried angrily and pulled his face hard against hers.

Her lips were hungry for his. When they touched, it was not enough, and she wrapped her arms around his head and pulled him brutally hard against her.

He moaned and tried to pull away. But, when he half succeeded, he pressed his mouth to hers again, this time with no extra assistance from her.

In fact, she now lay back in a kind of trance, as if all her muscles had lost the will to act. Only her head moved, this way and that, to double the wonder of that magical contact between them. She broke at last, fighting to breathe, and then kissed him lightly, again and again, between gasps for breath.

Soon she was giggling, too, and so was he. And then it became a game in which she moved her lips this way and that while he struggled to follow her and trap her once more. She never made it too difficult nor forced him to pursue her for too long, though.

Eventually she flipped him over onto his back and laid her head upon his chest. "We're mad," she murmured.

"I never doubted it," he replied.

"We'll never really suit each other, you know."

"But the fun is in the trying."

"It's going to be a long courtship."

He sighed heavily. "I'm used to that."

"You liar!" She rose on one elbow and hammered his chest with her fist, half-heartedly.

"It was the truth in one respect," he said. "I was in love and it wasn't requited — or not in any satisfactory form."

"Not in any form at all! Don't give yourself airs. I still don't know why I'm doing this — falling in love with a man who could be drowned at any time."

"Ah!" he said.

"What does that mean?"

"Why d'you think I needed this two hundred and twenty-five pounds, then?"

She rose onto both elbows and looked into his eyes. *"Two* hundred and twenty-five?"

"Including the hundred Mister Coverley gave me. It's enough to refit this vessel for trips round the bay."

"Honestly?"

"Next season — you'll see. The *Saucy Sal* — trips round Saint Michael's Mount — sea trips for sporting fishermen."

"So we really have got brandy somewhere aboard! Where?"

"Come!" He struggled out from beneath her and helped her to her feet.

"Ouch!' She walked gingerly and shook her feet to make the pins and needles go away.

He led her to the reserve tank where, once again, he screwed off the lid — or, rather, she noticed, he seemed to be screwing it *on.* And now she saw that the filler neck appeared to be rising with each full turn.

And finally he pulled it off — or out. Yes — the filler neck was *two* filler necks and the inner one, inserted on a right-hand thread, screwed out to reveal itself as a pipe with a blanked-off end. He carried it gingerly to the main fuel tank and poured it in.

"Waste not, want not," he said, returning with the two mugs and a cream dipper, the sort that dairymen carry on their rounds.

"I keep promising you that tot of brandy," he said. "It's high time I delivered."

It slipped down her throat like silk and came back with a sizzling afterburn.

The mugs went clattering to the deck as, once again, he put his arms around her. And now all the fight had gone out of her. All that resistance. All that common sense. What took its place was the thrill of his very being, and being *there* ... the ecstasy of feeling his lips against hers, the desire for him ...

The need to be his ... and him, hers.

Now and for ever.